The clone Andu knew only as Prime Alpha reached for her blaster. He hadn't noticed it before, but all this time the weapon had just been sitting there, unattended, on a small white table next to the hospital room door. Now, as Prime Alpha linked her long delicate fingers around the grip of the blaster and pointed it at his chest, Second and Third felt the cold touch of gray metal against their skin.

Andu stared down the barrel of the blaster with grave apprehension. He could see grim determination in the female clone's eyes.

Moving slowly now, so as not to spook her, he raised his hands above his head as if to surrender. He spoke in even, unhurried tones.

"Take it easy, Prime Alpha. I'm not an alien. I'm a human, just like you."

"We are not human," the clone replied. "We are Prime."

Other books by Steven Burgauer:

* The Brazen Rule - murder & mayhem in the year 2342

* The Last American - a country on the brink of disaster
    (the year: 2398)

* Fornax - treachery on the dark side (the year: 2425)

* In The Shadow Of Omen - Mars at its best!!
    (the year: 2433)

* Naked Came The Farmer - a round-robin murder mystery
    with contributions from 13 central Illinois
    authors

* The Wealth Builder's Guide: An Investment Primer

Available at finer bookstores everywhere, or write:
zero-g press, 6605 N Rustic Oak Ct, Peoria, Il, 61614

phone: 1-800-643-1327

e-mail: SCIFI20@prodigy.net

online: www.amazon.com   ,or
         www.barnesandnoble.com   ,or
         bradley.bradley.edu/~ dlb/steven.html

THE GRANDFATHER PARADOX

THE GRANDFATHER PARADOX

by
Steven Burgauer

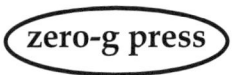

THE GRANDFATHER PARADOX

All rights reserved
Copyright © 1998 Steven Burgauer

Reproduction in any manner, in whole or in part, in English or in other languages, or otherwise, without written permission of the author and the publisher is prohibited.

This is a work of fiction. All characters and events portrayed in this book are fictional, and any resemblance to real people or real situations is purely coincidental.

Printing History
First Printing 1998

ISBN 1-892086-01-8

The name "zero-g press" and the "zero-g" logo are trademarks belonging to Steven Burgauer

PRINTED IN THE UNITED STATES OF AMERICA
10 9 8 7 6 5 4 3 2 1

For George Garland,
the man who introduced me to science fiction.

By the time Man reached out to the stars for the second time, memories of His first botched effort had long since receded into the dim past. In much the same way that the first Euros believed they had "discovered" the New World when in fact it had been found thousands of years earlier by migrating Asians, the space explorers of the second wave were scarcely even aware that there *had* been a first wave. Thus, it should have come as no surprise to anyone that when Man met Himself out there, He did not believe that was what He'd found.

PROLOGUE

BIRD-BEAST

It is a hot summer's day on the pampas of central Ancòn some twenty kilometers inland from the briny sea. A herd of small horse-like mammals are grazing peacefully in the warm sun. None of the animals are aware of the vigilant creature lurking fifty meters away in the tall grass. Most of the watcher's trim, feathered body is concealed by the lush vegetation. Its eyes—though set far apart on the sides of its disproportionately-large head—remain fixed on the herd. The head itself swings in rapid jerks, moving from side to side atop a long and powerful neck. Even without the benefit of stereoscopic vision, this reflex habit permits the stalker to keep a fix on her prey.

Before long the head drops down to the level of the grass. The creature edges forward. After several meters though, it stops, raises its oversized head once more and renews its surveillance. With cold, reptilian eyes the female bird-beast scans the herd for any sign that it has been spotted. Seeing none, she advances further. At a distance of perhaps thirty meters, the carnivore is ready to strike.

Scratching at the ground with her claw, the creature lowers its head to a large rock close by its feet. Completing her preparations, she rubs her cavernous snout against the boulder to sharpen the beak's bladelike edges. Back and forth she goes, until it's razor sharp.

Now the terrible bird-like beast bristles her feathers and springs from the tall grass. Propelled by two long and muscular legs, she dashes forward towards the herd at high speed. Within seconds, she is moving at close to seventy kilometers per hour! Her small wings, useless for flight, are extended out to the sides for balance and maneuverability.

Stricken with fright, the herd bolts in disarray as the predator bears down upon them. Undeterred, the attacker fixes her attention on an old male lagging behind the rest of the fleeing animals. Although the old male runs desperately fast, she quickly gains on him! Only moments later, she is at his side.

With a stunning sideswipe of her powerful left foot, the attacker knocks her prey off balance. Seizing the fallen male in her massive beak, she beats the hapless animal against the ground with repeated swinging motions of her giant head. All too quickly the victim loses consciousness, and the attacker swallows the limp body whole. Not too difficult a task considering the bird-beast's meter-long head and the half-meter-wide gape of her beak.

Stomach bulging, the gorged predator lumbers back to her round nest of twigs in the grass nearby and resumes incubating her eggs. There are two eggs in the nest, each the size of a basketball. Squatting down upon them, the mother grunts with satisfaction. Something approaching a contented smile is on her giant parrotlike face.

PART I

1
Mutiny

"Mates, I say we dump the bloody bastard out the airlock and let 'im *float* home!"

The speaker was a mammoth, carrot-topped man known only to the others as Red. He was a big hulk of a man with a short temper and a drinking habit to match. His audience sat cowed before him, holding their breath. The whole lot of them, the entire crew, had gathered in the mess to see whether or not they could muster the votes to declare a mutiny. One of Red's more timid co-conspirators was doing his best to voice his objections and put a stop to it.

"You actually expect us to just toss the Cap out the airlock?" the man asked, a look of surprise on his face. "That's not mutiny—that's murder!"

Red looked around the room. Though the ship itself was one of the newer T-Class cruisers—the T designating it as being outfitted with a tachyon drive—the ship's crew was quite ordinary: sixteen rough-hewn characters of questionable background.

"Why should you care what happens to him?" another man protested. "Lives or dies—it's all the same to me. We haven't been paid in weeks!"

"And we haven't passed anything but lifeless rocks for nearly a month now!" another chimed in, his closely-set eyes giving him a mean and stupid look. "I think we're lost!"

"Yeah, we oughtta turn back!" the second man urged, his greasy black hair falling across his shoulders. Though a big man himself, alongside Red he appeared of rather ordinary dimension.

"We're already so far off the charts, finding our way back may be impossible," the third man countered, clutching the bottle of Saronale he'd taken from the cooler. "If we kill the Cap, we may *never* get back home!"

"Hell!" Red exploded with fury, slamming his fist down on the table top. "We may never get back home either way. Didn't it ever occur to any of you velcroids that we might be stuck out here forever? Like the man said: lives or dies—it's all the same to me!"

"Shush!" the second man warned. "I think he's coming."

Captain Andu Nehrengel entered the galley from the cargo hold where he'd been working. A leather satchel hung from his belt. Placing his big muscular hands on the table, he looked around the room. He saw anger.

"What's the meaning of this?" he asked, making no attempt to hide the fact that he was armed.

Though not nearly as large as Red, Andu was a tall, slender man. He had dark hair, dark eyes, and a wiry build. He was the sort of big ugly-handsome galoot women went for and men took orders from, a man of considerable strength, a formidable opponent in battle. Even so, he left little to chance. Recognizing how restless his crew had become in the last few days, he no longer dressed without a sidearm. The safety was off.

"We're tired of being out here, Cap," the second man explained, an adolescent whimper creeping into his tinny voice.

"You volunteered, didn't you?" Captain Nehrengel barked, forming his fingers into a fist.

"But we was told it would only take two weeks to track down this damn signal we been following," Red pointed out as he straightened himself up to his full height and began cracking his knuckles one by one. He looked as if he were deliberating a big decision. "It's been two *months*, Cap'n Nehrengel."

"Yeah—Red's right! There's no one out here," the second man chirped, gesturing towards the viewport. The window was filled with pinpoints of light, some blurred, as they raced through the ether of space at unimaginable speed. "Who the hell knows *what's* out here? We oughtta turn back!"

"And so we shall," Captain Nehrengel agreed in a soothing tone. "But not before we locate the system we've been sent out here to find. We must be awfully close to it by now."

"Sorry, Cap, but that won't wash," Red declared, taking half a step backwards. In the next instant he brought his weapon to bear on Nehrengel's middle. It was a standard disintegrator powered by a tiny Fornax Battery. Though the safety was still on, at this range the Captain would have been melted to vapor long before he could have reached for his own blaster.

"We're not going any further," the big man said. "Either we turn around now or . . . "

"Or what?" Nehrengel said, bravely standing his ground, his dark eyes narrowing with derision.

"Or else we turn around without you," came Red's calm reply. In the shadows behind him, several of the other crewmen nodded their agreement.

"I see," Andu observed, accepting the futility of further argument. "Well then, you'll have to return home without me. Duty requires I complete my mission as planned. We haven't discovered the source of that transmission yet."

"Don't be a fool!" the third man objected. "Just surrender yourself peaceably and return to base with us as our prisoner."

"I can't do that," Andu replied, warily eyeing Red's blaster. "I swore an oath." Even as he spoke, there was the unmistakable click of metal against metal as Red switched off the safety on his blaster.

At the sound, a look of horror spread across the third man's face. Thinking that the big Irishman was about to pull the trigger, he was galvanized to words.

"You don't have to kill him, Red! Just give him one of the runabouts and let him be on his way! That way we can go along on ours."

"He's right," the second man parroted with uncharacteristic valor. "Let the Cap'n go. He deserves a chance!"

Red growled his disapproval. Oh, how he wanted to use his disintegrator on this Captain Andu Nehrengel! Oh, how he wanted to watch this man's torso get shredded into a thousand tiny little pieces! Only, it wasn't going to be. Red had backed himself into a corner of his own making. If he wasn't to have a mutiny of his own, Red had no choice now but to go along with the others and let the Captain live.

With the rest of the crew following closely along behind,

Red escorted Andu at gunpoint down to the cargo hold where the runabouts were stored. The *Drift On* wasn't much to look at—only twelve meters long and eight wide. Still, like her sister ship the *Sail On*, she had enough provisions onboard to feed a crew of four for a week and could maintain a top speed of 100,000 kilometers per hour for five days. Red took some consolation from the fact that this far out Andu's chances for survival were remote. Letting him have the runabout was as good as a death sentence!

"Okay, in you go, Nehrengel. Oh, and do mind your head," the big man jeered as he shoved Andu through the open hatch, leather satchel and all. "I wouldn't want you to get all banged up—and just before your long trip too!"

Laughing cruelly, Red slammed the hatchway shut and engaged the launch-track. There was a high-pitched whine from an electric motor as the mechanical arm extended.

Staring back at him through the viewport, the castaway swallowed hard. For the first time in all his travels across the galaxy, Andu Nehrengel found himself alone!

2
Space

Captain Andu Nehrengel sat in the cramped cockpit of the *Drift On*, his legs folded up beneath him, his leather satchel next to him on the floor. He had sat like this for six hours already, watching the monitor and staring out through the forward viewport at the vastness of space as it unfolded before him.

How to judge the dimensions of the cosmos? he wondered for the umpteenth time. Frankly, it couldn't be done! Can anyone picture a hundred million kilometers? A hundred billion? How 'bout a hundred million billion? Too vast. Even the word itself—space—was too short to convey much meaning. It should be something big like gigahectare, or zillionparsec, or billionlightyear—something that *sounds* big anyway.

How far out *was* he? Well, to begin with, how far out was he from *what*? He wasn't far from whatever lay just ahead, though he was rather far from what lay just behind. The Milky Way wasn't even a particularly large galaxy; yet over the course of his entire career, he had barely crossed one ten-thousandth of one of its spiral arms. So how far out *was* he? Perhaps two dozen light-years from the solar system, perhaps a little more. He didn't know for certain—he was off the map, as they say.

Back home, when the day ended, the blazing sun relinquished the sky to the pinprick glimmerings of a multitude of cousins. Earth's sky was of an intermediate type. It lacked the unbearable glory which filled the skies of the central worlds. There, star elbowed star in such blinding competition that the black of night was nearly lost in the explosion of light. But then it also lacked the lonely grandeur of skies out on the periphery.

The Grandfather Paradox

Out there, the unrelieved blackness was punctuated only at great intervals by the dimness of an orphaned star. Out there, so far from the center, the milky lens-shape of the Galaxy spread across the sky in such profusion, the distant individual stars were lost in a blur of diamond dust.

Though the naked eye could barely glimpse six thousand of these sparkling dots of light, Man had known for millenia already that the number of stars was beyond comprehension. The Milky Way alone probably contained 200 *billion* of these great spheres of shining gas, and it was only one galaxy among perhaps 100 billion. This, in a universe so vast that light—even at *its* great speed—took some thirty billion years to cross from one side to the other. How does a mere mortal comprehend such numbers?

Scattered like diamond chips across an ocean of black, the multitude of stars looked deceptively serene to the casual observer. Yet, each one of them was a creature of extraordinary violence. On the surface of a normal star, temperatures could range up to 50,000 degrees Kelvin; in the interior, even higher. There, in nature's own thermonuclear furnaces, the stellar fires raged at several million degrees Kelvin—hot enough to tear apart atomic nuclei and then forge them back together again into new types of matter.

Not only did the peaceful-looking heavens disguise the ferocity of its stars, they hid their enormous variety as well. Migrating through the galaxy—sometimes in binary pairs, or triplets, or even quartets—stars ranged in size from smaller than Earth to nearly as large as our entire solar system. Some expanded and contracted with regularity, growing brighter and dimmer with each oscillation; others remained virtually unchanged for eons.

Though their lives could be measured in billions of years, stars—like everything else in the universe—did in fact age and eventually die. Some went quietly, cooling into dark remnants of their former splendor; others collapsed and exploded in a shattering cataclysm. Yet Andu knew that even as old stars vanished, new ones were constantly being born. There were places—gaseous stellar-nurseries—where God worked His black magic on the elementary particles of the universe and created new stars. Not even Man, with all his learning, could yet duplicate such a feat. But for Andu, as he and his tiny ship rocketed through space, destination unknown, it was fun to think about. Perhaps a time would come when even that mystery would be solved. Perhaps he himself would solve it!

• • •

Meanwhile, Half A Million Kilometers Behind Him

Even routed through the nearest hyperlink, a distressing amount of white noise separated one person's voice from the other. At these distances it was impossible to have a conversation in the normal sense of the word. There was no room for niceties. An exchange like. . . How's it going? Oh, just fine. How's the kids? Oh, you know how difficult teenagers can be. And the wife?. . . might take 2½ days or more. Thus, this sort of banal back and forth was absent from space "talk." Questions were short and to the point; answers, staccato and bereft of detail. Most times, voice communications were out of the question and all talk-talk was in text.

The message was there waiting for him even before the grisly work was done. He had dumped Nehrengel overboard just as Chief Apostle Brigham Smith had wanted, but then came the hard part—killing the rest of the crew. It wasn't so much that he didn't enjoy killing—he did—it was just that it was messy. Everything floats in low-g, spit, pus, urine, semen, blood, everything! But most especially blood! He had tried to clean it up, but it was useless. Who cared anyway, this wasn't his ship!

Still, how was he supposed to answer Smith's message? It wasn't voice, it was text. And it had a terse edge to it, an urgency. He *had* to answer. Or should he let him stew? That just might serve the dirty bastard right, especially after all the trouble he'd put him through. In fact, this might be a good time to ask for more money! The arrogant bastard couldn't touch him out here!

The message, though clearly intended for Red, didn't begin with his name. Red had learned early on that Chief Apostle Brigham Smith was surreptitious, if not downright paranoid. The message, in fact, had no indication whatsoever from whom it came, nor for whom it was intended. Red knew, however, that it was for him:

> Power struggle continues here at home. Must have confirmation of success of your mission to hold locals in line. Immediate reply requested.

Red smiled. The timing couldn't be more perfect. Smith was at his mercy!

Power struggle continues here at home. That could only mean one thing: Chief Apostle Brigham Smith's little fiefdom was in jeopardy. Perhaps it was the Amerinds in the north. Or the Mexicans to the south. Who knew? Who cared? It didn't matter. Someone somewhere was putting on a full-court press to bring Smith down. To survive, he needed this mission to end in success. He needed Red more than Red needed him. And in that Red smelled opportunity!

The crew was already dead, Smith was at his mercy, and—at tachyon speeds—Nehrengel was only a blink ahead of him. Now was the time for him to play his trump card!

Red slid the keyboard out from its alcove and began typing. Like its predecessor, his reply was terse and to the point:

> A.N. on his way. Crew silenced. Task more difficult than anticipated, though. Will not pursue without additional funding. Advise amount soon, while A.N. still within tracking range. Confirm Zion National Bank, Colony One branch.

He read it over once, corrected a word he thought he'd misspelled, then pressed the send-button. Converted to dits and dahs, the message began its multimillion-kilometer trek back to Earth. It would be a day and a half before he had his answer.

3
Tachys

Thirty Hours Later

Former captain Andu Nehrengel woke with a start. Once again, a lump formed in his throat as he tried to make some sense out of his current situation. The man had been tossed off his own ship like so many bags of yesterday's garbage, and by his own men no less! And if that weren't bad enough, he was so far from the nearest outpost now, the list of places where he might possibly go, was exceedingly short.

The problem wasn't food—he had plenty of provisions onboard—no, the problem was power: he didn't have nearly enough of it. Andu was a million klicks from nowhere, and with his present battery reserves, he didn't stand a chance of making it back to Outpost Gamma alive, much less all the way back home. Thus, after a few fitful hours without sleep, he had come to a decision. The only sensible thing for him to do under the circumstances was to try and complete his mission. This, despite the terrible odds.

Thinking back through it one more time now, Andu adjusted his grav-chair, sat back, and tried to relax. After being thrown overboard he had dutifully set the runabout on the same course the mother ship had been following since they first left the solar system. He had sufficient charge in the batteries to keep this up for about five days. Then, unless he could find a suitable neutron source to refuel at somewhere along the way, he would be out of luck. At the end of those five days, he'd be like a piece of flotsam, adrift in space. And he would remain that way until his food and water ran out.

The water would go first because he needed the batteries to run the recycling plant. Then, within a few days, he'd die of dehydration. A lousy way to go, dehydration. There had to be a better way to die. Maybe he'd heat up Jenny, aim her at the airlock, and poof, it would all be over in an instant! Then again, maybe he was getting ahead of himself. Everything depended now on him either reaching his goal or else getting a recharge. If it was the latter, it would have to be *soon*.

Durbinium was funny that way. It absorbed energy from a nuclear source like a towel in water. And just like a towel, once it was squeezed dry it could be used over and over again for the same purpose. But if it should become *too* dry and allowed to drain down to nothing, it would become stiff as a board and forever after useless to sop up energy. Andu knew the physics and he knew he couldn't afford to let that happen. If he let the batteries run all the way down, he ran the risk of never being able to get them to take up a new charge again. Then he'd be dead for sure!

Anticipating the worst, Andu had grown more depressed with each passing hour. But then his luck took a turn for the better!

Though he didn't notice it at first, his forward viewport had begun filling with the fuzzy outlines of a spherical body. Lying directly in front of him and on precisely the same heading he had been following for the past day and a half, was a planet! Lo and behold, he had stumbled upon the very thing he was looking for: the only possible source of the signal he and his crew had been sent out here in the *Tachyon* to investigate! The telemetry matched perfectly, and from a distance anyway, the planet looked as if it might even be orbiting a Class M star, the sort most hospitable to life. And it was a good thing too, for he had at most 3½ days' worth of power left. He might just be able to make it!

But then what? If he got there alive, what was he supposed to do next? Put the runabout in orbit around the mammoth planet? Go down to the surface?

Andu's chances of finding this place had been so remote, it had never occurred to him to figure out what to do if he actually made it here. Now that he *was* here, what exactly was his best course of action?

Had the man still been in command of his own ship, the answer would have been simple. The T-Class cruiser *Tachyon*, the ship Andu had been captain of until the mutiny two days ago, would have been perfect for the job. Back on Mars the *Tachyon* had been expressly outfitted with exactly the right sort of equipment needed to home in on and accurately pinpoint the precise source of the radio signal; the *Drift On* was not. Had he still been in command of his own cruiser, Andu would have been able to make a detailed orbital survey of the surface, locate the city or other likely spot where the signal had originated, and land nearby, if necessary, to gather the appropriate data. Depending on what he found, he could then have radioed home for further instructions. Instead, he had no choice now but to make a visual survey of the surface from 10,000 kilometers up.

Much like his adopted home planet Mars, this place was a vast sea of green and brown, broken in places by the occasional splash of blue. If the colors meant the same thing here as they did back home, the green was vegetation; the brown, desert; and the blue, ocean. Then too, this place had white polar caps, their latitude and color suggesting an inhospitable stretch of snow and ice.

Like Goldilocks out for a walk on a cool summer's day, Andu wanted to land where it was just right—not too hot like down along the equator, nor too cold like up north at the pole. What he had in mind as a place to put down was a temperate zone in the middle latitudes of either hemisphere. What he wanted to avoid at all costs was a mountainous or heavily-wooded area.

After an orbit or two he picked out a spot that seemed just about right for what he had to do. He'd seen it from the air, a vast savanna located just south of a large inland sea.

Switching on the landing computer, he waited while the machine laid out a planet-wide grid he could use for navigation. Like any series of manmade longitude and latitude lines, the grid served as a reference point to help him find his way and to keep him from getting lost. By reading off the coordinates from the planet-wide grid and entering them into the landing computer, in no time at all he was able to select a landing site and make the switch to autopilot for the de-orbit burn. Less than thirty minutes later, Andu was on the ground.

Once the landing-sensors confirmed that he was on solid

ground, Andu powered up the runabout's external array. Right away the short-range scanners told him two very important things: the temperature outside was a muggy ninety-five galactic and the O_2 level was high enough to sustain a warm-blooded terran creature like himself. If the scanner didn't pick up any harmful trace-gases, he could go outside without a suit, something he very much wanted to do.

Andu had been a pioneer in the rebirth of space-travel, licensing the secret of his grandfather's Fornax Drive and helping to reopen the heavens to exploration after so many centuries of neglect. But dissatisfied with the pedestrian speeds he had been able to muster from the Fornax Battery, Andu had been the first to harness the tachyon, that once hypothetical particle of undefined mass named after *tachys*, the Greek word for swift. Unlike ordinary particles which acquired infinite mass as they were accelerated to light-speed, these superluminal particles possessed *imaginary* mass—at least in the mathematical sense of the word. Therefore, in a mirrored reflection of a "normal" particle, a tachyon could never travel at or below light-speed, but only *above* it, and with no upper limit on its velocity! Interestingly enough, instead of time slowing down as it would aboard a ship cruising just *under* light-speed, time onboard a tachyon ship would actually speed up! Thus, tachyon travelers tended to age slightly faster than their subluminal cousins back on Earth.

Traveling through hyperspace might be likened to a children's toy—the slinky. If the slinky were large enough, say the size of an entire galaxy, a traveler moving in a straight line along the coils of the slinky would probably not even realize he was actually tracing out a curved path. This, on account of the immense distances involved. Much the same illusion holds true, of course, for a hiker on the sphere we call Earth: the ground ahead of him always appears flat. Because the spiraling loops of the slinky are curved and tightly coiled, it takes the traveler a great long time to arrive at the far end. If he could somehow break free of the space-time fabric, however, and get *off* the coils, he could travel down the *center* of the slinky in a fraction of the time. This, in effect, is what Andu Nehrengel figured out how to do.

Andu's invention made him a wealthy man at a young

age, but neither wealth nor speed could satisfy his craving for adventure. In his drive for a new and more interesting challenge, he had joined in on the search for intelligent extraterrestrial life. It was the last great hunt of modern man. All of Earth's mountains had been conquered, the seas explored, the planets in the solar system visited, but the search for extraterrestrial life had come up pretty much empty-handed. It wasn't as if Earth held a monopoly on living things; to the contrary, other living planets had been found, and in the course of his many travels Andu had encountered life in countless other places. But *intelligent* life was something else again. Thus far anyway, the search had turned up little more than simple plants plus the occasional fishlike creature. Unlike the gruesome stories which had been bandied about for generations, the first aliens we met were not monsters but floating chlorophyll factories—water plants. And while these third-cousins to our own blue-green algae were oftentimes noxious, they were hardly the demons mankind had lived in fear of for nearly a thousand years.

And so it had remained.

Until now.

The unusual radio signal that had caught the researchers' attention was the first indirect evidence of intelligent life anywhere in this sector. It was what scientists had been hoping for since the SETI projects first began back in the twentieth century—a nonrandom, noncyclical, pattern of emissions separated at certain regular intervals by a recurring pattern of emissions.

Much as blotches of white space separate one typed word from the next on a printed page, the recurring emissions were thought to separate one alien word-idea from the next. No translation had yet been accomplished, though everyone agreed that the radio signal had almost certainly *not* come from any of a long line of known radio-transmitters like a pulsar or a Durbin anomaly. The regularity of *those* transmissions were legend! No, somebody—or something—had to be intentionally broadcasting. And somebody—or something—had to go out there to investigate. Grumpy and bored, Andu Nehrengel had been only too happy to oblige.

Taking the *Tachyon*, one of his newer T-Class cruisers, plus a dozen or more "volunteers" from his Martian tool-and-die factory, Andu had set out nearly two months ago to track down the source of this message. Unfortunately, he had neglected to observe the most basic rule of tracking: Never follow a trail unless you know ahead of time how long it is! Since radio waves were capable of traveling great distances given sufficient time, determining precisely how far he was away from the radio-source when he began, was an estimation problem of the first degree. Like any trans-galaxy traveler, Andu had to resort to an indirect method for calculating distance-to-source; though, in this instance, the usual techniques didn't seem to work. To begin with, the redshift was negligible. Then too, for some inexplicable reason, his attempts at triangulation failed. He ran it himself, three times, but each time it came up the same—inconclusive. It never occurred to him that someone might have been intentionally tampering with his equipment. And why should it? The way Andu had it figured, any race smart enough to be transmitting might also be smart enough to camouflage their presence. Either way, it had the making of a great adventure!

Eager to assemble a crew, Andu had lied to the men and told them the voyage would take two weeks at the outside. It had already been eight weeks at the time of the mutiny.

As he sat now in the cramped cockpit of the runabout contemplating his next move, Andu gazed out upon the primordial savanna surrounding his ship. It was a sea of tall coarse grasses, scattered trees, and the occasional watering hole. The nonwoody plants had hollow, jointed stems which were sheathed with narrow, bladelike leaves and petalless bland-colored flowers. As near as he could tell from inside the ship, the flat unbounded plain boasted not a single animal of any consequence. Still, the only way for him to know for certain was to get out there and investigate. That's exactly what Andu figured on doing.

Unsure how long he might be away from the ship or what kinds of trouble he might get himself into out there, Andu had no intention of venturing outside unprepared. He had learned his survival skills as a boy out on the scarred battlefields of Afghanistan, and he had learned them well. The centuries' old war had been terrible, leaving his homeland decimated and the hopes of his people shattered. All that now remained of the once fertile Afghan steppe were clumps of scruffy mountain vegetation and patches of stunted bushes, each clinging tenaciously for dear life to the fragile topsoil. Barren outcroppings and immense boulders dotted the devastated landscape. And like an untended boil, one swollen butte gave way to the next. The land was a tapestry of destruction quilted by an evil monster.

From the very beginning, Andu had been a reluctant warrior. That is, at least until that magical day his grandfather Fornax showed up at his doorstep and presented him with Jenny, the powerful durbinium-charged blaster Andu still carried at his side. In his gift of Jenny, Fornax had given Andu the means for changing history. By helping the beleaguered Afghan army win in their war against the Chinese, the tide of aggression was turned. And when the fight was over and the Chinese had withdrawn from his homeland, Andu set out in search of fame and fortune. It was that quest which had led him here today— wherever *here* was!

Gathering his materials together now, Andu went down the checklist as he packed his satchel. Each item had its importance, and before he dared leave the ship and go outside to explore the neighborhood, Andu wanted to be certain he wasn't leaving anything behind. As he methodically packed his gear, he was reminded of the mnemonic every soldier had to commit to memory as part of his wilderness training. Each of the letters in the word SURVIVAL was a rule to be obeyed in the field:

> **S**ize up the situation
> **U**se all your senses
> **R**emember your training
> **V**anquish all fear
> **I**mprovise
> **V**alue your life above all else
> **A**ct like the natives
> **L**ive by your wits.

A survival kit need not be elaborate to be effective, but at a minimum it should contain the functional items required to meet a person's highest priority needs of food, warmth, and shelter, plus an easy to carry waterproof case in which to transport these items.

Running down through his mental checklist, Andu took a

final inventory of his rucksack. There was a metal match, a snare wire, a polyglass collapsible shovel, a signaling mirror, a wax candle, a length of airline tubing, a solar blanket, a canister of oxy-tetracycline tablets to treat diarrhea or infection—oxy's in Army lingo, a box of condoms for water storage, a fishhook and line, a blade, a bottle of water purification tablets, a box of Acceleron caplets to promote rapid healing, a Chap stick, a couple of butterfly sutures, and at least a dozen Vaseline-saturated cottonballs to use as firestarters. All that plus Jenny and a handful of megaflares and his grandmother's diary (he never went anywhere without that!) and he was ready to go.

4
Chief Apostle Brigham Smith

Red-faced, Chief Apostle Brigham Smith bolted from his chair. He was furious! The veins in his head were near bursting. The old man's bony hands were shaking. Crumbled in his fist was Red's impertinent reply. He could scarcely believe what he'd just read. The lout wanted more money!

Chief Apostle Smith had never heard of such insolence! Not in all his days! Not from a commoner anyway. The audacity of the man!

Like an autocratic duke straight out of the Middle Ages, Chief Apostle Brigham Smith ruled a fiefdom complete with castle, moat, and drawbridge. After the Great War, what was left of America disintegrated into a series of competing fiefdoms, some religion-based like Smith's, some militaristic like the Southwest Protectorate, some hellbent for money like the Westcoast Consortium. But of all the districts that evolved after the War, Smith's was the most regimented. The Chief Apostle ruled it with an iron hand. He didn't expect insolence, and certainly not from an earthworm like Red. This mission Smith had sent him on was vitally important, though probably not in a way Red could ever fully grasp.

Three hundred years ago, at the start of the space-age, a shipload of Mormons set out from Earth intent on colonizing Mars. Their ship, the *Deseret*, went tragically off course and the pioneers never made it to their destination. They didn't die however, at least not right away, but endured for decades, drifting farther and farther away from the solar system. Though they were powerless to correct their drift, they made every effort to stay in regular contact with Church headquarters, first in the

U.S., then later in SKANDIA. Never giving up hope, they faithfully filed weekly reports of interesting observations they had made, both philosophic and scientific.

Though unintended, a long-duration spaceflight was the perfect laboratory for conducting all manner of fanciful experiments, from the mundane to the exquisite, in every field from chemistry to physics. The experiments numbered in the hundreds and the Mormons reported in on their results right up to the bitter end. Their final communiqué, circa 2285, was sent by one Brigham Young XIV, the last surviving member of the mission. Key portions of that transmission were later lost, though, when the Mormon bunker in SKANDIA was struck by an errand missile fired during a brief nuclear exchange between SKANDIA and her chief vassal state, the Republic of Germany. Only the cover page detailing the contents of the various sub-files survived the blast.

For nearly two hundred years it sat in a drawer gathering dust. Not until 2460 when a junior member of Viscount Nordman's staff uncovered it again, did anyone begin analyzing that sheet of paper's importance. And if not for the intriguing radio message received just six *months* ago, it might have remained a mystery forever!

The tantalizing message which so suddenly snapped the SETI researchers to attention had several distinctive features. The baud rate, which is to say, the number of code elements per second, was comparatively low. Then too, there were certain similarities to the message of 2285, similarities which, though important, only came to light after the fact: both messages were sent on precisely the same ultra-low frequency, both began and ended with precisely the same coded sequence, and both contained the same unambiguous, uncoded single word. That word, DESERET, suggested to the researchers that the aliens had received at least one of the tens of thousands of messages the SETI team itself had sent out in hopes of being heard.

All this they knew, and more. What they didn't know was how to decipher the thing. The message was a monster, a thirteen-bit transmission. To decode it required a thirteen-level etom. Problem was, such a machine hadn't been manufactured in over a century! To even find one still in working order took an exhaustive worldwide search. The word went out and, in what could only be termed a quirk of technological fate, the single working model was found in a sub-basement of the newly-rebuilt Mormon bunker now run by the impish Viscount Nordman.

Nothing short of a chance to decode this supposedly alien-transmission could dislodge the SETI team from their cozy mountaintop hideaway in the Hawaii Free State. But this might be the big break they'd been waiting for since late in the twentieth century. This might be first contact!

Thus, with pencils at the ready, and expectations high, off they went into the cold reaches of northern SKANDIA to see Viscount Nordman, that single uncoded word the only clue they had of the message's true meaning.

A code is different from a cipher, as different as night and day. Any computerman who has studied information theory will tell you that a cipher is a mathematical pattern, nothing more. One letter substitutes for another, the simplest being those where the alphabet is merely scrambled. A cipher can be made incredibly subtle, though, especially with the help of a computer. And yet, all ciphers suffer from the same weakness—they are nothing but patterns. If one computer can think them up, another can break them.

Codes, on the other hand, are quite different. Let's say the letter-group GLINK is in the current codebook. Does it mean "Aunt Minnie will be home for dinner" or does it mean "take pi to the fifth power"? There's no way to tell. The meaning is whatever you assign it, and no computer can analyze it simply by looking at a series of letter-groups. Even so, if you give a computer *enough* groups—plus a rational theory involving meanings, or subjects for meanings—it will eventually worry it out simply because the meanings themselves will ultimately show a pattern. But it is a problem of a different sort, and of a much higher order. If not for Nordman's thirteen-bit machine, the SETI people might have spent years trying to flesh out its meaning. As it was, they started down the wrong track, though through no fault of their own.

Viscount Nordman wouldn't have known what all the fuss was about if not for a fortuitous meeting between himself and Chief Apostle Brigham Smith just the month before. Pressured by inroads being made by the Amerind Nation of North America, the Chief Apostle had been in SKANDIA soliciting money and arms to help defend his fiefdom from invasion. Though he knew nothing of space-faring Mormons, he did know his history. Since well before the collapse of the United States, the quantitative study of history had been an official project of the Mormon church. Indeed, for the Church of Jesus Christ of Latter-day Saints, it had achieved the status of a science. Like the econometrics on which it was based, histometrics had a simple premise—take a big enough computer, the right equations, and the proper variables, and you could predict the outcome of an election, a war, even a revolution. To the survivors of the Great War in America, the question histometrics could answer was an important one: What was the very last moment in America's past that something, anything, could still have been done to halt the decline, to slow the downward spiral and prevent the carnage? When exactly was America's fate irrevocably sealed? What event, or series of events, was ultimately responsible for America's demise? Who, when, where, and what? Histometrics had the answer. Chief Apostle Brigham Smith of the Genealogical Institute outside Sane Lou was privy to the answer:

May 5, 2398. Lieutenant Lester Matthews steals a top-secret codebook from the hands of his dying grandfather, Senator Nate Matthews, Chairman of the U.S.'s Military Oversight Committee. Theft of that codebook eventually leads to the loss of the American fleet in the Pacific, irreversibly weakening the U.S.'s western defenses. Unable to recover from the blow, the nation is subsequently bombed into submission.

And the lesson from histometrics? If Nate hadn't been ill, if he hadn't been dying of Matthews Disease, Lester would never have managed to get his hands on that priceless codebook; the Chinese would never have been forewarned; and America would never have been defeated. One led to the next as surely as night follows day.

Chief Apostle Brigham Smith knew it to be true. Histometrics had proved it. His people had run the regressions. They had backfitted all the data. They had solved all the equations. There was no doubt about it. May 5, 2398 was the crack in time, the one that had sealed all their fates. And Matthews Disease was the culprit. If only time-travel were possible, Nate might have been cured ahead of time and America saved! If only.

It was all so much science fiction, however, until that fortuitous meeting seven months ago between Viscount Nordman and Chief Apostle Brigham Smith. That final communiqué, the one sent by Brigham Young XIV back in 2285, contained a tantalizing file, a hint of a truth yet to be known, a working theory of time-travel worked out by a shipload of doomed Mormons. Nordman's people had found it; but only Chief Apostle Brigham Smith had been smart enough to put two and two together. Indeed, of all the people in the know—himself, Viscount Nordman, the SETI team—only Chief Apostle Brigham Smith had figured out the truth: *the message-senders weren't aliens, they were Mormons!* More importantly, they were Mormons who were (hopefully) still in possession of the ship's full complement of files, especially Brigham Young XIV's proof showing why time-travel should be possible.

Smith knew instantly what had to be done: the original documentation had to be recovered at all costs! But more than that, no one else besides himself must learn the truth! Not Viscount Nordman, not the SETI team, not whatever dupe they found to chase down these mysterious aliens!

To keep to a minimum the number of persons who would eventually discover that these message-sending extraterrestrials were actually people, not aliens, Chief Apostle Brigham Smith hatched a diabolical three-step plan. First: to sucker Andu Nehrengel in, along with his tachyon ship and an expendable crew. Second: to have Red manufacture a mutiny and toss Andu overboard. Finally: to have Red murder the entire crew before following Nehrengel to his ultimate destination.

Meanwhile, to keep the SETI people busy long enough for him to get the mission off the ground and on its way before anyone recognized the subterfuge, Smith seized on the oldest trick in the book: a digitized machine-virus. This sleight of hand would send Viscount Nordman's ancient computer off chasing its own tail and prevent the thirteen-level etom from ever closing in on the answer. It would take a month or more of heavy-duty decoding work—templates and everything—before they realized that a systematic error had been introduced into the data. They wouldn't suspect sabotage, only the vagaries of a century-old machine.

Thus, it began.

Under the guise of mounting a SETI search halfway across the galaxy, the Church of Jesus Christ of Latter-day Saints, operating through its financial arm, the Zion National Bank of SKANDIA, came to fund the second space mission in Church history, this one aboard a T-Class cruiser belonging to one Andu Nehrengel. It was all an elaborate scheme, however; and if not for that radio message of six months ago, the one with the single uncoded word, time-travel might never have graduated beyond the status of an abstract theory!

None of this was known by Red, of course, nor by Andu, and therein lay Chief Apostle Brigham Smith's problem. How to control events half a galaxy away without revealing the very truth he wanted so badly to keep to himself? It wouldn't be easy, especially in light of his present power struggle against the Amerind Nation back home. But he had no choice! For Chief Apostle Brigham Smith, this scheme of his had taken on a life of its own. It had become an obsession. If time-travel were truly possible, the Mormons could go back in time and manipulate events more to their liking. Nate Matthews could be saved, and America along with him. The ship that had gone off course could perhaps be rescued, thus ensuring that Mars would become a Mormon homeland as the Elders had originally intended. Further back still, when Utah was but a territory, it might have extracted a better deal from the U.S. upon accepting statehood in 1896. The list was long, the stakes high, and it all rested on keeping Red in line and on track.

But how?

5
Life

As Andu stood on the cusp of setting foot outside, his mind rocketed back to the events of an earlier day. Beginning about two years ago, he had begun taking a keen interest in the question of extraterrestrial intelligence. Actually, it all started one rainy afternoon when he had nothing better to do than stay at home and view a drama-fiche. It was one of those stories about some invading alien-species who was threatening humanity's domination of the globe. Like nearly all such tales, the aliens rarely survive to see the credits at the end of the show. As a rule, they either die at the hands of the humans or else through an act of God—including the director! Depending on the script, earthquakes, volcanoes, even avalanches conveniently come to the rescue of humanity at the very last possible minute. But were such alien threats real, or were they imagined?

Andu wondered. So far, at least, all the alien life that had been found were nothing but plants. Which is not to say that those plants were always docile—they weren't—but they were hardly capable of interstellar space-travel! Still, in our fascination with life as being mobile, we sometimes forget about plants altogether. People who imagine life on Earth as consisting merely of animals moving against a green background seriously misunderstand what it is they are seeing. That green background is busily alive. Plants grow; they move; they twist; they turn; they fight for sunlight; they interact continuously with the animals around them, discouraging some with their bark and their thorns, feeding others to advance their reproduction, spread their pollen or disburse their seeds. What marvel of evolution, the burr, for instance?

Although people don't think much about it, plants evolved every bit as competitively as animals, and in some ways, *more* fiercely. Along the way, certain of them developed awesome chemical arsenals to achieve their ends—spores with deadly toxins; terpenes to poison the soil around them and inhibit competitors; alkaloids—some of which are deadly—to make them unpalatable to insects and other predators; pheromones to communicate with kin in distant parts of the forest. Plants even enlist animals in their defense. When attacked by caterpillars, certain flora release chemicals to attract wasps, the natural enemies of the invading caterpillar. Grazing bison secrete saliva which alters the metabolism of the very plant it's munching, thus hastening renewed growth. Being animals ourselves, we tend to forget how alive plants really are. But that still begged the question. Was terran life—humans in particular—in any real danger from alien-invaders?

To get his answer, Andu went to see his old friend Dr. Fosnach Chandra over at the university. Chandra was an exobiologist, recently returned from visiting the SETI team at the Hawaii Free State Observatory, there to deliver a series of lectures on alien biology.

"Not hardly," was the short answer. "Aliens have more to fear from us than we do from them!"

Clad in a dark, classically tailored suit and black shoes, Dr. Chandra approached with a slow but fluid gait. He shook Andu's hand firmly, unsmiling; he felt no need to ingratiate. Easing his lean frame into a chair, he slouched sideways and cocked his head. From this oblique angle it seemed as if his obsidian eyes could bore more deeply into his visitor than if he sat up straight.

"What, precisely, do you want to talk about?" he inquired, his voice still bearing the Indiastan lilt of his youth, this despite more than half a century's absence.

"I'd like to pick your brain a minute, Doc."

Chandra's dark eyes grew darker still. "A minute?" he fumed, jabbing one, then both, of his impossibly long forefingers at Andu. "You think you can summarize Homer's *Odyssey* in a minute? Newton's *Principia*? You think you can describe the Sistine Chapel to a blind man in a minute?"

Chandra's voice quavered with incredulity, disgust. "If

all you have is a minute to discuss a subject as vast as alien biology, I don't think it matters one way or the other whether you talk to me." He turned away with a harrumph.

"Figure of speech, Doc. What I meant was . . . "

Somehow the interview lurched forward despite the rocky start and Chandra slipped into the charming persona he was known for. The man dispensed jokes, anecdotes, and aphorisms, as well as generous smiles and laughter. But in that earlier moment of anger he had revealed his irrepressible passion, not only for scientific truth, but for beauty. Here was a man who, even at 83, was legendary for his work habits. He had been nurtured on ambition and couldn't help but exude a certain restlessness.

"So you say you viewed this drama-fiche. Why do you waste your time on such stuff?"

"I guess I'm bored," Andu replied. "While I'm intrigued by the possibilities of alien life, I'm frustrated by the fact that we've never found any."

"Silly boy. It is strange, isn't it, that a man should have a consuming passion to do something for which he lacks the capacity?"

"I beg your pardon."

"No need to beg," Chandra grunted. "T.S. Eliot. I wonder: was he talking about you? Life isn't interesting unless you're constantly striving against your own inherent, often insurmountable, limitations. We must join the battle in progress. Now, about those aliens of yours. Let me only say this: invading species are less likely to be threatened by heroic deeds or natural disasters than by their own poor fecundity."

"Huh?"

"Fecundity! Don't tell me you've never had *sex* before!"

"Boy, you're in rare form today, Doc."

"Opportunistic species, which is to say, those good at colonizing new environments, exhibit so-called r-selection. Their characteristics include small body-size, rapid growth, and large broods; all qualities which lead to a high r, a high intrinsic rate of growth in numbers. Such a rapid rate of increase can cause big problems—in real life, as well as in really bad movies. These rodent-like creatures, while most assuredly mettlesome, are not apt to be intelligent, nor able to arrive here under their own power."

"Stowaways?"

"Perhaps. But then compare them with the seemingly more dangerous k-type creatures. Here are species marked by slow development, large body-size, and reproduction later in life. They are good at competing in a stable environment, though not so good at colonizing a new one. Which is the bigger threat to our food supply: millions of r-type crop-beetles or the occasional k-type elephant? Just as we humans have found it exceedingly difficult to colonize foreign environments, so too will intelligent k-type aliens. If you think about it, Andu, we shouldn't be all that surprised to find the galaxy teeming with plants and r-type critters, but hardly any of the k-type variety."

"You make it all sound so logical, Doc. Why can't I accept that? Do we even know what it is we're looking for out there?"

"Now the shoe is really on the other foot! Do you think these SETI people are idiots?"

"Not at all, but for centuries now they've been scouring the heavens for some sign—*any* sign—of alien-intelligence. What have they found? Nothing. Not a thing. Nada. Isn't it possible that our inability to find any alien life is not so much a result of our perceptions as it is of our prejudices?"

"Now you've lost me," Chandra glowered as if the criticism were directed at him personally.

"Just because a frozen planet has no observable liquid water, and just because it seems to lack the necessary solar energy, does not mean the planet is dead."

"On this you get no argument. Even here on Earth, where the main source of energy is the sun, life is not confined strictly to those areas bathed in sunshine."

"That's what I mean!" Andu exclaimed. "There are more than a few instances where terran life draws its energy from sources *other* than the sun. Submerged volcanic heat-vents, the radiation given off by uranium deposits, even caustic chemical reactions deep inside potash fields. They've all proven capable of sustaining life! The same must hold true out there on otherwise inert planets, even frozen ones. Nuclear or chemical energy-sources might yield expressions of life *totally* foreign to us. Life might organize and thrive on everything from the electron-stripping action of cosmic rays to the gravitational potential of a falling body. And let's not forget the chemical energy of a highly-reactive atmosphere, or even the negative particle-flow out of a black hole."

"For God's sake, Andu, you're not telling me anything I don't already know! Whenever energy, plus matter capable of interfusing with that energy, come together in one locale—no matter how unearthly—and are allowed sufficient time to interact, life will result. It's inevitable. I proved it myself, years ago, in the laboratory. Now, as to whether or not that life will be intelligent, well, that's another subject. But life itself, especially in the form of those simple r-type creatures we've been talking about, should not be a rarity at all!"

"I'm sorry, Doc, but the question remains. Would we even know it if we saw it? I have my doubts. We may be staring blindly, even now, at tens of thousands of living worlds and not even know it. They say that some ten million viruses populate a single mill of unpolluted water; yet, from half a meter away we cannot see even one of them. What can be told, then, of a world half a *galaxy* away? It could be literally *bristling* with life, and we might not suspect a thing! Even good-sized creatures would be invisible to us on a world 100 light-years away, to say nothing of microbes."

"Curse our feeble instruments!"

"It has nothing to do with our instruments. Even a physical examination might not tell us much. An explorer might stumble across a seemingly inert 'rock' on a distant planet and not even recognize it *as* life. Farfetched? Not if he doesn't recognize that particular rock's method of respiration as *being* respiration! Worse yet, he might not even be able to recognize *intelligent* life if he stumbled upon it."

"Ah, the old flea-on-the-dog conundrum."

"Come again?"

"Surely you've heard of the flea-on-the-dog conundrum! A flea cannot 'see' the dog on which it's riding, thus, by analogy, we may be unable to 'see' any life-forms which are vastly superior to us."

"Yeah, I guess that's what I'm trying to say."

Dr. Chandra smiled. "I am reminded of a story I once read as a boy. It was written long ago—maybe as far back as the twentieth century—by a science-fiction writer of some note. As a story, it has practically attained the status of a fable, a parable really, about our own egocentricities."

Andu rolled his eyes, but Chandra ignored him, lacing his long fingers together and settling back in his chair to speak.

"Most tales involving encounters between humans and alien-intelligence make the assumption that the aliens will treat us as approximate equals, either as friends or as foes. As friends, they will be anxious to communicate and trade with us; as enemies, they will fight with us to the death, possibly killing or enslaving all of humanity. But this author put forth another, much more humiliating possibility—that alien-intelligence is so vastly superior to us and so indifferent to our very presence, as to be almost unaware of us. They do not even covet the surface of the planet where we live because they live in the stratosphere. We do not know whether they evolved here or elsewhere—and we will never know. Our mightiest engineering structures they regard as we ourselves regard coral formations—seldom noticed and considered of no great importance. We aren't even a nuisance to them! And they are of no real threat to us either, except that their 'engineering' might occasionally disturb our habitat, just as the grading done for a highway disturbs the occasional gopher hole. Some few of them might study us casually, as we study termite nests. Some odd duck among them might keep a few of us as pets. That is what happened to this author's hero. He got too nosy around one of their activities, was captured, and by pure luck kept as a pet instead of being stepped on. In time, he came to understand his predicament, except in one respect—he never did realize to its full bitterness that the human race could not even *fight* these creatures. He was simply a goldfish in a bowl; and who cares about the opinion of a helpless goldfish? I, myself, *have* a goldfish pond in my backyard. Perhaps those fish hate me bitterly and have sworn to destroy me. I won't even suspect it; I certainly won't lose any sleep over it. And it almost goes without saying that even the most esoteric knowledge of our science will not enable those goldfish to harm me. I am indifferent to them, and invulnerable."

Dr. Chandra went on. "The real lesson of alien biology, though, may turn out to be the myriad ways in which it has learned to take advantage of every crumb and morsel of available energy within its grasp. The competent use of energy rather than pure intellectual power may be the most remarkable quality of extraterrestrials."

"It's interesting that you should say that. If what you're saying is true, that might explain why all the aliens we've met so far are dumb, or else plants."

"Complex life requires complex energy. Whereas simple life-forms can generally convert solar radiation directly into useful calories, multicellular creatures capable of transportation almost certainly cannot. To build the complex materials necessary for *their* existence, multicellular creatures depend on a food chain built around plants and lower animals."

"Yes, but the higher up you go on the food chain, the scarcer edible living-structures become. As competition for those scarcer resources becomes keener further up the ladder, intellectual capacity inevitably becomes a more critical element in survival. By necessity, intelligence has to rise as you ascend the food chain. Let's face it, Doc, grazing doesn't require near the brainpower hunting does. Then too, it's almost axiomatic that as evolution proceeds, intelligence will rise right along with it."

"Ah, conundrum number two: Intelligence is inevitable! Sorry, Andu, but I couldn't disagree more. Whereas life itself may be spread profusely throughout the galaxy, *intelligent* life may not be. This is an important distinction. In point of fact, intelligent life may evolve only under the most special of circumstances. First, there must be sufficient energy-flow to adequately feed the base of the chain, but more importantly, there must be enough of an energy *shortage* at the top of the chain to drive a keen intellectual competition. Look at the dinosaurs. They were around here a lot longer than us primates, and yet there isn't even a single shred of evidence that they used so much as a tool, much less spoke or wrote or built cities. As you'd know if you had read any of my papers, creatures in a land of plenty don't *need* to be smart!"

"The stuff you write's way over my head, Doc."

"Must I spoon-feed you? Here, read this," Chandra said, tossing him a copy of his latest article. "Life is the interaction of matter and energy to produce a more orderly arrangement of said matter; evolution, the systematic search for the most efficient use of that energy; and intelligence, the evolutionary response to insufficient energy. Read it; learn something; it's all right there in my paper."

"What you said about the dinosaurs never occurred to me. I guess we were damn lucky sentient life ever sprouted here on Earth."

"Indeed! The question of whether or not intelligent life will arise—and where—is a bit like the old story of the laboratory parrot who is set to work pecking randomly and tirelessly at a keyboard, its talon occasionally pumping the SHIFT key. Most of what it 'writes' is unintelligible garbage, but once in a great while—purely by chance—it will render a sonnet of Shakespearian quality. Likewise, in a large and varied universe endowed with sufficient time, the conditions necessary for the development of intelligent life will occasionally be met, if only by accident. Unfortunately for us humans, these habitable islands are as few and far between as that parrot's sonnets."

Carefully folding Chandra's scholarly paper and putting it in his satchel, Andu said, "That sorta answers my other question too."

"Let me guess. Why does this particular location in the universe satisfy precisely the conditions necessary to support our existence? In other words, is there a God?"

Andu nodded.

"Dear boy, you must be kidding! If those habitable islands are as few and far between as that parrot's sonnets, then we shouldn't be surprised to find that the conditions necessary for life exist in precisely the same place as we do. Not only that, we shouldn't be surprised to find that every other locale nearby is not only hostile to life in general, but specifically hostile to intelligent life. Yet sometimes we *are* surprised, even perplexed. We're tempted by this seeming coincidence to invoke the divine, if for no other reason than because it appears as if the whole of our universe exists merely for our sake."

"Doesn't it?" Andu said, smiling.

"Even scientists manage to delude themselves sometimes—our SETI friends included. It has been shown, quite conclusively I might add, that fundamental physical properties can vary only within relatively narrow ranges and still allow for the development of life. Other sets of values give rise to universes which, while very often beautiful, would be completely devoid of living things."

"Give me a 'for instance'."

"If the electric charge of a particle as basic as the electron were only slightly different from what it actually is, life on Earth would probably not exist. Computer simulations have shown that had the charge been only slightly higher or lower than what it is, stars would have been either unable to burn hydrogen and helium as fuel to produce the radiant energy life requires, or else they would have been unable to explode as supernovae, thus depriving the galaxy of the heavier elements like oxygen and carbon which are the building blocks for our particular type of life."

"So what about God?" Andu asked at this point in the conversation.

"So what about him?" Dr. Chandra answered. "As a scientist, I would rather not invoke divine intervention to explain the workings of the world. Forgive me, but the whole history of scientific inquiry has been the gradual, if sometimes painful, realization that events can be explained in terms *other* than divine inspiration. Thus, we have now reached a level of understanding which permits us to postulate a universe that developed from completely random initial conditions, but which will nevertheless yield a number of regions suitable for the evolution of intelligent life. Just as that parrot may be expected to occasionally peck out a beautiful sonnet, even a random universe will occasionally bring together the necessary ingredients to cultivate life. All by chance, of course, and with nothing planned ahead of time—and certainly without any divine intervention!

"To a scientist, such a conclusion is important. It suggests that the initial state of this portion of the universe, the portion *we* inhabit, did not have to be chosen with great care by some higher being. In other words, no divine purpose is required to explain our existence!"

Andu smiled. It was the same smile he had given Chandra that day back in his laboratory. Now, as he stood in the airlock of the *Drift On*, his hand poised on the latch, his mind fixed on what he might find outside, he ritualistically crossed his fingers.

Forget divine intervention—how 'bout some old-fashioned good luck for a change!

6
Tracks

Every large rocky planet ever formed had done so according to the same scheme. Therefore, they all shared certain similarities. Each had tectonic plates; each, a molten iron core; each, a stable magnetic field. It was this last feature, the stable magnetic field, that Andu was banking on to help him find his way.

Even in an age of spaceships and tachyon drives, a magnetic compass was still a traveler's first line of defense in not getting lost. Though one of the earliest and simplest of navigational tools, no explorer in his right mind would set foot out on an uncharted planet without a compass in his hand, and a survival kit on his back. Even today, a thousand years after the fact, the story was still told of the one truly remarkable discovery that Christopher Columbus made, that of magnetic declination. Without it, practically no one could have duplicated his feat and made it to the New World!

Thinking now how it must have been back then, out there in the Atlantic, a thousand miles from nowhere, his crew practically in mutiny, their hopes dwindling with each passing day, Andu found himself identifying with Christopher Columbus. Though the story of civilization was too convoluted to make the comparison complete, Andu thought he understood how Columbus must have felt, how he himself felt.

Andu reached into his pocket. His fingers closed on a padded felt case. Inside was a handcrafted compass, practically the only thing his father had ever given him. Life back on the Afghan steppe had been hard, and possessions few; Andu treasured that compass almost as much as he did his grandmother's diary.

Gently unwrapping the compass from its felt case, he released the setscrew. Sure enough, the needle began to turn. Waiting a moment until it steadied, Andu twisted the outer shell until the needle pointed to zero degrees, magnetic north.

Lining up the direction-of-travel arrow with a distant tree, Andu took his first reading. To be certain of finding his way back again later, he activated the runabout's locator beacon and set his own pocket finder to the same frequency. Keeping his eye fixed on that faraway tree, Andu set off boldly through the tall grass.

Walking slowly so as to not turn an ankle, Andu found the going tough. The terrain was matted with clumps of upturned turf, and every so often, the ground was pitted with holes three to four centimeters in diameter. Had he been picking his way across a meadow back on Earth, he would have taken the holes as having been made by snakes. But snakes implied rodents, of course, and thus far anyway, he hadn't seen any evidence of such r-type creatures.

After proceeding for about a hundred meters he came into a clearing caked thick with wet mud. As he moved laterally across it, his boots sinking ever so slowly into the muck, Andu caught sight of a set of tracks at the far edge of the open space. Curious now, he advanced cautiously, his keen eyes darting back and forth watching for any sign of danger.

The giant pair of prints were set about a meter apart as if their maker had stood there motionless, hidden by the tall grass, waiting for the precise moment to spring. Each footprint had three claw-like toe marks out in front plus an additional one behind. But unlike any number of hunting carnivores back home, say, a cat or a wolf, animals with paws that were flat and padded, these toe marks were pointed and sharp like the talons of a hawk. In terms of their dimension, the bird-like prints were at least three times as wide as any Andu had ever seen or heard of back on Earth. If indeed the tracks *had* been made by a bird, the creature must have been enormous! Yet, he couldn't imagine such an immense beast ever being able to take flight. If it was a bird, it must have hunted on foot, like an ostrich, perhaps climbing the occasional tree for a better vantage point.

Andu smiled; he knew a little something about flight

dynamics. The physics had come to him naturally, as if he'd been born to it. But not wanting to stand still, he had entered the university after the war, intent on studying propulsion theory. There, under the wise tutelage of Dr. Chandra and others, he had conducted hundreds, if not thousands, of wind tunnel experiments. He had learned all there was to know about the mass-to-propulsion dilemmas posed when one doubled or trebled the proportions of a body or a machine. And then too, as part of his graduate work in ship design, he had learned that the study of such "scaling-up" problems dated back some eight hundred years to the early Modern era. In fact, it was Galileo himself who, in the early 1600s, first addressed the problem large land-animals faced in supporting their own bulk.

Galileo began his study by theorizing about the relationship between body size, body strength, and internal structure. He considered two animals which, while having basically the same body shape, nevertheless varied greatly in overall size. If, for instance, the larger animal were twice as long as the smaller one, it would also be twice as wide and twice as tall. Its volume was another matter, though. Rather than being double that of the smaller animal, it would be *eight* times as great—twice the length times twice the height times twice the width. Assuming the two creature were made of the identical substance, the larger animal would outweigh the smaller one by *eight times!* This made for a complication.

Whereas the volume of the larger animal had increased eightfold, the strength of its legs (or its wings, if it were a bird) had increased only by a factor of four—twice the length times twice the width. This was the scaling-up problem in its barest form—area versus volume, squared versus cubed. The strength of a leg or a wing could only increase in proportion to the area of its cross section, any increase in height contributing everything to weight but nothing to strength. In other words: *eight times the weight had to be lugged around by only four times the strength!*

As Galileo himself pointed out, this was untenable. If an animal became progressively larger without also changing its shape, it would eventually reach a size where it could no longer support itself. Confronted with this limitation, Nature compensated, of course, and did so by altering the internal structure of the beast so as to ensure that its weight *wouldn't* increase according to a cubic function. Birds evolved hollow bones. Big mammals took to the water. Really big birds quit flying altogether! As Chandra was fond of saying: Nature always found a way!

Andu nodded as if it all made perfect sense. He was still bent over the tracks he'd found in the mud at the edge of the clearing. Suffice it to say, any animal large enough to make *these* tracks could not take wing, no matter how bird-like its outward appearance! This beast obviously hunted on the ground. The question was: how big was it and what did it eat?

While he considered the answer, Andu thought back to his merchant marine days. The scaling-up problem applied to ships as well as animals, something he learned when he was first tinkering around with a suitable design for a prototype of his new T-Class cruiser.

In the realm of shipbuilding, estimates of the power required to propel a full-sized ship were arrived at well in advance of building the actual vessel. This was accomplished by running a battery of tests on a series of smaller-scale models, usually in a wind tunnel or a wave tank. No more unlikely a place than a wave tank led Andu to make a startling discovery!

In one of those stunning connections between disciplines, Andu discovered that the equation governing his propulsion calculations were one and the same as the equation Galileo had unearthed eight centuries earlier when he was trying to unravel the relationship between an animal's size and its strength. That such a relationship should even exist was uncanny! Who would have thought it? And the equation? $V^2/G*L$ where V was the craft's running speed; G, the acceleration due to gravity; and L, the length of the ship's hull, or in the case of an animal, the length of the creature's legs. How strange that he should now be engaged in an effort to judge the size and running speed of *this* creature!

Crouching down to study the impressions in the mud more closely, Andu pulled out his pocketknife. The largest blade was marked off in centimeters and doubled as a straightedge for map reading. He slid it in the hole and used it to measure the depth of the deepest claw mark. It went down all the way, more than ten centimeters!

Andu gasped. His own footprints were barely two

centimeters deep, and he weighed in at nearly 75 kilos!

Glancing around, Andu saw further evidence of the creature's size. Beginning from the spot where the beast had stood there at the edge of the clearing, a wide swatch of tall grass had been trampled flat as if the big animal had suddenly charged off in that direction.

It was anybody's guess what the damn thing had been chasing, or even if it had made the kill. But either way, based on the evidence, the thing looked to be big and mean and Andu wasn't taking any chances. Quickly folding up his pocketknife and putting it away, he unholstered his blaster. Carnivore or not, he wasn't about to risk meeting up with this bird-beast unprepared!

Peering once over his shoulder just to be sure, Andu crept judiciously forward. Since the trampled path headed more or less in the direction he was going anyway, Andu decided to follow it. If it should suddenly veer off in the wrong direction, he could always retrace his steps back to the clearing later on.

The path took him down a gentle slope into a lusher stretch of the savanna. Here, the ground beneath his feet became soggy, and the farther he went, the more bog-like it became. Now, with each step he took, his boots made a squishy sound in the mud.

Body on alert, he continued to slosh forward through the muck for perhaps another dozen paces. Then he stopped, unsure what to do.

Should he backtrack to higher drier ground, or continue in the direction he was going? Undoubtedly a marsh or lake lay hidden in the grass just ahead and it might prove interesting.

That's when he saw the droppings!

All else equal, the size of an animal's feces say a little something about the size of the animal. Consider the difference in size, say, between a cow-pie and a rabbit pellet. What goes in, must come out, and what Andu nearly stepped into was closer in size to the former than the latter. And it was fresh! Now he knew for certain that he wasn't alone!

Stepping over the still-warm pile, Andu continued following along through the trail of broken grasses until he arrived at the edge of a marsh. Draining it, about twenty meters farther along, was a brook. And, on the far side of the brook, lay an open field. There, he saw movement.

Catching his breath, he stood deathly still. Grazing there in the open field, just as content as could be, were about three dozen horse-like creatures, though of diminutive size. Andu wasn't close enough to them to make out much in the way of details, but one thing was for certain: these animals were not the owners of the claw-like feet that had made the pair of tracks he'd seen earlier. These animals were four-legged, and like their terran cousins, appeared to be chomping on the pampas-like grass. Their heads were big like a cow's, but their long legs and sleek body shape suggested they could run much faster, perhaps as fast as a deer or an elk. Instead of having a single, fly-swatting tail like an equestrian, though, these grazers sported *three* tails, each prehensile like a monkey's and each a third as long as the animal itself.

Andu moved out from the tall grass hoping to get a better look at the beasts. He stood there motionless, watching, waiting.

Suddenly, one of the "horses" looked up in terror as if it had caught a whiff of something horrible. Two of its three tails began flailing wildly around and the beast emitted a high-pitched squeal.

Thinking he'd been spotted, Andu dropped back into the grass and crouched down low where he couldn't be seen. The shrieking continued, however, and a moment later the entire herd bolted!

Andu swore. He was disappointed to see them go. Though he'd made no threatening moves, his presence there had obviously unnerved them. He was just about to swear again when it hit him: *They weren't running away from him, they were running away from something else!*

Jerking his head suddenly sideways to see what had spooked them, Andu shuddered in horror! A hundred meters away was the most fearsome-looking creature he had ever seen! It stood more than two meters tall, weighed perhaps fifty kilos, had a feathered body, and a huge parrotlike head with a giant scooped beak like a pelican. Speechless, Andu watched as it made its kill.

The bird-beast sprinted across the ground with unexpected swiftness. Its massive head swung from side to side in what could only have been an inbred hunting-technique designed to help keep its sidemounted eyes fixed on any quickly-moving prey.

With swift determination the bird-beast bore down upon one of the smaller three-tailed horses. It happened so terrifyingly fast, Andu could scarcely believe his eyes! Before he knew it, the creature had closed the gap and kicked the German-shepherd-sized "three-tail" to the ground with a single vicious sideswipe of a muscular leg!

The hapless victim squealed in anguish, its trio of prehensile tails twitching madly every which way. Thrashing around on the ground, the stunned herbivore tried to right itself using one of its tails like an arm. But before it could get back to its feet, the bird-beast had seized the "three-tail" in her massive beak and begun pounding it to death against a boulder.

Andu didn't wait around to see how it ended. Blaster still in hand, he was already running like hell back to his ship. Here was a creature he did not wish to meet again. Ever.

7
Bird-Beast

Sleep did not come easily that night. Though Andu Nehrengel would hardly have characterized himself as fearless, here was a man who wasn't prone to cowardice either. And yet tonight, this usually brave man was scared. Tonight, for perhaps the very first time since this whole caper began, he found himself painted into an uncomfortably tight corner.

Andu had neither the fuel nor the provisions to attempt a return home. Thus, if he were to survive at all, it would have to be here, and it would have to be now. Only problem was, this planet he was marooned on had turned out to be a mighty dangerous place. On top of that, he was no closer now to locating the source of that mysterious radio signal than when he first landed. What Andu needed was a plan!

For hours, he tossed and turned trying to fall asleep. Sunset had brought rain plus a howling wind. There had been two sunsets actually, as if the planet were in orbit around a double star. But Andu didn't have time to enjoy either. The storm buffeted his tiny ship, rocking his nighttime hammock to and fro. Cramped for space, he had been forced to string it across the galley doorway; though in doing so, he felt every tiny little tremor against the hull. When sleep finally did come, it was a fitful sleep, one invaded time and again by horrible images of that terrible beast pounding the life out of that helpless three-tail. And yet, as he drifted back and forth between wakefulness and slumber, a plan began to take shape in his mind.

It occurred to him that perhaps he could home in on the source of the radio signal using the ship's onboard receiver, plus two of her remote comm-units. If he set out the two comm-units, one on each side of the ship at a distance of perhaps two hundred meters, he ought to have a baseline long enough to triangulate the origin of the transmissions. The receiver onboard the *Drift On* would double as the third corner of the triangle.

Though he would have rathered not run the risk of meeting up with that bird-beast again, at first light he rolled out of bed and began making preparations to do just that! He had no choice really, not if he was to ever solve the riddle of the mysterious alien-message anyway.

With the sun just now peeking above the horizon, Andu clipped one of the two remote comm-units to his belt, undid the hatch, and headed outside. His blaster was clamped in his right hand, just to be sure.

Counting his steps as he went, Andu set off at a brisk pace. The morning air was hot and muggy, and a heavy dew lay on the grass.

His heading was ninety degrees due east of the one he had followed yesterday. Andu had done all the math ahead of time: since his stride averaged about one meter in length over flat ground, he'd have to stay on this heading for a count of at least two hundred. Only then could he assure himself of having a baseline long enough to make this stunt work.

He barely got a quarter of the way when something caught his eye.

Off to his left, about five meters away, was what could only be described as a nest. It was a shallow pit dug into the soft ground. In it were six, leathery, basketball-sized eggs. Judging by the claw marks in and around the nest, it almost certainly had been carved out by one of the bird-beasts!

Simultaneously curious and terrified, Andu bent down over the simple nest to study the rust-colored eggs more closely. Noticing, on several, a tiny hairline crack and movement within, Andu immediately assumed they were about to hatch. His first inclination was to torch the entire lot before they ever had a chance to. His only hesitation was a vague promise he'd made once to Dr. Chandra about needlessly destroying alien-life. Andu was just about to break that promise when he heard the sound of crumpling grass off to his left.

His heart stopped. *Not sixty meters away was a pair of adult bird-beasts!*

Still crouched down over the nest, blaster in hand, Andu peered out across the savanna. The ferocious-looking birds appeared to be tranquilly grazing; searching perhaps for nuts or berries, maybe insects. As the pair approached, they did so at a leisurely pace, the tall grass falling before them, the reed-like stalks being crushed beneath their feet.

Andu drew a sharp breath. He'd already seen what one bird-beast could do to an animal; what chance did he stand against *two*? None! None whatsoever!

Andu cursed his arrogance. He was too far from the ship to make it back there alive. If only he'd thought ahead! If only he'd thought to bring the emergency rocketsled along with him! If only . . .

For two long seconds Andu just stood there frozen, lost what to do. Then, looking around wild-eyed, he spied a solitary tree some forty meters away. With the bird-beasts blocking his retreat, the tree was his only chance!

Every muscle taut, Andu sprang to his feet and flew off in that direction at high speed.

No sooner had he begun to run, though, than the animals' heads popped up to see what was moving about in the tall grass.

As if drawn by instinct, both of them immediately gave chase, the larger of the two veering off to first stop and check on her eggs, the somewhat smaller one closing the distance between himself and Andu in a matter of strides. It would have all been over right then and there if not for Jenny. Just as the raptor-like creature was about to strike, Andu spun around and sprayed it with a plasma-pulse from his durbinium-charged blaster.

The results were startling!

Ionized by the hot stream of neutrons, the male bird-beast shuddered, then vaporized in a thick cloud of blue smoke!

Though the stench was horrific, Andu didn't have any time to waste being ill. By now, the mama-bird had satisfied herself that her eggs were okay and had taken up the chase. Though Andu had quite a head start on her, it almost wasn't enough. Perhaps two seconds longer and he would have been bird-beast breakfast!

Scrambling up the trunk of the mammoth tree like a monkey, Andu got above the bird-beast's reach in a thrice. The raptor's claws, while perfect for killing and maiming, were clumsy for climbing, and it couldn't pursue him up into the branches!

Though Andu was shaking with fear, he couldn't believe his good fortune. It made him think twice about simply blasting the she-beast to bits. On the off chance that she might leave of her own accord, he decided to wait her out and see. The last thing he wanted to do right now was attract more attention than he already had. Besides, he'd found a rather comfortable notch to sit in some ten meters up off the ground among the branches. The lofty perch afforded him a splendid view of the landscape and the surrounding countryside.

Andu could see all the way to the horizon. In the foreground was his ship. Beyond it, the creek and marsh he'd discovered the previous day. On the far side of the marsh was a lake he hadn't known about, in an area he hadn't yet explored. In the distance was a lush green valley, and beyond that, a range of low mountains. The area inbetween the lake and his ship was dotted with a dozen or more "nests." Working quickly, Andu made a mental note of their location so he'd be sure and steer clear of them if he ever made it out of this.

The female bird-beast circled the base of his tree for nearly an hour, never seeming to notice or care that in all the excitement her partner had vanished without a trace. After awhile, though, she started to get bored. And when a herd of three-tails wandered down to the brook to water themselves a short time later, the she-bird broke off her vigil entirely. Judging by the stealthy way in which she edged off across the veldt in their direction, it was clear she meant to have herself an early lunch!

Hustling back down the tree once she was safely away, Andu sped back towards the ship. He stopped only once, briefly, and that was to position the comm-unit he'd been carrying along with him since before he left the runabout early this morning. That completed, he couldn't reach the safety of the *Drift On* soon enough!

Unnerved by his latest close encounter with the bird-beasts, Andu slammed the hatch door shut and slumped exhausted into the nearest chair. His breath came in gulps. Sweat beaded up on his forehead. The walls of the tiny ship closed in around him. He felt faint.

For a long time Andu just sat there shell-shocked. Indeed, nearly a quarter of an hour passed before he could regain his composure. But once he had, his brain began to function like normal again.

Switching on the remote comm-unit he'd hurriedly placed during his hasty retreat, Andu commenced scanning frequencies for the telltale radio signal. Although the baseline was barely half as long as he had intended, it would just have to do. There was no way now he was going to risk his neck again by going back out there to set up a *second* unit! Anyway, if he boosted the gain sufficiently, one unit ought to be enough to do the trick. A crude triangulation was better than none at all, and even under the worst of conditions, a scan like this shouldn't take him more than a few minutes' time.

The essence of any triangulation was Euclidean geometry at its most elegant. The technique was based on the simple tautology that the sum of the angles of a triangle always totaled 180 degrees. If a would-be pathfinder were to take a heading on the third corner from each of the other two, and if the base separating corner one from corner two were of a known length, it would then be possible to calculate with some precision the distance from either corner out to the third. Andu had run such triangulations a hundred times before, even on occasion over stellar distances, but this was the first time his life depended on him doing it right!

Even as he spun the dials on his machine to home in on the frequency he wanted, Andu could see movement in the grass outside. A hundred meters away, in the field just north of his ship, a whole pack of bird-beasts had gathered for what could only be described as some sort of a town meeting. He watched their activity with growing apprehension through the forward viewport.

The congregation circled up as if they were conducting some kind of bird-beast ritual, perhaps a quasi-religious ceremony. While the others looked on, one of the bigger ones took centerstage and began performing a dance not unlike the nectar-dances of drone honeybees back home. And like a honeybee, it appeared to be directing their attention towards a new source of nectar: Andu!

With disbelieving eyes, he silently watched. As the

seconds ticked by, the dance got progressively more violent and the assembled crowd, steadily more agitated. The big one's head bobbed from side to side, then up and down. Each movement was punctuated by menacing claw-swipes and powerful leg-kicks. The violent outpouring went on for half a minute, and then, as quickly as it had begun, the dance was over. To Andu's horror, the pack now turned in his direction and began their approach!

They moved with intent, as if they meant to have him and his ship for supper. Unlike the hunting pattern he'd observed earlier, this time they exercised classical pack-hunting technique, fanning out in all directions in two-by-two formation, paramilitary style.

Andu's jaw dropped. Though their actions were unmistakably coordinated, he didn't have a clue how they were communicating. Gestures? Yes. Language? No! Grunts? Some. Telepathy? Maybe! End result? Extremely dangerous!

Though Andu was fairly certain the birds couldn't peck their way through the ship's polymerized hull, creatures this brazen couldn't be taken lightly. Whether or not these beasts knew it, they could still wreak plenty of havoc out there. Whereas the hull of the runabout had been built to withstand every space-hazard known to man, from gamma ray radiation on up to micrometeors, certain of his instruments were not. Andu had had to extend the high-gain antenna and the chromatic radio dish in order to run the triangulation he was working on; neither of which was tough enough to stand up to much punishment. Then too, there was a pair of finicky exhaust ports plus a dozen hypercritical maneuvering fins, each one essential, yet each relatively fragile. After seeing the pounding one of these bird-beasts had given a fullgrown three-tail, Andu didn't want one of them chomping on, say, his laser-guided landing array!

A low-pitched ping told him that the computer had a final fix on the frequency he'd been scanning for and had begun the necessary calculations. It couldn't happen fast enough to suit Andu, though. While he couldn't deny feeling a certain sense of security at being there inside the *Drift On* and safely out of the animals' reach, the whole experience was frightening, if not surrealistic. These creatures were aggressive like nothing he'd ever seen, and it was already on his mind to lift off as soon as possible and put down somewhere else. Even now, the animals were bearing down on him like a pack of rabid dogs. All he could think of was retracting the antenna and the radio dish and getting the hell out of there!

Moments passed, and the computer began spitting out x, y, and z coordinates relative to his current position. The corresponding 3-D image on the screen showed the source of the radio signal as being in the mountains several kilometers ahead of him, and at a much higher elevation.

Opting for a hardcopy to carry along with him, Andu hit the PRINT button and waited. A millisecond later, the still-warm paper was in his hand. But no sooner had he shoved it in his pocket than all hell broke loose!

One of the bird-beasts had leaped onto the canopy of the runabout and begun tearing at the roof with her claws!

Inside the tiny craft it sounded as if the creature were literally pulling the ship apart at the seams! Each slash of the claw, each swipe of the leg, reverberated like a buzz saw through the metal hull, terrifying Andu and sending him scrambling for the controls. Already primed to take to the skies, he acted without thinking!

Quickly gauging the direction and approximate distance to the mysterious source of the radio signal, Andu fired up the engines for takeoff, half expecting in his blind panic that the noise would scare off the birds.

It didn't.

Then, a second later, when another bird-beast sprang up on top and joined his brother in ripping at the skin of the ship, Andu went berserk, allowing his animal fears to take over.

Jolted to action by a sudden rush of adrenalin, he punched the ignition and jerked back on the joystick. His rapidly forming plan was to head for the range of mountains he'd seen earlier in the day during his brief tenure up a tree. It was a measured risk, but one he had to take!

The ship was less than a hundred meters in the air when Andu first realized he had a problem. Though he'd been pulling back hard on the joystick to ascend, all of a sudden the ship quit responding to his controls! The only thing he could figure was that one of the bird-beasts had bent a maneuvering fin or else jammed a pushrod. Either way, the result was the same. He suddenly found himself veering sideways at full speed, careening into the lake which lay barely a hundred meters below him and just to the southwest.

Andu hit the water hard.

He was slammed by the force of the impact against the bulkhead. Pain invaded his head. Blood oozed from the gash. For an instant, his vision blurred and darkness crowded in around him as the collision of man against metal raised a nasty knob on his skull.

Still under full steam, the craft shuddered violently as it spun, half into the mud, half into the water, popping a seam just below the surface. The airlock groaned under the pressure.

Struggling to right himself, the dazed man watched with some satisfaction as the two bird-beasts who had been riding up on top were flung into the water. Their stubby wings flailing wildly, they made a fruitless attempt to swim. But their claws and heavy weight made them rather unlikely ducks, and the pair promptly sank! The others, which had been in hot pursuit of the faltering craft, stopped at the water's edge, afraid to enter.

Understanding dawned slowly. Then it hit him. These beasts couldn't swim! They couldn't fly, they couldn't climb, they couldn't swim! That gave him a way out!

Bruised and dazed, Andu scrambled from his slowly sinking craft and jumped into the shallow water. He had his eyes fixed on the opposite shore. Slung over his shoulder was his survival knapsack; strapped to his belt was his blaster.

As he pushed forward through the water, he kept a nervous eye on the bird-beasts lined up on the lakefront behind him. They kept to the shore, making no attempt whatsoever to follow him into the water. Perhaps Andu could turn their shortcoming to his advantage!

Perhaps.

If the lake and the brook were an effective deterrent, maybe there wouldn't be any bird-beasts on the other side.

Maybe.

8
Survival

The water had been ice-cold, and when Andu dragged himself out on the opposite shore he was shivering.

The first order of business was to get warm and dry. Fortunately, he had everything he needed to start a fire right there with him in his rucksack, from a metal match to a supply of Vaseline-saturated cottonballs. The only thing he was missing was fuel.

Spying a good-sized tree a short distance away, Andu moved in that direction, gathering up anything that looked combustible as he went. Searching the ground at his feet and around the base of the tree, it wasn't long before he had assembled a rather respectable stack of tinder and small limbs. From these he built what outdoorsmen call a log-cabin-style fire. The interior was filled with tinder, and in keeping with its name, the exterior was framed up with small limbs like a log cabin. The front door was where the fire was lit, in this case by touching the hot tip of the metal match to one of his Vaseline-soaked cottonballs. Once lit, the cottonball would sustain a flame long enough to ignite the tinder within.

Less than ten minutes later, Andu had a roaring fire. Peeling off his wet clothes, he laid them out over a hastily-erected scaffolding above the flames. Inside of half an hour they were dry enough to put back on.

Focusing his attention once more on the low range of mountains in the distance, Andu set off for higher ground. If his earlier calculations had been correct, somewhere up there among the peaks was the source of the radio transmissions he'd come all this way to find.

From the printout in his pocket he estimated the distance to the base of the mountains at no more than ten kilometers. If the going wasn't too steep or the trail too rocky, he figured he could cover that much ground in no more than two to three hours.

As it turned out, the terrain was neither level nor smooth. Nor were the mountains as close as they first appeared. Some sort of physical anomaly had distorted the z vector, altering the scale by a factor of at least one-third.

The first half hour or so was easy going. But as the sun rose ever higher in the sky and Andu began to sweat, he came to the realization that he'd made a big mistake. He had been in such a hurry to put some distance between himself and the bird-beasts that he'd completely forgotten to stop and take any water along with him from the lake!

Turning around now to look back over the ground he'd already covered, Andu decided that rather than hiking all the way back down there he would have a go at applying his survival skills instead.

Even in an arctic clime, a person needs two quarts of water a day to survive; twice that if the weather is hot. On Earth, the usual suspects included snow, rain, ice, ground water, even dew. Then too, vines and the like were excellent sources, as were succulent plants, tree sap, and most fruits. But even in familiar surroundings, there was always a certain risk associated with ingesting an unknown foreign plant. The problem was compounded, of course, on an alien world where any number of exotic poisons might be present. Andu was smart enough to know that in most instances those risks far outweighed any possible benefit he might gain from consuming whatever little quantity of water those plants might hold. Besides, in any but the most extreme desert conditions, a trained survivalist like himself should have little difficulty finding an adequate and safe supply of water. All one had to know was where to look!

In rocky terrain, he knew to look for pools of standing water or active springs or seepage, even runoff; elsewhere, to dig in dirt near any vegetation or in a streambed, even a dry one. Along the coast, fresh water might be found behind the first dune above high tide. Here, though, caution had to be exercised. Andu knew better than to drink sea water, or for that matter, alkali water or urine. In nearly every locale, though, it was possible to evaporate ground water with a solar still. Indeed, this was by far and away the safest, most productive strategy for generating an adequate supply of drinking water—and the very method Andu had already settled on.

Opening up his survival backpack, Andu removed the equipment he would need and spread it out on the ground in front of him. Near the top of the pile was his lightweight polyglas shovel. Andu unfolded the handle and locked the blade into place.

The first step in building a solar still was to identify a suitable spot, one with relatively moist soil. This he did quickly and then began digging out a bowl-shaped pit one-and-a-third meters wide and a meter deep. At the bottom of the pit, in the center, he placed a shallow, cuplike container. Next, he lined the sloping walls of the pit with a few green leaves and some live shoots. Then he rigged a length of airline tubing, leaving one end curled up inside the cup and snaking the other end up along the wall of the pit and out over the top edge of the hole. That done, he stretched a sheet of clear plastic over the mouth of the pit and placed a small stone in the center of the sheet to form an inverted cone that hung down directly over the cup. Using clumps of loose soil he had removed earlier from the hole, he then weighted down the plastic all the way around the circumference of the hole, being sure to leave one end of the tubing free where he could later get his mouth around it like a giant straw.

Then the man stood back and let nature run its course. It wouldn't take long. Damp soil and green shoots could be very productive, especially when subjected to the kinds of temperatures a properly-positioned solar still could generate.

As the midday sun shone through the plastic canopy, the trapped solar heat would boil off the water from the moist soil and the green leaves, filling the inside of the pit with steam. The water vapor would condense on the underside of the plastic sheet, run down to the lowest point of the inverted cone and then drip into the shallow cup. There it would accumulate. To avoid disturbing the still while it was operating, the water could be sipped out through the tubing at regular intervals. Inside of fifteen minutes he'd had his fill.

While this stopgap measure would keep him going for

awhile, Andu needed to get up into the forests and find himself a more permanent source of water as soon as he could. That, plus food and shelter.

As he climbed steadily higher into the foothills, the terrain around him gradually transformed itself from savanna to forest. After the heat of the open field, it was a most welcome change. And yet, the cool darkness of the woods only served to remind him that nightfall would soon be upon him. Before long, he'd need to build or find shelter.

The trees around him were not unlike those of a terran pine forest: straight and tall and widely-spaced, each a thriving entity unto itself. And yet, the similarities only went so far.

Instead of an outerskin that was rough and furrowed like earth-bark, these colossal plants had an outerskin which was leathery like rawhide, perhaps to ward off burrowing insects or to help the tree retain water better. And rather than having needles like a conifer or veined leaves like a deciduous, each entire branch was a giant sun-gathering appendage. The "leaf," if it could be called that, was thick at the center where all the weight was, then tapered out horizontally into a thin, flat fin several meters wide. The fin extended out from the central core along the entire length of the "branch," beginning at the trunk and reaching all the way out to the tip of the limb some twenty meters away. The leaf-branches themselves were arranged in a stepwise fashion counterclockwise around the trunk of the tree. Had it been possible to view them from above, the tree and its series of leaf-branches might have resembled an enormous spiral staircase winding its way up to heaven step-by-step. From below, down on the forest floor, the arrangement made for a rather curious pattern of light and darkness, sun and shadows.

As night drew ever closer, the forest came alive with noises, all unfamiliar. These were the voices of creatures he never actually saw. A rhythmic chirping sound like that of a cricket. An occasional shrill screech like that of an owl or a hawk. Something which sounded a lot like moaning, though it might very well have been the wind swirling up through the staircase of flat leaf-branches. It was all quite unnerving, and when Andu spied a fallen tree trunk, he decided to appropriate it for lodging until morning.

Quickly gathering up several downed leaf-branches,

Andu leaned the lot of them against one side of the log, fashioning a rudimentary shelter two-and-a-half meters long. Matting additional leaf-branches plus hunks of leather-bark against the limbs, he soon had a warm, dry place out of the wind to spend the night.

Satisfied with his handiwork, Andu crawled in to sleep in the space between the log and the lean-to. Overhead, one very bright star lit the forest floor, throwing eerie shadows everywhere. A double star system, he thought as he closed his eyes. Figuring he would be hungry by morning, he had set out some snares before settling down for the night. Now he opened his eyes once more to see if they were still okay. With any luck at all, Mother Nature would provide while he slept.

• • •

They had met once, he and Smith. The Chief Apostle was a thin, severe-looking man with a temper to match. Each had taken an immediate dislike for the other, perfectly understandable under the circumstances, but hardly the basis on which to forge a lasting business relationship. Only now, with a hundred million kilometers separating them, could the two possibly hope to get along!

Red had asked for more money, and Chief Apostle Smith had had no choice but to comply. Now that he had it, now that his bank had confirmed deposit of the draft, Red could do what he pleased. And what he pleased was to kill the son of a bitch. Not Smith. Nehrengel!

To Red McIntire, Andu Nehrengel represented all in life that was wrong. Wrong color, wrong race, wrong religion. It was a battle that had been going on for more than a thousand years. Time and again, the light-skinned peoples of the world had made war on the not-so-light-skinned. The English on the Amerinds, the Russians on the Afghans, the Euros on the Negro, the Aussies on the Aborigine, the Nazis on the Jews. But each time, it was never quite enough. Each time, the lighter-skinned races had stopped just short of finishing the job. Each time, the darker-skinned races were punished, their numbers decimated, their young killed, their wives raped, but the race itself never quite exterminated. Each time, the problem was left for the next generation to solve, Red's generation. It couldn't be simpler. Andu was swarthy; Red was not. This was his chance to do his part, to fulfill his destiny as a white man, to hunt the darkie down and kill him!

The *Tachyon* had a definite fix on the *Drift On's* position; the runabout hadn't moved in more than a day and a half. If Nehrengel was still alive, if he hadn't burned up on reentry, or crashed trying to land, or been eaten alive by some local carnivore, Red could follow him. He could follow him and kill him. And he could do so in his own time, and in his own way. He'd have to leave the *Tachyon* in orbit—it was just too large and unwieldy to manage alone—but he could take the number two runabout to the surface. All he needed was to recharge the *Sail On*'s battery and load her with some gear. In a few hours, Nehrengel would be his!

9
Footprints

Remarkably, the night passed without incident. But in the morning when Andu awoke, his snares were empty. This was a big disappointment. Ordinarily, he had no trouble catching something to eat. Ordinarily.

Grumbling about his rotten luck, Andu gathered his belongings and set out on the trail. His stomach was growling loudly. He'd try again this afternoon to catch something, preferably something big and meaty like a three-tail.

Trying to imagine what it would be like to have a hot meal in his belly, Andu set off hiking at a good pace. His spirits were high, despite his hunger, and he made good time. Inside of half an hour he came out of the woods above the tree line. He was immediately greeted by the sound of rushing water. A mountain brook at last!

He washed his hands and face in the stream being careful to get as little water as possible in his mouth. Then, purifying what he drank with a few drops of iodine, Andu downed his fill, this time remembering to take some water along with him in the empty bladders he had stashed away in his knapsack. No wonder a week's supply of condoms was as much a part of a man's survival gear as his knife or his metal match!

Though Andu was still hungry, the water had tasted good. Refreshed, he resumed his trek to higher ground. After another half-hour's climb, he was up high enough to have a view all the way back down the way he'd come. It was spellbinding!

The lake was in the distance, blue and calm. Not far from shore sat the *Drift On*, gleaming in the morning sun and still sticking partway out of the water where he had left her. Except for the forest he had bedded down in last night, everything else was savanna, and it stretched as far as the eye could see.

Working his way laterally across a sloping ridge, Andu came upon an alpine-like meadow overflowing with color. Shutting his eyes for a moment he imagined he was back in the Alps of Zealand, hiking. Andu had been there once, after the war. Inescapable curiosity had drawn him there, a curiosity that was born on the steppes of Afghanistan with a visit from his grandfather, Fornax. Besides making a gift to him of Jenny, Fornax had also given him two things his grandmother wanted him to have: her diary chronicling a lifetime of scientific pursuit, plus the master key to the Matthews estate north of Auckland. Andu had gone there straightaway. It was on a side-trip afterwards that he had found himself high in the Zealand Alps. Eyes still closed, Andu remembered.

To Zealanders, the Milford Track was the equivalent of a pilgrimage to Mecca, something to be done at least once in a lifetime. To outsiders like Andu, it might be only the finest walk in the world. The Milford Track, in the heart of the South Island, was an apocalyptic, forty-kilometer hike through chattering rain forests and blithe fern-shaded meadows, along temperamental rivers and across blustery mountain passes, past giant hurrying waterfalls and quiet lakes, beneath vast cliffs and into deep decadent woods. There were so many landscapes, it was like crossing an entire uninhabited continent. It took four days to complete at an enjoyable pace, and best of all, could be done comfortably by anyone who simply enjoyed a long walk and didn't mind sharing a cabin plus a few meals with fellow trampers of every age. The hostels, spaced at sensible intervals along the Track, were comfortable and provided bedding, towels, and hearty food. All a tramper need bring were waterproof lightweight boots, two pairs of socks, a light slicker, and a very light knapsack packed with perhaps a sweater and little else.

In a flash, the memory passed and Andu was back in the present. When he opened his eyes now to drink in the beauty of the alpine meadow unfolding before him, that's when he saw them. For the longest moment he just stood there staring at them, thinking he was hallucinating. But when he blinked his eyes and looked for a second time, they were still there!

Just ahead of him and a little to his right, in a muddy spot where the mountain brook had recently overflowed its banks, was a set of footprints!

Gulping in surprise so hard he nearly began to choke, Andu instinctively drew his blaster. Ever so cautiously he advanced, his watchful eyes darting from side to side. These depressions in the mud weren't clawprints like he had seen down near the spot where he'd landed; these were *foot*prints! Only, these were no ordinary footprints. Unlike those a wild animal might make, complete with toes and pads and heels, these had the size and shape of a *shoe*! A bit undersized perhaps, like that of a small man, but a human-sized shoeprint nonetheless!

Thinking that perhaps he was lost and had been going in circles, Andu quickly compared the tread to his own. No more than a cursory examination was required—the tread wasn't even remotely similar in size or in style.

Thinking next that his mutinous crew had taken guilty and come looking for him, his heart leapt into his mouth. He was about to be rescued!

Jumping for joy, Andu yelled out to his men. They couldn't be far; all he had to do was run and catch up with them!

But before he could move, reality set in and his exhilaration faded. The mother ship had only one functioning runabout onboard, the one Red had set Andu adrift in to begin with, the one now sitting stuck in the mud several kilometers away. The other one, the *Sail On*, had been disabled by Andu himself the day before the mutiny. Smelling trouble, he had disconnected the laser-guided landing array; anyone trying to fly her now would almost certainly spin in and crash. As for the big ship, the *Tachyon*, nobody in his right mind would try to land a ship of that size on anything but a concrete-hardened tarmac. That's why the *Tachyon* had been equipped with a pair of runabouts in the first place!

Which brought him back to these footprints. They couldn't possibly belong to a member of his crew after all. Like a fool, he'd let his imagination get the better of him!

Too curious for words, Andu decided to follow the tracks. It seemed the logical thing to do, especially since they seemed to be moving off more or less in the direction he was headed anyway. It didn't take him long, however—no more than a few paces—to make a second startling discovery! *Almost every step of the way, the leading set of impressions was overlaid by a second, and sometimes even a* third *pair of prints*! He was following not one, but two, perhaps as many as *three*, similarly-sized individuals!

Though the closely-spaced footprints suggested the small troupe was traveling crosscountry in an unobtrusive, single-file line, judging by the clues they left in their wake, the makers apparently had no fear whatsoever of being followed. To the contrary, they'd left behind countless signs of their having been there–upturned clumps of lichen, broken stalks of grass, dislodged rocks, bits of broken branches. It seemed to Andu as if the bipedal primates–if that's what they were–had been feeding as they went. Along the trail there were berries, what looked like peach pits, broken foliage, even a fairly recent set of droppings–three closely-spaced piles to be exact. These were darn messy creatures he was following!

Everything about them made him more curious, though, and he couldn't help but be drawn along the littered trail behind them. The trail weaved back into the forest for a short distance and then back out again, crossing over into a clearing on the other side. With each bend in the trail, Andu climbed ever higher into the saddle of the mountain before him. Then, all of a sudden, after about a quarter of an hour of hiking, he knew he'd come to the end of the road.

Obstructing his path, about seventy-five meters ahead, was what could only be described as a wall. That it was manmade was without question. Rocks and boulders had been gathered and intentionally stacked there to provide a buffer separating what was inside from what was out here. Whatever intelligent life had built the wall either meant to keep something from getting in or something else from getting out. Either way the result was the same–curiosity practically demanded he investigate.

Andu drew closer. Judging by the crudity of the construction, it never occurred to him that the creatures inside would be armed, or if armed, that their weapons might be lethal. This proved to be a major miscalculation.

When Andu had approached to within fifteen meters of the stone wall, it happened. From three different locations among the boulders, a blonde head briefly appeared. Then, before he could dive into the bushes to take cover, each of the three creatures took careful aim on him with some sort of primitive blaster.

To his good fortune, the seemingly identical humanoids were not equally good shots; only one of the three managed to hit him. But one was enough. The projectile slammed into his leg with such force it shattered his femur above the knee! Blood splattered everywhere!

Andu screamed out in pain, collapsing to the ground in a crumpled heap. He had never felt anything so excruciating!

Blind with rage, the wounded man writhed around in the dirt, still trying desperately to make it to cover. In his panic, he slipped and smacked his head hard against a big flat rock.

An instant later, he was out cold!

10
Humanity

When Andu first came to, he thought he had died and passed onto the next world. Though not a believer himself, Afghan legend told of places beyond. Barely conscious, he recalled bits and pieces of strange tales of the hereafter, tales he had heard around the campfire as a boy, tales of demon gods and satanic women. Somehow, his present locale seemed to fit the ancient story in every detail.

Andu turned his head left and right, trying to get a better handle on his situation, trying to get his bearings. Everything was in a daze, and at first he couldn't remember. Then the fog began to clear and it all came rushing back. He had been shot! But why? And where was he now?

Andu was lying in some sort of bed and the bed itself was in some sort of medic-ward. Only, it wasn't like any hospital room he'd ever been in; it was like something out of another time!

Through foggy eyes, he could make out three nurses, blondes all. It was eerie. They were standing huddled together in a group having a conversation, only it *wasn't* a conversation—no words were being exchanged! Not only that, the three females appeared to be exact duplicates of one another. Identical copies! Try as he might, there was absolutely no way Andu could tell them apart!

Knowing that it was absurd, that no three women could possibly look that much alike, the prone man naturally assumed his vision had been blurred by the fall. A bandage was on his head, another on his leg. Pain was shooting like an arrow up through his entire frame.

Andu opened his mouth to speak but found he could not.

Though he was certain his lips had moved, he was equally certain he hadn't uttered so much as a syllable!

With great effort, the hurt man rolled onto his side to get a better view of his attendants. Again he tried to speak; again, nothing. Again he tried to distinguish one triplet from the other; again, no luck.

A frustrated groan issued from his throat and three heads turned his way. Seeing that he was stirring, one of the nurses came closer. She spoke in a strangely detached, almost disjointed fashion.

"The creature is alive," she said.

The other two nodded their understanding without saying a word.

By now his eyes were beginning to focus. Andu could see that the speaker was a perfect specimen of womanhood: big round eyes, firm uplifted breasts, blemish-free skin, straight teeth. From what little he could see of the other two, they were equally gorgeous. Exact duplicates of the first, if that were possible.

Struggling to lift himself up onto one elbow, he croaked out a few words. "My knapsack . . . where is my knapsack?"

Jumping backwards at the sound of his voice, one of the triplets shrieked. "It speaks! The creature speaks!"

Still unable to make any sense of his predicament, Andu spoke again. "Why do you call me a creature? . . . I am a man."

"Can it be?" the girls questioned, studying each other's eyes for confirmation.

Moving quickly away from him, the three again circled up in a huddle as if they meant to have another silent conversation. Just as before, it seemed as if no words were being exchanged, only thoughts.

Seeing his opportunity, Andu swung his legs out over the side of the hospital bed and sat up shakily. He had spied his rucksack on a chair, along with his blood-stained shirt and pants. Looking down at himself for the first time since he awoke, he realized he was stark naked and that his manhood had become the object of the girls' deliberations.

Covering himself with his bare hands as best he could, Andu limped painfully across the shiny tiled floor towards the chair and his things. What he was after, in addition to his clothes, was the Acceleron tablets he always kept with him in his survival pack. Acceleron was a wonder drug, a healing drug. It could help his body heal in a day what might ordinarily take a week; in a week what might ordinarily take months. Andu needed one fast!

Though the three clones eyed him warily, they didn't make any moves to stop him. Quite the opposite, in fact. They seemed rather relieved once he'd slipped his underpants back on again.

Exhausted by the effort, Andu leaned back heavily against a filing cabinet to catch his breath. "Why did you shoot me?" he asked, reaching for his knapsack.

While he waited for an answer, he rummaged through his survival gear searching for the tiny white pills. Swallowing one without benefit of water, he stood back to scrutinize the three women more closely. Pictures of beauty all, they were virtually indistinguishable.

"How do I tell you three apart?" he asked, extending them a friendly hand. "My name is Andu; what's yours?"

Lurching backwards to avoid being touched by his outstretched appendage, the girl closest to him stammered out a terse reply. "We are Prime . . . Prime Alpha; Prime Second; Prime Third . . . We shot you because we were afraid . . . We thought you were an alien . . . an alien invader . . . We had to protect ourselves."

"I meant you no harm," Andu said, bristling at the suggestion. It never occurred to him that in their eyes he might be an alien. Who would've thought it!

"We cannot read your mind," one of the clones said. "How were we supposed to know whether or not you meant us any harm?"

The clone Andu had identified as Prime Alpha reached for her blaster. He hadn't noticed them sitting there before, but all this time their weapons had just been sitting there unattended on a small white table next to the hospital room door. Now, Prime Alpha picked hers up and pointed it at Andu's chest. As she linked her long delicate fingers around the grip of the gun, Second and Third felt the cold touch of gray metal against her skin.

With grave apprehension, Andu stared down the rifled barrel of the blaster. He could see grim determination in the woman's eyes. Afraid of being shot for a second time, he raised his hands above his head in the classic poise of surrender, moving slowly so as not to spook her. He spoke in even, unhurried tones.

"Take it easy, Alpha. I'm not an alien, for God's sake. I'm a human, just like you."

"We are not human," they said in unison, "we are Prime."

Screwing his forehead into a frown, he said, "Oh, you're human all right—Prime is just a name; like Andu. The only thing that confuses me is how the hell you got here. What planet is this anyway?"

Alpha answered. "This is Ancòn."

"I see," he granted, though he didn't. "Now tell me, Alpha, how did you three *get* here?"

"We are descended from the great ones, the Terr-uns."

Andu caught his breath. What were the odds? They had to be vanishingly small. Terr-un was uncannily close to terran. It was too farfetched to be mere coincidence. These people must have come here from Earth. But how? And when? And where were their men?

"Are there others here with you?" he asked, already beginning to feel stronger as the first effects of the Acceleron took hold.

When his question went unanswered, Andu tried again. "Are there any other Terr-uns here besides yourselves?"

"There is only Prime. Prime Alpha. Prime Second. Prime Third."

Seeing that he wasn't getting anywhere fast, Andu tried a different tact. "I'm hungry. Is there anything to eat around this place?"

"Why, yes, of course," Prime Second replied, showing him the way. "Come with me."

As Prime Second led him out into the corridor, the other two followed close behind, Alpha still holding tight to her blaster. Sensing that the moment of tension had passed, Andu cautiously lowered his arms. A nearby broomstick caught his attention and he reached out for it, putting it to use as a makeshift crutch to help him get around.

Once they'd moved beyond the confines of the small hospital room he'd woken up in, Andu made an amazing discovery. This place he was hobbling around in was not a building like he first thought, but in fact a spaceship!

Let it only be said that Andu Nehrengel knew just about everything there was to know about spaceships, and he immediately recognized this as being one of Earth's N-Class cruisers circa 2200. The N-Class cruisers had been nuclear-powered (hence the "N" designation), though as far as he knew, none had ever undertaken a trip beyond the main Belt, much less out to a distant star system. Typically, the N's had been put to work delivering colonists and supplies to the Mars Station, but that was about as far as they ever went. It was a bit of a conundrum to figure out how one could have gotten out this far. And who could have possibly survived such a long trip at nuclear speeds? Certainly not these three! They were at least two hundred years too young to have been any part of the original crew.

Andu frowned. He couldn't help himself. He had plenty of questions, and damn few answers.

What they fed him, he had no idea. But it tasted good, and he hoped it was nourishing. Though the three women almost never talked aloud among themselves, Andu was nevertheless convinced they were in constant communication with one another. The whole idea was so farfetched; it hadn't occurred to him yet that they might be telepathic. Still, he couldn't help but think they were awfully interested in his reasons for being here.

Between mouthfuls of what could only be described as some sort of a spicy, homemade sausage, Andu remembered the radio signals which had drawn him here to Ancòn in the first place.

"Who have you been trying to contact?" he asked.

"Contact?" they replied in unison, not grasping his meaning.

"When I came to your planet . . ."

"Ancòn," one of the girls interrupted.

"Yes, Ancòn. When I came to your Ancòn, I was following a radio signal. I now have reason to believe that radio signal was emanating from this very ship. What I would like to know is: who were you trying to contact?"

"Yes, now I understand," all three women parroted, their flawless faces beaming with delight. "You heard our calling. We were calling the Great Ones. The Terr-uns."

Andu smiled. "I received your call. *I* am a Terr-un."

Revolted by the very thought, Prime Alpha jumped to her feet, her face consumed with horror. "That cannot be!" she shouted, knocking over her drink in the process. "You are not like us. You have that . . . that . . . *thing* between your legs!"

Blushing modestly, Andu instinctively bowed his head and looked down into his lap. That "thing" she had noticed was of course his manhood. It suddenly dawned on him: *these females had never seen a man before!* Would wonders never cease?

Clearing his throat to speak, he said, "Terr-uns come in two varieties—male and female; men and women. You are a woman. I am a man."

"No! We are Prime! Prime Alpha; Prime Second; Prime Third. You are *not* like us. You have that hairy thing hanging down between your legs. What function does it serve?"

Blushing for a second time, he answered. "To make a woman pregnant."

The blank stares Andu received in response told him the Primes didn't have a clue what he was talking about. But not one to give up easily, he tried again. "Terr-un men use their 'thing' to make Terr-un women pregnant. So they can have babies—*new* Terr-uns."

"No, that is not right!" Alpha returned, shocked by his explanation. "The *machine* makes new Terr-uns."

Now it was his turn to be surprised. "The machine? What machine? Show me this machine."

Cordially doing as he asked, the three Primes led him from the galley where they had been eating and into another part of the ship. By now, Andu thought he had it all figured out: the ship had either crashed or else soft-landed here in this secluded clearing halfway up the mountain. To keep the local creatures out, the girls, or perhaps their ancestors, had built the stone wall around the outside of the ship as protection. Yet, with each step, there was a new revelation.

The room they now took him to was a fully-functioning cryogenic lab complete with coffin-sized cubicles for long-term freeze, plus the appropriate monitoring arrays, computer terminals, and bio-maintenance equipment, all circa 2200. It occurred to him that if the ship had indeed been traveling at nuclear speeds rather than tachyon speeds, it might have arrived here on Ancòn only relatively recently. That might account not only for the young age of these girls, but also for their attempt to "call" home.

"This is where babies are made," one of the girls explained, showing him around the lab.

In front of him was a complicated apparatus of a sort he had never laid eyes on before. It was a dizzying maze of glass tubes, aluminum cylinders, rubber hoses, brass valves, and bio-sensitive diaphragms. Though the internal workings of the "machine" were hidden from view, Andu could see enough of it to believe it was a sophisticated incubator, perhaps one of those synthetic-uteruses Dr. Chandra had once told him about. They were all the rage two or three centuries ago.

What caught his attention, though, was not the synthetic-uterus, but what hung from the wall next to it—an info-terminal connected to the ship's mainframe.

"May I?" he asked, sitting in front of the darkened screen.

"By all means," Prime Alpha replied, powering up the terminal. "This is the Universal Well of Knowledge. The Great Ones left it behind for us. Hidden inside must be everything They ever learned, though we ourselves have read only a small portion of what They—in Their great wisdom—wanted us to know."

"How long may I remain here?" Andu asked, knowing he had his work cut out for him.

"As long as you please," the Primes answered, mouthing the words in unison. "I will leave you now—we have much to do."

Staring after them as they left the lab, Andu turned to face the antiquated keyboard. The screen flickered green before him. Centuries of accumulated wisdom awaited the touch of his eager fingers!

11
Genetics

The first screen Andu came to was like a road map. Roads already-traveled were marked out in red; places not-yet-visited highlighted in blue. It showed subject areas and files the girls had already read plus tens of thousands more they had not. A few were bookmarked as if of special interest, things that perhaps they wanted to return to later on. One immediately caught his eye and he clicked on it, only it turned out to be distressingly banal. He moved on.

Andu had seen the synthetic-uterus; he'd already figured out that these girls were clones: what he wanted to know was how they got here!

Activating the machine's search engine, he moved rapidly through the topics, narrowing the categories as he went. Under SCIENCE, he selected BIOLOGY; then, from that list, GENETICS; then, from the subsequent list, CLONING. Still, there were thousands of choices. How to narrow it further?

Thinking about the bio-maintenance equipment there with him, and the cryogenic cubicles, Andu had an idea. By cross-linking "space-travel" and "cloning" he could run a search using Boolean operators. This improved his results.

Looking first under CLONING-EXOTIC, then under CLONING-ZERO-G, he found a promising entry: CULT CLONING & THE LATTER-DAY SAINTS, A MODERN EXODUS. He clicked on it:

> Genetic tinkering was barely in its infancy in the last decade of the twentieth century. Nevertheless, once recombinant

techniques were mastered, the field took off with an explosion of activity. Much as the interstate highway system once paved the way to America's industrial might and the building of the railroads transformed the nineteenth century, the Human Genome Project sparked America to bio-technical preeminence in the twenty-first. This mammoth undertaking enabled scientists to locate every one of the hundred thousand or so genes which make up a human being while simultaneously making it possible to copy each gene, identify its chemical makeup, and determine its function. Moreover, the techniques developed for inventorying and cataloguing the human gene-map have since been used to develop a genetic archive containing the gene-maps of more than a hundred domesticated animals plus every food-grain of commercial importance.

While such research met with resistance and a fair amount of criticism along the way-- some asserting that trying to learn every letter of the genetic alphabet was tantamount to reaching for forbidden fruit, others claiming that such knowledge would engender Nazi-like eugenic measures--eventually the project was finished, irrevocably altering the future course of human history in the process. Once man was able to identify specific genes, he naturally sought to manipulate them. The means were never called into question, only the ends.

By early in the twenty-first century, biologists had developed reliable diagnostic screens for a whole host of genetic disorders including Alzheimer's Syndrome and cystic fibrosis. Though the cures didn't come nearly as quickly or easily as the diagnostic screens, by discovering which genes regulated what functions, the DNA mappers set the stage for repairing any and all dysfunctional lines of genetic code. More importantly, it was shown early on that there were no biological barriers to prevent plant or animal genes from being transferred into diseased people, thus helping them to do certain things better, like produce insulin or metabolize fat. Scientists even learned how to construct synthetic genes, genes Mother Nature never got around to building Herself, and then found a way to deliver them to patients using transplantable skin cells. Yet in spite of all its promise, there was a fly in the ointment.

To begin with, neither the scientists, nor the politicians, nor the public-at-large, could agree on what defined a genetic "mistake." Whereas a cure for say, diabetes, didn't arouse much in the way of controversy, the same could not be said of a "cure" for black skin, or a "cure" for brown eyes. It was just these sorts of "cures" which set off the twenty-first and twenty-second-century battles centered on the issue of genetic purity. Did people have the right to manipulate the genetic attributes of their offspring or not?

Radical groups like the Randomists insisted that the luck of the draw was God's way, that genetic knowledge was too powerful a weapon for mere mortals to wield, that power as awesome as that belonged in the Lord's realm. More moderate thinkers of the day believed that selecting the right genes for one's children was every bit as important as selecting the right schools for them.

The problem was, it was a rather short jump from deciding which set of genes was best for one's *own* children, to deciding that a particular set of genes was best for *everyone*'s children. This was particularly true in countries which already had a fairly homogeneous population, like SKANDIA, and in closely-knit religious communities like the Church of Jesus Christ of Latter-day Saints. Just as polygamy was--and still is--a controversial tenet of Mormonism, so too was genetic manipulation. Indeed, the history of Mormonism has long been one of an enigma wrapped up in a controversy.

Joseph Smith founded the Church in New York in the early 1800s after having had visions of God in which he was told he would be the instrument to restore Christianity. Because of religious persecution, the Church was forced to move first to northern Missouri, and later to Nauvoo, Illinois. In keeping with Smith's philosophy of securing a Kingdom of God here on Earth, missionaries were soon sent out to England, and to SKANDIA, with most of the converts eventually emigrating to the United States.

Although the Church prospered in Nauvoo, neighbors resented the Mormons, and for good reason. Not only did they vote as a bloc, they were constantly proselytizing. Then, when rumors spread that Smith had secretly introduced polygamy into Mormonism, the townspeople became irate. Feelings peaked while Smith was being held in a Carthage, Illinois jailhouse. Before it was over, an armed mob had shot him dead.

The head of the Church's Council of Apostles, Brigham Young, was voted leader to replace Smith, and he organized and directed an epic march from Nauvoo, across the Great Plains, over the Rocky Mountains, and on into the Great Salt Lake basin. It was an exodus in every sense of the word.

Though a full-scale war nearly erupted over the acknowledgement of polygamy as a Mormon tenet, in Utah the Church continued to grow. Eventually, the matter was settled when the U.S. Supreme Court denied that religious freedom could be claimed as the grounds for a plural marriage. By the end of the nineteenth century, Mormons had officially ended the practice altogether.

Despite the controversy, more than fifty thousand new settlers from the Midwest and from Europe soon joined up with them. Brigham Young himself helped found more than 350 new towns and cities as he sent colonizing parties all throughout the West. The enterprising Mormons built canals to irrigate the land, engaged in farming and home industry in an effort to become economically self-sufficient, and saw to it that members abstained from the use of alcohol and tobacco. In this new land, a land they called Deseret, community and self-reliance were their watchwords.

As for the importance of genealogy to the Church, this went straight to the heart of their beliefs. Faith was based on four books--the Bible, the Book of Mormon, the Doctrine and Covenants, and the Pearl of Great Price, all of which were considered scripture. Latter-day Saints believed in the eternal progress of humans from a spiritual state, to mortality, and then on to an afterlife where resurrected individuals would receive their reward. Because vicarious baptism for those who had died was such a distinctive Mormon practice, the Church laid great emphasis on carefully collecting and preserving genealogical records, that its members might undergo baptismal rites on behalf of their ancestors.

But there was more to the Mormons' interest in genealogy than merely doing research and keeping records. By the time the first human being was born on Mars in 2125, certain select members of the Church's Council of Apostles had already secretly convened on the grounds of the University of Utah at Provo to adopt genetic manipulation as a matter of principle. This was, of course, during the heyday of genetic engineering and cloning, and the possibilities seemed endless.

While efforts to "standardize" the flock were kept secret for a long time, when the news of such efforts first broke in 2182, there was a fierce public outcry, much as there had been three hundred years earlier at the first public hints of plural marriage. Though genetic choice itself had been legal for half a century already, this cloning of congregants went well beyond what the original framers of that legislation had in mind. Pressures against the radical Mormon sect built steadily, and by 2187 the stage was set for another great exodus, this time to Mars!

Gathering up contributions from like-minded people across the globe, a great sum of money was raised, enough to outfit an N-Class cruiser called the *Deseret* for a Mayflower-style voyage to the Red Planet. Only, the immigrants never reached their destination. The why-not remains a mystery to this day. Some contend it was sabotage, others that it was simply bad luck born out of haste, still others that the impact of a small asteroid was to blame. Suffice it to say, whatever the reason, by about six weeks out they were hopelessly off course with no way back. Their future now lay upon another path.

Once it was realized by those onboard that they didn't have enough fuel to rectify their trajectory, that they were now simply going to float out of the solar system and keep on going wherever the solar winds chose to carry them, the tenor of the entire mission changed. Hope became resignation and joy became despair. For decades they drifted like a piece of flotsam upon the cosmic ocean, carried by the waves and bounced from system to system by the vagaries of a dozen overlapping gravitational fields. Kept alive by vats of blue-green algae which cleansed their water and filled their bellies, they could only pray to someday being tossed ashore on some warm galactic beach in a neighboring star system.

Their faith was tested in a hundred ways, yet somehow the small band of pilgrims endured, surviving internal strife, close confinement onboard, and extreme isolation. Though some committed suicide and none lived long enough to reach the promised land, they used their many long years of involuntary exile to good measure, producing works of literature and art and music in staggering proportions; working out details of physics and biology and economics which never had even been attempted back on Earth; pursuing lines of inquiry no one had bothered to follow before--and would have been baffled by if they had. Saved for all eternity in the bubble-memory of this computer, these closely-reasoned theories of time-travel, of bio-silicon chip engineering, of chaos-dynamics, remain waiting to be extracted by someone who knows what they mean.

(Someone like me? Andu thought, as he read the closing paragraph.)

Eventually, everybody onboard the *Deseret* died, but not before cloning and placing in stasis, three copies of a single, genetically-flawless male plus three more copies of a single, genetically-flawless female. The ship was left on automatic pilot, programmed to soft-land itself in the event its long-range sensors detected a habitable earthlike planet.

Wide-eyed, Andu stared at the screen. For some unknown reason, either in the landing or in the transit, the male triplet perished. The only survivors of the voyage were the three women. Though the cryogenic freeze had slowed their aging, it hadn't halted it; thus, when they were "born," Prime Alpha and her sisters were some eighteen years of age. Fully developed physically, they nevertheless still harbored a childlike innocence born of a life devoid of experiences.

Mother of God! Andu swore, still staring at the screen. These women *had* never seen a man before!

As the truth slowly dawned on him, the color ran from his face. No wonder they'd been looking at him so strangely! No wonder they'd been so vigorously debating the usefulness of his male appendage!

And that wasn't the half of it! Unless he was entirely mistaken, they were at least partially telepathic. When one was hungry, they all were hungry; when one was angry, they all were angry.

He couldn't help but wonder: If one got horny, did all three of them get horny? For that matter, did they even *get* horny? Were they horny now? *He* certainly was!

Trying to put the thought out of his head, Andu nervously cracked his knuckles. Legions of unanswered questions remained. At the top of the list was one that had bothered him for some time: Why the Mormons of all people?

It was curious, but the world had turned out to be a very small place indeed. Here was living proof. Who would have guessed it? Not only had the Mormons played a central role in Prime Alpha's very existence, they had played an equally big role in the life of *his* family. The truth was, if it hadn't been for the Church of Latter-day Saints and their relentless record-keeping, Andu's grandmother Carina would never have learned of her ancestry. Andu knew from reading her diary that the one regret Carina had carried with her to the grave was never having been able to find a genetic cure for what killed her father—and eventually herself: Matthews Disease. Undoubtedly, if time-travel had been possible, she would have journeyed back in time to find Byron Matthewson, the last of her line to be clean of the defect. Alas, it was not to be. Time-travel was but a dream of science-fiction writers!

Pushing himself back from the machine now, Andu reached over and clicked off the power. The loud humming noise slowly subsided, leaving in its wake only the sound of his own staccato breathing.

For a long moment he closed his eyes. Then he heard it. A strange, sensual sound coming from just down the corridor. His manhood stiffened. *He knew that sound!*

12
Sex

What Andu saw from the open doorway made him gasp, first with surprise, then with excitement. He had never seen a woman masturbate before, and certainly not three all at one time.—It was electrifying!

Unsure what to make of his discovery, the bewildered man shrunk silently back into the corridor and pressed himself flat against the wall. Though his heart was racing, he didn't dare make a sound! The last thing Andu wanted to do right now was give himself away. If he spooked them, who knew what they might do? These three had shot him for less the *first* time around!

And yet, Andu couldn't just simply forget what he'd seen. These women—even if they'd never been with a man before— were still very much women, complete with carnal desires, unfulfilled fantasies, and all the right body parts!

Seeing them totally wrapped up in the throes of ecstasy like that—if only for a brief instant—couldn't help but make him stop and think. For some reason, out of the blue, Andu suddenly remembered his grandmother's diary. In her younger days, Carina seemed to have been preoccupied with sex, writing about it often, sometimes with startling frankness. Her favorite topic? The female orgasm. She called it the engine of evolution.

Though the details were lost to him now, Andu vaguely remembered one such diary entry. It began something like this:

Sex. What is it? Only a ritual as old as life itself! Next to food-gathering, mating is arguably the most basic, most ancient, most necessary activity a plant or animal can engage in. The human animal is no exception of course, though he long ago managed to elevate sexual intercourse from the mere making of babies into a rarified art form. Indeed, with the possible exception of the bonobo, man's closest living relative, *Homo sapiens* stands alone in the animal kingdom as having been the only species to have successfully separated sex from reproduction. And even there, some question remains. For, in keeping pace with the evolution of that oversized mammalian brain, something else evolved as well—heightened desires. Once humans had acquired sufficient intelligence to recognize that intercourse could be pleasurable—plus the right body parts to make it interesting—the prospect of regular sex would have been a pivotal force in drawing the man home from the hunt, thus strengthening an institution which figured so prominently in humanity's success, the nuclear family. Both men and women learned early on, maybe as far back as the first proto-human, that orgasm floods the brain with chemicals the soul finds addictive. Sex is the ultimate narcotic, and humankind its most enthusiastic junkie. But there was a hitch.

For women especially, dousing that raging fire wasn't always possible. In separating sex from reproduction, evolution had played a rather nasty trick on the human female. Now, compared with her male counterpart, the female found it relatively difficult to achieve a satisfying orgasm, sometimes even after vigorous sex.

But why should this be? Carina wondered. What Darwinian-style explanation could possibly account for such an unsatisfactory outcome?

Of all the many questions Western Civilization left unanswered, this certainly had to be one of the more perplexing. What conceivable motive could Mother Nature have had for interfering with a woman's ability to come quickly and easily? Indeed, besides making a woman feel good, what was the purpose of the female orgasm anyway?

Theories abounded, and for good reason. Unlike the male orgasm, where the biological purpose was self-evident, understanding the purpose of the female orgasm is a bit of a conundrum. Was it, as some had postulated, nothing more than a crude method for keeping a woman eager—and thus a man happy—so as to cement the bond between man and woman? Or was it perhaps a genetic relic, like the male nipple: useful to one sex, but not to the other, Nature had found no compelling reason to delete it? Or was it none of the above?

Andu himself couldn't remember whether or not his grandmother had ever worked out an answer. All he knew right now was that an involuntary bulge was growing in his pants and he couldn't talk it down.

Men's "things" were that way, always seeming to have a mind of their own, as if they were somehow disconnected from their owner. Maybe his grandmother had an explanation for that one too. If so, he'd never heard it. And even if he had, what good would it do him now?

Andu let out a weak groan. It was hard to separate fact from fantasy here, and he found his current situation embarrassing. Was his manhood reacting to the graphic, carefully-reasoned analysis he remembered from Carina's diary, or was it reacting to the sounds of three women in the next room working themselves up towards a frenzied climax?

A little of both, he guessed, still trying to talk his hard-on down. It wasn't listening.

Andu stood at attention now, outside the girls' door, thinking how the three must be right on the verge of cresting. He couldn't deny his feelings. He wanted to join them, to be a part of it. *But should he?*

A powerful force locked onto his subconscious now, and he began to act the whole thing out in his mind, from start to finish. The lump in his pants grew larger.

In concert with his thoughts, impassioned moans floated on the air, filling his ears. These were animal sounds, guttural sounds, sounds which had had their genesis in the jungle half a million years ago and which had then been raised to a fevered pitch out on the veldt. These were the sounds of a 100,000 years of primate evolution, of a thousand generations of yearning, of a lifetime of coaxing the man back from the hunt. These were the sounds of a woman, nay *three* women, in heat!

Andu peered cautiously around the corner, then just as quickly retracted his head.

Did he dare?

No, he did not!

Andu hesitated, the diary speaking to him still.

His grandmother wouldn't have blamed him if he'd

stepped into that room. If there was one thing she knew about, it was libido. By her own account, Carina had spent most of her adult life sexually frustrated, horny as she put it. Talk about the itch that couldn't be scratched—Carina wrote the book on it!

But for Andu there was a paradox: he wasn't sure if the usual rules applied. These women spread-eagle on the bed before him were clones. They'd had no mothers to teach them manners, no fathers to teach them right from wrong. They'd never seen so much as a *man* before! Who was he to intrude? All these girls had were desires. Hot, unfulfilled, carnal desires. And it was as if they were calling out to him now to join them, calling out to him with their mind, begging him to come inside and finish the job.

Andu no longer had the will to resist. Unable to contain himself even for another minute, he cleared his throat, straightened his clothes, and stepped into the dimly-lit room.

• • •

It went differently than he expected. Better than he feared. Worse than he hoped.

They didn't seem at all surprised by his entrance. It was as if the three had sensed his very presence out there in the hallway, as if they had read his very mind, digesting in an instant everything he had thought, then preparing themselves physically for what was to come.

They had never experienced hetero-sex before, but it didn't seem to matter; they knew exactly what to do. Legs spread wide and knees raised, they lay back on the bed, one next to the other like hors d'oeuvres lined up on a buffet table.

In their advanced state of arousal, no foreplay was required. If anything, Andu was the one in need of encouragement. And sensing that, they willingly complied. His leg still hurt like mad, and at first he was afraid of overdoing things so soon after the accident. They must have picked up on that because the three joined forces to will away his pain. Then, egging him on with their eyes and their smiles, drawing him in with their arms and their legs, they acted as if they expected him to do all three of them at once, this very instant!

He knew he couldn't manage it, no man could, not even with a short rest inbetween. Yet, as he mounted the one he believed was Prime Alpha, it occurred to him that the clones might be totally unaware of a man's physical limitations.

What *else* didn't they know? Andu wondered as he entered her. Did they have any idea how a man's member might feel thrusting back and forth inside them, how the hot rush of wet come might feel when it gushed out into the cavity between their legs, how unbundled and spent the man would be when it was over?

No, of course not! How could they? And what about the other two? Would they be angry because he couldn't perform for them as he had for their sister? Or were they so closely linked telepathically that when one came, they all would came?

Andu couldn't say.

• • •

How he wished afterwards that it could have lasted longer. The experience was so riveting, so electrifying, so stunningly singular, Andu knew he could never live long enough to repeat it. No matter how hard he tried to explain it to himself metaphysically, there was no getting around the truth: *he had just had sex with three women at once!*

A contented grin edged onto his face as he labored to relive the moment. Andu wasn't certain, but he didn't think they had exchanged so much as a single word from start to finish, not one! Only now, as he drifted off to sleep, did he think he heard one of them speak. Her voice was barely a whisper.

"So that's what that ugly thing hanging down between your legs is used for. Who would have guessed it?"

Indeed! the others answered, transferring their thoughts without benefit of speech.

Then all was quiet.

13
Attack!

The next morning brought another incredible round of love-making, only this time it was more measured, more deliberate than before. In fact, if not for their being hungry, they might have stayed at it all day!

But as the sun climbed ever higher in the Ancòn sky, the foursome gathered around a table for breakfast. It was a pleasant morning, and as the girls put out plates and napkins, Andu thought back over the past twenty-four hours. He remembered yesterday's session with the computer and the conversation that preceded it. Something they'd said still bothered him.

Turning his attention to the girl on his right, Andu spoke between bites of what could only be described as some sort of primitive unleavened bread. Despite their earlier intimacy, he still wasn't sure which girl was which. He thought this one was Prime Second.

"When we first met, you said you were calling the Great Ones, the Terr-uns. What I can't figure out is *why*. Why were you calling the Great Ones? What did you intend to ask them if they answered?"

The three exchanged glances as if the answer should have been obvious. Prime Second addressed Andu. "We want to know why the Great Ones sent us here. What do they expect of us? What are we supposed to be doing until they come to take us home? If we've been sent here to Ancòn for a reason, what is the reason?"

Andu didn't know what to say. Even as Second struggled to vocalize her thoughts, tears flowed from all three sets of eyes. It broke his heart to see them cry.

"Can't you understand?" she blubbered. "How can our life have meaning if it has no purpose? Can you blame us for wanting to know the truth?"

Andu shook his head.

"You, who call yourself a Great One. Have you no answer? What possible reason did they have for sending us here? Are we being punished? *What have we done wrong?*"

"Sweet Jesus, girls, you've done nothing wrong!" Andu exclaimed, doing his best to console them. "You're not being punished, for God's sake! You're victims, victims of a tragic mistake. Innocent victims. You've got to believe me, girls. No matter what you think, you've done nothing wrong! No one's punishing you!"

"How can you be so sure?" she asked amid a new explosion of tears. "What would you have us do? We want to go home; only we don't know the way. Do you?"

"Why, yes, as a matter of fact, I do."

"Will you take us then?" the three bubbled excitedly, speaking in a practiced unison so perfect it bordered on harmony.

"Well, yes . . . I mean, no . . . I mean, it's not that simple," Andu replied, stumbling through the answer.

"And why not?" came the indignant response.

"My ship isn't able."

"But you said you were a Terr-un, a Great One. You must have a great ship! All Terr-uns do. Or have you been lying to us? You *have* been telling us the truth about yourself, haven't you?"

"What reason would I have to lie? I'm a Terr-un just like I said, and I do have a great ship—or rather, I *did* have one. It was stolen from me. By my crew. I was set adrift in a *smaller* ship. It could never get us back home, though. Not from here, anyway. That's the God's honest truth."

"Oh." The dejected reply came in one word.

"The propulsion unit on the runabout is way too small," Andu explained, seeing how they weren't taking no for an answer.

"But our ship is big," Alpha said. "It has a big . . . a big . . ."

"Propulsion unit," Andu said, filling in the words she couldn't remember.

Prime Third nodded her appreciation. "Yes, thank you, that's what I was trying to say. Our ship has a big propulsion unit. Why couldn't we just take *our* ship? Why couldn't we just take the *Deseret*? All you'd have to do is point us in the right direction."

Andu acknowledged her with a perceptive grin. "Well, I know the way all right, but I seriously doubt whether this old bird can even still fly."

"Bird?"

"That's a figure of speech," he explained. "Back on Earth some animals walk, some animals swim, some animals fly. The ones that fly are called birds."

"Ah . . . and what is this Earth you speak of?"

Andu's voice showed surprise. "That's *my* planet. The planet where Terr-uns live. The planet you've been trying to make contact with."

"How far away is it?"

"Too far. Besides, I have a better idea. Rather than risk our necks trying to fly this bird halfway across the galaxy using outdated navigational equipment and without so much as a map to guide us, I suggest we first try something else. The foremost rule of wilderness survival is: if you should ever get lost, stay put! Let the search party find you; don't try to find them. Now, with that in mind, it might make more sense for us to have a go at boosting the gain on your transmitter. Properly amplified, we might stand a better chance of getting someone's attention back on Earth. That way they'd be *sure* to come looking for us. Otherwise, we're looking at a two to three month trip minimum at N-Class speeds to reach the nearest outpost."

"Your words are strange to us, Earth-man. What do you mean, 'boost the gain'?"

"Uh, amplify the signal using the power cells I have back on the ship."

One of the she's nodded her head as if she understood. "I think what he's suggesting we do is continue trying to call the Terr-uns just as before, only by using his power cells we should now be able to call them louder. Is that it? Is that what you're saying?"

"Yes," Andu replied, chuckling. "In a manner of speaking that's exactly what I'm trying to say. We'd most definitely be calling them louder."

"But why should they come?" Alpha interrupted. "Why should *anyone* come?"

"Because Terr-uns are good people. Don't forget, it was your calling which brought me here to begin with."

"Yes, so you've said," Prime Second snapped in a tone which could only be described as irritable.

"Listen, I know a man, a Dr. Chandra back on Earth. If we reached him, he'd be sure to send a rescue party."

"I don't see why we can't leave now. Where is your ship, anyway? The ship that brought you here."

"My runabout? It's half a day's hike from here," Andu said, pointing. "Beyond the forest. Down in the valley. Beside a small lake."

"No! We mustn't!" the Primes erupted in unison. There was genuine terror in their eyes. "Beyond the forest, down in the valley, there are bird-beasts! It is too dangerous!"

"I know, but I don't see as how we have any choice. We all have to go. The power cells are way too heavy for one man to carry alone. If this is to work, we'll have to join forces. Together, we can construct a skid, then slide the power cells one by one onto the rocketsled. After that, it'll be a simple matter to drag them with us back up here."

"But what about the bird-beasts?"

"I think by working together we ought to be okay. We'll just have to be darn careful and watch out for one another. Of course you three'll need to bring along your blasters," Andu said, remembering how handy they had been with their weapons that first day. Even now, a dull ache remained in his thigh where they'd shot him. "We can build a skid from branches we collect up in the forest on the way down there."

Silently weighing all the factors, the three girls slid trance-like into a telepathic discussion. Every once in a while, Andu actually believed his mind could make out a word or two of what was being said. Each time, though, he quickly decided he had to be hallucinating. If he himself wasn't telepathic, how could he possibly be "hearing" what they had to say? It didn't make any sense!

Nevertheless, even before they could break out of their huddle to give him an answer, he had an inkling of what their decision was going to be: Yes, if going down into bird-beast valley was the only way for them to get home, they'd chance it!

• • •

Another day of love-making and preparation passed before the journey began. If they had any hope whatsoever of making it all the way down to the ship and back up again to an elevation of relative safety, and doing so all in one day, they had to leave early, very early, even before the sun snapped above the horizon.

In the dark, Ancòn was a very creepy place indeed. Though Andu had spent a night here once already, on that occasion, sleeping on the ground, hidden from the blackness by his lean-to, it had all seemed so serene. Now, in the wee hours just before dawn, the alpine meadow and the pine-like forest were alive with sounds. Like before, he never actually saw any of the forest creatures he heard, but there was no escaping their presence. With each step they took, the four of them were greeted with fresh reminders that they were not alone. The trees were filled with hoots which might easily have come from an owl, plus guttural growls which sounded like they were coming either from a wolf or else a big cat, and grunts reminiscent of a bullfrog. It was unnerving to a degree an Earth-forest never could be.

Barely exchanging a word, the quartet walked in a single-file line, their blasters at the ready, their keen eyes alert for any sign of trouble. In their hands they carried lanterns, but these only made it worse, throwing eerie shadows down on the ground before them. On their backs they each shouldered a rucksack. Between them they were carrying a two-day supply of food and water, just in case.

At dawn, they stopped to rest and eat. Andu put his leg up on a big log. It had been giving him trouble for the past hour or so, and he was beginning to feel as if he were slowing them all down. Before they started out on the trail again, he scouted around for a sturdy branch to use as a walking stick. It helped take some of the weight off his leg and cushion the impact as they descended swiftly through the switchbacks and down towards the gleaming meadow below.

By this time Andu could already make out the lake in the distance. His ship was still there, sitting half-in, half-out of the water just as he had left her. Feeling the fool, he explained to the girls how it happened. They laughed at his story, and the tension was broken.

In the bright sun of mid-morning everything seemed tranquil, not dangerous at all. They moved with a giddy, almost carefree bounce to their step. There was nothing here to fear, nothing. That alone should have been warning enough.

All Andu knew for certain about the bird-beasts was that in his one encounter with them they had been deathly afraid of water. Here, on the other side of the pond, on the far side of the stream, he thought the four of them would be safe from attack.

This was a miscalculation of the first order.

To begin with, it never occurred to him that they might have been cunning enough to cross the stream without actually getting wet. Perhaps a dead log had fallen across the brook, offering them a natural bridge. Or perhaps the bird-beasts themselves might have been able to roll a log or boulder into the water at a spot shallow enough to allow them to ford the creek. Then again, jumping was another obvious possibility. At full gallop, these formidable flesh-eating terror-birds might have been able to manage a jump of five to six meters. How much of a barrier, then, was a puny little stream two to three meters wide? Not much, especially to a determined pack of hungry carnivores!

When the attack came, it was sudden and devastating. The bird-beasts were to the savanna of Ancòn what the sharks were to the seas of Earth—veritable eating machines! And, having no natural enemies themselves, these awesome engines of destruction usually fed at their leisure after making a kill.

The attack came from three sides all at once in a coordinated fashion. To his eternal shame, Andu was caught completely off guard. Even before he could level his blaster and fire, Prime Second and Prime Third had been taken down, their legs kicked out from under them, their broken bodies snatched up in the beak of a giant bird.

At first, their anguished screams didn't register. Nor did the splintering of shattered bone. But the blood did! It galvanized him to action!

Andu moved with alacrity. Shielding Prime Alpha with his body, he vaporized one of the rapidly approaching birds.

Then another.

Then a third.

He couldn't move fast enough; there were dozens of

them, closing in, swarming all over them like angry hornets!

Even as Prime Second held onto the last vestiges of life, one of the beasts began to gouge out her insides, making a meal of her while she was still alive!

Andu gagged, then threw up, then put Second out of her misery, frying her along with the bird-beast that was eating her.

There was no stopping him now. Andu went berserk. He killed everything in sight.

Pieces of bird-beast flew everywhere, filling the moist air with a bright-pink mist of blood and entrails. Those that he didn't kill on the first shot, he got on the second.

So much rage was pumping through his veins now, he didn't know when to stop. And long after everything around him was dead, he still went on pulling the trigger until the blaster registered empty, the contact clicking hollowly each time it met the electronic ignitor.

Exhausted by the effort, Andu fell to the ground, tears pouring from his eyes. The man would not live long enough to erase the memory of that terrible moment from his mind. Even if he grew old with age and went deaf, there was no way he would ever stop hearing those horrific sounds. Even if he went blind and became senile, he would never stop seeing those girls' terrified faces. Their look of shock and horror, their blood-curdling screams, would remain with him until the very day he drew his final breath.

Suddenly convulsed by another explosion of vomit, Andu got to his knees. His hands flew to his face. The gooey residue dripped to the ground from between his fingers.

For minutes he just sat there frozen, kneeling on the dirt, doubled over in agony. Only then did he realize he wasn't alone. A few feet away, curled up in the fetal position on the ground, was Prime Alpha. White-faced and motionless, but otherwise unhurt, she was scarcely breathing. Everything about her spoke of massive trauma, and yet he couldn't find a single mark on her body!

Scrunching down on the ground beside her, Andu flew into a panic. Was she hurt or wasn't she?

Then it hit him. *The woman was telepathic!*

Though unharmed herself, Prime Alpha had suffered through the trauma of the vicious attack every bit as much as her sisters had. Maybe more. The pain she must have endured had to have been excruciating! No wonder she showed every sign of having been ripped apart herself—in a way, she *had* been!

How exactly to understand pain? Someone breaks their leg and suddenly finds himself in agony. If the pain is sharp enough, the shock deep enough, they pass out on the spot. Otherwise, unless they are subjected to additional trauma, their body activates the pain-control mechanisms that humans have evolved over the past half-million years of trying to cope with accidents, shutting down the central nervous system and blocking out at least part of the pain from ever consciously registering inside their head. In fact, the system is so effective, countless accident victims claim to not even remember being hurt!

But how to understand pain if one is a telepath? It's not your leg that's been broken, it's your friend's; it's not *your* guts that are being gnawed on, it's your twin's. While their system shuts down and tries to cope with the injury, yours writhes in agony. While their system cuts off all signals to the pain-center in the brain, yours goes into overdrive, exploding in a megadose of hurt. While they die bite by bite, you live on, enduring the agony of each horrifying mouthful, time and time again. Overloaded, your system eventually can't take it anymore. It shuts down completely and you collapse to the ground in a crumpled heap, just as Prime Alpha had.

With his adrenalin pumping like a juggernaut now, all of this and more raced through Andu's mind in the moments following the accident. If ever there was a man desperately afraid of losing the only friend he had in this world—perhaps in this galaxy—Andu Nehrengel was that man. Clearly, he had no time to waste.

Andu sprang into action!

14
Final Entry

Prime Alpha didn't come out of her coma for nearly a week. In all that time, Andu only left her side twice—once to connect up the power cells and begin sending out a May Day; and a second time, now, to sit in front of the *Deseret*'s onboard computer and gather information.

After the brutal attack, he had strapped the unconscious Alpha—along with the power cells they'd come for in the first place—to the runabout's emergency rocketsled and taken off across the savanna at high speed. The adrenalin must've kicked in because under ordinary circumstances one man couldn't possibly have moved those heavy power cells alone. Andu managed it, though, and in the aftermath of the attack, when he was done rummaging through the hold for blankets and a first-aid kit, he powered up the rocketsled, then put it to good use transporting them both to safety.

The two of them were able to make a clean getaway, though for an instant, just an instant, he thought he had seen a streak across the sky, the telltale green vapor-trail of a tachyon ship! It wasn't possible, of course, and from that moment forward, the only thing on his mind had been getting the hell off this planet. And the sooner the better!

By sun-up this morning, Andu had decided that his best course of action would be to try and fly this old N-Class cruiser to the nearest outpost, at least a month away at nuclear speeds. But even that gambit was a long shot unless he first got himself better acquainted with how the ship operated. The duty logs seemed a sensible place to start.

The onboard data-retrieval system was archaic, but

serviceable. Everything was archived on erasable disks employing an *e*lectron-*t*rapping *o*ptical *m*emory, or etom for short. Though ancient, the etom was the first in a long series of innovations which improved upon the very earliest of information-storing schemes, those which relied on binary formatting for their success. In a binary memory-scheme a mark was either there (1) or it was not (0). The etom introduced shades of gray between the two extremes. No longer was it just simply a matter of on or off, plus or minus, black or white. With four distinct levels, one could write twice as much digital information on a disk and read it out twice as quickly; with eight levels, three times the data in one-third the time. This was a thirteen-level etom. In a few keystrokes, Andu brought up the final log entry. It was dated December 26, 2285.

The author, one Brigham Young XIV, had recorded the entry in an unusual way. Rather than being a mechanical log entry like Andu was used to, it was more along the lines of a book-film or a video-documentary. The author, an old man, had positioned himself before a video camera as if he was giving some sort of a speech. In his hands were a sheaf of papers, probably notes for what he intended to say on this, his final log. The lines in his face spoke of extreme old age, and looking at him Andu was reminded of the subject-file he'd read the other day, the one about CULT CLONING & THE LATTER-DAY SAINTS. Obviously, if everybody onboard the *Deseret* eventually died, maybe this fellow, the last fellow alive, had taken it upon himself to say something profound. If so, Andu wanted to hear every word.

The fellow cleared his throat now and began to speak. His gestures were slow and even, as if he were giving a sermon, rather than recording an entry in the ship's log.

"My days here in space are numbered. I am the last surviving member of an expedition which left Earth on Independence Day, 2187, to establish a New Kingdom of God on Mars. Regrettably, we were blown hopelessly off course by a flare in the solar wind, a flare so severe it confounded our instruments beyond repair. Though I myself cannot fathom the reason for such a calamity, it was of course God's will that this should happen.

"All of our party except myself have now died of extreme

old age. That I am still alive at this late date can only be ascribed to the fact that I was not even born when this voyage first began. My mother—God rest her Christian soul—came aboard pregnant. There were no others born after me. Once it was realized that we could never make it back to Mars, it was agreed there would be no further conceptions. Everyone onboard submitted to voluntary sterilization just to be certain. Only the clones we left behind in stasis will ever be capable of taking our places; and that is only if, God willing, our ship ever arrives on the cusp of a habitable land.

"As I look at my pocketwatch now, a watch handed down to me from generation to generation and reputed to have once belonged to Joseph Smith, our founder, I realize that I have been alone now for some six weeks already, ever since Mordecai died. I find it utterly senseless that I should remain like this until my natural end. Though the Scriptures tell us that suicide is a sin against the Lord, I believe He would make an exception in my case. If the God of Earth lives out here among the stars as He surely does at home, He should be able to see that I am far too old now to be of any further service to Him. Whether I live or whether I die can be of only trivial importance now in the never-ending battle between good and evil. My passing a little sooner or a little later can have no bearing whatsoever on the outcome of the titanic struggle between Himself and Satan. That He has even allowed me to live *this* long can only be for one reason. And now that I have completed in full the mission for which I was surely brought into this world, it is time for me to surrender my corporeal existence and join with the Great Almighty.

"What mission have I now completed, you ask? Only the job of showing under what circumstances time-travel should be possible. It can only be for this reason . . . "

Andu gasped and stopped the tape. He couldn't believe his ears. Did the man say *time-travel*? What would God want with a theory of time-travel? he wondered.

Scratching his head in confusion, Andu backed up the tape and started the paragraph over.

"What mission have I now completed, you ask? Only the job of showing under what circumstances time-travel should be possible. It can only be for this reason that the Lord our God has kept me around all these great many years. Why else? He had to be certain I'd live long enough to finish His work. And this I have now done.

"Although the more technically inclined listeners may wish to consult my detailed notes reprinted in their entirety in an appendix at the conclusion of this entry, for most viewers, the brief summary which follows should suffice to reveal the essence of what I have learned.

"Theory, unfortunately, precedes engineering, and there is no craft of this day capable of attaining the great speeds necessary to travel back in time. This may very well have changed, though, by the time my writings are discovered and read. Such has been the case over and over again in human history. Leonardo da Vinci invented the helicopter, but it took the twentieth century to build it; Isaac Newton, the calculus, but it didn't find practical application for another 250 more years; Charles Babbage, the mathematics underpinning the modern computer, but more than a century passed before more than a handful of God's children could lay claim to having ever seen one. What, if anything, will I be remembered for? I wonder.

"Life is strange that way—people are not always remembered for what they think they will be. Wasn't it the Talmud which said, 'We do not see the world as it is, we see the world as we are'? So it has been throughout recorded history. Epony, I believe, is the correct term for it; from the Greek, eponym.

"Think of all the science that has been named for its discoverer: the amp, a unit of electric current, after André Ampère; the curie, a unit of radioactivity, after Marie Curie; the hertz, a unit of frequency, after Heinrich Rudolph Hertz; the newton, a unit of force required to accelerate a mass, after none other than Sir Isaac himself; the watt, a unit of electric power, after James of the same last name.

"The list goes on and on, and not just in science, of course, but in many other disciplines as well. Take religion, for instance. They don't call it Christianity for nothing!

"Or how about economics? Here we have Occam's Razor—the simplest theory is the best theory; Say's Law—supply creates its own demand; and Sander's Paradox—every test measures *something*, even if it's not what you think you're testing for.

"And what about medicine? Paget's disease; the Apgar test; the Golgi complex; pasteurization.

"But wait, there's still more! The Buckminsterfullerene; the Bunsen burner; the Turing machine; the joule; to galvanize; durbinium; etc.; etc.; etc.

"Certainly it must have occurred to you by now that something is weighing heavily on my mind. That, dear listener, is undeniably the case. On this, the very last day of my life, the question which is vexing me is—For whom will time-travel be named? Will it be named for me? Will it be called 'Brigham Young XIV's Theory' of time-travel? Or perhaps, 'Young's Theory' of time-travel? In the future, will getting 'younger' take on a whole new meaning?"

At this, Young stopped and smiled. "But I digress, and for that I must apologize. It's high time I got back to the matter at hand—a comprehensive theory of time-travel.

"Albert Einstein made time-travel possible, at least conceptually anyway. Whereas Newton assumed that space and time were absolute and unvarying, Einstein described space-time as being relative, and as changing with the distribution of mass or energy in the vicinity. In his scheme, no longer were space and time independent.

"He went on to assert that if one were to view the universe as being a flexible sheet of discrete grid-points, out in the perfect vacuum of empty space such a sheet would in fact be a plane, flat and smooth, and devoid of even so much as a bump or a wrinkle. When we introduce objects with mass into the equation though, the picture quickly becomes rather more complicated. Each new body produces a dimple or a contour in that imaginary flat plane. The heavier the body, the bigger the dimple.

"A moon-sized planet, for instance, would make a shallow dent or impression in the grid-point plane; an Earth-sized planet, a deeper impression; a sun, a much, much deeper impression. This phenomenon has even come to have a name, and nowadays we usually speak of such dents in the plane of space as being 'gravity wells.'

"The term is meant to be descriptive. If viewed edge-on, a gravity well would have the appearance of an inverted mountain hanging down from beneath the otherwise smooth surface of the flexible sheet, a depression scooped out of the fabric of space like a dip of ice cream. For bodies of immense mass—say, a large planet or a sun—the well could be quite substantial, quite deep. The deeper the well, the more energy a traveler would have to expend to climb up out of it and get out into open space.

"Among the most important steps Einstein took in relating time to gravity was to build on the physics described two centuries earlier by Isaac Newton. It was well understood by then that an object moving through undimpled space would travel in a perfectly straight line. But what *wasn't* so well understood was what would happen when that space was pitted with gravity wells of varying depths. Einstein provided an explanation. He said that when we shoot a projectile out across *that* sort of space, its path is no longer a nice straight line, but becomes instead a course which is warped and twisted by the tortured curvilinear profile of the space it travels through.

"As the hypothetical projectile barrels through *dimpled* space, it exhibits complex behavior. Its motion gets bent, refracted if you will, by the prisms in that flexible sheet, the prisms we have now come to call gravity wells.

"If the object's velocity is sufficient, it will ricochet off any number of small dimples, sliding through the contours forming the upper reaches of each well, and zoom out the other side, careening off in a new direction. On the other hand, if its velocity is *not* high enough, or if the well it encounters is exceptionally deep, the object in question will drop into the cavity, never to be seen or heard from again. Lacking the energy to 'crawl' back up the wall and out the other side, it will eventually come to rest at the bottom of the well. On yet the third hand, if the circumstances are just right and the forces precisely balance, the object will neither glance off nor sink into the well, but go placidly into orbit instead.

"When we speak of a physical object such as an asteroid or a spaceship, this chain of reasoning seems abundantly clear. Yet somehow, the common sense of it all seems to melt away and become suspect when the same argument is applied to a photon phenomenon such as light. Part of the problem is, of course, that for all its inherent brightness, we cannot see light for what it really is. And we certainly cannot see light the way *nature* sees it!"

Andu nodded his head. He had experienced the same measure of disbelief himself when he first invented his tachyon drive. What Brigham Young XIV said made sense.

"To begin with (and contrary to longstanding belief), light is made up of tiny particles, particles we refer to as photons. While there has been a lively debate in the scientific community over the years as to the true nature of photons and as to whether or not they are in fact endowed with a measurable mass, the simple fact is, light behaves as if the case were proven.

"Thus, when light passes unperturbed through that flat, undimpled, Newtonian type of space I described earlier, it proceeds in a nice straight line much as a *physical* object would. However, if we contour that space, if we pepper its fabric with countless gravity wells, then according to General Relativity those depressions will affect not only the straightline motion of *physical* objects, they will work their black magic on a beam of light as well. And, as one might expect, the effect will be especially noticeable in the vicinity of a particularly massive object like a star or a black hole.

"Now, as a scientist ever curious to learn more, the question can be reduced to a testable proposition, namely, to what extent will a beam of light be bent when it passes in the vicinity of a heavy mass?

"Well, the answer must obey the identical principles already set forth for describing the motion of an *ordinary* object through a gravity well. Which is to say, the degree to which a lightbeam will be bent is a function of only two variables—the mass of the object being passed and the distance of the pass. Should a beam of light encounter an extremely heavy object such as a black hole, and do so at very short range, the beam may actually be bent so drastically as to fall *into* the hole, never to be seen or heard from again. Indeed, it is for this very reason we call these super-massive objects black holes to begin with; even light cannot escape their clutches! Of course, for encounters with less massive objects, the bending would be that much less severe.

"In Einstein's physics, light-speed was posited as the greatest speed at which an ordinary object could move. Though this proposition was later called into question by Durbin—the very same man who suggested that General Relativity was all wrong, that objects *could* attain a velocity in excess of light-speed—for Einstein's purposes, the hypothetical maximum was a realistic enough assumption to support the cause of astrophysics research well into the next century. Yet, in spite of this one shortcoming, what Einstein did in relating time to light-speed was brilliant! To understand the essence of his genius, consider the following thought-experiment:

"An observer at rest measures the speed of light. Using his most sophisticated measuring-device, he comes up with a rather precise number. At the very same instant, an observer in motion—say, onboard a swift spaceship—likewise measures the speed of light with *his* most accurate instrument. He too comes up with a number. Upon comparing results, both observers agree they have arrived at the same figure!

"Now, it almost goes without saying that such an outcome stretches credulity. A simple, everyday example should help to explain why:

"At one time or another, most of us have had an occasion to ride a moving sidewalk. (I, myself, never have—for reasons that should be obvious—but that doesn't make the analogy any less sound.) For, in riding that moving sidewalk, we have all observed the identical phenomenon. If a rider stands motionless on the horizontal escalator as it lumbers forward, he will not be surprised to learn that his forward speed relative to a fixed observer is precisely equal to the speed of the sidewalk itself. If, on the other hand, he is strolling *along* the sidewalk in the same direction as the sidewalk itself is traveling, he will not be surprised to discover that his forward speed relative to that same observer on the platform is now the arithmetic sum of his walking pace *plus* the velocity of the sidewalk. No concept in physics could be simpler! Only, in our earlier thought-experiment, this is not what happened. In that instance, when the two observers independently did their best to calculate the speed of light, they both came up with the *same* answer. Thus, the paradox. If, like the moving sidewalk, the spaceship had forward velocity of its own, how in the world could the passenger *onboard* the spaceship have arrived at the identical answer as the *stationary* observer?

"Well, of course, he shouldn't have, and it took an Albert Einstein to offer a solution to this seemingly intractable problem. What he came up with was pure genius!

"Albert suggested that, despite what their instruments were telling them, it was actually *time* which was traveling slower as the moving observer sped up, not light which was traveling at precisely the right speed to accommodate its observer.

"Careful and detailed experiments have in fact borne this proposition out, though the differences remain negligible until one has attained a speed very nearly that of light, perhaps in excess of 90%. A hypothetical traveler carrying a timepiece of any kind—a wristwatch, a pendulum, a water clock, it doesn't matter—soon discovers that as his velocity approaches the speed of light, the timepiece will begin to run slower as compared with a timepiece in a stationary frame. To the light-speed traveler, time would appear to pass normally, but for each hour that his clock advanced, *years* might pass for someone back in a fixed frame. In fact, compared with his brother sitting back home on Earth waiting for him to return, the space-traveler would age more slowly!

"Tying this all together then, what do we have? We know that as a traveler's velocity approaches light-speed in open space—which is to say, in space devoid of any outside gravitational influences—that time will slow. And though it has been impossible to prove (see my Appendix A for a summary of several such attempts), we have it on good authority that at light-speed itself, time—as duration—will slow to zero. Now, if we have learned nothing else from three centuries of studying physics, it is that—with one exception—all forces in nature are symmetrical. What goes up, must come down; what swings to, must swing fro; there is matter, and there is antimatter; there are right-handed amino acids, and there are mirror image left-handed ones; mass and energy are conserved, as is angular momentum. The list goes on and on. Symmetry must hold for time as well!

"If it is true that in the approach to light-speed from below, time slows, it must likewise be true that in the approach to light-speed from above, time will also slow. Only at light-speed itself, is time still. Or, to put it another way, if you begin from light-speed where time is at a dead stop, and either speed up or slow down, time will resume moving forward in the customary fashion.

"Though not entirely complete, a picture would perhaps help clarify what we have learned thus far."

Here, Brigham Young XIV stopped and held up a hand-drawn graph done on white poster board:

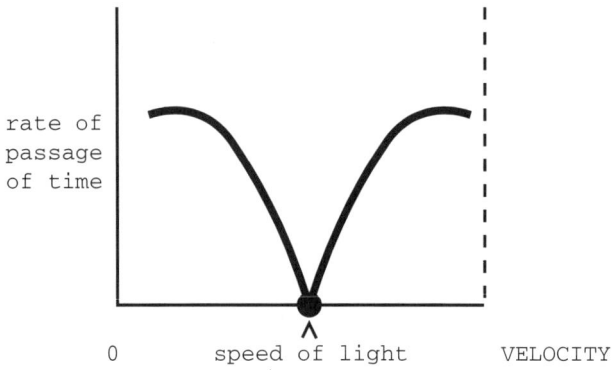

"The graph, while preserving symmetry, is incomplete. For one thing, the 'tails' of the time-curve are conspicuously absent. For another, the graph has no scale. The first is more easily handled than the second, though to fill in either would require leading you through page after page of tedious equations, something which I am loathe to do. Thus, I offer you a choice.

"If you wish to familiarize yourself with the mathematical underpinnings of what follows, feel free to consult my Appendix B before continuing. If, on the other hand, you are willing to accept it on faith that I have spent the past fifty years checking and rechecking my math, then simply continue viewing. You can always check the math later on.

"My equations tell us two things. First, beginning at the far left, as we approach zero velocity from above, the arrow of time resumes its upward climb and accelerates asymptotically towards infinity. On the far right of the graph, as we move out towards infinite velocity, the rate of passage of time also accelerates, again driving upwards toward infinity. In both cases, a consistent symmetry is maintained either side of light-speed.

"Now, if we superimpose these constructs on our original graph, the relationship between time and velocity is brought into sharper focus."

Here, Young brought up a second chart:

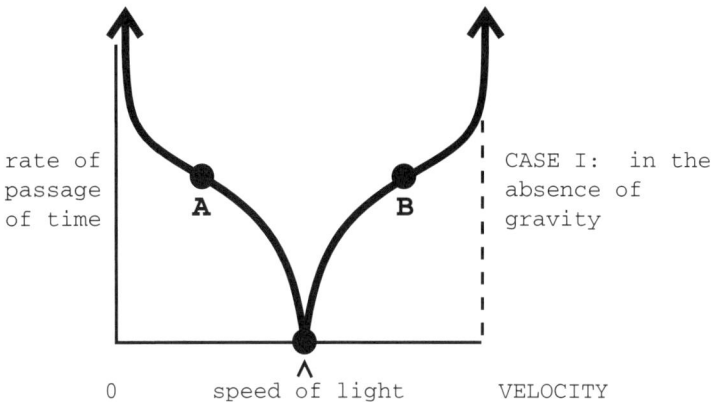

"What can we conclude from this? Several things. First: In the zero-g-space we posited at the outset of this discussion, there are two zones—one above light-speed, and one below—where time edges forward at a leisurely enough pace to support the chemistry of life. We exist perhaps at point A, while an alien, but equally successful race may exist out at point B. It would, however, be just as difficult and confusing for us to live in their supra-light-speed world as it would be for them to exist in our infra-light-speed world. I doubt that either one of us would survive in the others' world.

"As you may have noticed, thus far I've intentionally avoided saying anything specific about the *shape* of the time-curves, though I have drawn them as smooth and regular. Any number of possibilities exist. The left and right-hand portions of the time-curve might be hyperbolic tangents. They might be a series of downward-sloping line segments. Or two parts of a perfectly symmetrical half-circle. Or even none of the above! In fact, the time-curves might not even be smooth at all, but riddled with countless bumps and irregularities I can only guess at! The point is, I've drawn them as I see them, uniform and smooth, their regular shape dictated by a physicist's intuition that steadily increasing amounts of energy are required to reach light-speed, whether from above or below.

"As you, the viewer, have undoubtedly recognized by now, motion across a zero-g plane is a special case. Life (along with just about everything else) takes place on planets and in solar systems; that is, where there is mass and gravity. Just as accelerated motion affects the duration of events, so too does gravity. As a matter of fact, the effects of acceleration and of gravity are indistinguishable. Physicists call this property the Principle of Equivalence. A clock placed near a massive body runs more slowly than one placed farther away. That this is so has been repeatedly demonstrated by actual experiment. Gravity bends light, slows time, and thus alters the position of the time-curve on our graph. The extreme case of gravity bending light is, of course, the black hole. Here, gravity is so intense, light cannot escape at all, and time—along with everything else within the event horizon—clocks down.

"I know, dear listener, that by now you must be terribly bored with my explanation, and for that I am truly sorry. Be assured, though, that the end is near. I have already laid out for you all the physics that is required. In just a moment you will see why—aside from engineering a speedy-enough craft—there should be nothing in God's physics to prevent us from time-traveling into the past. The logic of it goes something like this:

"If, when traveling at light-speed in zero-g, time slows to zero; and if, when in the presence of gravity the passage of time is inexorably reduced further; then, what is the effect on the progress of time when traveling at light-speed in the *presence* of gravity?

"The answer couldn't be more obvious! Already at zero in the *absence* of gravity, the passage of time is reduced even further in the *presence* of gravity. It becomes negative! Relative to someone standing outside the spaceship, *time begins to flow backward*!

"Is this possible? Why yes, of course it is! That this should be the result becomes clearer when we add the effect of gravity to the picture we've already drawn of (dare I say it?) Young's Time-Curves. They are shifted downward by an amount equal to the Durbin coefficient. To wit:

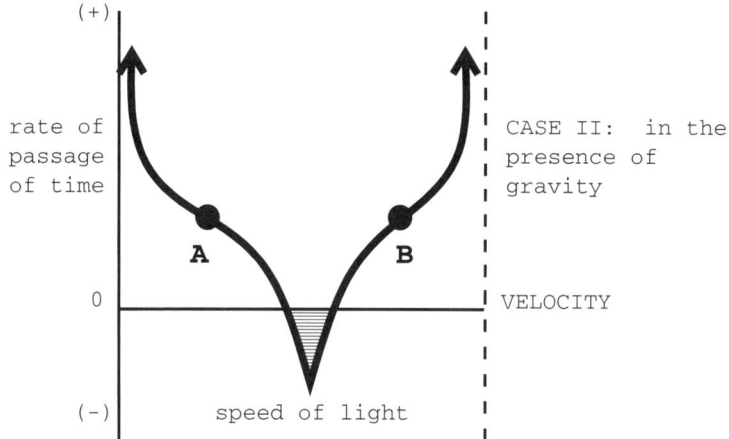

"Looking now at the shaded, V-shaped pocket straddling either side of light-speed, we find a zone where negative time-travel should not only be feasible, but unavoidable! Think about that for a moment because the implications are staggering!

"As Albert Einstein himself once pointed out, traveling at light-speed is all but impossible for a physical object. Indeed, accomplishing that particular feat would require the expenditure of an infinite amount of energy. Now, all of a sudden, we have found a way around what has seemed an insurmountable barrier! *So long as you are in close enough proximity to a sufficiently heavy mass, and go fast enough, negative time-travel will result. And all without ever having to actually attain light-speed*!

"Could any other result be as intellectually satisfying? I think not. If all that's required to travel back in time is getting a man and his spaceship into that V-shaped zone, then it will be only a matter of time until someone attempts it. Indeed, only two conditions must be met: (1) his velocity must be near, but not quite light-speed, and (2) his travel must take place under the influence of an enormous gravitational field. Difficult perhaps, but not impossible.

"So there you have it, faithful listener. My mission here in this world is now complete. The clones are in deep sleep, the ship is on autopilot set to land if the bio-sensors sniff out a satisfactory world, and the education disk is in place if the clones survive and reach an age at which it would do them any good. I may now in good conscience go to meet my maker. The only question remaining for me is whether or not there *is* one. A maker, that is.

"A devout man always, I can't help but wonder whether there really is a God or whether it hasn't all been a gimmick foisted on us by small men with dangerous minds.

"I ask you: If God can prevent evil, but doesn't, then how can we call Him all-loving? If God *intends* to prevent evil, but cannot, then how can we call Him omnipotent? If God intends to prevent evil, and furthermore is *capable* of doing so, then how can evil even exist in the first place?

"And what of free-will? If God is omniscient, then He knows ahead of time precisely what each person will do in a given situation. If that is the case, a person has no alternative but to do what God already knows he *will* do; thus, free-will is nothing more than an illusion.

"Not to put too fine a point on it, but if one 'chooses' to commit a sin, how can it be said that he sinned freely? If I now choose to commit suicide, is it not God's will that I do so?

"Circles inside of circles, and it all ends up the same. A life of solitude is a purgatory of the worst sort. A life without love is no life at all. Goodbye, sweet world. May the Lord forgive me for what I am about to do.

"Respectfully, Brigham Young XIV"

And then the screen went blank.

15
Fornax

Andu moved away from the machine, stunned by what he'd just learned. The words "time-travel" echoed through his head, triggering a rush of memories. He couldn't stop them. Back he flew, year by year, back in time to his earliest days as a freedom-fighter in the Afghan resistance. What had it been now, fifteen years? No, seventeen! Was it possible? Could it really have been that long?

While it felt as if a lifetime had come and gone since, Andu remembered every grisly detail as if it were only yesterday. He had been a young, frightened man at the time, a man caught up in the middle of a desperate war. On this particular day, the day that it happened, he had been hiking with the rest of his unit back towards their mountainside hideout following a punishing battle. They had been caught in an ungodly rainstorm along the trail and were now all drenched to the skin and shivering. Finding it difficult to stay warm, Andu thought it curiously ironic that he should be fighting to defend a flag he paid scant allegiance to or risking his neck in support of cherished ideals he barely endorsed. He resented being there and desertion was on his mind.

Flopping onto his sagging bunk after yet another day of killing the enemy, Andu lay there wet and cold, licking his wounds and mourning the death of his closest buddy. He was in a black mood. Though they had won the confrontation with the Chinese regiment, Andu's unit had suffered heavy casualties. That included the loss of his best friend and bunkmate.

Andu had almost talked himself to sleep that night when all of a sudden he was startled to attention by an unfamiliar swooshing sound outside his tent. It was unlike any noise he'd ever heard, and his first reaction was that it was the enemy, there to bushwhack him!

His heart pounding, Andu drew a sharp breath. But before he could roll over and even make a move to defend himself, he opened his eyes to behold an elderly gentleman standing there at the foot of his cot, leaning against a tentpole. This was a man Andu had never laid eyes on before, albeit one he was unlikely to soon forget. To this day—seventeen plus years later—that amazing old coot still haunted his dreams.

Though Andu was fairly alarmed by this stranger's mysterious appearance, the man did not threaten him in any way. To the contrary, supported by a knotty old pine cane, the bloke hobbled in from out of the rain and handed Andu a mammoth sheaf of papers. Yellowed and tattered, the pages were bound in a frayed folio of tooled red leather. Their ragged condition bespoke of great old age.

Then, before turning abruptly and heading back out into the storm, the man spoke to Andu in a broken, fractured sort of tongue. He wore a jagged smile. "Ma nome is Sven Rutland de SKANDIA. Dis is vor you."

Andu was understandably suspicious of this leathery-skinned old fellow, and who could blame him? Still, he wasn't quite sure what to make of the old guy. Though the man's accent was peculiar and in a class by itself, it certainly didn't strike him as being even vaguely SKANDIAN.

"Heh, old man," Andu remarked, taking hold of the bundled sheaf of papers he had just been given and shaking them in his hand for emphasis. "What is the meaning of this?"

In the worst impersonation of a SKANDIAN accent Andu had ever heard in his life, the man before him answered. "Vo grandmudder vanted vou to 'ave it."

"Drop the fake accent, gramps," Andu ordered, his tone suddenly caustic. "Ma grandmudder . . . I mean, my grandmother, has been dead for years. My dad told me she died even before I was born."

"Nonsense, Andu," the man countered, speaking to him now in plain, ungarbled English and calling him by name. "Your father told you that just so you wouldn't ask too many questions about your past. In fact, your grandmother has only just passed away within the week. And that is why I am here today."

Even as he spoke, the old man dug at something buried deep down inside his pocket. "Oh, I almost forgot," he said, pulling it out and tossing it across to Andu. "This is for you as well."

Snatching the small object from out of the air, Andu opened his hand to find an oddly-shaped custom-made key resting in his palm. By the time he looked up again, his uninvited guest had already pivoted on his cane and was tottering towards the open flap of Andu's tent.

This whole sequence of events was just too much for Andu to bear, and he found himself coming completely unglued.

"Heh, stop!" he shouted, before the old fellow could make it outside. "How come you know my name? And if *you* knew my grandmother, how come I never did?"

Pausing at the entrance to Andu's tent, the prehistoric gentleman tried to clear things up. "Because she lived on Mars . . . with me."

Andu chuckled with disbelief, mocking the other man with his reply. "Sure, pops, and I'm the Emir of Afghanistan."

Tired of listening to the old duffer, Andu turned to toss the sheaf of papers into a wastebasket. But before he could, a bony hand had reached out from across the tent and grabbed his wrist with the fierceness of someone half his age.

"You stupid dunce!" the man exclaimed, his eyes all afire. "This is your *heritage*! You must read it, Andu! Do you think I came all this way to have you *trash* it? Indeed! Is every Nehrengel that was ever born a stubborn jerk?"

Andu was startled by the outburst, and even just a little bit scared. Unsure what to say, he barely managed to stammer out a question. "You knew . . . my father?"

"*And* your grandfather," he said, loosening his grip on Andu's arm. "You might say I rescued him from the clutches of the Overlord not far from here."

"Sure," Andu snapped, reassuming his cocky stance. "You and what army?"

"Just me and Jenny," he said, a sphinx-like grin filling his face.

"*Jenny*?" Andu asked, perplexed. "What kind of a man takes a woman into battle?"

Producing a queer-looking gun from under his coat, the mysterious old fellow smiled. "Andu, meet Jenny. With this blaster you can defeat an entire army without losing so much as a single man."

Considering his own, rather meritorious accomplishments on the battlefield that day, Andu abruptly dismissed his guest's ridiculous claim with a contemptuous bob of the head. "What are these papers anyway, old-timer? And what is your real name? It certainly isn't Sven whatever-you-said."

"These papers, as you call them, are Carina's diary."

"And who, my good friend, is Carina?"

"Your grandmother, you dolt!" the old fellow bellowed, his tone one of exasperation. "As for me, I was once a soldier just as you are now."

"You?" Andu blurted out, confounded by the possibility. "You're a fossil!"

"Indeed," he answered, his voice flat. "A fossil named Fornax."

"That was my grandfather's name."

"So I'm told."

"He was a hero."

"Yes—I was."

"I don't believe you," Andu said, though somehow he did. "And this key?" he asked, all at once curious. "What is *it* for?"

"Carina, that is, your grandmother, inherited a great estate near Auckland, an estate which for many years served as a halfway house for fleeing immigrants. Since all of her children, save your father, remained with her on Mars, she wanted him to have it. No freedom-fighter was more tenacious than her son, your father, but when he died in the Indiastan revolt, we agreed the Auckland estate should pass to you instead."

When Fornax had finished with his spiel, he placed Jenny on the table next to Carina's diary, patted it lovingly on the stock as if it were his own flesh and blood, then hobbled from Andu's tent still leaning heavily on his time-worn cane.

Too shocked by the proceedings to try and stop him, Andu just sat there on his bunk with his mouth agape. Not until he was cued by a repeat of the strange swooshing noise that had accompanied his grandfather's arrival, did he come to his senses and rush from his tent. By then, the old man had disappeared from sight.

Had the setting sun not been unceremoniously shoved aside by the invading night, it might have witnessed the departure of this truly remarkable relic of a man. But to this day, Andu had no idea how he got there nor by what means he left. Nor did he ever see or hear from his grandfather again.

Although the young soldier was confused and exhausted by the day's events, he barely closed his eyes that night. Until the next morning when he set off with Jenny clenched tightly in his fist, Andu lay in his bunk mesmerized by every word his grandmother had recorded in the course of her long and thrilling life. He was so riveted by what she had to say about Fornax, that he read it from cover to cover twice, the second time paying particular attention to those passages she'd devoted to him. And, like a bedside Bible, Andu had revisited those selections several times since, even committing some of them to memory.

When Andu awoke with a start that next morning, everything was clear. Though tired and bleary-eyed, he understood perfectly why Fornax had come, and more importantly, what he expected Andu to do. As was most assuredly Fornax's intention, Andu immediately put Jenny to work in their beleagured country's battle to be free. She marked a turning point in the war. And, as his grandfather had promised, that awesome gun *could* defeat an entire army!

With Andu leading the charge, and with Jenny gripped in his capable hands, he was able to liberate his tiny, landlocked province from the clutches of the Overlord for the first time in more than two generations!

For his accomplishment, Andu was hailed as a hero by his countrymen. But the real hero was Fornax. Not only had he saved his grandson from making the mistake of a lifetime by deserting, he had saved his country from another century of fruitless warfare. Afghanistan could never have succeeded in winning against the Chinese if not for the gift Fornax bestowed upon Andu that night seventeen years ago.

Not long after the truce was signed, Andu set off for Auckland determined to make some sense out of what he had learned about Fornax from Carina's diary. By then, his grandparents had become an enigma, a mystery begging to be solved.

He began with the odd-looking key Fornax had given him that same blustery night. Andu found it hugging the bottom of his footlocker along with some dirty socks and a pair of worn-out fatigues. But without so much as an address to go on, Andu didn't have a clue where on the island to begin searching for his grandmother's estate.

As it turned out, he didn't have far to look. In fact, the provincial land office on the outskirts of town proved to be his first and only stop. They knew the place well and were more than happy to have somebody come along and claim it and take it off their hands. The magistrate warned him up-front though that the property was a trifle rundown.

In Andu's estimation, the man's appraisal bordered on a serious understatement of the estate's true condition. The buildings were old and the grounds unkempt, the shingles loose and the gutters drooping. Even so, Andu had no difficulty imagining how, in its prime, without the jumble of weeds and the tapestry of cobwebs, the manor must have been palatial. Regrettably, the years had not been kind and when Andu found it, the once proud estate was little more than an assembly of rotted timbers and decaying masonry.

For a couple of hours he stumbled about the property unsure what it was he was looking for or how his grandmother could have thought she was doing him a favor by bequeathing him this dump. Andu was just about to throw in the towel and go home, when it happened—he found the *Tikkidiw*!

The gleaming spacecraft out of another time was moored in a dilapidated woodshed. Silent, it seemed to be patiently waiting for his arrival. Outside, peeling white paint littered the unmown grass; inside, a tattered decal of a butterfly still emblazoned her hull. Opening the hatch, Andu discovered a ledger chronicling the ship's travels, plus a mammoth set of logbooks tallying the names of the many thousands of immigrants his grandfather had carried to freedom over the years. Only then did he begin to grasp the full measure of the man who had once called himself Fornax Engels.

Yet, in spite of everything he'd learned thus far, Andu barely had half the story. He still had a lifetime of questions which had to be answered about his grandmother, Carina Matthews. Time and again he went back to her diary. Time and again he revisited it with only one purpose in mind, to reread her entry dated October 5, 2433, some fifty-five years ago.

It was *that* entry which had come to mind now when he moved away from the archaic, data-retrieval machine with the words "time-travel" on his lips. Carina had often lamented her inability to go back in time, to find a cure for the genetic defect which had robbed her family of long life. Now, all of a sudden, thanks to Brigham Young XIV, Andu Nehrengel might just have it within his power to fix what she could not!

Slipping back into the other room where Alpha still lay in bed, out cold, he opened his grandmother's diary and turned to that page.

16
Byron

October 5, 2433

    Carina had narrowly escaped the nightmare of Sane Lou with her life and was now deep inside the Genealogical Institute having a conversation with a man named Brigham Smith. The Institute was a project of the Church of Jesus Christ of Latter-day Saints, and Chief Apostle Smith was its sole proprietor.
    Thinking about it now, Andu couldn't help but chuckle. The world was funny that way. Sometimes the past came ripping through to the future in the most unexpected of ways. Here he was in 2488 sitting inside a space vehicle built by the Mormons three hundred years earlier; there Carina had been, fifty-five years ago, talking to an elder from that very same Church. She had come away from that meeting with information, important information, information dating back to a distant ancestor of hers who had lived—and died—in the 1860s; here *he* was, more than half a century later, dredging up that same information in contemplation of testing out a time-travel theory worked out by yet another Mormon, Brigham Young XIV. Clearly, if Andu was to entertain the risk of making a trip back in time, it only made good sense to have a destination; and his grandmother's diary gave him one—May 1862.
    Her father Sam was dying and the culprit was a genetic defect, the same defect Andu was afflicted with. Carina had journeyed there to the Institute in search of answers. Her idea for a cure was to find a compatible donor not infected with the bad gene, and it didn't take long for her and Chief Apostle Smith to agree that the most likely donor-candidate would be a family

member from an earlier generation. Tapping into the Institute's genealogical database that day the search took them back to the mid-1800s and one Byron Matthewson. Carina had recorded the details of that conversation in her diary as faithfully as she could:

```
     We were seated in the Institute's meeting
room located deep within a cavernous underground
bunker.  The room was modestly furnished with a
large  board-of-directors-style  table,  plus  a
dozen or more straight-backed chairs. Tasteful
music played in the background. Chief Apostle
Brigham Smith had taken a seat at one end of the
rectangular, cherry-wood table.  I sat across
from him.  The others there in the room with me
were Sister Siona, BC, and Doctor Killjoy.
     Of the three, perhaps only Sister Siona
needs an introduction.  She was on her way to
Mars with BC, but this side trip to the Institute
had  delayed  their  departure.   The lines in
Siona's face made her look older than she
actually was, but then she hadn't had an easy
life.  The hospital ward she headed was run by
an  order  of  nuns,  only  these  weren't  your
ordinary nuns; these gals had sex, got married,
drank like fish, and cussed like kickboxers.
When it suited her, Siona's vernacular could
suddenly swing from her Sunday best to her
locker-room worst.
     The meeting began badly.  Brigham Smith
was a thin, severe-looking man who might have
been happier as a preacher back in the wild days
of the Old West than here in the twenty-fifth
century. He viewed the Institute as his private
fiefdom. I took an immediate dislike to the man,
and he was more than happy to reciprocate.  It
was evident from his demeanor that he didn't
care much for visitors, and certainly not for
women—-at least not nosy women like me, armed
with loads of nettlesome questions.
     Within  easy  reach  of  where  Smith  was
```

seated at the table was an info-terminal and an oversized keypad. He switched the unit on. The screen flickered briefly then shone a pale green as it awaited his commands. The entire depository was at his fingertips: millions upon millions of documents collected over the course of six centuries of American history--birth certificates, baptismal records, marriage licenses, divorce decrees, death certificates, even adoption proceedings.

Placing my hands flat on the smooth tabletop in front of me, I shivered involuntarily; the polished wood felt uncommonly cold to the touch. Pursed on the edge of my lips was a name, a name my father had given me, a name *his* father had given him, a name that was part and parcel of the Matthews' legend.

Brigham Smith's eyes were upon me as I began to speak. "As luck would have it, I happen to know the name of an ancient ancestor. He was originally from around here, as a matter of fact. Private Byron Matthewson of the Eleventh Cavalry. Died in the War Between the States."

"That's wonderful!" Brigham chirped, his eyes lighting up for the first time. "Not that he died, of course, but that he was in the military. Even in those days, the militia kept fairly good records."

His fingers glided swiftly over the keys as he began entering search parameters into the giant computer. Somewhere down the hall, hidden from view, eighteen pairs of magnetic drives began whirring as the machine canvassed millions of entries for a match.

"How did you come to learn of this fellow?" Smith asked, his eyes fixed on the screen.

"My father—-the man's like a walking history book."

"Lucky for you," Smith murmured approvingly.

"Men like that are rare. You did say Matthew*son* didn't you?" he asked. "Not Matthews."

I nodded, nervously cracking my knuckles as he worked.

"Now, if I recall my U.S. history correctly, the War Between the States dates to the early to mid 1800s." His fingers were poised on the cusp of depressing the ENTER key.

"1860s, to be precise." This was Sister Siona correcting him. She was something of a history buff.

Tabbing backwards, Smith adjusted his entry. "All our data is stored by decades. I'll set the range as 1860 to 1870 and see what we get."

The machine responded almost instantly to his inquiry. Skimming nearly as fast down through the biographical information, Brigham Smith read aloud from the screen, summarizing what was there as he went:

"According to the *Adjutant General's Report/Illinois*, Volume 8, covering the five year period from 1861 to 1866, a Byron Matthewson is listed on page 290 as having enlisted in the 11th Cavalry, Company B, January 8, 1862 and having died at Vicksburg, May 1862. His residence prior to enlistment is shown as Trivoli, Illinois."

"That's *it*?" I exclaimed, disappointed. "That's all you can tell me?"

"My dear, that was nearly six hundred years ago! I've already just told you a great deal."

"There must be more!" I insisted. "Father's name? Mother's name? Children? Wife? Where in the Sam Hill is Trivoli anyway?"

"Patience, my dear. There *is* more. Like I said, the Army kept good records. And keeping track of family trees has been a project of the Church since the days of Joseph Smith. Don't forget, Mormonism really got its start not far from here, in Nauvoo. And one branch of the Church was even headquartered in northeastern Missouri for the next three hundred and fifty years."

By now I'd grown weary of Brigham Smith and his constant recounting of Mormon history. The only subject which was of interest to me was the life and times of one Private Byron Matthewson. "Where did he die?" I asked. "And when?"

Though my tone was an impatient one, the Chief Apostle didn't seem to notice. He resumed reading from the screen.

"The *Adjutant General's Report* includes a 'History of the Eleventh Cavalry.' Let's see whether it sheds any light on our Byron:

"In October of 1861, Robert G. Ingersoll of Peoria and Basil D. Meeks of Woodford County obtained permission to raise a Regiment of Cavalry and commenced recruiting at Peoria that very month. Twelve full companies were raised and this Regiment of Illinois volunteers went into Camp Lyon, Peoria, about November 1, 1861. They were mustered into the service of the United States on December 20, 1861. The Eleventh Cavalry—-that would be Byron's unit—- was under the command of a Major James Johnson. The Regiment remained at Camp Lyon until February 22, 1862, when they broke camp and marched to Benton Barracks, Missouri, arriving there March Third. Shortly thereafter, the recruits were armed with revolvers and sabres; one battalion was issued carbines."

"This is wonderful!" I exclaimed, taking notes as he talked. After so many setbacks, I found it hard to believe I was finally getting somewhere. "Do go on."

"On March 25, the Regiment proceeded to the Tennessee River where, on April 1, the First

Battalion landed at Crump's Landing. The balance of the Regiment landed the same day at Pittsburg Landing on the west bank of the Tennessee River about ten miles above Savannah; they camped about two miles from where they put in."

Even as Smith spoke, a computer-generated map popped up on the televideo screen, each location he mentioned being illuminated in turn. By keeping an eye on the screen, it was easy to trace the Regiment's movements crosscountry.

His reading of the salient facts continued. "The Third Battalion, which included the Eleventh Cavalry, encamped on the north side of Snake Creek. On the sixth and the seventh of April, the Regiment was engaged in the great battle of Shiloh, a bloody contest between the forces of General Ulysses S. Grant and General Albert Sydney Johnston. Following the death of Major James Johnson in battle on May 22, 1862, there were mass defections from the ranks of the volunteers. In the months ahead, the Regiment participated in operations throughout southwestern Tennessee and northern Mississippi."

"Wait a second!" I interrupted, looking at my notes. "Something doesn't jive here. I thought you said Byron died at *Vicksburg* in May of 1862? That's way down here," I said, pointing to the computer-generated map. "Now you're saying they were engaged in the battle of Shiloh in *April* of that same year. That's way up here," I said, pointing again. "There's an inconsistency here. According to this map, Vicksburg, Mississippi, was deep in Confederate territory at the time. How in the world did they fight all that way in just over a month? And didn't I see on that earlier screen a list of all the pivotal battles of the war? Wasn't the big fight at Vicksburg in 1864, not 1862?"

Flipping back to the previous window, Smith

exclaimed, "By George, you're right! The Battle at Vicksburg *was* in 1864! Which is not to say there weren't any minor skirmishes there before the big one. It says here in the commentary on the Eleventh Cavalry that one company of this Regiment, Company G, was detached from the rest of the unit in the fall of 1862, and this Company alone (out of this Regiment) served in the Vicksburg campaign of 1864. That's curious because Byron was in Company B, not G. I have to admit, this is all a bit confusing."

For a moment, neither of us said a thing. Then, like a flash of light, it hit me! "Maybe Byron didn't die at Vicksburg after all! Maybe, he died at *Pittsburg!*"

"As in, Pittsburg Landing?"

"Exactly."

"Or maybe he was captured," Brigham suggested, offering up what in his estimation was a more sensible alternative. "It says here that prisoners of war were taken to Vicksburg for recording, then held there indefinitely."

"Indeed curious," I replied, scratching my head. "Were there any other volunteers from his hometown?"

"Trivoli?"

"Yes. It seems to me that the younger the man, the less inclined he would be to volunteer alone."

"Good point," Smith agreed.

Flipping down through the computer-generated pages of the *Adjutant's Report*, he fell upon an interesting entry. "Yes, here's a Frank Hitchcock; residence—-Trivoli, Illinois; enlisted—-September 3, 1861. That's four months before Byron, by the way. Well, I'll be! It says he deserted, May 1862."

"May 1862, eh?" I remarked. "Byron dies, so his buddy Frank deserts?"

"Looks that way."

"Or maybe they *both* deserted, only Byron gets listed as a casualty because some buffoon misidentifies the body."

"So where did the two of them go?" Smith asked, thinking my interpretation of events farfetched.

"Home," I answered in my best it-ought-to-be-obvious voice. "It's May. It's Spring. These people were farmers no doubt. There were crops to put in."

Smith nodded as if it all made perfect sense.

"What information do you have on his family?" I asked, reveling in the challenge of unraveling yet another mystery.

"Well, let's see. By all rights, Byron would still have been living at home in Trivoli during the time of the 1860 census. So let's find out what the computer has to say about our friends, the Matthewsons."

Punching a few buttons and manipulating a couple of dials, Brigham Smith set the machine to work scanning through the voluminous decennial census records. At light-speed it flew backwards, first to the exact decade, then to the right state, then to the correct county, and finally to the proper township. The screen flickered once, and he began to read.

"Here we go: On the rolls of August 1, 1860, a Matthewson family is listed with a rural address. Two parents plus seven children. Father: Benjamin Matthewson, age 48. Mother: Elizabeth (Betsy) Matthewson, age 39, born New York."

"That's quite a difference in age, wouldn't you say?" I murmured.

"Not for those days. Anyway, Elizabeth may have been a second wife. We'll check for that possibility in a moment. But I can tell you one thing for sure—-they were pretty well off. The census lists their real estate holdings—probably farm ground—as being worth $6000; their personal effects are valued at $1500."

"That doesn't sound like much."

"Silly girl, it's all out of context. Not only do these figures probably underestimate the true extent of their wealth—after all, some taxing body undoubtedly based their levies on these highly-subjective self-appraisals—but there has been nearly six hundred years of *inflation* in the interim."

"What difference should that make?"

I hated to ask the question because it only served to point up my naiveté regarding all things financial. But how else was I supposed to learn?

"In the genealogy business, one can never lose sight of the old maxim that time is money. Compound interest, my dear; it's powerful stuff."

"How so?"

"I take it you are unfamiliar with the Rule of 72?"

"'Fraid so."

"Why doesn't that surprise me? Well, no matter. You divide a given rate of interest into the number 72 and that tells you how long it takes for a sum of money to double. At six percent, for instance, money doubles in twelve years. Twelve times six makes 72. At six percent then, how many doublings per century?"

I quickly did the math. "Twelve goes into a hundred, eight times. With four left over."

"And don't forget those leftovers because they add up fast, especially at six percent. Okay, eight doublings per century, but over how many centuries?"

"Six."

"So that's forty-eight doublings."

"Plus the four years remaining from each century, makes twenty-four more, or two more doublings. Fifty in all."

"Precisely!" he exclaimed, his fingers flying to the computer's keypad. "Now, if we take $7500--which is the six thousand in real estate plus the fifteen hundred in personal assets—-and double it fifty times, we get . . . wait a moment . . . wait a moment." He let out a low whistle. "Eight point four four four times ten to the eighteenth."

"Wow."

"Wow indeed. Assuming, of course, I entered the figures correctly, that would be a one followed by eighteen zeroes."

"That's an impossibly large number."

"Granted, but don't just automatically assume they were living on easy street. In those days, the agrarian way of life was brutally hard and completely unmechanized. They no doubt had their setbacks along the way. And having enough hands to help with the chores was always a challenge. In fact, the August 1860 rolls show this couple as having seven children: Byron, age 20; Nancy, 16; Charles, 12; Mary, 7; John, 5; Sarah, 3; and Elli, 8 months."

"Sounds as if Lady Matthewson couldn't keep her knees together," I quipped immodestly, wondering whether all the women in my line had been equally lusty.

"It's a woman's duty to bear children," Brigham returned, deadly serious. "And to do so without complaint. Now, can we concentrate on the matter at hand?"

"By all means," I answered gravely.

"If Byron were twenty when this census was taken, that would have made him perhaps twenty-two when he died . . . "

"You mean when he deserted, don't you?" I corrected him. This late in the game I wasn't about to be swayed from my version of events. "What else can you tell me about Byron's parents? When were they married, for instance?"

"Give me a minute to switch reels," he said, his fingers clicking merrily away at the keyboard. "Once the switchover is complete, it'll be a snap for us to check the marriage records. Let's see now: If Benjamin was 48 years old in 1860, he couldn't have been married before, let's say, 1827. And if Byron was age 20 in 1860 like the census says, he would have to have been born by 1840 or so. Assuming he was born in wedlock—which is a big if for those days—we can safely use 1840 and 1827 as the upper and lower limits for our search. Benjamin was almost certainly married between those two years."

It took a moment for the computer to complete its trace. "Here we go . . . Illinois . . . Peoria County . . . it's arranged alphabetically by last name. Here!" he exclaimed, slowing the scrolling screen down to a crawl. "Benjamin Mathewson—spelled here with one 't'—married Dorothy Thompson on November 4, 1838. The marriage was certified by a James Hitchcock."

"That would fit in nicely with Byron's birthdate having been sometime in 1840," I remarked, "but I could have sworn you said earlier the mother's name was Elizabeth."

"Yes, you're right. Here it is in the 1860 census—Elizabeth (Betsy)."

"Maybe Dorothy died."

"Then there would have been a second marriage," Brigham replied enthusiastically.

With each layer of the Matthews' mystery that we peeled back, his opinion of me seemed to steadily rise. It was obvious, though, that he was unaccustomed to working in tandem with a woman of my keen intellect.

"Listen, Carina," he said, "if you could

stay awhile here in my world, I could sure use a tenacious researcher such as yourself."

I gave him an icy stare. Had I said it, the unspoken answer might have come out something like, "You have got to be kidding!" But I didn't say it. Instead, I kept it businesslike. "How do we find out whether or not there *was* a second marriage?"

"Let me check," he said, obviously peeved by the rebuff. "Nancy, child number two, was age 16 in 1860, so let's run a scan of the marriage records from 1840, the year of Byron's birth, to 1844, the year of Nancy's birth. Wait a minute . . . wait a minute . . . Here it is!" he said, pointing excitedly to the screen. "Benjamin Matthewson to Betsy Holcom. February 9, 1842. Witnessed by N.P. Cunningham, Minister of M.E. Church. Here Matthewson is spelled again with two t's."

"So Dorothy must have died giving birth to Byron . . . or else shortly thereafter."

"It would appear that way."

"Which means, of all the Matthewsons, only Byron had Dorothy's genes. All the rest of us, me included, carry Betsy's."

"How can you be so sure?" he objected.

"It makes perfect sense," I answered. "Was Byron married? Did he have any children?"

Checking his data-files, Smith shook his head, "No, none that I can find."

"So Byron might very well have been the last Matthewson not to have been sickened by the damaged gene."

"If that were the case, that would make Betsy the carrier."

"And it would mean I'm out of luck. If only we could time-travel," I mused outloud before abruptly switching gears. "Did I hear you say James Hitchcock performed Benjamin's first wedding?"

"I believe it said 'certified' but, yes, a James Hitchcock is listed as the witness of record."

"And didn't you say that a *Frank* Hitchcock, also of Trivoli, deserted the very *month* Byron was supposedly killed?" I cross-examined, eagerly playing the part of the detective.

"What are you getting at?"

I practically bubbled with enthusiasm. "What are the odds? Don't you see? These families *knew* one another. Frank deserted; so did Byron. It *has* to be." My mind was made up.

"Let it not be said you don't have a rich imagination, little one. Here, let me print this out for you," Smith offered, touching a key. A few feet away, the nearly silent printer spat out a page with a dozen or more lines of closely-spaced type.

"Now, if only we could time-travel," I said again, accepting the sheet he handed me. On it were all the details about Private Matthewson's life—his father's name, his mother's name, their rural address, the date of his supposed death, and his place of burial. I carefully folded the sheet Brigham Smith had given me, plus my own notes, and slid them into my pocket. I had to make doubly sure to carefully record these historic details in my diary once Siona, BC, and I began the long trip back home.

"Time-travel indeed!" Brigham Smith harrumphed.

Yes, Andu thought, putting the diary aside, time-travel indeed!

The yellowed piece of paper Smith had given her fell to the floor. Reaching down now to pick it up, Andu slowly unfolded the sheet. Somewhere in the margin Carina had scribbled a note. Apparently, on a subsequent visit to Earth, she had happened across a copy of the State of Illinois archives. The annotation said that after the Battle of Shiloh, Byron Matthewson was supposed to have died onboard the steamer *Decatur* bound for Pittsburg Landing, Tennessee.

Although these names and places meant nothing to Andu, he tucked that information away in his head for future reference. Now if only Prime Alpha would snap out of it, he would travel with her back in time, find Byron Matthewson, and perhaps persuade the man to let Andu harvest a sample of his DNA. It mattered in a way Andu had never fully admitted until now—his very *life* depended on it!

Like his father, like his grandmother, like his great-grandfather, like every Matthews as far back as they knew, Andu Nehrengel had a defective gene. But unlike so many other defective genes, this one couldn't be fixed, at least not by any of the conventional means.

The remedy of choice in this day and age was the viral-repair-engine, the VRE. Properly understood, a viral-repair-engine was simplicity itself. Like any virus, a VRE would invade virtually every cell in the body. But what was unique about these viruses—aside from their being manmade—was that they would only attack a cell's mitochondrial DNA. This avoided any risk of damage to the germ cells, plus—and here is where it really got exciting—as part of their attack, they could alter the body's metabolic factories in a deliberate, predetermined fashion. These laboratory-engineered viruses had been intentionally designed to edit just enough lines of mitochondrial code to remedy whatever metabolic dysfunction the host was afflicted with!

This delivery system worked extremely well, and over the years scientists worked out several thousand metabolic remedies. Unfortunately, untold millions more—including Andu's—had not yet succumbed to a solution.

Andu learned the bad news only weeks before setting out on this trip: the VRE he'd been given wouldn't "take."

Though death was by no means at hand, Andu didn't stand a chance of living out a normal life-expectancy. The realization was devastating, especially to a vigorous, adventure-some man like himself. Closing in on age 40 already, he'd be lucky if he made it to the ripe old age of 70, much less the 120+ that was typical for men of his century. That, as much as scientific curiosity, had probably cinched his decision to complete work on the *Tachyon* and set off in search of extraterrestrials. What did he have to lose?

Andu was just about to shed a pitiful tear for himself when, outside, a few hundred meters away, a terrific crash rocked him back to reality.

17
The Crash

Everything seemed all right at first. Some minor buffeting, but nothing out of the ordinary. Certainly nothing bad enough to make Red hit the panic button. The man wasn't expecting trouble, nor had he planned for any.

The descent was fast, but not so fast as to alarm him.

Not at first anyway.

And even when the descent accelerated, he had no reason to suspect the laser-guided landing array. Why should he? Unless someone tampered with it, there was no way for the unit to go out. And who would be fool enough to tamper with the thing? A member of the crew? Not likely; they were all dead. Nehrengel? When would he have had the time? No, there had to be some other explanation! Maybe it had something to do with the high-gain signal he was picking up.

Before starting down, Red had orbited the big planet for more than a day trying without success to get a fix either on the source of the original SETI signal or else on the *Drift On*'s homing beacon. All he'd gotten for his trouble was static, hours of it. He had just about been ready to call it a day and head for home, when there was an explosion of activity on the radio band. A massively-strong signal had begun pounding out a universal May Day followed by a short coded message. Even a blind man could follow a transmission of this magnitude to the surface!

Calling himself lucky, Red had dropped out of orbit and started down. Now though, he was beginning to feel ill. His stomach was doing somersaults. For some reason or other the craft had acquired a nasty spin. Only he didn't have the first clue why. Nor did he know what to do about it.

Not suspecting the laser-guided landing array, he fumbled for a long time with the controls. This was a mistake of the first order. But then Red McIntire didn't have a first-rate intelligence. He had spent the lion's share of his flying career on the ground, not in the air, and then filling out requisitions rather than becoming proficient with runabouts like the *Sail On*. That lack of training was about to catch up with him.

By now the descent had become so rapid, he felt the g-forces tugging at his chest. He could see the ground. It was a green blur, and it was rushing up to meet him at high speed!

Moving to avert a crash, he switched to manual control. The descent slowed, but not nearly enough. He was already too close to the surface to prevent the inevitable!

The landing was hard, very hard, though not so hard as to kill him. The nose of the craft dug into the ground, splintering on impact. Dazed, Red staggered from the ship bleeding. He found himself in a forest, a forest of unusual trees, trees ringed by a spiral staircase of flat, strangely-shaped leaf-branches.

There were sounds all around him, unusual sounds, scary sounds. He heard a growl nearby, then a screech like an owl. Benign creatures otherwise, these beasts could read his mind. They knew he was hurt.

Red stumbled forward, then fell to the ground. He could hear breathing. Nearby.

It wasn't breathing, it was hissing. Like a snake.

Red was scared. He knew he was going to die. He had no idea how painful an end it was going to be.

The snake-like thing screeched and reached out for him. It had dozens of octopus-like tentacles to hold its prey. Two of the rubbery appendages grabbed him around the torso, another round his leg. He pulled away, but the spidery arms held him fast.

Red screamed bloody murder, but by then the tentacled-snake had already begun spraying him with sulphuric acid to break down his body parts. The pain was excruciating!

Then he heard a familiar voice.

"Jesus, Red, is that you?" Andu gasped. The sound of the crash had brought him out of Alpha's ship and down the trail into the forest.

"Help me, Nehrengel! This . . . this . . . *thing*'s got me.

It's eating me alive!"

Andu drew his blaster and aimed at what looked like the tentacled-snake's head. Blood was pouring from Red's chest and abdomen. The acid had eaten through the epidermis and was now attacking the muscle and inner organs.

Andu fired. Bits of yellow goo flew everywhere, and the air filled with the stench of rotten eggs. The creature heaved and convulsed in great agony, then expired with a great sigh. But it was already too late for Red. The acid was dissolving his body right before Andu's very eyes!

Red was screaming for mercy. Andu didn't dare touch him for fear of the acid.

"I'm sorry!" Red cried. "I killed them all. Smith set the whole thing up. Brigham Smith!"

"*Brigham* Smith?" Andu shouted, not believing his ears. Could it be one and the same? The man from Carina's diary? What were the chances?

"Hah! The man's crazy!" Red exclaimed, coughing up a mouthful of blood. "Wants to change the past, he does. Histometrics I think he calls it. Now put me out of my misery, you bastard! Or don't you have the guts?" His voice faded away in a sick gurgle of phlegm and body fluids.

"The ship. What about the ship?"

Extending a weak finger, Red pointed towards the sky.

Andu nodded and squeezed the contact. In the next instant, the air filled with acrid entrails.

Andu turned away. It hadn't occurred to him until now that Red's arrival had changed everything. He had his ship back!

What only hours before had seemed like an impossibility was now within his reach. *In Red's death was the means for him and Prime Alpha to time-travel!*

18
Neurons

For the first time in her life, Prime Alpha was alone, truly alone. No more voices in her head, no more unspoken conversations, no more having six hands to carry out the instructions of two.

Prime Alpha had never experienced oneness before. Her whole life had been always as one of three. Now everything had changed.

It was eerie. And utterly frightening!

As she floated back and forth between consciousness and unconsciousness, Prime Alpha tried to decide what was real and what was imagined. But in her present state, she found it impossible to distinguish between actual events and imagined ones, between true memories and mere dreams, between actual fears and terrifying nightmares. Surrealistic was the only way to describe her condition.

Andu, too, found it disconcerting. Nothing made any sense anymore, nothing at all! Not the mutiny, not the sudden appearance of Red, not the involvement of Brigham Smith, not the girls' telepathic powers. That, least of all.

How, then, to understand the brain?

Of all the organs in the body, it has been the one least susceptible to study, the one which cannot be transplanted, cannot be regenerated, cannot be replaced. And why is that? What is it about the brain which makes it so irreplaceable?

Closely allied to this question, of course, is the one of memories. How are they formed? How are they stored? How do they die?

A memory is formed—imprinted, as they say—when the

brain alters its wiring, establishing a new connection with other brain cells, or, in some cases, strengthening existing ones. To accomplish this transformation, chemical receptors located on the surface of each brain cell are brought into play. These receptors operate much like signal-boxes, opening and shutting chemical "doors" to allow in the energy a cell needs to fire an electrical charge, thus laying down a memory-trace.

The process of encoding a memory begins in the hippocampus, an evolutionarily-ancient part of the brain. The hippocampus is the Grand Central Station of memory. It dispatches arriving trains of thought either to short commuter runs that are quickly forgotten—names of party guests, for instance—or else to more permanent destinations in the brain where important things like a spouse's name or a home address is stored. When the hippocampus receives the same message several times or else once with emphasis, it will change an incoming message from a short-term commuter to a long-distance traveler.

As one might expect, young brains accomplish all these feats more efficiently than old ones. It took science quite a long time, though, to answer the question why.

Part of the reason has to do with those "doors." On the surface of every brain cell is a gateway which regulates the passage of electrically-charged particles into or out of each cell. Under normal circumstances, calcium bursts in through one of these doors and, in its rush, helps to carry an electrical charge from one end of the cell to the other. But should some of those doors begin to leak, the calcium molecules would start to dribble in rather than rush in, thus diminishing their capacity to ignite an electric charge. Without a sudden surge of current, the message doesn't get through and no learning ever takes place.

This type of memory decline can be especially severe in older people. As cells age, the chemical doors begin to loosen. Though drugs have been developed which act like gaskets to combat the worst effects of this "leakage," the process itself is irreversible.

The chemical signal-box which sits on the surface of each cell "decides" whether or not to fire an electric charge through a given cell, thus helping to blaze a memory-path. It is not a capricious decision. When a neurotransmitter races between cells yelling, "Heh, pay attention, there's something important coming here," it opens up certain doorways on the cell's surface, thereby letting in energy-carrying sodium particles. These positively-charged particles act like batteries, building up that cell's electrical charge. Once a critical point is reached, a biochemical "spark" is ignited, changing that cell's connections to the surrounding cells: a memory pathway has been forged!

Just as the brain has a mechanism for stitching memories together, it also has a mechanism for *un*stitching them. The neurotransmitter *beta amyloid*, for example, disassembles memories that are no longer needed. Its normal role within the brain is to help us forget things we don't want to remember, or else to erase memories which no longer serve any useful purpose. As we age, however, some of us produce too much beta amyloid, causing new memories to dissolve before they can be solidified, sometimes even dissolving *old* memories that are still useful. Fortunately, in most instances, this can be combated with mega-antioxidants.

Since all of this neuro-processing is going on down at the cellular level with neurons sitting in close physical proximity to one another, how to understand telepathy, something which works at a distance? To a man like Andu, a man of science, it seemed a stretch of the imagination to believe that neurotransmitters could physically "jump" from one body to the next. And yet, that was the only explanation he could think of which fell safely within the realm of normal physics and which didn't resort to some kind of paranormal interpretation.

Needless to say, the phenomenon he had observed taking place between the three girls had to have something to do with that sodium/calcium reaction, but what? And how? How did those electrically-charged ions manage it? How did they manage to transfer themselves from one individual to the next?

Had the girls been touching one another when they telepathed? Or, if they hadn't been touching, had they perhaps been in close enough proximity so that, like a moth, they had exchanged some sort of airborne pheromone? Maybe they had been genetically engineered from the start with some sort of supersensitive "antenna." Or maybe they had just lived together so long that, like good friends, they knew one another's thoughts without even vocalizing them.

Whatever it was, whatever it *had* been, it was no more. Now the whole thing was past tense. For the first time in her life, Prime Alpha was alone!

It would have been easy for her to blame Andu for what had happened. He, after all, had been the one who'd assured her everything would be okay; he had been the one who was the uninvited guest; he had been the one who had failed to properly anticipate the danger. And yet, she knew it wasn't his fault. She and her sisters had lived on Ancòn long enough to know about the bird-beasts; they, after all, had been the ones who had shot Andu down without just cause to begin with; they, after all, had wanted to leave the planet as much as he had. Who could say who was to blame?

One thing was certain, though, and she realized it when she first came to: she *still* wanted to leave! Thus, it was with this objective in mind that Prime Alpha tried to explain herself in their first conversation after she woke up.

She was still very weak from her ordeal and preferred that the room lights remain dimmed. He didn't have to see her tears to know that she had been crying.

"I belong somewhere," she said in a halting voice from her bed, "but I certainly don't belong here. I belong in *some*time, but I certainly don't belong in *this* time. Oh, Andu, Andu, what will become of me?"

The words were barely out of her mouth before he knew what he was saying. "Perhaps I can convince you to join me in an adventure."

"What sort of an adventure?" she asked, her spirits suddenly perking up.

"A crazy sort. Perhaps even a dangerous sort."

"Danger seems to be your middle name. Tell me, Mister Andu, what exactly do you have in mind?"

"There is someone I would very much like to help," he answered, hoping she would take him seriously.

"I can see no harm in that," she nodded agreeably.

"That someone has been dead for more than fifteen years."

Firing off a confused look in his direction, Prime Alpha swung her long beautiful legs out over the side of the bed and got up. After so many hours on her back, it felt funny to stand.

At first, she was unsteady on her feet. Andu came up beside her and lent her an arm. Together, they hobbled across the room to a chair.

Exhausted by the effort, she gratefully took a seat. It took her a minute to catch her breath. Then she spoke.

"If that someone you're talking about has been dead for fifteen years, I don't see how we can be of much help to them."

"We can't. That is, not unless we first travel back in time."

"Ah, so you've been reading the ship's logs, have you?" The remark was phrased more like a statement than a question.

"Yes, I have," Andu answered, wondering from her tone whether he had broken some unwritten rule.

"Ever since we first woke up, we've been reading what the Great Ones left behind for us. It was all laid out quite simply. There was an education disk complete with instructions. But that one about time-travel really baffled us; it made no sense whatsoever."

"I'm not surprised. Without a solid background in physics it might just as well have been Greek. However, I do have a background in physics, and I believe it is possible. To time-travel, that is. Anyway, I'd like to give it a try."

"What difference would it make? Everyone knows history can't be changed!"

"Oh, but I think that it can," Andu objected. "And there's only one sure way to find out."

"For goodness sake, who could possibly be that important? Why would you be willing to risk an almost certain 'right now' for a terribly uncertain 'back then'? A former lover?" she asked, jealousy coloring her face. "A long-dead wife?"

"My grandmother."

"Your *grandmother*?!" she exclaimed, her cheeks reddening with embarrassment. "You must have loved her very much," she added, quickly recovering.

"Actually, I've never met her."

"Now I'm really lost."

"It gets worse," Andu explained. "In order to save my grandmother, I don't mean to travel back the few short years to *her* time—at least not right away—I mean to travel all the way back half a millenia, to the nineteenth century."

"Whatever for?" Though her face was flush with excitement, Alpha was clearly perplexed.

"To find a distant ancestor. One who has an undamaged copy of a certain gene. I mean to bring a copy of that gene forward in time from the nineteenth century to the twenty-fifth and give it to my grandmother back when she was young, say fifty years ago. My grandmother was a geneticist; she'll know what to do with it."

"When and where in the nineteenth century do you plan on going?" Prime Alpha questioned, raising and lowering her foot several times to improve the circulation in her leg.

"The United States. 1862. A place called Illinois."

"From what I understand from the education disk, my people got their start in the United States. At just about that time. Before they moved to Utah, my people *lived* in Illinois. Perhaps they could give us a hand when we arrive," she said, warming to the idea.

"So you'll go?"

"I have no reason to remain here," she said, again testing out her legs. "Besides, I wouldn't mind seeing the beginnings of what I was eventually the product of. Like I told you before, I belong somewhere, but I certainly don't belong here."

"Well then, it's settled!"

"Not so fast, Mister! Even if physics permits us to time-travel, common sense does not. We'll never make it!"

"You'd better explain yourself," Andu demanded.

"Don't worry—I intend to."

And she did.

19

The Grandfather Paradox

By this time they had moved to a lounge in another part of the ship. They were already comfortably seated when Prime Alpha began to speak.

"Let me tell you a story," she said, "something I will call the 'Grandfather Paradox.' Imagine, if you will, a girl named Margaret. She . . . "

"Heh, I like that name!"

"I like that name too. I may even adopt it as my own someday. Now will you please pipe down so I can finish my story?" she scolded, though playfully. "Where was I? Oh, yes. Imagine a girl named Margaret. She keeps a time machine in her garage. Last night she used it to travel back in time sixty years to visit her grandfather when he was still courting Margaret's grandmother. Margaret convinced him of her true identity by relating to him family secrets that he himself knew, but by this age had not yet revealed to anyone else. Though this disclosure left him stunned, worse was yet to follow.

"When the grandfather told his sweetheart over dinner that night that he had just met their future granddaughter, the lady's response was to not only doubt his sanity, but to take offense at his presumption. They never married and never had the baby who would have grown up to be Margaret's mother."

At first, Andu didn't know what to say. After a moment's hesitation, he stammered out a reply. "So how can Margaret be sitting here today, telling us of her adventure? If her mother was never born, how could *she* have ever been?"

"That's the paradox!" Alpha beamed. "Of course, the real question is this: when Margaret returns to the past, will she or won't she be able to bring her grandparents' romance to a premature end? Now think carefully about it before answering because either answer can lead to certain baffling problems."

"How so?"

"If Margaret can prevent her own birth, logic has been defied to such a degree, no amount of reasoning can reverse the contradiction. If, on the other hand, she *cannot* act to prevent her own birth, that inability in and of itself conflicts with common sense. After all, what is there to prevent Margaret from behaving as she pleases? Will some strange paralysis grip her every time she tries to act a certain way? Is free-will lost in time-travel?"

"Well, of course not!" Andu exclaimed.

"And I would agree, but you still haven't answered my original question: can she upset her grandparents' romance or not?"

Making up his mind, he answered. "She cannot. Margaret may visit her grandfather just as you have suggested. She may even convince him who she is. But instead of Margaret's grandmother-to-be becoming incensed by what he tells her of his meeting with Margaret, she grows concerned about his state of health. He is very touched by her compassion and proposes to her right on the spot. She accepts. Far from *altering* the past, Margaret becomes a part of it."

"That's ludicrous!" Alpha objected. "She wasn't even *there* the first time!"

"Someone was."

Exasperated, Alpha said, "Okay then, if the Grandfather Paradox doesn't convince you, perhaps the Knowledge Paradox will."

"The *what*?"

"The Knowledge Paradox. Listen and you will learn," she said, demanding Andu's full attention. "An art critic from the future visits a nineteenth century painter who is regarded in the critic's own time as a great artist. Seeing the painter's current works, the critic finds them amateurish and concludes that the artist has yet to produce those inspired paintings which so impressed future generations. The critic shows the painter a book of reproductions containing those later works. The artist contrives to hide the book, forcing the critic to return to his own time without it, and then sets about meticulously copying the reproductions onto canvas."

"Yes, I see what you're getting at," Andu interrupted. "The reproductions exist because they were copied from the paintings, and the paintings exist because they were copied from the reproductions."

Prime Alpha nodded. "Though there's no inherent contradiction here, there is still something very wrong. The Knowledge Paradox purports to give us paintings without anyone actually having to expend the artistic effort. The problem applies equally well to paintings, scientific articles, pieces of machinery, even living organisms. The knowledge required to invent the artifacts must not be supplied by the artifacts themselves!"

"I honestly don't know how to answer you," Andu said, scratching his head. "Obviously, there is no such thing as a free lunch; not here, not anywhere else. Knowledge can only come into existence as the result of problem-solving processes. Biological evolution. Human thought. Maybe the paintings ascribed to the mediocre artist were never his to begin with. Poof, the paradox disappears!"

"My, but aren't you the clever one! I guess what you're trying to say, though, is that the only paradoxes which can arise from time-travel are the ones we ourselves create."

"Yes, something like that."

"That's all well and good, Andu, but how do we get there? I mean, how do we *physically* do it?"

"Ah, I thought you might get around to asking that," he answered. "But I must warn you ahead of time: it's a rather lengthy story."

"As you can plainly see, I have nothing else to do today," she said, crossing her long legs and getting comfortable.

"In that case, let's get started."

20
Gravity Well

Andu began at the beginning, with Brigham Young XIV's theory of time-travel. Though the physics were confusing for her, he did everything in his power to keep her focused on just one important principle: if they could find a way to approach light-speed while in the presence of a super massive body, time should begin to flow backwards. That is, for them relative to everyone else in the universe. How far, and how fast, were the topics presently up for debate.

"But I thought you said an *infinite* amount of energy would be required to reach light-speed?" It was an unending stream of questions like this which had kept the discussion alive this long.

"Ordinarily, yes, but we don't have to get quite all the way up there to make this work. Anyway, if we execute a slingshot, it just might be possible."

"Now you've really lost me!" she exclaimed. "This is the first I've heard anything about a slingshot."

"It's more of a metaphor than an actual device," Andu hurriedly explained. "But it's a relatively simple maneuver. We've been doing this sort of thing for centuries. All the way back to the dawn of the space-age, scientists have been sending out satellites and intentionally putting them close—but not quite into—the gravity well of a big object. There they'd get an energy boost and then be slingshot back out the other side. Preservation of angular momentum and all that. Indeed, this is precisely how many of our earliest space-probes were able to reach the outer planets, not to mention the Oort Cloud. We spun them first around Jupiter, and then around Saturn, and then on out. We made the planets' gravity wells work to our advantage. In fact, if you want to know the truth, that's probably how you got out here as well. The *Deseret* wouldn't have had the necessary velocity to escape the solar system if it hadn't accidentally been slung around Jupiter or Saturn or perhaps even both of them, on the way out."

"I never knew that."

"No, I suppose not, but it's the only possible explanation. Otherwise, I don't see as how you could have made it here to Ancòn in the first place. Now maybe—just maybe—we can apply that very same technique to get us where *we* want to go. Not to put too fine a point on it, but if we approach a black hole, not at light-speed perhaps, but at as near to light-speed as we can manage; and if we can get in close enough—though not so close as to be sucked into the thing—we ought to get slingshotted out the other side at or perhaps even a little above, the speed of light."

Prime Alpha frowned and shook her head. "All I'm hearing is ifs and oughts, ifs and oughts. We could die performing this little stunt, couldn't we?"

"It's a distinct possibility," Andu admitted.

"And how are we going to manage it in this old ship?"

"That's the beauty of it—we won't have to! While you were old cold recovering from your shock, a member of my crew brought my ship here to Ancòn."

"That's wonderful!"

"Maybe not as wonderful as you think. The man who brought it, killed the rest of my crew, and he himself died when he landed. Not only that, to get us up into orbit where my ship is, I'll first have to make substantial repairs to the runabout that's stuck in the mud down by the lake. But if I work at it . . ."

"Ifs and oughts, ifs and oughts. Can't you do better than that?"

"You have to understand something, Alpha—this time-travel stuff is not an exact science. But if it does work, and we do live through it, for us, time will begin to roll backwards. From our frame of reference, the normal passage of time will become negative."

"So what happens, we become babies again?"

Andu chuckled. "I hardly think so. Our own personal time can't go backwards; it can only go forward. We are, after all, only flesh and blood. We live in linear time. Our bodies will continue to age, just as before. We will still die in the ordinary fashion. When you and I time-travel, we are not going to change our *body*'s time; no, what we're going to do is change the time in which our bodies *exist*. Which is to say, relative time. This is no fountain of youth we've discovered here; we won't get any younger; we can't go back and relive our childhood; no, all of that is science-fiction! What can happen—what *must* happen—is that we will reappear at an earlier time. Not at an earlier time vis à vis our bodies, because that's irreversible, our bodies are what they are—but at an earlier time vis à vis the universe!"

"Andu, you're scaring me! How do we stop? How do we keep from going back too far? I don't want to end up in the age of dinosaurs, for goodness sake!"

"Nor do I. But rest assured, I've already given that problem some thought. As you pointed out, if we go back in time, we don't want to go back to just *any* time, we want to go back to a time of our choosing. Otherwise, it's all kind of a moot point, isn't it. But how to accomplish that? As I've already said, this time-travel stuff is nothing if not an inexact science. We know that after so and so long we need to brake, to slow back down again from our near-light-speed velocity, only what we don't know is when—*when* should we apply the brakes?"

"Couldn't we just set a timer or something?" she offered.

"If you think about it, you'll see that that won't work."

"And why not?"

"Because any clock we carry onboard the ship with us to tell us when it's time to brake will—if it runs at all—be running backwards to match its surroundings. No, what we need is something objective by which to judge what I'll call, for lack of a better term, absolute time. Something *outside* the ship."

The look on her face told him she was perplexed. "How can you do that? How can you measure 'absolute' time?"

"The only method I've been able to come up with thus far uses a celestial body which emits time references in a regular fashion, one which will remain unaffected by our motion."

"What are we talking about here?" she asked, more confused than ever.

"We are talking about a pulsar."

"I don't know what that is."

Andu explained. "A pulsar is a rapidly spinning neutron

star which gives off radiation in rhythmic pulses. Several thousand of these anomalies have been catalogued over the years and their pulse rates carefully measured and recorded. Most of them fall within the range of 1 pulse every four seconds to as much as 1 pulse every three-*tenths* of a second. They're easy to track, even over long distances, because the pulses are given off over a wide range of radio frequencies."

"Fine and dandy, but how does that help *us*?"

"We may be able to use one of these pulsars as a metronome to count off how much time has elapsed since we made the jump to light-speed. That way, we'll know precisely just when it's time to brake." Even as he spoke, a tiny satisfied grin began to erupt on his face. Andu had figured out a way to get around the time measurement problem onboard a light-speed ship!

"Now I'm beginning to see," Alpha smiled. "You are the clever one, aren't you?"

"Why thank you, my dear," Andu said, taking a bow.

"So how do we do it?"

"Well, before we can even start, we first have to select the right pulsar to use as a measuring rod. We need to know with great precision exactly how many beats of the metronome pass per minute of 'real' time. Only then can we hope to determine how many beats of the metronome we must account for as we slip backwards toward the year we want to arrive at. If, for instance, there's one beat of the pulsar per second, that would be sixty per minute, thirty-six hundred per hour, something on the order of eighty-six thousand per day, or thirty million per year! If we want to go back, say six hundred years, that comes to eighteen billion beats, give or take a few."

"How in the world are we going to keep track of eighteen billion anything? You must be *crazy!*"

"Perhaps I am, but either way, we'll have to set up a monitor of some sort—a giant adding machine maybe, or else a recording device of some kind. A photoelectric eye, perhaps; aimed in the right direction, but sensitive to radio-waves rather than light-waves. One thing is for certain, though: whatever we come up with has to operate without our supervision."

"Oh? And why is that?"

"Because in the course of our trip, as time rapidly reverses, I don't know what will happen to us. We may pass out, for all I know. But this much I'm sure of: the machine or monitor or whatever else we set up, has to keep an accurate count of how many pulses have ticked off since we first left our own time. Not only that, the machine must be programmed in such a way that if we *do* pass out, the spaceship will automatically brake at just the right moment after counting out just the right number of beats."

"But I thought you said this was an *inexact* science. Now it's beginning to sound rather precise to me."

"Not at all!" Andu countered strenuously. "Pulsars don't keep exact time, at least not over periods of several hundred years."

"Wonderful. Just wonderful," she said, her voice laced with sarcasm. "How far off are they?"

"Could be off by as much as fifteen microseconds per year."

"Fifteen microseconds! Why that's hardly anything!" she exclaimed, drawing herself closer to him. "A microsecond is only what—a millionth of a second?"

"True enough, but fifteen per year is fifteen *hundred* per century. You and I are headed back six centuries. Those errors add up fast. All I'm saying here is that even if we do all the math right and even if none of our equipment fails, instead of going back precisely six hundred years we may wind up actually going back 602 or 598. We won't know exactly *how* many years we went back until we physically pop the hatch and go out and buy a newspaper."

"This just keeps getting better and better," Alpha interjected. "Certainly . . . "

Cutting her off midsentence, Andu said, "Now before you go getting yourself too worked up, I should mention two other problems we face. The first has to do with getting safely out of this solar system, and the second with finding our way back to Earth."

"What's wrong with this solar system?"

"I didn't realize it at first, but this is a double star system."

"What's the significance of that?"

Andu explained. "Planets in double or triple star systems would be excluded from certain vast regions within which they could not orbit safely. Any planet inside this immense zone would eventually be tossed out by gravitational interactions. Just one more example of that slingshot effect I told you about earlier. For a double star system, a planet could circle either near one of the two stars or else far away from both of them. For a triple star system, a planet could orbit close to either one of the paired stars, or in a large region around the single member, or far away from all three."

"How do you know this is a double star system?"

"Because the planet has life. Higher level star combinations—triples and quadruples—are orbitally unstable and will eventually fly apart. It's highly unlikely that they would hold together long enough to permit anything but the very simplest life-forms to evolve."

"Oh? And why is that?"

"Because if the three stars of a triple system were to ever come close enough together, they would eject the star of lowest mass, leaving behind a stable pair. The same holds true for all higher level combinations. As a result, double star systems would seem to be the norm, the rule rather than the exception. Living on a planet like Earth which is in orbit around a solitary sun, gave early terrans a distorted view of the cosmos. Now we know, of course, that even our system is a double, only the Sun's partner is a black hole way beyond the edge of our solar system."

Alpha frowned. "That still doesn't explain how you know *this* system is a double."

"Binary star systems have widely varying characteristics. Stars of some double-dwarfs may be nearly touching one another; others can be as far apart as a third of a light-year. Those in close proximity may circle one another in less than a day, whereas the most widely separated doubles may take as much as ten million years to complete a single orbit. I ask you: have you ever seen an Ancòn sunrise?"

"A few times, I guess."

"On a world orbiting at a safe distance from a tightly-bound binary, the daytime sky would contain a pair of suns separated by a small distance. On a world orbiting one of a pair of suns—and depending upon the inclination and distance separating the two—there would be seasons, perhaps long ones, when both sides of the planet would be illuminated. Of course, the 'night' sky would never be as bright as the day sky."

To make his point, Andu took out a piece of paper and drew her a picture:

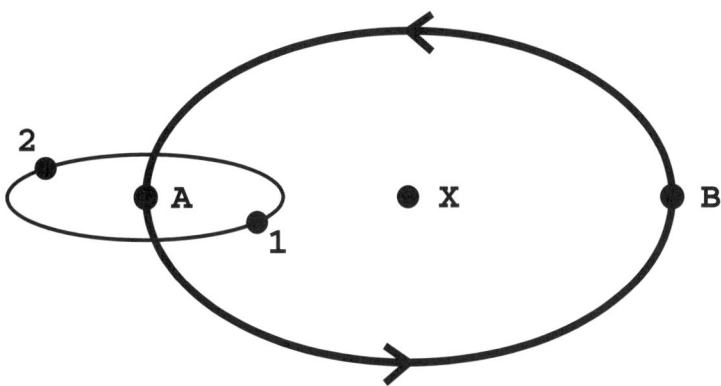

"Stars A and B orbit their common center of gravity X. The planet orbits star A and is now in position 1. Now, I ask you: have you ever had nights here on Ancòn that weren't dark?"

"Yes, all the time! My sisters and I called them no-nights. They ended just before you arrived."

"I'm not surprised. Nights without darkness can occur in polar regions on planets circling either a single sun or a tightly-bound binary, but never in a temperate zone like this. To have no-nights at this latitude, Ancòn must be in orbit around one of the two stars in a binary pair."

"Okay, you've convinced me! But what I fail to see is what this has to do with us getting safely out of this solar system."

"I'm afraid my ship is in an unstable orbit around Ancòn. Like you said, the no-nights are over. That means the planet is now at position 2. With both suns tugging on the ship through part of its orbit, the orbit itself is decaying. It's becoming more and more egg-shaped with each pass. It won't be long now before the orbit deteriorates completely and the ship crashes, either into the planet or else into the closer of the two suns. If we don't leave soon, we may be stuck here forever!"

"You said earlier that there were *two* problems. The first one sounds bad enough; what's the other one?"

"Location. This neat little parlor trick of ours won't alter our actual location one little bit. All we'll be doing is changing our time coordinates, not our physical coordinates. Traveling back through time can help us accomplish a great many things, but scooting across the galaxy in an instant certainly isn't one of them. Just as time-travel is no fountain of youth, it's also no magical wormhole. Time-travel or no, we still must physically cross millions of kilometers of open space to reach our destination. And we still must do so in the ordinary fashion—one meter at a time."

"I understand perfectly," she said, delighted to finally have a chance to squeeze in a word. "But if you're smart about it—and I know you will be—while we're zipping across the galaxy at light-speed making our time-jump, we can simultaneously be using that speed to quickly get us where we want to go."

"On this you get no argument, but we're still going to have to travel through linear space in the customary fashion. And we're still going to have to chart a course through each and every gravity well that lies between here and Earth."

"Sounds like we have our work cut out for us," she sighed, reaching across to him with her hand. Caressing his knee, she beamed a mischievous smile.

"We have no time for that right now," he said, gently nudging her away. "If we can manage to get up to my ship, we need to search the computer's star-atlas for a suitable black hole that we can use to slingshot us up near light-speed. Then we must identify a pulsar which will be visible to us throughout the entire trip, one we can use to reliably measure absolute time. And then, just to make things interesting, it would be nice if we could choose a trajectory which would allow us to do as you've suggested—brake when we're near not only our physical objective, but our time objective as well. I'll have to use the global positioning satellites of my own time to triangulate the longitude and latitude of the place we're headed for."

She answered him with a curious stare. "Look, Andu, I have faith in you, I really do. I'm sure you'll figure out all the details and we'll make it okay. Actually, none of that worries me. What concerns me about this parlor trick, as you called it, is something different."

"Now what's troubling you?"

"Let's say we make it safely back to the Earth of 1860—what then?"

There was surprise in Andu's voice when he answered. "Silly girl! What kind of a question is that? We land. We find

Byron. We leave. What could be simpler?"

Her response was immediate and crisp. "Land? Are you crazy?! We can't just land *anywhere*! It's 1860 for God's sake! We have to set down in a place and at a time where we won't be noticed. From what I gather, these people don't even know anything about space-travel! What I mean is, they may have their theories or ideas about such things, but they certainly don't know anything at all about traveling through time! We have to find a way to land unobserved, keeping our ship hidden and camouflaged. So you see, smart guy, it's not as simple as you pretend."

Andu nodded his head thoughtfully. "You couldn't be more right," he said. "And we'll need new identities, won't we? I guess it goes without saying that names like Prime Alpha and Andu Nehrengel weren't in vogue back in the 1860s. Along with everything else, we'll have to find a way to learn about names current to the time. Maybe you can be Margaret after all. Like in your story."

"And what about clothing?"

"That could be a problem."

"Not if we do some research it won't. The *Deseret* has a fairly complete history-disk, and I should imagine your ship does as well."

"As a matter of fact it does."

"I have another idea," she said. "There are some ancient drama-fiche recordings onboard that we might be able to use to help us. My ancestors must have brought them along as entertainment, although most of them date to the twentieth and twenty-first centuries. Perhaps we could view a few of them to get a better idea of their dress and customs."

"Isn't there anything older?" he asked. "A lot could have changed between the late 1800s and the year 2000."

"Well, there are the printbooks," she said. "There may be as many as two dozen onboard."

"Now you're talking!"

"It's a fairly complete collection of early American works. They're up in the Captain's quarters on the main deck. I remember reading some of their names: Twain, Hawthorne, Cooper."

"Okay, then. That's where we'll start."

21
Life is But a Dream

Fifty Meters Above The Event Horizon
Of Cignus Minor, A Black Hole

Suppose the past exists only in books and documents. A world without memory is a world of the present:
Arriving home at night, each man finds a woman and children waiting at the door, introduces himself, helps with the evening meal, reads bedtime stories to the children. Likewise, each woman returning home from her job meets a husband, children, sofas, lamps, wallpaper, fireplace that are all wonderfully new to her. Late at night, the wife and husband do not linger at the table to discuss the day's events, their children's school, the bank account. Instead, they smile at one another, feel the warming blood, the ache between the legs as when they first met fifteen years ago. They find their bedroom, stumble past family photographs they do not recognize, and pass the night in lust. For it is only habit and memory which dulls the physical passion. Without memory, each night is the first night, each morning the first morning, each kiss the first kiss.

· · ·

In this world, time flows backward:
A withered woman sits in a chair hardly moving, her face red and swollen, her eyesight nearly gone, her hearing no longer, her breathing scratchy like the rustle of dead leaves on stone. Years pass. There are few visitors. Gradually, the woman gains strength, eats more, loses the heavy lines in her face. She hears

voices, music. Vague shadows gather themselves into light, and lines become tables, chairs, people's faces. The woman makes excursions from her small house, goes to the market, occasionally visits a friend, drinks tea at the café in good weather. She takes needles and yarn from the bottom drawer of her dresser and crochets. She smiles when she likes her work. One day her husband, with whitened face, is carried into her house. Within hours, his cheeks become pink, he stands stooped over, straightens out, speaks to her. Her house becomes their house. They eat meals together, take long walks, tell jokes, laugh. They travel through the country, visit friends. Her white hair darkens with brown streaks, her voice resonates with new tones. She goes to a retirement party in the school auditorium, begins teaching history. She loves her students, argues with them after class. She reads during her lunch hour and at night. She meets friends and discusses history and current events. She helps her husband with the accounts of his business, walks with him to the foot of the mountain, makes love to him in the grass. Her skin becomes soft, her hair long and brown, her breasts firm. She sees her husband for the first time in the library of the university, returns his glances. She attends classes. She graduates from that same auditorium, her parents and sister crying tears of joy. She lives at home with her parents, spends hours with her father walking through the woods by their house, helps her mother with the dishes. She tells stories to her younger sister, is read to at night before she goes to bed. She grows smaller. She crawls. She nurses. She is born.

• • •

    Suppose time creeps forward so slowly as to be imperceptible. People live forever.
    In such a world, the population of each city splits in two—the Laters and the Nows:
    The Laters reason that there is no hurry to begin their classes at the university, to learn a second language, to read Voltaire or Newton, to seek promotion in their jobs, to fall in love, to raise a family. For all these things, there is an infinite span of time. In endless time, all things can be accomplished; thus, all things can wait. Indeed, hasty actions breed mistakes. And who

can argue their logic?

The Laters are everywhere. They can be recognized in any shop or promenade. They walk with an easy gait and wear loose-fitting clothes. They take pleasure in reading whatever magazines are open, or rearranging the furniture in their home, or slipping into conversation the way a leaf falls from a tree. All day long, the Laters sit in cafés sipping coffee and discussing the endless possibilities of life.

The Nows are different. They note that with infinite lives they can do everything they can imagine. They will have an infinite number of careers, they will marry an infinite number of times, they will change their politics time and time again, raise a thousand families, write a hundred books. Each Now will be a lawyer, a bricklayer, an author, an accountant, a painter, a physician, a farmer. They will constantly be reading new books, studying new trades, mastering new languages. In order to taste the vast infinities of life, they will begin early and never slow down. And who can question their logic?

The Nows are easily spotted. They are the owners of the cafés the Laters sit in, they are the college professors, the doctors and nurses, the politicians, the people who constantly rock their legs whenever they sit down. They move through a succession of lives, eager to miss nothing. When two Nows chance to meet in the marketplace next to the fountain, they quickly compare the lives they have mastered, exchange information, and hurry on their way. When two Laters meet at the same spot, they ponder the future and follow the parabola of water with their eyes.

Ironically, in such a world no one is happy, not the Nows, not the Laters. With infinite life comes an infinite number of relatives. Grandparents never die. Nor do great-grandparents. Sons never escape from the shadows of their fathers. Nor do daughters of their mothers. No one ever comes into their own. No enterprise is truly new; all things have been attempted by an antecedent in the family. Indeed, all things have been accomplished, and the multiplication of achievement is divided by the diminishment of ambition. This is not a happy world. No person is free, for it is only in death that the weight of the past is lifted. This is the paradox of infinite life.

· · ·

To every thing there is a season, and a time to every purpose under heaven:
> A time to be born, and a time to die;
> A time to plant, and a time to reap.
> A time to kill, and a time to heal;
> A time to break down, and a time to build up.
> A time to weep, and a time to laugh;
> A time to mourn, and a time to dance.

A time to cast away stones, and a time to gather stones together;
> A time to embrace, and a time to refrain from embracing.
> A time to seek, and a time to lose;
> A time to keep, and a time to forsake.
> A time to rend, and a time to sew;
> A time to keep silent, and a time to speak.
> A time to love, and a time to hate;
> A time for war, and a time for peace.

• • •

For every time there is a world, and a world for every time:
> A world of now, a world of then;
> A world of tomorrow, a world of today;
> A world of the future, a world of the past;

A world where everything's possible, a world where everything's not.

The world that we dream of, though, is the one world which *doesn't* exist.

To cross from it to the other is to cheat the gods and invite their anger.

He who does so, does so at his own peril!

PART II

22
Upstream

It was May 20, 1861, and the game was straight poker. Armed with their new identities, the two time-travelers were onboard the steamer *Nebraska* headed north. Zebulon Leavenworth was at the wheel, and he was agitated. They had heard war-talk at each stop along the way, and although they'd avoided a confrontation so far, at Memphis they had barely escaped the blockade.

Andu and Prime Alpha had set the *Tachyon* down in a marsh outside Caruthersville in southeastern Missouri, then sent it aloft again remotely, this time placing the ship in a polar orbit where it wasn't apt to draw the attention of the few telescopes of the time. They could recall the *Drift On* in an emergency using the slender metal device Andu kept hidden in his shirt pocket.

After stealing a fresh set of clothes from off a farmer's clothesline, they proceeded next to the docks to await the arrival of the next riverboat. There they made a shocking discovery. *They had arrived on Earth nearly a full year ahead of time!*

It couldn't be helped, of course, and the pair might still need every spare minute of time to track down Byron Matthewson before it was too late. Just catching up with the man would require two parts luck and one part ingenuity. Their plan was to first make their way upstream to Hannibal, then crosscountry east to Peoria. But even before that, they needed currency to replace what little they had raised selling some of Alpha's things. Hence, the game of chance.

All they had for collateral was a pocketwatch they had found among Brigham Young XIV's belongings. It had the name of Joseph Smith inscribed in block letters on the back, along with a date—September 22, 1827—and the words, "On To Deseret." Though the watch was simple and unadorned, it had been enough of a stake to get them seated at the table.

Prime Alpha had sized-up the game fairly quickly, pointing out in an aside to Andu that here was an instance where being telepathic was bound to be of some help.

To the three other men and one woman seated around the table, Andu was Henry Blake and Prime Alpha was Margaret Hoolehan, two names they had decided on after viewing several episodes of a twentieth-century drama-fiche about a mobile army surgical hospital unit caught up in the middle of some war. Henry and Margaret were traveling as husband and wife-to-be on their way to visit friends in Hannibal. Margaret had now won four hands in a row, calling one particularly good player's bluff, and tempers around the table were beginning to flare. She and Henry had only been invited to join the game in the first place because the two had given every indication of being rubes ripe for the picking. Thus far, though, it wasn't quite working out that way for the other players, and the ones who had been looking forward to doing the picking were beginning to get a little hot under the collar.

Off to one side, watching their every move, was a man, yet unintroduced, but young and attractive in every way. Margaret had noticed him right off. Good-looking and sandy-haired, he seemed more than a little curious about the progress of their game. At times, a cigar hung from his mouth, and to Andu it seemed as if the other bystanders paid him more than the usual deference. He gave the impression of being very much at home here, as if he belonged.

Indeed, despite the talk of war in the air, everyone onboard looked as if they belonged. And why not? What was a riverboat if not a floating palace? Or was that too strong a term? Perhaps not.

If a worldly man of the times were to compare these boats with the crown jewels, or the Taj Mahal, or the Matterhorn, or some other priceless wonder he himself had seen, then, in that context, he might have been reluctant to describe these boats as magnificent. But the people of the time could only compare these boats with things they *had* seen; and thus measured and judged, the steamboats *were* magnificent—certainly finer than anything they had ever seen on shore!

Every town and village dotting both banks of the river from Baton Rouge to St. Louis had its finest dwelling, a mansion its wealthiest and most conspicuous citizen called home. It was an edifice easy to describe: large, grassy, front yard; white fence, paling with age; brick walk from gate to door; big, square, two-story wood-frame house, painted white and porticoed like a Grecian temple, though in this instance the imposing fluted columns and Corinthian capitals were a sham, having been made from white pine and then painted; an iron knocker on the front door, plus a brass doorknob, the latter being sorely discolored for lack of polish.

Inside: An uncarpeted hall of planed boards. Opening out of it, a parlor—fifteen feet by fifteen—with ingrain carpet and a mahogany center-table. On it, a lamp with green-paper shade, standing on a sort of gridiron made of brightly colored yarns by the young ladies of the house, and called by them, a lamp-mat. Several books, piled and disposed with cast-iron exactness according to an inherited and unchangeable plan. Among them, Tupper, much penciled; maybe *Ivanhoe*; a book of original "poetry" of the Thou-hast-wounded-the-spirit-that-loved-thee breed; two or three goody-goody works of the chaste and innocuous sort.

Further along inside: A polished, airtight stove (a new and most deadly invention), complete with chimney-pipe which passed through a board that closed up the discarded, but perfectly good, old fireplace. On each end of the wooden mantle, over the fireplace, a large basket of peaches and other fruits, all natural size, done in plaster rudely, or in wax, and painted to resemble the originals—which they didn't. Hanging over the middle of the mantlepiece, an engraving of George Washington crossing the Delaware. On the wall by the door, a copy of it done in thunder-and-lightning crewel by one of those same young ladies, a work of art which would have made the good General hesitate about making that crossing could he have foreseen what advantage was going to be taken of it!

Next: A piano with music piled on it—bound and unbound—and on a stand nearby. Frantic work of art on the wall, pious motto and all, done on the premises, sometimes in colored yarns, sometimes in faded grasses; progenitor of the "God Bless

Our Home" of modern commerce. An outrage in watercolor, done by the young niece who came on a visit long ago, and since died. Pity too, for in time she might have repented of this sin.

Other works of art framed in black mouldings on the wall, conceived and committed on the premises by the same young ladies. Landscapes, mostly; done with grim, black-and-white crayons, the name of the criminal conspicuous in the corner: a lake, a solitary sailboat, petrified clouds, trees on a distant shore, an anthracite precipice. Lithograph—Hannibal Crossing the Alps. Lithograph—The Grave at St. Helena. Steel plate—The Battle of Bunker Hill. Copper plate—Moses Smiting the Rock. In big gilt frame—slander of the family in oil. Opposite, also in gilt frame, grandpa and grandma, at age thirty and twenty-two, stiff, old-fashioned, high-collared, puff-sleeved, and glaring pallidly out from a background of solid Egyptian night.

On the table and elsewhere: spread-open daguerreotypes of dim children, distant cousins, unknown aunts, and forgotten friends, in all attitudes except their customary ones. Each of them too much combed, too much fixed up; each of them rigidly uncomfortable in their Sunday clothes born of a style most would now find hard to believe ever were in fashion. Husband and wife generally grouped together with husband sitting, wife standing, her hand on his shoulder, both preserving for posterity their faint toothy smiles.

The rest of the house: Horsehair chairs which kept sliding out from under you. Bedrooms with rag carpets. Bedsteads of the "corded" sort, sagging in the middle and needing to be tightened. Snuffy featherbeds not aired-out often enough. Cane-seat chairs. A splint-bottomed rocker. A wall-hung looking glass the size of a school-slate. An inherited bureau. A washbowl and pitcher—possibly, but not for certain. A brass candlestick and tallow candle. Nothing else. Not a bathroom in the house; and no visitor likely to come along who'd ever seen one.

Without exaggeration or embellishment, the home just described was the residence of the principal citizen all the way from the suburbs of New Orleans to the edge of St. Louis. And yet, when that same citizen stepped aboard a big fine steamboat, he entered a new and marvelous world, one that could only be described as magnificent.

On the texas deck above, extending only part of the boat's length, were the officer's quarters. In front of the texas rose the twin chimneys—one engine for each wheel, one chimney for each engine—sometimes reaching as much as a hundred feet above the water, the chimney-tops cut to mask a spraying crown of plumes, all painted red. On the texas deck stood the pilothouse. In this glass-enclosed cage, the pilot stood behind the great spoked wheel, communicating with the engine room through bell ropes and a speaking tube. On a bench behind him, other pilots, traveling free to have a "look" at the river, might sit and talk shop.

In that age of ineffable gaudiness, not even the pilothouse was strictly functional. Carved and fretted as though some lunatic carpenter had run wild with a scroll saw, it might look from the outside like a Turkish minaret or a medieval turret. The interior could be grand, a sumptuous glass temple with room enough inside to hold a dance. At a minimum, there would be showy, red and gold window-curtains, a wheel with costly inlaid work, bright brass knobs for the bells, a leather-cushioned bench for visitors, and the inevitable stove and spittoon. There might even be a tidy white-aproned black "texas-tender" to bring up tarts and ices and coffee during mid-watch. Unutterable pomp!

Still up-top: Pilothouse, hurricane deck, and boiler-deck, all ringed by guards, all garnished white with wooden filigree-work of fanciful design. Gilt acorns topped the derricks, gilt deer-horns covered the big bell, and a gaudy symbolic picture crested the paddle-box. The boiler-deck, painted blue, would be big and roomy and furnished with Windsor armchairs.

Inside: Looking down her long, gilded saloon was like gazing through a splendid tunnel. A porcelain knob hung on every stateroom door, and an oil painting as well, by some gifted artist. Curving patterns of filigree-work, touched up with gilding, stretched overhead all the way down the converging vista. An endless array of prism-fringed chandeliers, each an April shower of glittering glass-drops, lit the way. Lovely rainbow-light fell everywhere, splashing down from the glazed and colored skylights. In a word, the whole resplendent tunnel was a bewildering and soul-satisfying spectacle!

In the ladies' cabin the floor was covered with a pink and white Wilton carpet, soft as mush, and glorified with a ravishing pattern of gigantic flowers. As for the Bridal Chamber (the animal who invented the idea being still alive and unhanged at that day), there were not enough words left to describe it, for by now, the tottering intellect of any hosannaing citizen was overawed!

Every stateroom onboard had its couple of cozy clean bunks, and perhaps a looking glass and a snug closet. Sometimes there was even a washbowl and pitcher, and part of a towel, though only an expert could tell it from mosquito netting. Generally, however, these things were absent and the shirt-sleeved passengers cleansed themselves at a long row of stationary bowls in the barbershop where there were also public towels, public combs, and public soap.

To all but that most conspicuous and wealthy citizen of the shore, the one living in that superior dwelling-house, the steamboat just described *was* a floating palace. To call it anything less would have been a gross miscarriage of justice!

But of all the things which set that superior dwelling-house of the shore apart from the most complimented boat of the times was the people—gay and interesting; each a story unto himself.

It was May 20, 1861, and the game was straight poker.

23
The Grand Game of Poker

Poker and American history are inseparable. And like everything American, poker's antecedents are mixed. Some elements of the game are believed to have come from *As Nas*, an ancient Persian card game; others, from *Poque*, a French pastime. Other cousins include the English card game *Brag*, and the French game *Ambigu*. Indeed, the whole family of bragging games in the West are said to descend from an Italian game, *Primiera*, after which it disappears into antiquity, probably along the same gypsy trail over which playing cards themselves were brought into Europe from the East.

The conjuncture of *As Nas* and *Poque* is thought to have taken place among sailors in New Orleans back in the early nineteenth century. Americans are also believed to have made their customary mispronunciation of French by dividing *Poque* into two syllables, thus: Po-que, later corrupted to poker.

Originally, *Poque* was played with hands of three cards from a deck of thirty-two and contained such combinations as pairs and three of a kind. The Persians played their *As Nas* with hands of five cards from a deck of twenty, the cards being ranked lion, king, lady, soldier, and dancing girl. The theory, never proven, has been that *As Nas* was grafted onto *Poque* to form the original twenty-card deck of New Orleans-style poker. Though some of the present combinations were missing, the draw and the full deck were soon added, with stud, straights, and flushes to come later.

From New Orleans, poker went up the Mississippi River along with the steamboats, and by the 1840s it was the principal card game of the frontier. The gambling spirit was so much a part of the frontiersman's character, the game soon overlapped into real life.

Poker was often played for unlimited stakes. According to legend, plantations, slaves, even gold mines, backed up a man's word at the table. If a bet was higher than a man's resources, he had—by universally-accepted rule—twenty-four hours in which to raise "call" money. During that time, the cards were sealed and held by an arbiter.

Poker and professional gamblers became as much a part of the American folklore as cowboys and Indians, sheriffs and bad men, hustlers and losers. Surprisingly, though, the game did not achieve even moderate respectability until after the Civil War. Then, in the gambling boom which accompanied the era of fortune-seeking, poker came into its golden age. By then, the public had already expressed its kinship with the game by absorbing its language. Every American, poker player or not, knew what it meant to be in the chips, to have an ace up the sleeve, or in the hole, to call a man's bluff, to stand pat, to put their cards on the table, to be in a situation where the chips were down, or to reach the end of one's life by cashing in their chips.

The real substance of poker, however, is not the cards but the money. Unlike other card games such as bridge or gin where knowing the cards is everything, poker concerns itself only with the management of money. Its spirit is the bluff; its supreme objective, the inducement of a bet against an "unbeatable" hand. Thus, poker is a game of strategy where the cards—being of agreed-upon rank and sanction—are the instrument. Their random distribution according to the luck of the deal creates the chancy situation which is the entire basis for the game. That, plus the fragmentary knowledge each player has of the other players' hands. Money exerts the discipline; the bluff raises it to a high plane of conflict. Winning a bet achieves the aim of the game: the acknowledged triumph over an opponent!

Though the play of the cards can be learned from a book, it is usually learned by experience from old hands at the price of lost pots. Indeed, the game is more difficult to describe than it is to play. A knowledge of mathematical probabilities will not make a good poker player, though a total disregard for them *will* make a bad one. Every poker player knows better than to draw to an inside straight, yet few can resist the temptation of drawing to an open-ended one. This, despite the poor odds. As any sharp player will attest, the probability of making it is but eight in forty-seven! And even if you *are* successful, one of your opponents may do better!

Despite the game's Byzantine nature, all varieties of poker take on only one of two basic forms—draw or stud. Either you are given the opportunity to improve your original hand by discarding and drawing new cards, or else you must play out the original hand.

The five essential movements of draw poker—anteing, dealing, betting before the draw (or dropping out), discarding and drawing, and betting again after the draw—give the game a special complexity. Since the draw puts more cards into play, the hands often run the whole gamut of rank making for spectacular play!

Stud poker, on the other hand, is fast, tight, and almost purely strategic. With one card turned down and four showing, the unknown element in each player's hand is at a minimum. Thus, each round of open cards produces a series of simple, clear correlation probabilities. This fine-drawn game leaves the real play to the representations made by the players. With winning hands seldom rising above two pair or three of a kind (the chance of a full house, for instance, being no more than one in six hundred ninety-four), the game is generally won by a high card or else a single pair. When there are several players, it is not unusual for at least some of them to be frozen out even before they have been dealt a complete hand of five cards. For those who like their poker neat and clean, stud is the game!

As already suggested, the bluff is the quintessential heart of the game; its fundamental purpose, to engender uncertainty between the players. In poker, one has cards, chips, and conversation. The cards are known only to their holder, and he "represents" their value to his opponents in the form of chips bet, plus comments made. When the representation is false, that is called bluffing. Indeed, in the absence of such misrepresentation, the highest bet would always signify the best hand and the lower hands would always decline the issue. In that event, there would never be any real betting, and hence, no game. It would then no longer be poker, but ordinary gambling.

In the real game, of course, no one ever knows what cards

his opponents may be holding, except by dint of the available strategies. The most common bluff is to represent a low hand as being high, especially when the circumstances favor such a misrepresentation. The objective here, at least superficially, is to win the pot by forcing the retirement of a higher hand. But should that strategy fail (and it frequently will), and one be caught in an unsuccessful bluff, its higher purpose may still be realized. The payoff arises from the confusion such play causes in the minds of one's opponents with regard to *future* representations. Thus, the game is dynamic; it depends upon a *series* of plays. As a result of that failed bluff, sometime down the road when one's hand *is* strong, it will be suspected of being weak and a large bet will be forthcoming.

Despite its potential for success, bluffing is in fact hazardous and expensive. It must be calculated so as to either win, or else cost relatively little to lose. The player who never bluffs seldom gets a big pot and many of his best hands go abegging. He is inevitably a loser. The player who bluffs often, and expensively, is never able to recoup his losses. He too is a loser.

Since each of the players is engaging in the practice of bluffing at one level or another, confusion is rampant at the table. Close attention must be paid, not only to the pace of the game, but also to the laws of probability, the habits of each player, and any situations which might develop to give one or the other player the advantage. This would extend to any of a dozen myriad forms of cheating, from cards up the sleeve to handsignals. It goes without saying that telepathy was unheard of in those days and would never be suspected as a means of communication.

The corollary to bluffing is referred to as "calling" the bluff. Here again, variation is the key to success. A man who always calls is rarely bluffed. Now that might be a distinction to be proud of, if not for the fact that as a result, all his calls will be against strong hands and he will always lose. Likewise, a man who consistently drops out in the face of strong representation will always lose as well, for he will be bluffed completely off the table!

Thus, as in so many enterprises, the mark of a good poker player is deception. The poker hand must be concealed behind a mask of inconsistency at all times. The good poker player must avoid set practices and, on occasion, even go so far as to violate the elementary principles of correct play. His pace must be suited to the company—tight in a tight game, liberal in a liberal game—though some players may be strong enough to bull their way through an entire game, from the opening deal to the final ante. When a good player thinks he has a winning hand, he makes the kill with more skill and alacrity than a conservative player would believe possible or prudent!

In a way, then, poker is like war, only less violent. Deception—or as some would call it, the proper use of imperfect information—is one of the essential ingredients in the making of a fortune or the winning of a military campaign. So said Machiavelli. Others, like Clausewitz, the master of modern military science, found uncertainty to be the essence of any military situation. He was the one who looked upon war as the continuation of politics by other means. With each combatant uncertain about the strength of his enemy, and with all the news he gathers from spies or otherwise, exaggerating the threat posed by his opponent, the military leader must guard against acquiring a false impression of his opponent's resources. To avoid blowing the risks of doing battle out of proportion, the leader cannot take new intelligence too seriously and thus must constantly be on the lookout for it from the beginning. To be prepared is to have a strategy. Winning is only what happens if one doesn't lose. This is a psychological subtlety few people appreciate!

Despite his brilliance, Clausewitz did not provide us with a general theory of strategy. From start to finish, his analysis remained stubbornly within the confines of military situations, bounds far too narrow to encompass the more complex realities of economics or of politics. To handle those sorts of "games" required a whole new approach.

The concept of strategy was first laid out by one of the chief participants in the development of the atomic bomb, the young, and at that time already great, mathematician, John von Neumann. In collaboration with the eminent economist, Oskar Morgenstern, he wrote a landmark piece entitled, *Theory of Games and Economic Behavior*. Though largely written in the special notation of the mathematician, there is nothing mysterious about the observations to be found there. Indeed, its triumph is that each and every one of its conclusions were arrived at by that rigorous medium we call logic. To wit:

Imperfect information creates uncertainty among individuals, not only in games, but in society as well. To see the dynamics of uncertainty at work, one need only reflect upon the relations between partners at a bridge table, or opponents in poker, or traders on the floor of the stock exchange, or a housewife on a shopping tour. Wherever uncertainty exists, strategies are employed either to clarify the information, or else to obscure it further. The theory of games as put forth by von Neumann deals therefore with deception, particularly *counter*deception, and with strategies lending themselves to clarification. Yet the theory itself is formal, and thus neutral. Being non-ideologic, it is as good for one man as it is for the next. And although deeply involved in the mysteries of value, it does not intrude on the province of ethics. Nor can it tell anyone his desires. It may be able to predict, however, what one can get; and how one can go about getting it.

Just as poker and American history are inseparable, so too is game theory and nearly all of modern science. Genetics, bio-mechanics, chaos, algorithms, all owe a debt of gratitude to game theory. Indeed, game theory has spawned a dozen different disciplines, including quantum mechanics, econometrics, tactical simulation, virology, and, of course, histometrics.

The strategic situation in game theory lies in the interaction between two or more persons, each of whose actions is based on an expectation concerning the actions of others, and over whom he has no control! The outcome is dependent upon the personal—and oftentimes unpredictable—moves of the participants. And regardless of the amount of information given them, in the final analysis, the players generally act on hunch; which is to say, they gamble without being able to calculate the risk.

Take a duel, for example. Two men, back to back, each with a pistol and one bullet. They walk away from one another a certain number of paces, turn, and then either fire or begin walking back towards their challenger. At the farthest distance apart, the chances of a hit are less than with each succeeding pace they take back. To fire and miss would be to give their opponent a sure kill at any range he chooses. To hold fire too long would be to risk being shot before ever having an opportunity to shoot himself. Thus there are two "maximums," and they conflict with one another. To have the first shot or to have the better shot. Except under extraordinary circumstances, a dueler cannot have both. The question each combatant must answer is: when to shoot in order to obtain optimum strategic value?

As esoteric as this problem may sound, the traditional duel is a model for a number of military situations, not the least of which is that of two aircraft entering each other's range in combat. It can also be configured to include the problem of dueling tanks, especially where the situation is further complicated by "silent guns." Whether or not the guns are actually noiseless is not the issue; the term refers to any case in which a given combatant doesn't know whether or not his opponent has fired until the shell itself actually hits. And by then it may be too late!

But I digress. Suffice it to say, a high-stakes poker game onboard a riverboat was like a duel, only executed with money instead of pistols!

24
The Game

It was May 20, 1861, and the game was straight poker. Five men and two women were seated around a big wooden table in the main parlor of the riverboat *Nebraska*. Included among them was one Margaret Hoolehan and her fiancé, Henry Blake. They were on their way upriver to visit friends of theirs in Hannibal, Missouri. Margaret had won four hands in a row now and tempers around the table were beginning to flare.

Off to one side, watching their every move, was a man, yet unintroduced, who had caught Margaret's eye. A cigar hung from his lips. Smoke curled up past his sandy-colored hair. Though he couldn't have been very old, perhaps twenty-six, there was an air of authority about him that she liked.

The rubes, if that's what they were, seemed to be having a jolly good time. Only, it had been at the expense of the more accomplished players at the table. This was the source of all the friction.

Consider, then, how a number of free men—or women, as the case may be—gather in a somewhat friendly atmosphere of blue smoke and blue chips, and, rapt in the study of five dealt cards, proceed throughout the night to engage in a strategic tug-of-war for the purpose of securing at least a portion of one another's wealth. This is poker of the draw variety—five cards down and but a single opportunity to improve the composition. Except for the telepath in the circle, each man alone is privy to the secret of his own hand, knowing the rest only as his money talks.

It begins with the ante. Each player places a set number of chips or money on the table to form the pot. A player must hold a pair of jacks or better to open the betting. Moving clockwise around the room from the opener, each player must make one of three decisions: to fold, which is to say, drop out of the game until the next deal; to call, which requires he match the most recent bet to stay in the game; or to raise, which means he'll not only move to match the current bet but to increase it as well.

Once this first round of betting is concluded and all the players have either matched the highest raise or else folded, those remaining may discard up to three cards, drawing a like number in an attempt to improve their hands. After all the players have drawn, the player who originally opened the first round of betting is charged with opening the second. The other players in turn may then check (momentarily pass the turn), call, fold, raise, or re-raise.

When the betting is over, the players who have not folded reveal their hands in the showdown, beginning with the last person to have raised. The player revealing the highest hand wins the pot, though in an attempt to provide disinformation, a losing player may intentionally choose not to reveal his hand.

The ante was $2 and the man to Margaret's immediate left was the dealer. Billy Bob, he called himself, and his breath smelled of garlic. Going around the table clockwise, it was Margaret, Billy Bob, Patrick, Olivia, Henry, Big Joe, and Nathanial. Big Joe was the accomplished gambler of the bunch, the one who had—in the last hand—accused Henry of peeking at his cards and then somehow signaling their content to Margaret. In that particular instance Big Joe had tried bluffing, only Margaret had called his bluff, winning the hand in the process.

In a game as complex as poker, the number of cards one drew in the draw could itself be a great source of disinformation. For instance, taking one card might mean that your hand was very, very good, say four of a kind; or it might mean that your hand was less good, say three of a kind, though by your action you're hoping to convince everyone else that it *is* four of a kind; or it might even mean that your hand was very, very poor, say a pair of deuces, though here again, what you're trying to do by drawing one card is make everyone else *think* it's something good like four of a kind or four to a straight flush. In other words, taking only one card may or may not mean a thing!

In three different ways now, in three different hands, Big Joe had tried to bluff Margaret. Each time it ended the same—his gambit failed. *No matter what he tried, the woman couldn't be bluffed*! Big Joe didn't know how she was doing it, but he was convinced Margaret was cheating. And her boyfriend was helping! He'd said as much after the last pot.

Billy Bob was the dealer. He slowly passed out the cards, one at a time, clockwise around the table. As was her habit, Olivia chattered away the whole time. Daughter of an east coast banker, she had the money for the game, but not the brains. Sitting between her and Billy Bob was Patrick, a fiery Irishman and a natural-born gambler. Across the table from Billy Bob and slouched in a chair between Margaret and Big Joe was Nathanial, a Missouri boy on the way to St. Louis and then upriver to Keokuk to see about a job. Billy Bob didn't think Margaret was cheating and—garlic pouring from his mouth—had come to her defense as he passed out the cards. Privately though, he couldn't figure her and her man-friend out; they definitely weren't from around these parts!

Five cards dealt, the betting began. Billy Bob himself had jacks or better to open, and he did, betting $3. Patrick called. So did Olivia. Henry folded. Now it was up to Big Joe. He took his time then raised Billy Bob $2. It was $5 to Nathanial; he folded. In rapid succession, Margaret, Billy Bob, and Patrick called. Olivia folded. No one having raised Big Joe, the first round of betting closed and the draw began.

Patrick took two. Big Joe, one. Margaret, two. Billy Bob himself, three. Now, if all was what it seemed and no one was attempting to bluff, the hands might look like this:

Patrick took two on account of the three of a kind he held, hoping to increase it to four, or at least pick up an ace "kicker." Margaret, the same. Big Joe already held four of a kind, hoping only to improve his side card. Billy Bob, having opened, obviously held a pair; by drawing three, he hoped to garner a third to that kind, or perhaps even a second pair. If he was really lucky, he might be able to turn it into a full house!

But all was *not* as it seemed. In poker, it never was. Patrick held a low pair plus a high face card. Big Joe had four to a Queen-high flush. Margaret, three of a kind. Billy Bob held a high pair.

Patrick drew two unrelated cards, not improving his hand in the least. Big Joe didn't round out his flush, but did pair up one of his hole cards. Margaret drew cards no better than what she discarded, leaving her with three of a kind. Billy Bob picked up a pair.

Having already set the stage in the first round by raising and then again by taking just one card, Big Joe was the man to beat. Billy Bob checked. Never faint, Patrick bet $2. Big Joe saw Patrick's $2 and raised him $2 more.

By this time a small crowd of passengers had gathered around the table. The gentle thump-thumping of the paddle-wheel filled the silence. It was Margaret's turn and she could feel the eyes of everyone upon her. The man who had been watching the game from off to one side, the man puffing on the cigar, had come to stand behind her, watching closely for any sign that Henry might be signaling her with regard to Big Joe's hand. But Henry didn't dare budge or even blink, lest he be accused again of cheating.

It was $4 to Margaret. Without further delay, she saw Big Joe and raised him $4 more. Holding two pair, Billy Bob stayed in for $8. Patrick folded, although reluctantly. Big Joe didn't hesitate. He matched Margaret's raise and raised her $10 more.

Margaret didn't flinch. She knew Big Joe hadn't filled out his flush; that all he had was a pair. She knew that all he was trying to do was buy himself a pot; this, despite the lesson he should have already learned.

Smiling, Margaret saw his raise and raised him $10 more. Hurried whispers filtered through the crowd.

Billy Bob couldn't take it any longer. Two pair was an okay hand, but certainly nothing up against what could only be a full house or perhaps four of a kind. Billy Bob folded. Now it was just Margaret versus Big Joe.

Having had enough himself, Big Joe would just as soon have followed Billy Bob out of the game, only pride wouldn't let him. This was a *woman* for Chrissake!

Gritting his teeth, Big Joe saw Margaret's raise and raised her $25 more! If he couldn't be bluffed into submission, maybe she could!

But Margaret wasn't about to back down now. And why should she? She and Andu needed the money, and she knew she held the winning hand.

But Margaret also knew when enough was enough. She met Big Joe's $25 and called.

What happened next was perfectly predictable. When Big Joe laid eyes on her three of a kind and knew for sure that he'd lost, he went berserk!

Grabbing Henry by the back of the shirt, Big Joe sent him sailing across the table. Chips and cards flew everywhere! Henry's pocketwatch fell to the floor and Henry himself landed in Margaret's lap, nearly toppling the both of them from her chair. When Henry next looked up, a huge knife was in Big Joe's hand, a big Buck Henry with an ivory handle. The other hand was knotted in a fist.

When Big Joe wasn't gambling or drinking or womanizing, he was fightin'. It didn't matter who or what or where or why. Indians, Negroes, Chinamen, Catholics. Nothing much beat a good fight, especially against a mark as easy as Henry.

But before Big Joe could unleash his intended assault, a hand was on his shoulder restraining him.

The voice was unhurried, but forceful. "That'll be enough, Joe," the man said, clamping down hard on Joe's wrist. "Zeb won't tolerate no fighting onboard, you know that. He's the Pilot and he makes the rules. If you don't stop what you're doin' right here and now, it's over the side for you!"

"But these two were cheating, Sam. Everybody could see that."

"I couldn't," Sam replied, taking the knife from Big Joe's hand. "And I'm the only one who matters."

"What are you saying?"

"I'm saying the game was fair. You lost fair and square. No signals. No cards up the sleeve. Nothing."

"That can't be!" Big Joe complained in a disbelieving voice.

"It can be . . . and it is. Now leave them be," he said before bending down to pick up Henry's pocketwatch. To Henry himself, he extended a hand. "Here, let me help you up. And you, my dear lady," he said, turning on his Missouri charm. "May I buy you a drink?"

"I don't drink with strangers," she replied cooly.

"The name's Clemens. Samuel Clemens. See? Now we're no longer strangers."

25
The River

The three of them sat in a small lounge off the main parlor. A ribbon of lightning flashed in the distance. It was May here in the heartland, and another late-spring rain was about to get underway.

The river was wide, the product of an exceedingly wet spring. So wide and so close they could almost reach out and touch it! Banks brimming with water, the big river was full, and frequently, more than full. The water poured out over the land, flooding the woods and the fields for miles into the interior. In places, it was as much as fifteen feet deep! Several generations would pass before a deluge of equal magnitude would be seen in these parts again.

The present flood put all the unprotected lowlands underwater, from Cairo to the mouth. It broke down levees on both sides of the river in a dozen different places. And in some regions south, when the flood was at its highest, the Mississippi was seventy miles wide!

The cost of the flood in lives lost and property destroyed was staggering. Crops were wiped out, houses washed away, and shelterless men and cattle forced to take refuge on isolated elevations here and there in both field and forest.

Everywhere they turned there were signs of men's hard work gone to ruin, all to be done over again with straitened means and weakened courage. A melancholy picture, and a continuous one; hundreds of miles of it, in fact.

Sometimes the beacon lights stood in water three feet deep. Like tiny candles wading in some thick brown soup, the beacon lights stood alone against the night, alone out on the edge of dense forests which themselves extended for miles inland without farm, or wood-yard, or clearing, or break of any kind. This meant that the keeper of the light, in order to discharge his trust, had to come a great distance in a skiff, and often in desperate weather. Yet, the work was faithfully performed no matter what the weather, and not always by men—sometimes by women, if the man was sick or absent.

The loneliness of this solemn, stupendous flood was impressive—and depressing. League after league, and still league after league, it poured its chocolate tide along between walls of solid forest and shores without tenants. With seldom a sail or a moving object of any kind to disturb the surface or break the monotony of the blank watery solitude, the night came. But the next day it would be the same—the same majestic, unchanging serenity, the same tranquility, the same lethargy. The big muddy river was a symbol of eternity, the realization on earth of all that was longed for by both priest and prophet.

To Margaret, when she stared hypnotized out the glass, the great river was filled with poetry and grace and romance. All she knew was Ancòn and its puny streams and inconsequential lakes. Nothing in her experience could compare with this. Despite the gathering storm on the horizon, she beheld a wonderful sunset. Before her very eyes a broad expanse of river turned blood-red. In the middle distance the red hue brightened into gold, a tawny yellow through which a solitary log came floating, black and conspicuous. In one place, a long slanting mark lay sparkling upon the water; in another, the surface was broken by a series of boiling, tumbling rings, all tinted opal. Where the ruddy flush was faintest, there was a smooth spot which was covered with graceful circles and radiating lines, each traced ever so delicately upon the water. The shore to her left was densely wooded, and the somber shadow which fell from this forest was broken in one place by a long ruffled trail that shone like silver. High above the forest wall a clean-stemmed dead tree waved a single leafy bough which glowed like a flame in the unobstructed splendor flowing like a highway to the sun. The reflected images of woody heights and graceful curves filled the scene near and far, and with each passing moment, the dissolving light steadily enriched it with new marvels of color.

Like one bewitched, Margaret drank it in. She stood;

then sat; then stood again; all in a speechless rapture. This world was new to her, bold and new. She had never seen anything like it in her life. Never.

The same could not be said for the affable man standing beside her. Samuel Clemens—experienced riverboat pilot—was also looking out the glass. But he saw the same scene differently.

For him, the romance and beauty were all gone from the river. Whatever value any feature of it once held for him had long since vanished. By the learning of his trade, everything he saw out that window had been reduced to the amount of usefulness it could furnish a man toward the safe piloting of a steamboat. Just as a seasoned doctor can no longer see the lovely flush in a beautiful girl's cheek, for fear it might be a sign of disease, Samuel Clemens could no longer take note of the glories and the charms which the moon and the sun and the twilight wrought upon the river's face. He looked upon that same sunset without rapture, commenting upon it inwardly in an almost clinical fashion:

The cloudless sky and brilliant sun means that we are going to have wind tonight and tomorrow. That floating log means that the river is rising. That slanting mark upon the water indicates a bluff reef which is going to kill somebody's steamboat one of these nights, especially if it keeps on stretching out like that. Those tumbling "boils" show a dissolving bar and a shifting channel. The lines and circles in the slick water over yonder are a warning that that troublesome place is shoaling up dangerously. That silver streak in the shadow of the forest is the "break" from a new snag, and it couldn't have found a better spot to fish for a steamboat. That tall dead tree, the one with the single living branch, is not going to last long. And isn't it a shame, because without that friendly old landmark, how is anybody ever going to get through this blind place at night? He shuddered to think!

Looking at the world this way, it made Sam wonder. Had he gained or lost by the learning of his trade? He'd made a valuable acquisition mastering the language of the water; that much was true. But he'd lost something else as well, something which could never be restored to him as long as he lived. A sense of wonder. Of innocence.

The sky blinked with sudden energy! This time, the crack

of lightning was closer. The brilliant flash snapped Clemens out of his reverie and he nearly dropped Henry's pocketwatch overboard. He had been holding onto it all this time, ever since he first picked it up off the floor after the fight. Now, before handing it back to him, Clemens took a moment to study the inscription on the back, wryly committing the details to memory. Faintly amused, Clemens gathered himself together and cleared his throat to speak. His cigar had gone out in the meantime.

"You're not from around these parts, are you?" he said.

The question had more the quality of a statement than a question, and it was delivered with a self-assured swagger. It made Andu nervous, and he stole a worried look in Alpha's direction.

"No sir . . . I'm from Afghanistan."

"And where, pray tell, might that be?" Clemens asked, not missing the anxious exchange of eyes.

"Due east and a bit south," Henry replied, being intentionally evasive.

Clemens was not the sort to be lied to. "Now don't that beat all! I been east and I been south, but I've never heard of your Afghanistan."

Henry was quick to respond. "Until I stood here today, I'd never heard of such manners before either!"

"Well then, let me be the first to apologize. But before I do, let's just straighten one thing out, shall we? You two aren't going to visit friends in Hannibal like you said, are you?"

"Whatever do you mean?" Margaret exclaimed. "Are you now calling us liars, along with cheats?"

"That, ma'am, I am. You see, I'm *from* Hannibal. Grew up there. Know everyone in town. Everyone knows me. So a name if you please. Who is it you're going to see there?"

Silence was followed by stammering. "Well," Henry said, "you see . . . we just . . . said that. To make conversation. Actually, we're headed for Peoria."

"Ah, know it well!" Clemens replied.

"We don't. Will you show us the way?"

"Perhaps. Perhaps. May I call you Hank?"

"Is that short for Henry?"

Clemens nodded. "Henry was my brother's name, and I'd rather not share it with you."

"Then by all means."

"Tell me, Hank, why the poker? And why involve Margaret here? You two don't strike me as the marrying kind—at least not to each other."

Margaret blushed. "You're a good judge of character, Mister Clemens. And as for the poker, we needed money. I seem to have, shall we say, an empathy for the game."

"Ah," Clemens sighed knowingly. "Poker's not a game, Miss Hoolehan, it's a way of life."

"Sir?"

"Like the law of gravity, like all great thoughts, the truth is quite simple—and always has been. The game is a travesty on life. Shrewdness, cunning, deception—hardly a game for a woman. Conscious strategies, bold aggressions, suspicious appraisals. In this game, all the repressed values of a competitive society are let loose and placed first in the order of priorities."

"You sound cynical," Hank observed.

"Indeed I am. Poker is less a game than an extension of the corrupt practices of life itself. Perhaps this is why it is customary for players to settle accounts at the conclusion of play, before they leave the table, before they go home for the night. The error is not in the nature of the game, but in the playing of it too hard, in the inadmissable garbling of the graces of life."

"But if it is an abomination, then why is it allowed?"

Clemens chuckled and ordered another whiskey. "And for whom do we legislate morals? The impulse to gamble is a part of the ineradicable irrationality of modern man."

"Why irrational?" Hank argued. "It is, after all, a fair game."

"Not in the least!" Clemens boomed, the alcohol beginning to talk. "The winners cannot possibly win as much as the losers lose!"

"That's patently ridiculous!" Hank objected. "In every game of poker, winnings exactly balance losings."

"In money-sum only," Clemens said.

"How else then?"

Clemens smiled. "The value to a man of a given amount of money varies according to the amount he already has. That is to say, with the odds even and the game square, a given sum of money has not the same value when it has been won as when it has been lost. The winner cannot win as much as the loser loses."

"Huh?"

"Since a given sum of money means more to a poor man than to a rich one, the gambler is in a worse position if his opponents' capital greatly exceeds his own. Poor men should not gamble, and rich men should do nothing else. But rich men gain nothing by gambling with one another. And not until the poor man sits down at the table does the rich man find opportunity. Is it any wonder then, that the very same people who buy insurance also play games of chance? Or that people crowd into glittering, fame-and-fortune businesses where the total number of members divided into the total earnings is less than the wage of a modest but secure civil servant? Good Lord, man, the small chance of a large payoff is what has settled practically the entire continent! Poker is nothing if not a reflection of the American dream!"

Spellbound, his listeners nodded. But they did not understand, at least not yet. This thing called America was too far removed from their own experience for them to fathom or appreciate.

26
The Frontier

All night long they talked—about war, about Negroes, about the frontier. It began with a question: "Why do you smoke?"

"It's not as if I haven't tried to stop before, but you have to understand, things are different out here on the frontier. We do as we please, not like back East. It takes a certain willpower to break the habit. When I was a cub-pilot I made up my mind not to chew tobacco any longer. In fact, I have that last plug right here in my pocket," Clemens said, unbuttoning the flap. "Not wanting to throw it away and burn any bridges as it were, right here it'll stay, as a reminder, until it's a powder if necessary, but I'll never chew Kinnikinnick again. As for smoking, when I was a young man in Keokuk, I decided once to stop, and I was firm in my resolve, at least until I decided to resume again."

At that, Hank chuckled. "I don't understand Kinnimuck, or whatever it was you said."

"Kinnikinnick—a smoking mixture. Or some say, Killickinick. It is composed of equal parts tobacco stem, chopped straw, old soldiers, fine shavings, oak leaves, dog fennel, cornshucks, sunflower petals, the outside leaves of the cabbage plant, and any refuse of any description so long as it costs nothing and will burn. After the ingredients are thoroughly blended, they are run through a chopping machine. Then the mix is sprinkled with fragrant Scotch snuff, packed into various seductive shapes, labelled 'Genuine Killickinick, from the old original manufactory at Richmond,' and sold to pioneers and Indians for a dollar a pound."

"Thank the Lord you quit!" Margaret exclaimed. "That

sounds just awful! Though it does bring one question to mind. You said it was different out here on the frontier. Different how?"

"Such a question!" Clemens harrumphed disapprovingly. "You mean to tell me you came all the way from Afghanistan—wherever that is—to America, and you don't know anything about the *frontier*?"

Margaret nodded.

"Well, no matter—I shall answer. In American history the frontier has always been the westernmost area of settlement at any given time in the expansion of the nation. It began in 1607 with the settlement of Jamestown and hasn't ended yet. All the attitudes, all the principles, everything associated with this process form the foundation for the American idea, the American myth."

"Like what?"

"Rugged individualism. Conquest. Law and order. Progress. Free enterprise. The right to bear arms. Need I say more? The American frontier has always been at the edge of free land, at the meeting place between savagery and civilization."

"Savagery?"

Clemens nodded. "Geography and hostile Indians have generally determined the boundaries of a particular frontier. The junction of the tidewater region and the piedmont marked the frontier of the 17th century. Then, within the next hundred years, pioneers pushed the settlement line out to the base of the Alleghenies. During the American Revolution, settlers crossed the mountains into Kentucky and Tennessee. From there, they ventured into Illinois Country. Pioneers poured through the Cumberland Gap and down the Ohio. The next wave even moved beyond the Mississippi and out to the edge of the arid plains. But there, the westward migration has run into some trouble."

"What kind of trouble?"

"Near the 98th meridian, the forested area gives way to rolling prairies, and farther beyond, the prairies merge with the Great Plains. But out there, at the higher elevations, it's too dry to raise crops. That's why, for a long time now, settlement has been halted at the bend of the Missouri and along the eastern boundary of Indian Territory. But soon, this too will change. The discovery of gold in California about a dozen years back has caused hordes of settlers and prospectors to pass through the

Great Plains, over the Rocky Mountains, and across the Great Basin. They're now at the very edge of the Pacific Ocean, and all of a sudden, the line separating the settled region from the unoccupied zone has moved back to the Rockies. For all practical purposes, ma'am, the last remaining frontier now lies between the mountains to the west and the prairies to the east. This great expanse, bordered on the north by Canada and on the south by the Rio Grande, is America's last frontier."

Except, of course, outer space, Andu thought wryly.

"That's incredible!" Margaret exclaimed. "For the first time in my life, I'm beginning to understand my own people."

"Indeed. And I may be one of those moving west myself, if war ever comes to Missouri."

"But what made all those people move?" she asked. "What was the lure?"

"The lure?" Clemens echoed. "Worn-out land, economic impediments back home, the availability of roads and canals and riverboats, the coming of the railroad, the dream of adventure and romance. Moving towards the setting sun became a compulsive urge, like gambling. And once a body caught the fever, no logical argument against pulling up stakes and moving on could change his mind. For millions of Americans the frontier was the place to go simply because it was there. For the more adventuresome, six or seven moves during a lifetime was not all that uncommon.

"The fur trappers and the traders; they were the first to venture out into any new territory. They opened the trails into the wilderness and did so decades ahead of those who would follow. Only later did the miners come, and the cattlemen and the farmers. The trappers and traders preferred solitude to association with other settlers; they adapted to the ways of the Indians and took Indian women for wives or concubines. Most operated as 'free' trappers, exchanging their yearly catch of furs at the nearest trading post and getting guns, knives, traps, whiskey, tobacco, and other supplies in return.

"These mountain men, as they came to be called, spread disease and whiskey among the Indians, as well as ruthlessly exploiting the beaver and other furbearing animals. Yet, despite their shortcomings, these men played a significant role in opening each successive frontier. As they got older, some of them served as guides for emigrant companies; others settled down to raise livestock or farm. To this day, Jim Bridger, one of the more renowned and free-spirited of the mountain men, still operates a famous trading post in South Pass, Wyoming.

"After the trappers came the cattlemen; and after them, the miners. The mining frontier advanced in a less orderly fashion than that of the traders and herdsmen, sometimes lagging far behind the line of settlements as in the Georgia of the 1820s, other times leapfrogging ahead long before communities of settlers had arrived. This was the case with lead mining in Illinois and Missouri, and more recently, in the goldfields of California."

Here Clemens paused and took a long tug at his drink. When he resumed with his story, there was a hint of pride in his voice.

"The California Gold Rush is a tale all its own. Set off by the discovery of gold on the American River in January 1848, it has involved the largest migration of people over the longest distance in the briefest span of time in the history of the world! Nothing before or since can compare!"

"But gold's not like corn; you can't eat the stuff. How do all these miners manage to feed themselves? Weren't there any farmers?"

"Ah, the scourge of mankind—the farmer. After the trappers and the miners and the cattlemen, of course came the farmers. But unlike their predecessors, *these* high-minded folk set out to conquer the land, not compromise with her. Trees had to be eradicated like weeds, and Indians too. They had to be exterminated like varmints. And all in the name of cultivating the soil."

Clemens sighed, speaking only again after a long pause. "Soon the frontier will be no more."

"You seem sad," Margaret observed.

"Wouldn't you be?"

Margaret winced. She could feel Clemens' pain. It was welling up inside her. This was the flip side of the telepathic coin, and there was no way to shut it out.

Andu winced too. He and Margaret were close; her pain was his pain. He had to change the subject.

"Why the sudden talk of war?" Hank asked, redirecting

the conversation.
"Ah," Clemens nodded. "The Negroes."
"And what are they, these Negroes?"
"What indeed!" Clemens answered. "Are you two from outer space? You don't know what a *Negro* is? They're people. Black people. Coloreds, actually. But people nonetheless. People with strange habits, many of whom are slaves."
"My Lord!" Margaret exclaimed. "You stand here all puffed up with pride over your mountain men and your pioneers, yet in the same breath you tell me your people kill Indians like varmints and enslave Negroes like dogs! I don't know if I like your America."
"Nor I, somedays," Clemens admitted. "And there are plenty others besides me. And so soon there will be war."
"What did these people do to deserve being made slaves of?"
"I don't rightly know. But I can tell you this much: they're not like you and me."
Margaret couldn't believe her ears. "If cut, do they not bleed? If whipped, do they not cry?"
"Indeed they do; but then so does my dog."
"What kind of logic is *that*?" Hank angrily objected. Back home in his native Afghanistan, Andu had seen enough persecution to last him a lifetime!
Clemens explained. "In my schoolboy days I had no aversion to slavery. I was not even aware that there was anything wrong with it. No one objected to it in my hearing. The local papers said nothing against it. The local pulpit taught us God approved it, that it was a holy thing, that the doubter need only look in the Bible if he wished to ease his mind. Then, to make matters doubly sure, he would read the texts aloud to us. The slaves themselves, if they had an aversion to slavery, were wise and said nothing. In Hannibal where I grew up, we seldom saw a slave misused; on the farm, never!"
Margaret narrowed her eyes, giving him an I-don't-believe-you look.
Clemens picked up on it right away. "I assure you, ma'am, there was nothing about the slavery of the Hannibal region to rouse one's slumbering humane instincts. It was the mild domestic slavery, not the brutal plantation article. Cruelties were extremely rare—and exceedingly unpopular. To separate

the members of a slave family and sell them to different masters was a thing not well liked by the people. It was not often done, except in the settling of an estate. Indeed, I have no recollection of ever seeing a slave auction in that town, though I'm suspicious now that that might have been because the thing was such a commonplace spectacle, not out of the ordinary at all. I do vividly remember seeing one thing, however: a dozen black men and women chained to one another and lying in a group on the pavement. They were awaiting shipment to the Southern slave market. I must confess, those were the saddest faces I've ever seen.

"Then, too, there are some Negroes who *aren't* slaves. They hail us along the river sometimes. We'd be traveling through a region that was woodsy, and we'd come upon a group of highwater-stained tumble-down cabins populous with colored folk and no whites visible anywhere. There would be patches of dry ground here and there, grassless patches; a few felled trees; and a skeleton herd of cattle, mules, and horses, all eating the leaves and gnawing the bark, no other food being within reach for them in that muddy and flood-wasted land. Other times, we'd come upon a single, lonely, landing-cabin; near it, the colored family that had hailed us. Little and big, old and young, there they'd sit, roosting on a scant pile of household goods. In their midst lay a rusty gun, some bedticks, a chest, some tinware, two stools, a crippled looking glass, a venerable armchair, and six baseborn and spiritless yellow curs attached to the family by strings.

"Black folk must have their dogs, you see; can't go anywhere without their dogs. Yet the dogs themselves are never willing to come aboard; they always object. So, while we wait, they are dragged, one after the other, in ridiculous procession, all four feet braced and sliding along, their head likely to be pulled off, the tugger marching determinedly forward, bending to his work with the rope over his shoulder for better purchase. Sometimes a child is forgotten and left on the bank; but never a dog."

"You talk about the river as if you've lived it," Margaret observed. "What is it that you do anyway, Mister Clemens?"

"Well, ma'am, if your friend here is agreeable to buying me another round, I'd be privileged to answer that question for you."

27
Childhood

"When I was a boy growing up in a small village on the west bank of the Mississippi River, there was but one permanent ambition among me and my comrades. And that was to be a steamboatman. Oh, we had transient ambitions of other sorts, of course, but they were just that—transient. When a circus came and went, it left us all burning to become clowns. Then, on another occasion, when the first Negro minstrel-show came to our section, it left us all suffering to try *that* kind of life. And now and again we all had hopes that, if we lived long enough and were good, God would permit us to be pirates. These ambitions faded out, each in its turn, but the ambition to be a steamboatman always remained.

"Once a day, a cheap, gaudy packet arrived upward from St. Louis, and another down from Keokuk. Before these events, the day was glorious with expectancy; after them, the day was a dead and empty thing. Not only the boys, but the whole village, felt the same way. I can picture that old time to myself even now, just as it was back then:

"The white town drowsing in the sunshine of a summer's morning. The streets empty, or pretty nearly so. One or two clerks sitting in front of their Water Street stores asleep: chins on their breasts, hats slouched down over their faces, splint-bottomed chairs tilted back against the wall. A sow and a litter of pigs loafing along the sidewalk, doing a good business in watermelon rinds and seeds. A pile of skids on the slope of the stone-paved wharf. And—except for the fragrant town drunkard asleep there in the shadows—nobody around to listen to the peaceful lapping of wavelets against the wood flats.

"Then there was the river: the great Mississippi, the majestic magnificent Mississippi, its endless mile-wide tide rolling swiftly along, shining in the sun. Far away on the opposite shore, dense forest. Above the town and again below it, each 'point' fixing a boundary to the river-glimpse, turning it into a sort of sea, still and brilliant and lonely.

"Presently, a film of dark smoke appears above one of those remote 'points.' Instantly, a Negro drayman, famous for his quick eye and prodigious voice, lifts up the cry: 'S-t-e-a-m-boat a-comin'!' and suddenly the scene changes!

"The town drunkard stirs, the clerks wake up, a furious clatter of drays follows. Every house and store pours out a human contribution and, in a twinkling, the dead town is alive and moving! Drays, carts, men, boys, all go hurrying from many quarters to a common center—the wharf. Assembled there the people fasten their eyes upon the coming boat as if it were a wonder they were seeing for the first time."

As Clemens spoke, Margaret watched him with her eyes, feasting on every little gesture, every little nuance. As if in a trance, she was hypnotized by his every move, by the way he carried himself, by the slightest inflection in his voice. He noticed her approving look and commented upon it in his own way.

"The approaching boat is a rather handsome sight. Like you, ma'am, she is long and sharp and trim and pretty. She has two tall, fancy-topped chimneys with a gilded device of some kind swung between them; and perched atop the texas deck behind them, a fanciful pilothouse all glass and 'gingerbread.' The paddle-boxes themselves are gorgeous, decorated either with gilded rays or else with a picture above the boat's name. The boiler-deck, hurricane deck, and texas deck are fenced and ornamented with clean white railings. There is a flag flying gallantly from the jackstaff and the furnace doors are open, the fire glaring bravely. Great volumes of the blackest smoke you ever saw are rolling out of the chimneys, a husbanded grandeur created by throwing in a bit of pitch pine just before arriving at town. The pent-up steam is screaming through the gauge-cocks. The upper decks are thick with passengers, and the crew is grouped on the forecastle. The captain stands by the big bell, calm and imposing, the envy of all. The broad-stage is run out over the port bow, way out, and a deck hand stands poised on the end of it with a coil of rope hanging from his hand. He waits for the signal. Then, as if on cue, the captain lifts his hand. A bell rings. The wheels stop. Then, a moment later, they turn back, churning the water to foam. Finally, the steamer is at rest.

"Next comes the scramble: the scramble to get aboard, to get ashore, to take in freight and to discharge it, all at once and all at the same time, and all facilitated from beginning to end by the yelling and cursing of the mates. Ten minutes later the steamer is under way again, only this time with no flag on the jackstaff or any black smoke issuing from the chimneys. After ten more minutes the town is dead again, and the town drunkard asleep once more by the skids."

Here Clemens paused and leaned back in his chair. It was getting late, he was drunk, and his eyelids were drooping. Yet despite the late hour, something inside him urged him to press on. It was as if someone were desperately prodding him to finish his tale.

"Boy after boy managed to get on the river. The minister's son became an engineer. The doctor's son became a 'mud clerk.' So did the postmaster's. The wholesale liquor-dealer's son became a barkeep aboard a boat. Four sons of the chief merchant became pilots along with two sons of the county judge. I, being no less capable, wanted the same. And why shouldn't I? Pilot was the grandest station of them all! Even in those days of trivial wages, a pilot had a princely salary—anywhere from a hundred and fifty dollars a month on up to as much as two hundred and fifty dollars a month. And no board to pay! A mere two months of a pilot's wages would pay a preacher's salary for a full year! Though it took some finagling, that's what I finally did become—a pilot."

"Finagling?" Hank asked, unsure of the strange word's meaning.

"You know—wrangling, dickering, bargaining. Give me a minute and I'll lay out the whole story for you. It was not so long ago, you see—about four years—and I remember it well. I was actually on my way to Brazil at the time, when I got sidetracked. Circumstances found me onboard the riverboat *Paul Jones*. The pilot, Horace Bixby, then a man of thirty-two, was at the wheel and looking out over the bow of the *Jones* at the head of Island No. 35 when he heard a slow, pleasant voice—*my* voice:

"Good morning," I said.

Bixby was a clean-cut, direct, courteous man. "Good morning, sir," he said briskly, without looking up. As a rule, Mr. Bixby did not care for visitors in the pilothouse. This one—me—presently came up and stood a little behind him.

"How would you like a young man to learn the river?" I said.

Bixby glanced over his shoulder and saw in me a rather slender, loose-limbed young fellow with a fair complexion and a great tangle of auburn hair. "I *wouldn't* like it," he said. "Cub-pilots are more trouble than they're worth. A great deal more trouble than profit."

I was not discouraged. "I am a printer by trade," I went on in my easy, deliberate way. "It doesn't agree with me. I thought I'd go to South America."

Bixby kept his eyes on the river, but I could see that a note of interest had crept into his voice. "What makes you pull your words that way?" he asked, "pulling" being the river term for drawling.

I took a seat on the visitors' bench. "You'll have to ask my mother," I said, more slowly than ever. "She pulls hers, too."

Pilot Bixby woke up and laughed. He had a keen sense of humor and the manner of my reply amused him. Encouraged, I decided to have another go at it. "Do you know the Bowen boys?" I asked. "Pilots in the St. Louis and New Orleans trade?"

"I know them well," he said. "All three of them. William Bowen did his first steering for me; a mighty good boy, too. Had a Testament in his pocket when he came aboard; in a week's time he had swapped it for a pack of cards. I know Sam, too, and Bart."

"Old schoolmates of mine in Hannibal. Sam and Will especially were my chums."

"Come over and stand by the side of me," Bixby said. "What is your name?"

I told him and the two of us stood looking out at the sunlit water.

"Do you drink?" Bixby asked.

"No."

"Do you gamble?"

"No, sir."

"Do you swear?"

"Not for amusement; only under pressure."

"Do you chew?"

"No, sir, never; but I *must* smoke."

"Did you ever do any steering?" was Bixby's next question.

"I have steered everything on the river but a steamboat, I guess."

"Very well; take the wheel and see what you can do with a steamboat. Keep her as she is—toward that lower cottonwood snag."

At this point Clemens paused again and smiled, this time at Margaret. These were good memories he was resurrecting and his face beamed.

"And so it began," Clemens said. "Bixby's terms were steep, but I agreed to them. Bixby had a sore foot that day and was glad of a little relief. I was often at the wheel, that trip, while he sat there directing me and nursing that sore foot of his. By the time we'd reached New Orleans, I had forgotten all about the Amazon and had entered in upon the small enterprise of 'learning' twelve or thirteen hundred miles of the great Mississippi River with the easy confidence of that time of my life. I was determined to be what I am now—a pilot—but if I'd really known what I was about to require of my faculties, I would not have had the courage to begin. At the time, I supposed that all a pilot had to do was to keep his boat in the river, something I did not consider could be much of a trick since it was so wide. Now I know better, of course."

"You must be quite the pilot," Margaret said approvingly. "Is this your boat?"

"No, ma'am, it is not. On this trip, I am but a passenger, like yourself. Zebulon Leavenworth—he's the pilot—though I did promise him I'd take the 4 a.m. watch. He knows my ability, and yes ma'am, I am quite the pilot."

"And modest, too," Hank jibed.

Clemens smiled. Perhaps prosperity and prestige *had* gone to his head. Still, he had passed through a laborious apprenticeship and was already earning much more than his father or his brother ever had. He felt himself any man's equal and a good deal better than most. Though his brother Orion was ten years his senior, Sam claimed position as head of the family, and his claim had been accepted. He was a man well established in a responsible, honored, and lucrative profession, and he met the requirements of his role. He liked the company of women, as he would all his life, and he enjoyed flirtation. That he was flirting with Margaret was clear in every syllable he uttered.

"If I seem to love my subject," he said, "it should be with no great surprise, for I love this profession far better than any I ever followed before—or probably will after—and I take measureless pride in it. The reason is plain: in these days a pilot is the only unfettered and entirely independent human being that lives on the Earth! Kings are little more than hampered servants of parliament and the people; parliaments sit in chains forged by their constituency; even the clergy is but a hostage, unable to freely speak the whole truth without regard for his congregation's opinion. Freedom of the press? Think again! The editor of a newspaper cannot be independent, but must be content to utter only half or two-thirds of his mind; indeed, writers of all stripes are but manacled servants of the public. In truth, every man, woman, and child has a master, and each worries and frets in servitude. But the Mississippi riverboat pilot has none!

"The captain of the ship can stand upon the hurricane deck in the pomp of brief authority; he can give five or six orders while the vessel backs out into the stream; but then that skipper's reign is over. The moment that boat is underway in the river, she is under the sole and unquestioned control of the pilot. He can do with her exactly as he pleases, run her when and whither he chooses, even tie her up to the bank whenever his judgment says that that course is best. His movements are entirely free. He consults no one. He receives commands from nobody. He promptly resents even the merest suggestion. Indeed, the law of the land *forbids* him to listen to commands or suggestions, a rule which only makes good sense considering how the pilot knows better than anyone else how to handle his boat.

"So there you have it, Margaret, the novelty of a king without a keeper, an absolute monarch who is absolute in sober truth and not by a fiction of words. I suppose you will have guessed by now that given a pilot's boundless authority he is a great personage—and that is true. He is treated with marked courtesy by the captain and with marked deference by all the officers and the servants. This deferential spirit is quickly communicated to the passengers as well.

"By long habit, pilots have come to put all their wishes in the form of commands. It gravels me to think that some day I'll have to put my will in the weak shape of a request instead of

launching it in the crisp language of an order."
"And why should *that* be?" Margaret asked, seeing the disappointment in his eyes.
Clemens answered with a sigh. "Alas, it seems as if my riverboating days are about to draw to a close."
By now it was 4 a.m., and his turn for the watch. Hank and Margaret followed him upstairs.
One can never see too many summer sunrises on the Mississippi. They are enchanting. First, there is the eloquence of silence, for a deep hush broods everywhere. Next, there is the haunting sense of loneliness. Of isolation. Of remoteness. For you are far from the worry and bustle of the world.
The dawn creeps in stealthily. The solid walls of black forest soften to gray as vast stretches of the river open up and reveal themselves. The water is glass-smooth; it gives off spectral little wreaths of white mist. There is not the faintest breath of wind, nor stir of leaf. The tranquility is profound; infinitely satisfying. Then a bird pipes up, and then another, and before long the pipings explode into a jubilant riot of music. You see none of these birds, however, but simply move through an atmosphere of song which seems to sing itself.
When the light has become a little stronger, one of the fairest and softest pictures imaginable develops like so many frames of film before your very eyes. The first frame, intense green, is of the massed and crowded foliage close by. Paling shade by shade, the color changes the further away you look. Upon the next projecting cape, a mile or more off, the tint has lightened to the tender young green of spring. Upon the cape beyond that, it has lost almost all color. And upon the furthest one, miles away and just under the horizon, the water is a mere dim vapor, hardly separable from the sky above.
With more light still, the whole stretch of river becomes like a mirror, a canvas really, on which the curving shores, receding capes, and shadowy reflections of leafage are all painted in, soft and rich. The finished sketch is a masterpiece!
And when the sun gets well up in the sky and distributes a pink flush here, and a powder of gold there, and a purple haze over yonder where it will do the most good, you grant that there is a god and you have seen something worth remembering!

28
Pilot

Clemens stood there, firm and tall, leaning out over the rail, staring at the rising sun. He was a slender, fine-looking man, well-dressed—even dandified—with his patent leathers, his blue serge, white duck, and fancy striped shirt. Though he was clean-shaven now, at times, he heightened his appearance by wearing his beard in the atrocious muttonchops fashion, then popular, but becoming to no one, least of all him. Judging by the way Margaret hung close to him, it was clear she had grown fond of the man. He turned from the rail to speak.

"Well, you two have listened to me blither on and on all night long talking about myself. But where I come from, turnabout is fair play. So tell me, Hank, what do you do for a living? And you might compliment me with the truth this time."

"I'm a pilot, too," Andu answered. "Only of a different sort of ship . . . a spaceship."

"Well, how silly of me to ask!" Clemens exclaimed. "Next I suppose you'll tell me you're from another time as well; that you're nothing but a Connecticut Yankee in King Arthur's Court!"

"King Arthur? I don't understand the analogy," Andu replied. "But, yes, I *am* from another time. The year 2488."

"Hah! The tales you tell are taller than my own! Indeed, if it weren't for your swarthy skin and funny accent, I'd take you for my very own brother."

"You said earlier that I reminded you of him," Hank noted, grabbing at the opportunity to change the subject. "What became of your brother?"

"A sad story, I must confess—the saddest I've ever had to endure—certainly the saddest I've ever had to relate."

"If it's too painful, then don't!" Margaret cried, sensing his intense feelings.

"It might help to talk about it. Let me try, anyway. I was still a cub-pilot at the time—Bixby had gone on to another boat—and I was working under one William Brown. Looking back on it now, those months on the *Pennsylvania* were the unhappiest in my four years on the river. Brown was a petty tyrant—surly, stupid, and ignorant—and he made the lives of his subordinates miserable with his incessant faultfinding. I was his favorite target—no doubt because he envied my bright intelligence and playful humor—but his curses and angry explosions had to be endured, no matter how unjustified."

"Why did you put up with it?"

"A pilot holds despotic authority over his cub," Clemens replied. "But there was one provocation which proved intolerable. That was the abuse of my younger brother Henry. He had shipped aboard the *Pennsylvania* as third clerk. One day, Henry appeared on the hurricane deck and shouted to Brown to stop at some landing or other, a mile or so downriver. Brown, who was slightly deaf, did not hear him, though, and when the boat went past the landing, Captain Klinefelter came to the pilothouse to ask if my brother had delivered Brown the order. Brown denied it, of course, though I myself clearly heard him do so. At the time, Brown cursed me, but the episode seemed to be over. That is, until an hour later when Henry entered the pilothouse on another errand. That's when the real trouble began.

"Brown started in on my brother straightaway, demanding to know why he hadn't told him that they were to land at that particular plantation. Henry replied that he *had* told him. Brown said it was a lie. I said, 'You lie, yourself. Henry *did* tell you.'

"Furious, Brown instantly ordered Henry out of the pilothouse before attending to my own insubordination. But then, as my brother left, Brown—with a sudden access of fury—picked up a ten-pound lump of coal from next to the stove and sprang after the boy. I jumped inbetween them with a heavy stool, knocking Brown to the deck and then pounding the prostrate man with my fists until he struggled free and sprang for the wheel. By then, the *Pennsylvania* was heading downstream at full speed, unattended. Banished from the pilothouse, I refused to leave, mocking Brown's illiterate English until he had been silenced.

"There was, of course, a reckoning to come. Captain Klinefelter summoned me to his cabin, shut the door, and took inventory of what had happened. I admitted that I had fought Mr. Brown, had struck him with a stool, had knocked him down, and pounded him. 'I am deuced glad of it!' exclaimed the captain. 'You have been found guilty of a great crime, and don't you ever be guilty of it again on this boat! But,' and he smiled, 'lay for him ashore!'

"Though Captain Klinefelter must have thoroughly disliked Brown, I was relieved of duty. The immediate consequence was that I left the *Pennsylvania* when she docked at New Orleans. When the *Pennsylvania* went north again, it left without me; though Henry was still onboard as a clerk. I traveled north as a passenger on the *A.T. Lacey*. Two days out, when the *Lacey* touched at a landing, we got the news that the *Pennsylvania* had blown up at Ship Island with more than a hundred and fifty lives lost."

Margaret caught her breath, and tears came to her eyes. Clemens struggled forward to finish his story.

"The *Pennsylvania* exploded at six a.m., June 13, seventy miles south of Memphis and three hundred yards from shore. Four boilers blew up. The blast and scalding steam instantly killed the firemen and most of the deck passengers. The whole forward part of the boat, including the texas deck and the pilothouse, was destroyed. Like most such accidents, this one seems to have been caused by negligence and recklessness. According to testimony given at the coroner's inquest, one boiler was known to have leaked badly and had to be watched constantly. Even so, shortly before the explosion, the *Pennsylvania* had successfully raced one steamboat and was preparing to race another. The engineer had given orders to fire up the boilers to the limit, to avoid being passed. The fire was as strong as any they had ever had and could not have been made any stronger.

"Within one minute of the alarm, the boat was wrapped in flame. Many passengers were trapped. More than two hundred people were killed right away, and many others died later on. It was the worst disaster of all my years on the river.

The body of Brown, the pilot on duty, was never found. My brother Henry had been blown into the river, then, despite suffering internal injuries, had swum back to the *Pennsylvania* before it caught fire. He was taken off in the flatboat and finally carried to Memphis with the others.

"While the boat I was on steamed north past wreckage and the occasional floating corpse, all I could do was wait in suspense, hearing first that Henry was unhurt, then later on that he had been fatally injured. In Memphis I realized at once that my brother's case was hopeless. There was nothing to be done," Clemens stammered, the bitter memory still painful. "Six days after the explosion, Henry died."

By now there were tears in Clemens' eyes. To explain meant to place responsibility. In his Calvinist universe there was no place for accident. Would Henry even have gone on the river at all if Sam had not first set the example? Would Henry have clerked on the *Pennsylvania* if Sam had not been there first? Therefore, wasn't Sam responsible for everything which followed? Hadn't Sam's advice to Henry in case of disaster—to rescue passengers, then see to his own safety—contributed to his brother's death? Hadn't Sam's fight with Brown been about the only occasion in his adult life when he had resorted to physical violence? If only he'd kept his temper!

Margaret felt the pain as if it were her own, and when she came to him and touched his hand, she drained it from him, making it hers.

"It's not your fault," she said. "If not for that fight, right now you'd *both* be dead!"

She had read his mind and he knew it, but before he could open his mouth to object, a terrible thundering roar exploded right in front of them taking full possession of their faculties.

Their ship had been fired upon!

29
Secession

In the fateful presidential election of 1860, Samuel Clemens had cast his vote for John Bell of Tennessee, nominee of the short-lived Constitutional Union Party which stood for both union and slavery. Bell was the candidate for men who did not want to choose up sides, and he carried most of the Border States. Like most pilots, politics did not interest Sam particularly, and he was no more prepared for civil war than most of his fellow citizens. Traveling that great commercial highway, carrying people and cargo from both North and South, the pilots did not believe that political differences would be allowed to interfere with the nation's trade, nor that those differences could not be settled peaceably at the polls or else in the halls of legislation, rather than out on the streets with guns. As late as March of 1861, only two months before the present, Sam had renewed his pilot's license as per usual.

Yet signs of the coming catastrophe were visible everywhere. In December, the Memphis *Daily Avalanche* had reported that Sam's old commander, Captain Klinefelter—known by all to be a Union man—had been "waited on" in New Orleans by a "committee" who gave him six hours to put off his freight and leave the city on pain of being hanged if he disobeyed. By that time, the State of Mississippi had already set up batteries at Vicksburg and was stopping southbound boats for inspection. In late January of 1861, Louisiana declared the Union a failure and seceded. Among the pilots, however, there was no clear consensus as to what rights a State had in this regard, or even what the real meaning of secession might be. Until recently, comparatively few of them believed it meant war—and certainly not young Samuel Clemens! Indeed, a letter he wrote from New Orleans on February 6, 1861—a date *after* Louisiana had already seceded from the Union—contained no mention of war or of any special excitement in that decidedly southern town.

But such things would come soon enough. President Lincoln was inaugurated on the fourth of March and Fort Sumter was fired upon six weeks later. Men had begun to speak out. And to take sides!

There were pilots who would go with the Union; there were others who would go with the Confederacy. Horace Bixby was one of the former and in due time would become chief of the Union River Service. Montgomery, another pilot Clemens had once steered for, declared for the South and later commanded the Confederate Mississippi Fleet. Though these men were all close friends, a good many were not at all clear as to their opinions. Their discussions—though warm—were not always acrimonious. Living as they did, both North and South, they saw various phases of the question and hence, divided their sympathies.

Samuel Clemens was of the less radical element. He knew there was a great deal to be said for either cause; furthermore, he was not bloodthirsty. He'd given the matter some thought and decided that a pilothouse, what with its elevated position and glassed-in transparency, was a poor place to be in the middle of a fight. And yet, until just ten days ago, he had been piloting the *Alonzo Child*, a boat whose owners and crew were strongly Confederate. This all changed, though, when the *Child*'s flamboyantly secessionist captain decided to pull his boat off that route. Suddenly, Clemens was out of a job and had no choice but to return to St. Louis by other means. That is how he found himself a passenger aboard *this* boat, Zebulon Leavenworth's boat, the *Nebraska*.

Though they didn't know it at the time, the *Nebraska* was to be the last boat to pass through the Union blockade above Memphis. At Cairo, Illinois, they had seen soldiers drilling, troops later to be commanded by General Grant. It was only now, as they came steaming up toward St. Louis with those onboard congratulating themselves on having come through the checkpoints unscathed, that the unthinkable happened.

Abreast of Jefferson Barracks, they suddenly heard the boom of a cannon and saw a great whorl of smoke drifting in their direction. At the sound of the cannon, Margaret fell back against Andu even as Clemens sprinted up the three steps to the pilothouse.

Zeb was at the wheel, squinting into the morning sun. He seemed oblivious to what was going on around him. Though the signal had obviously been intended as a thunderous "Halt!", he had kept straight on.

Less than a minute later, there was another horrendous boom, and a shell exploded directly in front of them, this time breaking out most of the glass in the pilothouse and destroying a good deal of the upper decoration. Stunned, Zebulon Leavenworth fell back into a corner with a yell.

"Good Lord Almighty!" he said to Clemens as Andu and Margaret came around the corner. "What do they mean by that?"

Clemens stepped to the wheel and brought the big boat around. "I guess they want us to wait a minute, Zeb."

In due time, they were examined and passed. But in the space of those few minutes, their entire world changed. The *Nebraska* would be the last steamboat to make the trip north from New Orleans to St. Louis, and Clemens, after his recent stint onboard the *Alonzo Child*, was never to pilot a steamboat again. Here it was, May 21st, 1861, and his piloting days were over!

• • •

They had arrived in St. Louis, shaken but unhurt, and were now at the house of Pamela Moffett, Sam's sister. Zebulon Leavenworth lived near the Moffett's in St. Louis, and Sam had just returned home from talking with him. He had a sour look upon his face.

After their encounter out on the river with the cannon, this secession business was beginning to look rather serious. There was a pressing war demand for Mississippi riverboat pilots, and Sam was now intent upon hiding out, afraid he'd be pressed into service against his will. The dreamy easy romantic existence of a pilot had suited him exactly, and he was on tenuous ground in deciding what to do next with his life.

His sister Pamela was there with him in the front room, along with his new friend Hank Morgan and his niece Annie. Not feeling well, Margaret had gone upstairs to lay down.

The time had come to take sides. For some, the choice was clear and easy, but for Samuel Clemens of Hannibal, Missouri, it was anything but. His family had held slaves, though that had been long ago, and his brother Orion was now an anti-slavery man who had campaigned for Abraham Lincoln. Sam could not simply follow his state, for Missouri was a border state, divided within itself, and would soon fight a brief and bloody civil war all its own to decide the matter. Thus, even at this late date, Samuel Clemens wavered. He had been a Union man in the fall, then a Rebel, and would eventually end up as a Union supporter. Of one thing he was certain: *he would not serve as a pilot on the Union River Fleet!* That exploding shell had taught him the vulnerability of a glass-enclosed pilothouse. And to make matters even worse, after this morning's talk with Zebulon Leavenworth, Sam was now obsessed with the fear that he might be arrested and forced to act as the pilot on a government gunboat while a man stood by with a pistol ready to shoot him if he showed the least sign of a false move.

"But Uncle Sam!" his niece Annie spoke up suddenly. "What will you do if you quit piloting? That's all you've ever wanted to be your whole life long!"

"Your uncle's quite resourceful, little one," Pamela Clemens Moffett told her daughter. "He could be anything he chooses. He already has a proven knack for writing and storytelling. Perhaps he could take up farming? Like his own Uncle John Quarles."

"Hah!" Clemens roared. "Me? A farmer? Not very damn likely! Let me tell you something, dear sister. Four out of five of my former pilot-friends who quit the river chose farming as an occupation. This was not because they were particularly gifted agriculturally and thus more likely to succeed as farmers than in any other industry; no, they chose farming because that life was private and secluded and away from the interruptions of undesirable strangers—just like the hermitage of the pilothouse had been. I imagine another reason they chose it was because, on a thousand nights of black storm and danger, they noted the friendly twinkling lights of each solitary farmhouse as the boat swung by. No doubt they pictured to themselves the serenity and security of such refuge, the coziness even. By and by, they came to dream of that retired and peaceful life as the one desirable thing to long for, the one thing to anticipate, to earn, and at long last, to enjoy."

"Why, Samuel, you have such a way with words!" Pamela teased. "Didn't I tell you he had a knack for storytelling?"

"Shush, dear sister, and let me finish, for the story is hardly half over. Not one of those pilot-farmers astonished anybody with their successes. Their farms did not support them; they supported their farms. Believe me, if I've seen it once, I've seen it a dozen times. Long about the first of spring, the pilot-farmer disappears from the river and isn't seen again 'til the next frost. Then he reappears, combs the hayseed out of his hair, and takes a pilothouse-berth for the winter. In this way he manages to pay the debts which his farming has achieved during the agricultural season. Alas, his river bondage is but half-broken! He is still the river's slave, only now it's just for the *hardest* half of the year. Sorry, Pamela, but that sort of life is just not for me."

His sister smiled, knowing how Sam craved adventure. "Well, if not farming, then what about going west with our brother? Orion received his commission from the President a few weeks ago. Even as we speak, he's trying to scrape together enough money to pay the fare."

Sam nodded as if he already knew all about it. "We spoke of his appointment when I was here for a few days at the end of April. Even now, I find it hard to believe Orion's to be the secretary of the Nevada Territory! I told him then, and I'll tell you the same: going west holds some appeal for me. But whether I do or whether I don't, I must first go up to Hannibal. William Bowen still owes me $200 on account of that boardinghouse he built for his mother to run. It's three stories high, if you can believe it, and has twenty rooms! Not only that, some of us have been talking about taking up arms and joining with the rebels."

"Sweet Jesus, Samuel! Are you out of your head?!" Pamela exclaimed. "That's Union territory up there! And even if it weren't, have you no regard for our brother? Who do you think gave him his appointment as secretary? None other than Abraham Lincoln himself! How is Orion gonna explain to Mister Lincoln that his brother's a rebel? No, Samuel, this is something you must not do!"

"Pamela, I grew up with those boys; Sam Bowen and I are friends. And Orion will have his appointment no matter *what* I do. Anyhow, I promised this fellow here I'd get him and his girl up to Hannibal, and then onto a coach for Peoria."

"Oh, I just love that town!" Pamela bubbled excitedly. "The actors. The actresses. The minstrel shows. Vaudeville. What's that they always say? If it'll play in Peoria, it'll play anywhere. Are you and Margaret one of them? Actors, I mean?"

"No, ma'am," Hank answered, in the way he had heard others say it. "We're on our way there to see relatives."

"Don't believe a word he says, Pamela. Next, he'll have you believing he's from another time; another place. Actually, the details aren't important. When I go to Hannibal, Hank and his girlfriend are going there with me. I'll be back in time to join Orion and Mollie when they get on the boat to go west."

Pamela shook her head. "I don't think Mollie and Jennie are going with him—at least not right away. That's why he's so set on *you* going with him. Plus, you always seem ripe for an adventure."

"Well, we'll just have to see about that. In the meantime . . . "

"Uncle Sam! Uncle Sam! Come quickly!" the maid yelled from the top of the stairs. Everyone in the Moffett household called Sam "uncle" regardless. "And bring your friend along too. I think she's got the fever!"

"Lord, no."

30
Fever

Two Days Later
May 23, 1861

The two men were walking along a riverfront trail north of town. The day was hot and muggy and both men wore short sleeves. Hank carried a satchel under his arm, a satchel he had never once let out of his sight since he and Clemens first met. Clemens was just about to comment on that fact when they were buzzed by an enormous horsefly.

The morning was thick with bugs. All sorts of them. In every imaginable shape and size. Big ones; small ones; winged ones; hairy ones. Hoppers; crawlers; creepers. It was annoying. The pesky little buggers were everywhere!

Brushing one from his hair and another from his mouth, Andu thought of Mars, the home of his tool-and-die factory. Unlike Earth, Mars had comparatively few insects. This was by design, of course: the colonists had been very picky about the animals they brought along with them when they came. Only, this was one of those good/bad stories you hear so much about. Whether one cared to admit it or not, insects were what made an ecosystem work!

It was Dr. Chandra, Andu's no-nonsense friend, who had put it all in perspective for him. Like so many people, Andu was a confirmed bug-hater. The only good bug was a dead bug; or so he said. Chandra couldn't disagree more, especially when the subject turned to the terraforming of the Red Planet.

"You must open your eyes," Chandra said, warming to the subject. "Besides the vital job of pollination, insects do many things for us. They recycle nutrients, enrich soils, even dispose of nature's trash. You know, the icky stuff like entrails and carcasses and dung. Let's face it, Andu, insects have been an inextricable part of our human society almost from the beginning. Waxes, medicines, dyes, silk, honey; they all came to us courtesy of one insect or another. We've used them at various times in our past to do all sorts of things for us—convict murderers, catch fish, rid us of weeds, even other insects. I tell you . . ."

"I love your enthusiasm, Doc, I really do. But aren't you forgetting something?"

"Oh? And what is that?"

"The all-too-familiar downside to our buggy companions."

Chandra glowered. "I hadn't forgotten it; I just hadn't gotten around to bringing it up yet! But you're absolutely right about that downside. Insects have always been a major vector of disease, both in animals and in plants. Their ravages have even changed the course of human history on occasion. Louse-borne scourges have been known to influence the outcome of wars every bit as decisively as any manmade weapon. Typhus, for example. Negrolitis, for another. Indeed, recorded history has seen three pandemics of plague, including one in which a third of the population of Europe was killed."

"Yes, yes, yes. But what does this have to do with the terraforming of Mars?"

"Silly boy! No ecosystem could possibly be considered complete without them!"

At the time, Andu didn't argue. While it was undoubtedly true that no ecosystem could be considered complete without them, it was equally true that the daunting ability of insects to carry disease and to strip plants of their foliage made them far too formidable a beast for an ecosystem as young and fragile as Mars's. Even here on Earth, there were days like today when the usefulness of *any* insect might be called into question. For all Andu knew, one might have even been responsible for making Margaret sick!

"Don't worry about her so," Clemens said, seeing Andu's faraway look.

For half an hour already the two men had been walking single file along a narrow riverfront trail north of town. Every few steps or so a horsefly would buzz them, lighting on their legs or their arms, or the back of their neck, then sinking their vise-like mandibles into their skin and refusing to leave without taking with them an adequate offering of flesh. Now, while Clemens talked, Andu swatted at one of the monsters with his satchel.

"My sister Pamela is married to a prosperous merchant—Will Moffett. I assure you, Margaret will get the best medical care St. Louis money can buy. It's curious, though. You don't see scarlet fever much in adults. It's an infectious disease which affects mainly children."

"Why 'scarlet'?"

"On account of the bright-red skin rash that develops."

"But it came on her so fast!" Andu exclaimed, swatting at another fly.

"Scarlet fever develops rapidly. High fever; rapid pulse; headache; muscle pain; nausea. Then the rash."

"And then?"

"The skin starts to peel."

"Is it lethal, this scarlet fever? Could it kill her?" Andu asked, thinking how much pain he had already caused this precious young girl.

Clemens shook his head, uncertain how to answer. "Truth is, I don't know. There is definitely a risk, although I think the chance of death is small. I'm no doctor, mind you, but I do know that the toxins affect several organs, including the heart and the kidneys, sometimes causing permanent damage. A few patients develop pneumonia, even meningitis. Some die. In my experience, though, scarlet fever is by far the most dangerous to young children. What I don't get is how Margaret contracted it in the first place. At her age, she shouldn't have even been susceptible."

Hank stopped dead in his tracks. The pieces of the puzzle suddenly seemed to be coming together!

Clemens stopped too. "What's wrong?" he asked.

"It's my fault," Hank mumbled. "Margaret's never been immunized. Against *anything*."

"Huh?"

"What I mean is, she's susceptible to just about everything, every disease. It never occurred to me before. She wasn't born here. Lord, even a simple cold might kill her!"

"What are you saying?" Clemens stammered, dumbfounded by what he was hearing.

"I told you I was from the future, didn't I?"

"Twenty-four hundred something or other."

"Yes," Andu nodded. "And so is she. Only, she isn't a terran."

"A *what?*"

"Margaret's human like you and me, *only she wasn't born here!* Not on Earth, I mean."

"Let me guess," Clemens said, brushing an insect from his cheek. "Mars? Saturn?"

"Ancòn."

"Where's . . . how do you say it . . . Ancòn?"

"A few solar systems over. In the twenty-second century, Mormon colonists escaping persecution here on Earth were blown off course. Margaret . . ."

"Did you say Mormon?" Clemens interrupted.

"Yes. You've heard of them?"

"Indeed I have. The Church of Jesus Christ of Latter-day Saints was hatched not so very far from here. Across the river in Nauvoo, I believe. Their leader, one Joseph Smith, was martyred just down the road a piece, in Carthage, Illinois. It made all the papers at the time, though I was too young when it happened— maybe only 9—to have paid it much nevermind. Now I may be forced to catch up on my reading. Orion and I will be going through Mormon country on the way out to Nevada; that is, if I decide to join him. He tells me that Deseret is what they call their utopia; what the rest of us call Utah. Which reminds me. How did you come to be in possession of that pocketwatch?"

"Pocketwatch?"

"You know the one. I picked it up off the floor that day after Big Joe tossed you across the poker table onboard the *Nebraska.* The inscription said something about 'On To Deseret,' plus a date. Tell me: are you one of those future-type Mormons?"

Andu was just about to shake his head and say "no" when Clemens exclaimed, "Geez, what am I saying? You're not from the future—and neither is she!"

"I'd enjoy the opportunity to try and prove it to you," Andu said, thinking about the watch and kicking at a stone in the path.

"Clemens beamed. "How can you prove that which isn't true?"

"When you have eliminated the impossible, all that remains, however improbable, must be true."

Clemens thought a moment. "What sort of proof do you have in mind?"

From inside his satchel, a satchel he had never before opened in Clemens' presence, the man from the future produced Jenny. "See that grove of trees?"

He pointed across the river, a kilometer or more away.

"Yes."

"Well, keep your eye on them."

Andu pointed the blaster, adjusted the sight, and an instant later, the trees disappeared in a puff of blue smoke.

Clemens was stunned. "Oh, Heavenly Father!" he exclaimed, the color draining from his face. For seconds he just stood there, gaping at the spot where the grove of trees used to be. When speech finally returned, the words came slowly. "All that remains, however improbable, must be the truth?"

Andu nodded his head. He must have struck a chord somehow with Clemens because the man stopped and leaned heavily against a nearby tree. For an instant, he squeezed his eyes tightly shut and remembered.

How many nights had he stood there, up in the pilothouse, when the stars were blazing or when the moon on the water made the river a wide, mysterious way of speculative dreams? How many? He'd lost count. Sam was always speculating. The planets and the remote suns had always been a marvel to him. His love of astronomy—the romance of the unknown, the vast distances of the cosmos, its endless possibilities—it all began with those lonely river-watches and would never wane. For a time, one summer, a great comet had blazed in the heavens, a wonderful sheaf of light that glorified his lonely watch. Night after night he watched it as it developed and then later grew dim. Intrigued by what he'd seen, he eagerly read whatever literature came his way about comets, both then and afterwards. Like nothing else could, the mythical magic of space fired his imagination!

On those long nights Clemens speculated about many

things: life, death, existence, creation, the ways of Providence, and of Destiny. It was a fruitful time for such meditation, and out of such vigils grew larger philosophies, philosophies which had room for notions like space- and time-travel. Thus, if ever there was an audience willing to believe, it was Samuel Clemens.

"Why are you here?" Clemens finally asked.

"Dare I tell you the truth?"

"If you please."

"Okay. In the coming war, a distant ancestor of mine will die. I am here to take him back to the future."

Again Clemens was flabbergasted. "You know where and when? How is that possible?"

Andu reached into his satchel for a second time and pulled out the ancient diary that once belonged to his grandmother. Flipping rapidly through the pages, he found the entry he was looking for. "Died May 1862. Onboard the steamship *Decatur*. At or near a place called Pittsburg Landing. Following the Battle of Shiloh."

"There was a battle at Shiloh? I mean, there *will* be?"

"Apparently so," Andu said, shrugging his shoulders. "Do you know where Pittsburg Landing is?"

"Let me see. Pittsburg Landing. That would be well up the Tennessee River, I believe. When we board the boat for Hannibal, I can point it out to you on a river map. We should be able to find one in the pilothouse. There's usually a locker filled with them on every boat. But answer me this, Hank—if that's your real name—why go to all this trouble? What possible good can come from traveling back in time to find this fella? I figure it must have been a hazardous trip just getting here, and thus of the utmost importance, but who *is* this man? Of what conceivable value could he be to you?"

"Like I said, I need to take him back to the future with me."

"Then why wait for him to die? Why wait around here until next May? Why not grab him right now, while he's still alive and kicking? And how in the world is Peoria mixed up in this? She's on the Illinois River, for Heaven's sake! Nowhere near the Tennessee. The Illinois flows into the Mississippi; the Tennessee into the Ohio. Near Paducah."

"Let me see if I can explain."

And so he did.

About Carina Matthews. And Byron Matthewson. And the Grandfather Paradox. And time-travel. And Afghanistan. And Mars. And Fornax. And Prime Alpha.

When he was done, about the only thing Clemens could mutter was Andu's earlier logic. "All that remains, however improbable, must be the truth?"

Andu nodded.

"And Carina's father, your great-grandfather, was named for me?"

Andu nodded again.

"Well, frankly, I don't see as how I can refuse to help my namesake's great-grandson. Lord only knows what you're going to do hanging around here in 1861 for twelve months, but if you'll agree to help me collect the $200 Will Bowen owes me, I'll gladly give over part of it to you; enough, anyway, to cover your expenses for a week or two."

Clemens continued. "Now, not to put too fine a point on it, but if there really is a spaceship orbiting up there about the north star as you said, and if you really are from the future, one would think you'd have some sort of future-type medicine onboard that spaceship which might help this poor Mormon waif you've taken under your wing. You don't have to impress me, mind you, and I really don't care to go aboard the damn thing, but if it's up there and if there's a way to recall it, I'd dip into that bag of tricks you got there and save that poor girl."

Andu nodded and reached into his satchel for the remote. Clemens was right, and he said so.

"You know, for an out-of-work riverboat pilot, you sure do pack a lot of old-fashioned common sense. I can see now why someone might want to name their son after you."

All Sam could do was smile. Old-fashioned common sense indeed!

31
Cub

Two Weeks Later; June 4, 1861
On The Way To Hannibal

    For Samuel Clemens, that sandy-haired fellow now in his mid-twenties, the Mississippi River began in Hannibal, Missouri. He had grown up there. As a boy, he had roamed its hills and its woods, almost at will, and never once had he been disappointed. There was the cave with its marvels, the creek where he'd learned to swim, and of course the river itself.

    It was the river which meant more to him than all the rest. Its charm was permanent. It was the path to adventure, the gateway to the world. The river, with its muddy islands, its great slow-moving rafts, its marvelous steamboats, its stately current that swung endlessly down to the sea, that's where he wanted to be. He would sit by it for hours and dream. He would venture out onto it in a surreptitiously-borrowed boat when he was barely strong enough to lift an oar out of the water. He had learned all the river's faces, and each of her moods. He felt its kinship. In some occult manner he may have recognized it as his own alter ego—that unrelenting tide of life with its ever-changing sweep, its shifting shores, its unforgiving depths, its shadows, its gorgeous sunset-hues, its solemn and tranquil exit to the sea.

    His hunger for life aboard a riverboat became a passion. To be even the humblest employee onboard one of these floating enchantments would be enough. To become an officer would be to enter heaven. To become a pilot, well that would make him nothing less than a god. And to think that now it was over!

    Maybe he should end it all right here and now. Just step

into the water and let himself be sucked under by the current. It wouldn't be hard. As a boy, he had seen it happen more than once. He had seen two playmates drown; they went down without so much as a whimper. He himself had, on occasion, been dragged ashore more dead than alive, once by a slave-girl, another time by a slave-man. Yes, that would be the easy way out. But, no, killing himself wasn't the answer. His piloting days might be over, but there were other adventures to be had. Indeed, a month or more back, when the war was barely two weeks old, he had returned home to Hannibal, just as he was doing now, to size up his buddies about forming a regiment of rebels. Maybe that's what he would do after all!

"What's it like, Sam?" Andu asked, seeing the far-off look in his new friend's face.

"What's *what* like?"

"Being a pilot? Living along the river?"

"You should know, Hank—you're a pilot. What's it like living up there among the stars?"

"I guess it's hard to describe unless you've actually been there—unless you've actually done it."

"See? There you go. Same as a riverboat pilot. To most everyone else, the river is just muddy water."

"And space, just a cold vacuum."

"See? It's the same. We're brothers under the skin, you and me. Only difference is, my career's over; yours is just beginning."

"If I can get home, that is. Traveling through time is a bit more complicated than all that."

"What could be more complicated than navigating a river the size of this one? Have you ever seen such power? Such hazards? Lord, Hank, it took me a long time to learn this river. And I was fortunate—I had a good teacher. Horace Bixby. Widely respected and highly-competent. How did you learn about space?"

"You had your Bixby. I had my Fornax."

"Your what?"

"My Fornax—my grandfather."

"Oh, yes, you told me about him. Now tell me about Margaret. Did the medicine you gave her help? Will she be okay now?"

"I'm no doctor, Sam, but I think so. By leaving her with your sister while we run up to Hannibal and back, that'll give her some time to recuperate before the two of us move on. So tell me about this Bixby fellow."

"Don't mind if I do. Started on the river at age 18 as an unpaid 'mud clerk'; I imagine he'll still be on it the day he dies. Most pilots hold just one license; Bixby holds three. One for the Missouri, one for the Ohio, and the third for the lower Mississippi. It was the lower river, the portion from St. Louis to New Orleans, that he was to teach me. There, the traffic is heaviest, and year-round navigation the rule.

"Like I said, I was lucky. I came to the river at precisely the right time. The steamboat business was at its zenith and only beginning to feel the first rumblings of competition from the railroads. Lines of communication still ran north and south, and boats on the Mississippi and her tributaries still carried passengers, corn, and cotton from the Middle West and upper South down to the Gulf, bringing back with them on the return trip foreign luxuries, staple goods, tools, and machinery.

"It was free enterprise at its most anarchic, with every boat for herself. The river, though well-traveled, remained uncontrolled and unimproved throughout its entire length, with not a single beacon light or even a buoy from St. Louis on down to the Gulf! Safety regulations existed, of course—spelled out by the federal government and the insurance companies—but they were enforced haphazardly, or not at all. The traffic itself was hazardous, and the life expectancy of a Mississippi riverboat measured barely four years.

"There were countless ways to destroy or otherwise incapacitate a boat. Running aground was routine, hardly taken seriously except for the time lost unloading her cargo so the boat could float free. Of a much more permanent nature were accidents where a boat was damaged beyond repair. Its bottom could be ripped out in a collision with a snag or a reef or even an abandoned wreck. Sometimes they caught fire. Sometimes they even blew up!"

"I remember you said your brother Henry died that way."

Clemens nodded. "The boats are all wooden. They carry flammable cargo—cotton, hay, turpentine. The furnaces are always lighted; the engineers, often incompetent. Boiler explosions happen all the time. They start fires, and the fires themselves are usually uncontrollable."

"And I suppose all these hazards only added to the romance of piloting?" Andu teased.

"Precisely!" Clemens smiled, a twinkle in his eye. "Though varying widely in size and in luxury, all the boats I steered were of a pattern. They were flat-bottomed sidewheelers, some up to 350 feet long. The flat bottoms reduced their draft, and the side wheels, with their gaily-painted wheelhouses, provided more maneuverability than a single wheel at the stern. The shallow hold would be filled with cargo, while up on the main deck, the furnaces, boilers, and high-pressure engines shared space with more cargo, assorted livestock, and deck-passengers traveling cheaply. Higher still, the misnamed boiler deck accommodated the more genteel travelers. The amenities included nicely-furnished cabins, the ladies' saloon, and the dining room, or main saloon. The degree of grandeur determined a boat's status.

"Above, on the texas deck, stood the glass-enclosed pilothouse. In this sanctum, the pilot reigned supreme. On his skill depended the safety of the boat, its cargo, and her passengers. There was—still is—none better than Horace Bixby. I'll never forget that first trip with him upriver. It was a leisurely voyage of nine days' duration, punctuated with stops at river towns and wood-yards along the way, there to pick up fuel which had been cut from the limitless forests bordering the river. A boat could land anywhere she pleased, even at individual farms or plantations. It simply ran its bow aground and threw a gangplank ashore. The lazily-spinning paddlewheels held the boat in place against the current while passengers either got on or off or cargo was dropped or picked up.

"For me, learning the river meant committing to memory the names, shapes, and locations of countless landmarks: reefs, shoals, islands, points, bends, even individual snags! It meant learning the passages that were safe under any conditions and the 'chutes' that could only be taken when the river was at flood stage. It meant learning the *true* shape of the river, and learning it so well that I could navigate on instinct alone, even through fog or darkness, never mistaking shadow for solid shore. The difficult part for me was that the river wasn't something which could be learned once and forever. Its shape changed constantly, and for many reasons. The river ate away at its own banks. Landmarks appeared and then vanished without a trace. From out of nowhere would come a new bar or a shoal, even a snag. Islands might be washed away overnight. Then again, they might suddenly be joined to the mainland. Entire sections of river might become stranded by cut-offs slicing through a bend in the river. Fact is, a pilot had to constantly *renew* his knowledge. And while essential, even knowledge wasn't enough; a pilot had to have the confidence and courage to judge a new situation and act on it instantly!

"Learning the river would have been an enormous task for any man, and it was almost impossible for me. Ever since I was a little boy, I have always been too impatient, too absent-minded, too easily distracted. That I finally succeeded, proved the strength of my ambition."

"But you must have had your accidents?" Andu remarked.

"Oh, sure, once or twice. Nothing real serious, though. Bixby said I was a good pilot, and I took pride in that. But there *was* this one time."

Though Clemens tried like the dickens to suppress it, a rambunctious grin popped up on his face. Even at this age, his storytelling style combined parody, humor, and personal satire.

"Yes, there was this one time. I was steering the *City of Memphis* under Captain Montgomery. Now there was one tough bird. The man was always cool. Nothing, I mean nothing, could disturb his serenity. On that occasion, I was bringing the boat into port at New Orleans, expecting orders from the hurricane deck at any moment. But none were forthcoming. By then, I had stopped the wheels. There my authority and responsibility ceased. It was evening—dim twilight—and I could see the captain's hat perched up on the big bell. I supposed the intellectual end of the captain was in it, but such was not the case. Unbeknownst to me, the captain was out napping on the texas deck.

"The captain was very strict; therefore, I knew better than to touch a bell without orders. My duty was to hold the boat steady on her calamitous course and leave the consequences to take care of themselves—which I did. The seconds passed and we went plowing past the stern of one steamboat after another, getting closer and closer. The crash was bound to come very soon now—and still that hat never budged!

"Well, by about this time, things were becoming exceedingly nervous and uncomfortable. It seemed to me that the captain was not going to appear in time to see the entertainment. But he did! Just as we were walking into the stern of a big old steamboat, he stepped out on deck and said, with heavenly serenity, 'Set her back on both,' which I did—though a trifle late. We went smashing through that other boat's flimsy outerworks with a most prodigious racket."

"Wow!" Andu exclaimed. "I bet that one cost you!"

"The captain never said a word to me about the matter afterward, except to remark that I had done right, and that he hoped I wouldn't hesitate to act in the same way again under similar circumstances."

Andu burst out laughing.

"Like I said, Montgomery was nothing if not made of steel."

The words drained slowly away. In their place was the wind; the beginnings of a thunderstorm. It possessed an old-fashioned energy which had long been familiar to Clemens, though not to Andu.

The storm blew into the river valley riding a raging wind. The pilot had seen the tempest coming and had already given orders to tie up the boat to the bank. Now, while everyone else stayed below, Sam and Andu watched the progress of the storm from upstairs in the pilothouse. It was at once frightening and exhilarating!

The wind bent the young trees down, exposing the pale undersides of their leaves. The air grew cold. Gust after gust followed in quick succession, thrashing the branches violently up and down and from side to side. The swiftly alternating waves were either green or white depending on which side of the leaf was currently exposed, and they raced after one another like bikers chasing through the last leg of a crosscountry course.

Within seconds, the picture became surreal. No longer were the visible colors entirely natural; the tints had become charged with a leaden-tinge laid down by the solid cloud-bank overhead. The river was leaden, all distances the same. Even the far-off ranks of whitecaps had lost their lustre and were now painted dull-gray, shaded by the dark, electric atmosphere through which their swarming legions marched.

The thunderpeals were constant and deafening. Explosion followed explosion with only the briefest of intervals inbetween. The reports grew steadily sharper and higher-pitched, becoming progressively more trying to the ear. The lightning was as emphatic as the thunder, producing chilling effects which enchanted the eye and sent shock waves of apprehension coursing through every nerve in the body.

Now the rain poured down in amazing volume! The ear-splitting thunderpeals broke nearer and nearer. The wind increased in fury and began to wrench off branches and treetops and send them sailing away through space. The pilothouse set to rocking and straining, cracking and surging. Then, just when it seemed as if it were about to be torn from the boat and flung in the river, the tempest was over, passing as quickly as it had begun!

In the next minutes, the sun peeked through the clouds and a rainbow formed in the sky above their heads. Andu nodded as if he understood. Nothing in the galaxy could quite compare with the power of a summer rainstorm out on the river!

32
Rebel

June 20, 1861

They were a raucous bunch, these Marion Rangers, and Andu didn't know what to make of them. This was no army like he was used to, certainly not like any he'd grown up with during his days as a freedom-fighter back in Afghanistan. No, this was more like a great big campout complete with fishing gear, banjoes, and stories around the campfire!

Union forces had invaded Missouri shortly after he and Sam arrived in Hannibal, and on June 12 Governor Claiborne Jackson issued a proclamation calling out fifty thousand militia to repel the invaders. Clemens, plus more than a dozen of his boyhood friends, had promptly answered the governor's call; though, with Hannibal under control of Union Home Guards, they had had to organize secretly.

Their "battalion" consisted entirely of an irregular squad of young men all about Sam's age, mostly pilots and schoolmates, including Sam Bowen, Ed Stevens, and Ab Grimes. Andu was accepted into the circle without hesitation; any friend of Sam's was good enough for them. They named themselves the "Marion Rangers," after their county, and stole off into the woods, meeting in a secret spot on the slopes of Bear Creek Hill. They elected their officers—common practice in the early days of the war—and marched off into the night.

Sam had been elected second lieutenant, but that counted for little among men who had grown up together, each one firmly convinced he was as good as the next. To a man, these fellows were young, ignorant, good-natured, well-meaning, trivial, full of romance, and given to reading chivalric novels and singing forlorn love-ditties.

The army had a good enough time that first night, marching through the brush and vines on their way towards New London. By morning, though, this sort of thing had grown rather monotonous. When they took a look at themselves by daylight, what with their nondescript dress and their shabby accoutrements, they looked more humorous than patriotic. Nevertheless, they were received cordially in New London by Colonel Ralls, a veteran of the Mexican War. The colonel swore them into Confederate service with an old-fashioned speech full of gunpowder and glory, then belted a sword around the second lieutenant, a sword he himself had worn in the battle with Mexico. Duly fortified, the tiny battalion formed up in a line and marched off to a shady and pleasant piece of woods four miles away. There they took up a strong position with a low ridge of wooded rocky hills behind them and a purling, limpid creek out in front. Promptly, half the command was in swimming, and the other half out fishing.

The picnic atmosphere didn't last long, however. It rained, there were enemy sightings, false alarms, panics, and unnecessary retreats. Each was punctuated by quarrels as the would-be heroes came to see themselves in a less and less heroic light. The "officers" tried to goad the privates into performing various and sundry disagreeable duties—cooking, cleaning up, standing guard—though much of the time they met with limited success. At moments of crisis, of which there were several, the whole company, a little democracy, would hold a council of war.

The men obtained mounts for themselves, which only served to make retreating that much easier. But now that the battalion was a cavalry, they went in search of a new camp. Clemens had a yellow mule named "Paint Brush," but he rode it like a city boy and developed a saddle boil. Then he sprained an ankle leaping out of a barn when the hay the Rangers had been sleeping on caught fire. Now, between the boil and the sprain, he had been rendered useless as a soldier, unable to either walk or ride. For Samuel Clemens of Hannibal, Missouri, the war was over!

But *before* it was over, Andu learned of yet another side to this riverboat man he had befriended. Not only was Clemens a colorful storyteller, he was also a budding writer! Sam had a pocketful of letters, all written under a pseudonym and all published in the New Orleans *Daily Crescent* at one time or another earlier that same spring. Written in the guise of a loutish bumpkin, one Quintus Curtius Snodgrass, the letters satirized Confederate army life with such irreverence, just having them on his person might be considered by some a court-martial offense. Even so, that night as the dozen or so men huddled around the campfire, Clemens held the letters to the flickering light and proceeded to read from them at length.

    Clemens himself was a sight! He looked like a vagabond, what with his four-day-old beard and a bandage wound around his ankle. And he was barely able to move on account of his swollen ankle and equally swollen butt. But now, with the light of the fire dancing off the shiny parchment, he pulled out the first letter, cleared his throat, and began to read. At times, his voice was as comical as the words he'd put down on paper:

    "Hints to Young Campaigners with the Manual of Arms: In entering the drill-room, men should at once seize their muskets and fall in, or try to do so. There will, of course, be a series of hand-to-hand and shoulder-to-shoulder combats as to whom is to get up towards the front of the line, for the space of about half an hour. But it is just as well for the officers not to interfere with this innocent amusement, as by the time the half hour has elapsed, the big men will have beaten and pushed the little men into submission.

    "After the company be formed the men should maintain the strictest decorum, and during the calling of the roll, give their entire attention to the Sergeant. Privates of an economical disposition who are smoking when called to an attention and who are unwilling to throw away an unfinished cigar, may be allowed to moisten the lighted end with their saliva and put it away for another and better opportunity. Should they desire to place it in their cartridge box, they should be careful to thoroughly extinguish the fire, as an explosion would cause much confusion in the ranks.

    "While at an attention the hands and arms should under no pretence be removed from the side, except when necessary to the execution of an order. In coming to an 'order arms,' and particularly should there be strangers watching the drill, great care should be exercised that the muskets be all brought down to the ground at the same moment. Should any man find that he will probably be behind time, it is proper that he should bring the butt down upon his neighbor's foot, which will effectually deaden the sound."

(A hearty round of laughter brought Clemens up short, and for a moment, he forgot all his pains. An admiring audience suited him just fine!)

"In preparing for the tented field, it cannot be too forcibly impressed upon the mind of the young campaigner that if they have any regard for their personal comfort at all, the only number they should not forget is *number one*. Never refuse to eat or drink, for in active service one never knows when he may get another chance. An empty stomach is a poor thing to fight on!

"Before going into action, it is also usual for men to adopt their fatigue dress, not only for the ease and freedom of limb, but because it is certainly a shame and a sin to have bullets put through broadcloth and gold lace, when flannel answers all the purpose.

"It is well for the officers, when their companies are forming up on the eve of an action, to see that the most determined and courageous men be placed to the rear, as when the word 'charge' is given it frequently occurs that the courage and knees of some fail them, and then if the rear-rank men have their orders, they may, by a gentle and continued application of the bayonet, induce the more timid parties in front to advance, thereby saving the credit of the company.

(Again, boisterous laughter. This time, though, Clemens remained deadpan. He was beginning to enjoy the role of orator.)

"Officers who have been married men for any length of time are usually too rash and anxious to throw away their lives and those of their men, and thus should not be put in charge of a skirmish.

"In deploying as skirmishers it is necessary to display all sorts of agility and regard to personal safety by getting behind any tree that may present itself, or by lying on the broad of one's back.

"It is gratifying to privates to know that in these skirmishes their officers are entirely out of harm's way, remaining either with the reserve, or, at all events, so many paces to the rear as to be undiscernible to the naked eye.

"When the bugle sounds a retreat, it is expected that every man will obey the call with alacrity. Remember that discretion is the better part of valor. The time in which boys were wont to fight and conquer giants has long since passed away, and in these degenerate and matter-of-fact days, one who dies for his country when it is entirely unnecessary, and his country hasn't asked him to do so, gets laughed at for his pains.

"In attacking a fortress, it is well to hang back a little. You can be examining the lock of your musket or taking an imaginary stone out of your shoe. Let the eager ones get in first and draw the enemy's fire, after which you may enter with comparative impunity and take your full share of the glory.

"In entering a hostile city, especially where they have riflemen stationed on the housetops, it is wise to keep a sharp lookout lest any of these stuck-up individuals tumble from their airy roosts. Though riflemen are considered light infantry, should one of them land on top of you, you would probably find them decidedly heavy.

"After an action, it is the duty of the officers to prepare a full and accurate list of the killed, wounded, and missing. The term 'missing' is pleasantly and conveniently ambiguous as it may either signify that the individual has been taken prisoner or that he has run away. And should the latter supposition have been the case, it is by no means necessary that his friends and all the world should know of his little indiscretion. A judicious officer will therefore place his name under the appropriate heading."

By now the mood around the campfire had shifted from lightheartedness to solemnity. Andu was no longer paying attention to what Clemens was saying, but was thinking instead of Byron Matthewson. What had actually become of the man? Had he died at Pittsburg Landing like the *Adjutant General's Report* said, or did he desert from the service the way Carina had it figured? Either way it was time. Time for Andu to move one. Time to find Byron. This wasn't Andu's war; this wasn't even Clemens' war. This war belonged to someone else; it was time for *both* of them to move on!

For days already, the tiny battalion had been having a

jolly good time filled with schoolboy antics and juvenile horseplay; but that cooled down decidedly now. In no time at all, the fast-waning fire of forced jokes and crude hilarity died out altogether, and the company became silent. Silent and nervous. And soon, uneasy and worried. Apprehensive.

Every few days the rumor had come, the rumor that the enemy was fast approaching, that he was hovering in the neighborhood. "Let him come!" the more boisterous ones had said. "We are committed!"

But each time the rumors that came turned out to be false, and thus, so far, no one's bravery had ever been tested. Until now.

It was late, and there was a deep, woodsy stillness everywhere. They had bunked down for the night in a big old log-stable, but there, on the forest floor, the veiled moonlight was just barely strong enough for them to mark out the general shape of objects in the dark. Presently, an almost noiseless movement began in the dark as each man in turn, crept to the front wall and pressed his eye at a crack between the logs. One by one they went, their hearts in their throats, each taking their turn staring out beyond the horse-troughs where the forest footpath came through the woods into a clearing.

Suddenly, a muffled sound caught their ears, a sound they recognized as being the hoofbeats of a horse, maybe several horses! Could it be the enemy? they wondered, their hearts racing. Here and now?

As if to answer their frightened questions in the affirmative, a shadowy figure suddenly appeared before them in the forest path. Its shape was so murky and out of focus, so blurred, it could have been made of smoke. The shadowy figure was a man on horseback, and it seemed to Sam and the others that there were more horsemen behind him.

"The enemy!" someone shouted.

Adrenaline is powerful stuff, and in the next instant a half-dozen Marion Rangers got hold of their guns in the dark and pushed them through slender cracks between the logs. Dazed with fright, somebody yelled, "Fire!", and it seemed as if there were a hundred flashes and a hundred reports.

Sam had been one of the ones to pull the trigger, and when he saw the man fall down out of the saddle, his first feeling was one of surprised gratification. Like an amateur sportsman, his first impulse was to run out and pick up his game.

Somebody shouted, "Good—we got him! Wait for the rest!"

But the rest never came.

A long time they waited. And listened. But still no others came.

There was not a sound, not even the whisper of a leaf; just perfect stillness—an uncanny kind of stillness—all the more uncanny on account of the damp, earthy, late-night smells now rising and pervading it.

Then, wondering if the man was still alive, they crept stealthily forward out of their hiding place to take a look.

Up close, the moon revealed him distinctly. He was lying on his back with his arms flung out to either side. His mouth was open and his chest was heaving with long painful gasps. The front of his white shirt was all splashed red with blood.

Clemens was appalled! The thought shot through him that he was a murderer, that he had killed a man, that he had killed a man who had never done him any harm! It was the coldest sensation he would ever feel.

Along with a couple of his buddies, Clemens was down beside him in a moment, helplessly stroking the man's forehead and babbling that they would have given anything, including their lives, to undo the damage and to make the man what he had been only five minutes before. All the boys seemed to feel the same way, hanging over him, full of pitying interest, saying all sorts of regretful things and doing whatever little they could to help console him. In their grief they'd forgotten all about the enemy. All they thought about now was this one forlorn unit of the foe.

Clemens glanced over at Andu for help. But none was offered. Andu had killed before; Clemens never had. Andu knew the face of war; Clemens never would.

The dying man mumbled and muttered like a dreamer in his sleep, about his wife and his child too. That's when Clemens realized that this thing he had done did not end with just this one dead man, it fell upon *them* too—a wife with no husband, a child with no father.

The others would say it couldn't be helped, that he was

killed in fair and legitimate war. But Clemens knew better. The man was not in uniform; he wasn't even armed! This was a part of war Clemens had never figured on.

The thought of that man got to preying upon him—that night, and every night. Clemens could not get rid of it. He could not drive it from his mind. The taking of that unoffending life seemed such a wanton thing. Indeed, it seemed an epitome of war itself, that all war must be just that—the killing of strangers against whom you feel no personal animosity, strangers whom, in other circumstances, you'd be willing to help if you found them in trouble, and who would help you too if you needed it.

Unlike some, Clemens was not mentally equipped for this awful business. War was intended for men, and he was little more than an overgrown child. Fortunately for him, there was a way out, a way he'd known about from the beginning: joining up with his brother Orion to go west! Of all the places in America, only out there, among the savages and the cactus, could he possibly hope to escape the war; of all the places in America, only out there, among the mountains and the high mesas, could he possibly hope to launch a new career, one not already sullied by the memory of the disastrous events just concluded.

Clemens had done his share—killed one man, exterminated one army, as it were. Now someone else would have to go out and kill the rest. For him, the war was over!

33
Orion

June 29, 1861

Governor Claiborne Jackson had been driven to the Arkansas border, Missouri was in Union hands, and Confederate militiamen were free to go home without facing charges of desertion. Brief and inglorious though it might have been (from the standpoint of a Southern patriot anyway), the military career of one Samuel Clemens had come to an end. His days of doubt and hesitation were now over, and soon he would escape to the West to sit out the war in safety. Sam was not alone in this enterprise; indeed, the history of the next generation would largely be written by men who found more pressing things to do in 1861 than fight.

Though Samuel Clemens had resigned from the war, in a bitterly-divided Missouri there wasn't much room for a healthy, single male of twenty-four who preferred to stay neutral. Escape was the only answer, and his hopelessly impractical older brother made it possible.

For perhaps the first time in his life, Orion had been on the winning side and now had influence where it counted. He had campaigned for Abraham Lincoln, and Lincoln's old friend Edward Bates (in whose office Orion had once studied law) had become the new president's Attorney General. For his loyalty, Orion was rewarded with an appointment, that of Secretary to the newly-formed Territory of Nevada. Sam knew Orion had no money for stage-fare, of course, and would look to his younger brother for help. Thus, he and Andu set off together for Keokuk, where Orion lived. From Hannibal, it was a short trip north.

The people of the upper river, as it was called, were somewhat different from those Andu had met below St. Louis, and especially below Cairo. From St. Louis northward there were all the enlivening signs and presence of an active, energetic, intelligent, prosperous, and practical nineteenth-century population. These people weren't dreamers; they were doers. And they were living a wholesome life.

Quincy was a notable example—a brisk, handsome, well-ordered city filled with people interested in art, letters, and other high things. In uncountable ways it had the feel and the aspect of a model New England town—broad, clean streets; trim, neat dwellings and lawns; fine mansions; stately blocks of commercial buildings; ample fairgrounds; a well-kept park; a library; a couple of colleges; some handsome and costly churches; and a grand courthouse with picturesque grounds to match. Keokuk, Iowa, where Orion and his wife and daughter lived, was much the same, only smaller.

Sam had lived and worked there in Keokuk for a year before setting out to be a riverboat pilot. This was nearly five years ago. Unfortunately, he did not have the fondest memories of those days. Working as a typesetter alongside his brother Henry in their brother Orion's printshop for five dollars a week, plus board, Sam found himself trapped in a job without any future. Even at this late date all he remembered were the long hours and the mettlesome bugs. Now, when one lighted on his head and threatened to get tangled in his hair, it dredged up all sorts of old memories. Smiling, he turned to tell Andu the story in that spin-a-yarn voice of his:

"I often worked after-hours in Orion's shop. One night I stood working at the little press until nearly two o'clock in the morning. The air was still and the flaring gaslight over my head attracted every variety of bug known to man. To their credit, they all had the same praiseworthy recklessness about flying into the fire. At first they came in little social crowds of a dozen or so, but it wasn't long before they had increased in number until a religious mass meeting of several millions was assembled on the board before me. The meeting was presided over by a venerable beetle who occupied the most prominent lock of my hair as his chair of state. While he read the minutes of the previous meeting, innumerable lesser dignitaries of the same tribe clustered around him, keeping order, and at the same time endeavoring to attract the attention of the vast assemblage to their own importance by industriously grating their teeth. And the mosquitoes? Lord! Two of them could whip a dog; four could hold a man down—butcher him if help was slow in coming!"

Hearing Sam's tale, Andu couldn't help but laugh. In this particular respect anyway, nothing much had changed in the past five years. Just like that morning a month ago when he and Clemens were hiking north of town, there was no escaping the bugs. For the people of the river it seemed as if the moths and other pests were a perpetual plague, especially during the summer months. It was late June now, and when Andu Nehrengel and recently-retired second lieutenant Samuel Clemens stepped off the boat in Keokuk, the bugs were out in mass, hanging around their faces and making a regular nuisance of themselves. For a moment, Andu thought he'd be sick!

They didn't seem to faze Orion, though; he was still flush with the triumph of his appointment as Secretary. And as Sam expected, the only thing separating Orion from his new post was the price of a ticket west. Fortunately, Sam had saved enough out of his pilot's salary to afford it, and so they struck a bargain. If Orion would agree to overlook Sam's recent brief defection from the Union and appoint him as Orion's own unofficial secretary, Sam would supply the funds for both their overland passages.

The offer was a boon to Orion. He was always eager to forgive, and the money was vitally necessary, for he couldn't possibly swing it on his own.

But it was no less of a boon to Sam. He was undeniably eager to travel. To cross the continent by stagecoach, to see buffalo and Indians, desperadoes and Mormons, mountains and deserts, to reach the land of gold and silver—such a prospect for adventure would have tempted Samuel Clemens even without a war at his heels. Plus, after four uninterrupted years of piloting, he might have been ready for a vacation. As Sam admitted later on, he intended a three-month holiday, thinking that by that time the war would be over and the river open again to traffic.

It was decided almost from the start that Orion's wife and daughter would stay behind in Iowa until a suitable place could be prepared for them out west. That decision made, Orion moved with dispatch. In the briefest possible time he had packed his belongings, meager though they were, including one thing a man of his station could not be without, a large unabridged dictionary. Then Andu and the two brothers were on their way to St. Louis for final leave-taking. If all went well, within days they would set out for that great mysterious land of promise—the American West. It was July 4, 1861.

• • •

Though it had only been a matter of two months since the mutiny, only a matter of eight weeks since Red and the others shamelessly cast him adrift in the runabout, Andu had aged a lifetime. By now he should have learned to expect the unexpected, but nothing in his experience could have prepared him for what was to come next.

The news that Sam, Orion, and Andu were on their way back down river towards St. Louis reached the Moffett household ahead of them. When Sam and Andu first left for Hannibal back in June they said they'd be gone only a matter of days; it had been nearly a month! Up and down the river friends of Sam's had been on the lookout for him since before Independence Day. When he was spotted in Quincy three days ago, news of his sighting had raced to St. Louis on the next boat.

Because Sam himself didn't own a home or even have an address he could call his own, his sister Pamela's house was as much his place as it was hers. Truth was, after so many years out on the river, and after his brief stint as a soldier, it felt good to be home. For her part, Pamela played surrogate mother whenever the opportunity presented itself. Like today.

"Where have you been off to, dear brother?" Pamela exclaimed, casting a disapproving look in Sam's direction as the three men came strolling up the walk. With her hands planted firmly on her hips, she spoke in her best mother hen voice.

"To war and back," Sam answered, grinning from ear to ear.

It was obvious he was still favoring the ankle he'd twisted that day jumping out of the burning barn, but it didn't dull his enthusiasm. Taking his sister's hand in his own, Sam danced a little jig in the front yard. Up on the porch, and looking much better than before they left, was Margaret. He winked at her mischievously.

"What do you mean, to war and back?" Pamela said, stopping Sam in his tracks and looking to Andu for confirmation. He nodded, but remained silent.

"The North won," Sam chuckled, jabbing his brother playfully in the ribs. Though Sam was a Southerner and certainly had no wish to fight against the South, neither did he wish to fight for slavery. What he wanted more than anything else, was not to fight at all!

"I'm to be Orion's secretary," Sam said. "Secretary to the Secretary! In about a week's time, and without any unnecessary delay, he and I are going to a country so new, all human beings, regardless of previous affiliation, are flung into the common melting pot and recast in the general mold of pioneer!"

"I'm going with you," Margaret announced, stunning everyone into silence and putting an end to the carnival atmosphere.

Andu's jaw dropped. It was *this* announcement that he'd been unprepared for. Somehow, ever since that day he landed on Ancòn, ever since that day he found her and made love to her, Andu had always assumed she'd be right there with him every step of the way. It had never occurred to him—not even once—that their lives might lie along separate paths. Even when he went back to the *Tachyon* to get her medicine that day after she came down with scarlet fever, it was in his mind that they would find Byron together. It had even crossed his mind once or twice along the way that given some time, they might be married, maybe start a family. Now, to learn that she was going west with Clemens brought him up short.

"You're *what*?!" he exploded, his face reddening. "Is she out of her head?" he asked, turning to Pamela for help.

"No, that elixir you gave her did the job just fine. The fever passed quickly. What ails her now can't be solved with any old pill."

"What then?" Andu asked, looking to Clemens, hoping he'd try and talk her out of this.

Seeing the exchange, Margaret got vocal. "Now don't try and change my mind, you two! I've had plenty of time to think about this. In any event, Hank and I already had this talk a long time ago, even before we came aboard the *Nebraska*."

Pulling Andu off to one side, she said, "Sweet, sweet, man: I don't know where I belong—or even when. All I know is I don't belong in your world, not six centuries in the future anyway. There's a slim chance though that I might just belong in *this* one. While you were gone, Pamela told me about *my* people. They live in a place called Utah. She also told me that Sam and Orion have to pass through Utah Territory in order to get out to Nevada where he is to be Secretary."

Andu shook his head, as if in disbelief. He wanted to tell her a thousand things, but the words just wouldn't come.

"Please understand," she said. "I simply *must* go west with them. They can leave me off in a place called Salt Lake City."

Andu frowned.

"Now I know what you're going to say, Andu, but it wouldn't be fair if you tried to stop me. After everything we've been through together, I think you owe me that much."

Andu looked at her now with tears in his eyes. He didn't have the heart to say no. Involving her in this entire time-travel escapade had been his idea from the start. And now he was going to lose her!

"I'm not going west," he said, averting his gaze.

"I know," she answered, her tone flat.

"We'll never see each other again," he murmured.

"I know."

"But I love you," he said, taking her hand one last time.

"I know that too," she smiled. "But I'll carry you with me all the days of my life."

Could it be? he thought, his spirits suddenly rising.

Her look said yes.

"Don't worry," she sighed. "I'm sure our Mister Clemens here will protect me from harm." By this time, she had motioned for Sam to come over and join them.

"Whatever the question is, the answer is 'yes'," Clemens quipped.

"I leave her in your capable hands," Andu said, his voice cracking.

"I don't understand," Clemens replied. "You actually want her to go *with* us?"

"I don't see as how I can stop her."

"The West is no place for a woman. And how is she

supposed to pay the fare? It's not cheap you know."

"I'll chip in on that," Pamela piped up. "My husband Will's a prosperous man; we can afford it."

"How can I ever pay you back?" Margaret asked, unaccustomed to such generosity.

"Well, child, you really don't have to. But if you're feeling charitable, I seen that pocketwatch your friend Hank here is toting. And Sam told me what was written on the back of it. I think if Hank's willing to give it up, it might be worth something to those Mormons you're going to see. Maybe you or Orion could put it to good use once you reach Salt Lake. You never know when you may have to buy yourself out of a peck of trouble."

"I guess it's settled then," Clemens said.

Andu nodded, but without conviction. He reached into his pocket and dug out the watch. Turning it over to look at the inscription on the back, he placed it in Sam's outstretched hand.

"Don't worry, Hank. I'll take good care of her," he promised. "I give you my word."

34
The West

July 18, 1861

  The three travelers stood on the dock waiting to board the riverboat *Soux City* for the five-day journey upstream from St. Louis to St. Joseph, Missouri. St. Joe, as it was called, was the jumping-off point for the West. From there they would take an overland coach to their ultimate destination, Carson City. Eleven years later, Samuel Clemens—writing now as Mark Twain—would capture the glamour of that twenty-day journey west in his book *Roughing It*:
  The first thing they did on that glad evening when they landed in St. Joseph was to hunt up the offices of the Central Overland and Pike's Peak Express Company. There, shelling out one hundred and fifty dollars apiece, Sam bought their stagecoach tickets. Then, acting on instructions from their "conductor," they proceeded to ruthlessly pare down their belongings to meet the per person twenty-five pound luggage limit. For Sam and Margaret, it wasn't much of a chore. But for Orion, who was still lugging around that enormously heavy dictionary, it was an impossible task! Left behind were the swallow-tailed coats, the stove-pipe hats, and the patent leather shoes; on went the stogie boots and the rough woolens. Now, they were ready!
  Sam was armed to the teeth with a pitiful little Smith & Wesson seven-shooter. It carried a ball like a homeopathic pill, and it took the whole seven to make a dose for an adult. Still, Sam thought it was grand. To him, it appeared to be a dangerous weapon. It had only but one fault—he couldn't hit anything with

it! One of their conductors practiced with it awhile on a cow, and as long as the animal stood still and behaved herself, she was safe; but as soon as she went to moving about, and he got to shooting at other things, she came to grief. Sam's brother, the Secretary, had a small-sized Colt revolver strapped around his waist for protection against the Indians; though, to guard against accidents, he carried it uncapped.

The coach was soon loaded, and in they climbed. They had with them two or three blankets as protection against frosty weather in the mountains, although in the matter of luxuries they were modest, taking along none save some pipes and five pounds of smoking tobacco. That, plus two large canteens to carry water in between stops and a little shot-bag full of silver coin for daily expenses. They could refill their canteens at way-stations along the way, as well as buy the occasional breakfast or dinner. Such was the sum total of their personal effects.

Thus, on the morning of July 26, 1861, Samuel Clemens and his brother Orion left St. Joseph, sharing their coach with one fellow passenger, twenty-seven hundred pounds of mail, a volume of U.S. statutes to aid the new Secretary in his duties, and a huge unabridged dictionary. In his pocket Sam also carried his total life savings of eight hundred dollars. Had they known, poor innocents, that a dictionary of equal value could be bought in San Francisco on one day and received in Carson City the next, they would have left the ponderous thing behind!

Their coach was a great swinging and swaying affair of the most sumptuous description—an imposing cradle on wheels—and it was drawn by six handsome horses. Alongside the driver sat the conductor, the legitimate captain of the craft, and he was accustomed to giving orders. It was his business to take charge of the mails and the baggage, and to care for the passengers and the express matter. Sam, Margaret, and Orion were the only passengers this trip, and the three of them sat crammed together inside on the back seat. The rest of the coach was filled with mailbags, a great perpendicular wall of them, stacked up to the roof, for they were carrying along with them three days' worth of delayed mails.

Through Kansas and Nebraska they followed the winding Platte River, crossing hundreds of miles of open prairie at a steady eight to ten miles an hour, making a bed of the mailbags at night, and stopping only long enough to change the horses or allow the passengers time to gobble down a meal of slumgullion, prepared no doubt from condemned army bacon.

Heading steadily into the sunset, following it from horizon to horizon over the billowy plains, the trip was an inspiration by day.

By night, however, the passage was decidedly less exhilarating, what with the uneven mailbags for a bed and the bounding dictionary for company. They would stow the unwieldy volume where it would lie as quiet as possible and place the water-canteens and the pistols where they could find them in the dark if the need arose. Then they would smoke a final pipe and swap a final yarn, after which time they would stuff the pipes, the tobacco, and their bag of coin in caves or snug holes among the mailbags, and make the place as dark as a cow's insides—to paraphrase their conductor's more colorful language. All closed up like that, the coach was as dark as any place Clemens had ever been. Nothing, save their own shapeless forms were even dimly visible. Finally, the three of them would roll themselves up like silkworms, each in his or her own blanket, and sink peacefully off to sleep.

Youth loves that sort of thing of course, despite its inconvenience. And sometimes, in the middle of the night, the clatter of the pony express rider would sweep by, carrying letters at five dollars apiece and making the overland trip at double their speed. Just a quick beat of hoofs in the distance, a dash and a hail from the darkness, the beat of hoofs again, and then only the rumble of the stage and the even swinging gallop of the horses.

There was a buffalo hunt while repairs were being made to the coach; an encounter with authentic Westerners, booted and spurred and mustached, with six-shooters at their sides and bowie knives in their boot-tops; and a chilling conversation with a genuine desperado, a killer named Slade, a killer who was later hanged by vigilantes in Montana but who was presently a division superintendent for the stage company.

Each day brought a new adventure. The three travelers witnessed a fistfight between their conductor and a gang of drunken stage-drivers. They were thrilled by a midsummer snow when they crossed the Continental Divide at South Pass. And then, just before arriving in the Great Salt Lake Basin, they met up with a Mormon emigrant train, its members plodding along on foot behind wagons that had come as far in eight weeks as they themselves had come in one.

This would be the last stop for Margaret. After two weeks of dust and sagebrush and jackrabbits and coyotes, they had arrived in Salt Lake City—clean, prosperous, and industrious. With Margaret in tow, Orion paid an official visit to Brigham Young. Young made it his business to show them the city and the life there; Orion, to learn his host's attitude toward secession. This was at President Lincoln's specific request. He needed to know the Mormon take on slavery, and whether or not they would enter the war on the side of the South or remain neutral. The question of statehood had already come up twice—once in 1850 and again in 1856—and now, if Brigham Young could be persuaded to remain neutral, Lincoln would agree to support Utah's petition for statehood next year, in 1862.

To curry Brigham Young's favor, Orion made him a gift of the pocketwatch Andu had given him earlier to help defray the cost of Margaret's ticket west. The words on the back of the watch, "On To Deseret," probably did more to advance the cause of peace in the West than anything Lincoln himself could have ever done or said. As for Margaret, she was happy either way. For the first time in her life, she was among her own. Here, she would stay.

Then they were off again—Sam and Orion—this time wisely taking along their own provisions. Writing years later as Mark Twain, Clemens said, "Nothing helps scenery quite like ham and eggs. Ham and eggs and after these a pipe—an old, rank, delicious pipe—ham and eggs and scenery, a 'down' grade, a flying coach, a fragrant pipe, and a contented heart—these make happiness. It is what all the ages have struggled for."

As the coach rolled west from Salt Lake City, plowing through the deserts of alkali and sand, the passengers often walking behind to relieve the horses, the war must have seemed very far away indeed. On that last stretch, they saw their first Indians—treacherous, filthy, and repulsive. Then, on August 14, the twentieth day out, they reached Carson City, miniature capital of the new territory and Orion's new home.

But all of this was yet to come, for they stood now on the dock in St. Louis waiting to board the riverboat *Soux City* for the five-day journey upriver to St. Joseph, Missouri. There were goodbyes to be said and best wishes to be offered. With regard to Margaret, Andu was at a loss for words. Her mind was made up, and *he* had a mission to complete. He kissed her on the cheek and patted her on the bottom for good luck. Then Clemens pulled him aside.

"I suppose, dear space-traveler, that it is a little presumptuous of me to offer advice, but I mean to anyway, as I often find myself a good judge of character. I am leaving the war behind; you are just entering it. I am content with this world; you will eventually be going back to yours. How should one take life, I ask? Here, let me tell you:

"Take it just as though it were an earnest, vital, and important affair, because it surely is. Take it as though you were born to the task of performing a merry part in it, as though the world had awaited your very coming. Take it as though it were a grand opportunity to do and achieve, to carry forward great and good schemes, to help and cheer a suffering, weary, even heartbroken brother. Now and then a man stands aside from the crowd, labors earnestly, steadfastly, confidently, and straight-away becomes famous for wisdom, intellect, skill, greatness of some sort. The world wonders, admires, idolizes, and it only serves to illustrate what others might do if they take hold of life with a purpose. The miracle, or the power that elevates the few, is to be found in their industry, their application, and their perseverance under the promptings of a brave and determined spirit."

Andu nodded his understanding with a smile, then they shook hands warmly and Samuel Clemens bid him adieu. They would never set eyes on one another again.

PART III

35
Byron

New Year's Day: January 1, 1862

For Byron Matthewson of Trivoli, Illinois, the call to arms had come late. Not late as in he was too old, for he was only 22, but late as in the War Between The States had already been in progress for eight months before he decided to answer its call.

Byron was a reluctant warrior, pushed to join by his mother and by his minister. But then she really wasn't his mother; nor was Jim Hitchcock actually a minister. *His* mother was dead, had been for twenty years, and the minister, well he was nothing but a blowhard. Indeed, not a Sunday went by that he didn't stop to remind young Byron after church that his own son Frank had joined up months ago already. But then how could Byron forget? There had been a big to-do at the church that September day, complete with firecrackers popping and big drums beating. But Byron hadn't been impressed, not in the least. Frank was a fool if ever he'd met one, and his father the minister, a bigger one still.

The Reverend Hitchcock had preached that day about duty and honor and all those sorts of things, but never once breathed a word about blood or sweat or tears. He had railed at the top of his voice for fifteen minutes about devotion to flag and to country, but had said nothing at all about death or dismemberment. He had gone on and on about bravery and heroism, but never said a thing about laying waste to humble homes with a hurricane of fire or of slaughtering innocent woman with their babes at their breast. As far as Byron was concerned, it was all a big lie, every syllable Hitchcock had uttered!

Byron's mother, Dorothy Thompson, would have understood, but then she was already dead, having died when he was still very, very young. *This* woman, this Betsy Holcom as everyone called her, was a New Yorker; and everyone knows how patriotic *they* are—especially when it came to spilling someone *else's* blood! No, Byron really didn't want to go, but his dad was too old, and his brother Charlie, at age twelve, was too young: It had to be him. Trouble was, Byron's thoughts were everywhere but here.

Ever since his cousin had sent him that clipping from the Keokuk *Gate City*, Byron had had it on his mind to go west rather than enlist in this here civil war. Two months already and still he hadn't been able to get that fella's haunting words out of his brain. What was his name? Well, it was printed right here on the bottom of the clipping. The man, one Samuel Clemens, had written a letter to his momma from Carson City out in the Nevada Territory. The letter was dated October 26, 1861, and—with Jane Clemens' permission—had been published in the *Gate City* on November 20. Byron had read it aloud so many times already, the paper was beginning to tear at the folds:

```
Dear Mother:
        You asked me in your last to tell you
about the country--to tell you everything just
as it is--no better and no worse--and to let
nonsense alone. Very well then, ma, since you
wasted a considerable portion of your life in
an unprofitable effort to teach me to tell the
truth on all occasions, I will repay you by
dealing strictly in facts just this once, and by
avoiding that "nonsense" for which you seem to
entertain a mild sort of horror.
        . . . it never rains here, and the dew
never falls. No flowers grow here, and no green
thing gladdens the eye. The birds that fly over
the land carry their provisions with them. Only
the crow and the raven tarry with us. Our city
lies in the midst of a desert of the purest, most
unadulterated and uncompromising sand. Nothing
but that fag-end of vegetable creation, the
```

sagebrush, is mean enough to grow in such infernal soil. To understand what it would be like to travel through a sagebrush desert, take a lilliputian cedar tree for a model and build a dozen imitations of it with the stiffest article of telegraph wire you can find. Then, set them one foot apart and try to walk through them. Provided the floor is covered twelve inches deep with sand, you get the idea. When crushed, sagebrush emits an odor which isn't exactly magnolia and isn't exactly polecat, but a sort of compromise between the two. It looks a good deal like greasewood and is probably the ugliest plant that was ever conceived.

I said we are situated in a flat, sandy desert. True. And surrounded on all sides by such prodigious mountains that when you stand at a distance from Carson and gaze up at them awhile, and--by mentally measuring them and comparing them with things of smaller size--you begin to conceive of their grandeur and to feel their vastness expanding your soul like a balloon, ultimately, to find yourself growing, and swelling, and spreading into a colossus--I say when this point is reached, you look disdainfully down upon the insignificant village of Carson, reposing like a cheap print away down yonder at the foot of the big hills, and in that instant you are seized with a burning desire to stretch forth your hand, put the city in your pocket, and walk off with it.

. . . When my old friends ask you how I like Nevada, what reply shall you make? Tell them I am *delighted* with it! Tell them it is the dustiest country on the face of the earth; but then I rather like dust. And the days are very hot; but you know I am fond of hot days. And the nights are cold; but one always sleeps well under blankets. And it never rains here; but I despise a country where rain and mud are fashionable. And there are no mosquitoes here; but then everyone knows I can get along without them.

When my old friends ask you how I like Nevada, ma, tell them I never liked any country so well before; and my word on it, you will have told them the truth.

. . . For the present, good-bye.

S.L.C.

Carefully folding the newspaper clipping in half and then in half again, Byron slipped it into the back pocket of his coveralls. Outside, the January wind was howling.

Could anything be worse than an Illinois winter? And to think that it wasn't even half over yet! Just the thought of two more months of snow made him tighten up inside and shiver. Could this place called Nevada really exist? he wondered, trying to imagine the hot, desolate land Clemens had described. What was a desert like anyway? All Byron had ever seen was prairie. Forests and river and prairie. Hot and humid in the summer. Cold and damp in the winter. Like today.

And just what kind of soldier would he make anyway? It was anybody's guess. Byron had never killed anything in his life; nothing, that is, that couldn't be eaten. But then a squirrel gun wasn't quite the same as a musket, was it? And when it was all said and done, what difference would it make? Everyone agreed the war would be over soon—four or five months at the outside— and then he would go. Pack up his things, and go west. Get away from his mother. And his fears. And his loathing. Go where no lines had yet been drawn; where land was for the asking.

Yes, that's what he would do! Take the wagon into town next week, and join up. And when it was all over, by May or by June, he would head west!

• • •

For an unmarried young woman, Utah was a lonely place; for an unmarried, *pregnant* young woman, Utah was a nightmare.

Margaret had no family—none whatsoever—and in this

land women were practically second-class citizens, beholden to their men—nothing at all like she had been led to believe. Here, men regularly took two or three wives, if they could afford it, but scarcely any one of them cared to be around a fallen woman like herself.

The man Orion had left her with, Brigham Young, wanted nothing to do with her once he discovered she was with child. She fit the Mormon "look" okay, and that's why Young had taken her in, but anything less than a virgin didn't fit his master plan and in no time at all he had her shipped off to a place that was little more than a convent.

Margaret hated it there and promptly ran away. Then, lost and alone, she wandered around for weeks until finally, in September, she was taken in by an industrious, Mormon frontier family, the Parkers. Childless themselves, the Parkers had agreed to feed and house her, at least until the baby was born. And so it had remained. Until now.

Though Margaret wasn't due for another month yet, she was already beginning to feel the weight of giving birth to a bastard child in a world where gunslingers and lawless bandits roamed free. And if that weren't enough, this thing called winter was taking a terrible toll on her. Margaret was depressed.

Nothing in her experience could have prepared her for a January in North America. Ancòn got cold, but never like this. Ancòn had its blustery nights, but nothing to compare with a Utah blizzard. From time to time, in the higher elevations of Ancòn, there would be frost. But never snow. And certainly not feet of it! No, winter here on Earth was an abomination! Short days, gray skies; when would it ever end?

Again Margaret fought back the tears. What she wouldn't have given for Andu's comforting touch or for Samuel Clemens' neighborly smile. If only she had a man, if only she had a companion, everything would be okay. Margaret had said as much to Mrs. Parker—Minnie, she liked to be called—just the other day. It hadn't gone well.

Minnie had turned out to be a miserable, small-minded woman, not at all sympathetic to Margaret's plight. The most she could offer was to take the child herself and raise it as her own, but only if Noah himself agreed and only if she herself was unable to get pregnant in the months ahead. The two of them tried every night, Minnie and Noah, and it made Margaret sick, their tired grunting noises in the dark, but where was she to go? The cabin only had two rooms.

Minnie was obviously jealous of Margaret's fecundity, and if given half a chance, would probably have changed her mind about taking Margaret in in the first place. Then too, Noah had begun to eye her in a way that made Margaret feel uncomfortable. If she could have left at this late date she probably would have. But where was she to go? What was she to do? Margaret couldn't raise the child alone, not out here on the frontier. The child needed a father. She herself needed a husband. Maybe Minnie was right after all. Maybe, for the sake of the child, she *should* give it to them to raise. Maybe the last name Parker beat no last name at all.

Maybe.

36
Glimpse

January 2, 1862

According to the "Muster and Descriptive Roll, Regiment of Illinois Volunteers," page 15, John G. Lawrence of Brimfield, Illinois, enlisted in the Eleventh Cavalry, Company B, on January 2, 1862. This, Andu Nehrengel knew because he had spent the past three weeks learning all there was to know about the Civil War, and about the United States of America in the latter half of the nineteenth century.

It only made good sense to do so. After Sam and Margaret left for the West with Orion, what was he *supposed* to do? Twiddle his thumbs for five and a half months, waiting around until Byron showed up in Peoria to enlist? Sit around playing poker and swatting flies until the ten months had passed and it was time for Byron to die? Not hardly! Andu Nehrengel was a proactive person; sitting around waiting for someone else to die wasn't exactly his cup of tea. The only catch was, to learn about the past meant journeying into the future. But not *too* far into the future: he didn't want to accidentally get lost!

Time-travel was an inexact science, this much he already knew. Nevertheless, with each jump he made, Andu was getting better at it. He went ahead to the turn of the century, and from that vantage point read about the past. It wasn't pretty.

This Civil War of theirs had turned out to be a titanic struggle far worse than anything Andu could have ever imagined; certainly far worse than anything his little Afghanistan had ever endured. It was like a giant poker game, this war, a game in which both sides had decided to bluff, and in which both sides had had their bluff called. Something on the order of a million dead, perhaps three times that many wounded. Brother against brother at every turn. A great nation torn asunder. And one of the worst battles of all, was the battle at Pittsburg Landing, the Battle of Shiloh.

Andu quickly realized that if he was to have any prayer whatsoever of rescuing Byron from this horrible calamity, of getting him out alive and back to the future intact, he would have to be right there on the battlefield beside him. *He would have to enlist in the same unit!* Thus, the "Mustering Report of Illinois Volunteers."

John G. Lawrence of Brimfield, Illinois, was recorded there as having enlisted in the Eleventh Cavalry, Company B, on January 2nd, 1862, just six days before Byron Matthewson himself enlisted. In the case of John G. Lawrence, the Mustering Report was devoid of details—no physical description, no age, no address. As far as Andu could tell, John G. Lawrence was just an unimportant nobody. And today, January 2nd, 1862, Andu was going to take his place. All he had to do was transport the man to another time, perhaps another place. This, Andu had already done, depositing the bewildered fellow in 1901.

What would become of John Lawrence? How would he manage in the year 1901? These were questions Andu had asked himself.

The answer? Andu didn't know, and what's more, he didn't care. And why should he? According to the Mustering Report, John G. Lawrence would not live out the year. So, in a way, Andu was doing the man a favor. As for himself, knowing the danger he was walking into, if Andu had had any brains, he would have just walked away right then and there. Forgotten about Byron, forgotten about repairing his defective DNA, zipped out west to pick up Margaret, then gone home with her to raise babies. But he couldn't.

Andu knew without being told that if he snatched up Byron at any other time than at the Battle of Shiloh, if Byron didn't "die" a hero the way history said he would, that the entire Matthewson line might be changed in an unpredictable, and perhaps terrible way. Chaos theory practically guaranteed it. Small perturbations led to unknown consequences. And then there was the Grandfather Paradox. If he wasn't there the first time, he couldn't have been there the second. No, Andu had to see it through. He had to scoop Byron up from the battlefield, and he had to do it in such a way that the man would be listed as a casualty, just as history had recorded it.

His trip to the "future" was a busy one. Besides dropping off John Lawrence in 1901 and digging up some information on the Civil War, Andu did one other thing—plotted a speed course back to his own time. When the moment came for him to return home, he wanted the shortest possible route already keyed into the computer. Travel through hyperspace was nothing if not tricky, and after he'd come all this way Andu wasn't about to risk leaving anything to chance. For all he knew, Byron might be wounded and near death when he found him. Just in case, Andu wanted to have virtually everything in place so that at the last minute all he would have to do was punch a button and, whoosh, he'd be on his way home. Only there was one little problem.

The question had been nagging at him ever since he and Margaret first landed back in May of 1861, a full *year* off their intended mark. How could he have been so wrong? How could he have missed his target by as much as one year out of six hundred? Sure, time-travel lacked the precision of say, laser surgery, but the mistake itself was just too big, even granting that the pulsar they'd chosen as a metronome didn't keep a constant beat. No, he had missed something important, or rather Brigham Young XIV had. And it was not until Andu sat down at the ship's controls to plot a speed course back home that it occurred to him what that something was.

Just as the time-curves were themselves symmetrical either side of light-speed, so too must gravity observe a certain symmetry where light-speed was concerned. That is, at subluminal speeds—speeds below the speed of light—every object with a mass attracts every *other* object with a mass. Which is to say, gravity bends motion in the direction of the mass, if only slightly. But if we've learned nothing else in the last thousand years of searching for the truth, it is that the Universe is built on a series of astonishing symmetries. What that means in this context is that at *supra*luminal speeds, what was once positive ought to now be negative. What was once a pull, ought to now become a push; what was once a plus, ought to now become a minus. Thus, above the speed of light, gravity would no longer be a force for attraction, it would be a force for *repulsion*! Every object with a mass would repel every *other* object with a mass! Now, admittedly, the differences would be slight. Pull or push, gravity is a weak force to begin with. Then too, it wouldn't have much time to reveal itself, not at the speeds Andu would be traveling at anyway. Even so, the differences, while slight, would be enough to throw off his calculations a few parts of a percent.

Andu's insight into the problem was brilliant, and in more ways than one. Not only did it hold out the prospect of making time-travel less error-prone, it also offered up the possibility of making it that much less dangerous. If, instead of an attractant the force of gravity was a *repellent* above light-speed, the likelihood of a collision with an unknown or unseen object was sharply reduced.

And it was a good thing too, because although astronomers had catalogued with some precision the position of nearly every star in our sector, what they *hadn't* catalogued, what they knew practically nothing about, were the tens of thousands of asteroids orbiting around each of those stars, not to mention the millions of comets and untold numbers of black bodies. Hitting just one of these unseen objects at light-speed would destroy the ship and everything in her in under a trillionth of a second. And while the laws of chance unquestionably operated in Andu's favor—space, after all, was so huge that the chance of striking *any* object larger than a grain of dust was vanishingly small—luck wasn't good enough. Given enough trips, it was a catastrophe waiting to happen!

Now though, thanks to Andu's insight, the risk parameters had changed. Now he knew better. *Now he knew that the chances of collision were zero*! Nada. Nothing. The ship and any sizable object in her path would repel one another. They would tend to move apart, allowing the ship and her crew safe passage!

Although by this realization the trip had become infinitely safer, it hadn't become any easier. The last thing Andu had set out to do while he was in the future was to learn what had become of Margaret. If he had understood her meaning correctly in their last conversation together before she left, Andu had become a father sometime in February, 1862. But nothing he could learn during his brief stop in 1901 to drop off John

Lawrence could tell him anything about her—or his child. The few records he did find were spotty and incomplete, not helpful at all. But then he didn't have much to go on. For all he knew, she'd married somewhere along the line and changed her name. Even when they were together, Hoolehan was just an alias.

Although Andu was sorely tempted to try and find her, to try and make contact with her there in the future, he didn't dare. She might be dead, for all he knew. At the very least, she'd be an old woman some sixty years of age. Lord, even his son or daughter would be forty years old—older than he was now! For all he knew, *they* might have children. Talk about a Grandfather Paradox! He wasn't prepared for such an eventuality.

Nevertheless, on another level, Andu had come to a momentous decision. If he succeeded, if he found Byron and got him safely back to the future, he would return for her as soon as possible.

And why not? Margaret had a sort of ability which was rare in men and hardly existent in women—the ability to say a humorous thing with the perfect air of not knowing it to be humorous.

There was no getting around this. She was, after all, the woman he loved!

37
Desperate

February 12, 1862

What would motherhood be without a husband? Or childhood without a father? The time was at hand, and still she had no answers!

Margaret knew Andu wouldn't come; not that he *wouldn't*, but that he couldn't. She had hoped that perhaps Clemens would. They had exchanged letters once, back in December, and she had practically begged the man to marry her. But he wouldn't hear of it and had politely refused. She wasn't his problem, after all, and all he wanted was to get rich quick, mining for silver up there in the mountains of Nevada. Until he'd made his fortune he didn't even want to *talk* marriage, not to her nor to anyone else!

"It shouldn't be too long now," he wrote, "and some of my claims will be paying handsomely."

When she asked whether she could at least come visit him, he said no. He was dirt poor, and until he could afford to entertain a woman in "high-tone" style, he didn't want any woman guests. And as for marriage, it was totally out of the question until he had plenty of money. Clemens even went so far as to describe what he meant by living in "high-tone" style:

"A married woman deserves to have a house fit to live in—-and servants to do her work. You know it is all very well for a man's wife to talk about how much work she *can* do, but actually *doing* it is a thing that doesn't suit my notions.

That part of the business belongs to the servants. I am not married yet, and I never *will* marry until I can afford to have servants enough to leave my wife in the position for which I designed her, namely, as a *companion*. I don't want to sleep with a three-fold Being who is cook, chambermaid, and washerwoman all rolled into one. I don't mind sleeping with female servants as long as I am a bachelor (to the contrary, I enjoy it!), but *after* I marry, that sort of thing will be 'played out,' you know. No, Madam, I am anxious for you to stay put just where you are until the first July *after* the Millenium!"

Margaret was crushed, and the tears flowed. Sam had been her last, best hope for salvation. With but days to go now before the baby was due, and no husband in sight, Margaret began to panic. What good could come of a bastard child? And even if she gave up the child to the Parkers, what kind of parents would they make? Noah was a brute and Minnie a nagging witch. Was having a last name for her baby worth the risk of subjecting him to them?

• • •

The idea had come to her in the days following the delivery. She had seen it as if in a dream. The trip back across the prairie, the trip back downriver from St. Joe, the arrival in St. Louis at the Moffett house. But at that point the vision got blurry. After St. Louis, what then? She knew Andu meant to find Byron onboard the steamship *Decatur* in May of this year, but how would *she* get there? What would he be up to until then? And where?

It was all so confusing. All Margaret wanted from life now was for her and Andu to get back together again. But could she make it across the prairie alone? A single woman with no money, no friends? Clemens had warned her not to try.

A pretty girl like her, alone, in a wagon, was taking an awful chance, he said. Orion's wife Mollie had begged her husband to let her come out to Carson City on her own, and join him there now that he was settled in, but he'd refused—and with good reason. The trip crosscountry was long and hazardous, especially for a woman. Clemens was present when Orion wrote his wife back, and what he said applied every bit as much to Margaret as it did to Mollie:

> Traveling across the plains sometimes develops the damndest in people. But of all the ways of traveling for a woman, the very last I have even tried is a stage. Half the time for three weeks it will be so dark in the stage you can't see your hand before you. The stage is rolling and tumbling, you may be asleep, your man company awake, but pretending to be asleep. His hand wanders over you. If you catch him he snores or yawns sleepily, and you don't know whether he was asleep or awake. They say the worst enemy a woman has is *opportunity*, and if I didn't know you to be incorruptible, I would be almost doubtful whether to sleep with you or not, if you came three weeks of dark nights, through a wilderness, with only a man acquaintance.

But for Margaret, traveling by stage wasn't really a choice. There was only one way of getting east, and if traveling as a woman was too dangerous, maybe she'd have better luck traveling as a man!

She looked at herself in the mirror and laughed. Then she looked down at her chest and laughed even harder. Hah! Me pass for a man? With breasts like these? Swollen up to twice their normal size with milk? Not a chance! A very fat man, then? In a big, winter coat? Maybe.

And how would she pay the fare?

Maybe she'd just have to reprise her role as poker player extraordinaire; only this time not as Margaret Hoolehan, greenhorn from back East, but as say, Edgar Jenkins, high roller from Salt Lake City. Yes, it just might work! All she'd have to do is steal a grubstake from the Parkers, kiss the baby goodbye, and set off for St. Louis.

But would Andu understand, she wondered, or would he be angry? This question weighed heavily on her mind in the days before she left. She would, after all, be abandoning their boy. *His* boy! But couldn't the two of them come back for him together later on?

Alone, she was powerless against the Parkers. They wanted the boy for themselves, had in fact already given him a proper Mormon name—Robert Leroy Parker. They'd throw her out soon enough anyway—or worse. So why not leave of her own accord? Yes, that made sense. Andu might be angry, but he couldn't fault her logic.

Margaret knew how to find her way back to the Moffett's all right, but how to proceed from there? How could she find her way onto the steamship *Decatur*? As a nurse perhaps? A volunteer to aid the wounded? Yes, but how would she go about finding the boat itself? What route did it run? What stops did it make? Who was its pilot? There was no way for her to know!

The woman was just about ready to give up the whole scheme without ever really trying, when it occurred to her that Pamela Moffett would know! Sam had friends all up and down the river. Some of them still piloted boats for the North. Indeed, some of them made their home right there in St. Louis! The boat she had met Sam on, the *Nebraska*, had been piloted by a man who lived just down the street from the Moffett's, Zebulon Leavenworth. Surely, *he* could help her!

Her mind made up now, Margaret gathered the boy to her breast. There would be no looking back. As soon as the baby was stronger. As soon as the weather broke. Then she would go!

• • •

The soldiers broke camp on February twenty-second and marched from Peoria, Illinois, to a place in Missouri called Benton Barracks. They arrived there on March third. It was a cold, brutal march and the Eleventh Cavalry was four men shorter by the time they arrived. It wasn't that the horses they'd been given were poor—to the contrary, they were good steeds—it was that the men who rode them were not equally good riders. To begin with, most of the enlistees were unaccustomed to the sheer length of the ride. But then also, the trails they had to follow in the snow were not so well defined. Back during basic training at Camp Lyon in Peoria, they'd been taught several useful things, but how to handle a horse on an icy slope was not one of them. That sort of accident accounted for two of their losses to date. The other two were straight-up defections, horse and all.

When they left Peoria to head south, it had only been a month-and-a-half since Byron joined up, yet already he felt awfully alone. Granted, Frank Hitchcock was there from his hometown, but Byron didn't like him much, and it seemed the feeling was mutual. Three others from Trivoli were there as well, and Byron knew them all: Robert Jones, age 45, brown hair, blue eyes, dark complexion, and old enough to be his father. Hardly the sort Byron could get close to. Then there was John Kimsey, age 21, and dumber than a brick. Last but not least, John Manning, age 20, nice fellow but dangerously gung-ho. Johnny didn't much care whether or not he lost a leg so long as he got to kill some damn Southerners.

No, none of these men were the sort Byron wanted to share a beer with, much less a foxhole. He had met one fella though, a strange dark-complexioned fella from Brimfield named John Lawrence. They had become friendly. Even joked with him that he had two first names, John and Lawrence. But then, in his own way, John Lawrence himself was an outcast. Maybe it was 'cause of his dark skin. The man wasn't Negro-dark, mind you, not like a slave, but he certainly was a lot darker than anything the local crop of farmboys had ever seen. This had gotten him into trouble back at Camp Lyon and was about to again.

It began as they were unloading the horses after the long trip down from Peoria. One of the recruits who was already there in camp, a big Italian-looking fellow from St. Louis, came up from behind John Lawrence and started to pick a fight.

"What, we got niggers joining up with us now?" the big man said, shoving Andu as hard as he could.

The shove caught Andu off guard, and he lost his footing in the mud. Kicking and swearing as he went down, Andu landed spread-eagle on the ground at the man's feet.

"What the hell? Have you lost your mind?"

The big man laughed.

This made Andu angry.

Slowly getting to his knees, he turned to face the man. Though his hands were cold and wet, Andu's cheeks were red with anger.

In any other situation, he might have pulled out Jenny and vaporized this buffoon on the spot. Instead, Andu suddenly reached out with one hand and yanked the man's legs out from under him.

The bully fell to the ground, his back making a hard slapping sound against the wet mud as he fell. He gasped for air, his breath having been knocked out of him.

In the next instant, John Lawrence was on top of the man, his hands at his throat, ready to squeeze.

The bully struggled to get free, but John Lawrence had a firm grip and wouldn't let him loose.

"Don't judge a man by the color of his skin," Andu said, suddenly realizing that whatever else it might be about, this Civil War wasn't about abolishing slavery. "If I ever hear you use that word again in my presence, whether you're talking about me personally or someone else, I'll kill you. Understand?"

Without waiting for an answer, Andu got up off the prone man and went back to finish grooming his horse. While he worked, Byron kept a steady eye on the other man until he got up and quietly disappeared into another part of the camp. Excitement over, he turned to lend John Lawrence a hand.

The look on Byron's face said it all. Even though his new friend was covered in mud, it didn't seem to faze the man. Byron was impressed. John Lawrence had a mental toughness about him that raised Byron's own flagging spirits. Ever since he'd joined this man's army, friends had been hard to come by. It wasn't so much that people were *un*friendly—because that was hardly the case—it was more that people were scared. And not to show their fear, they didn't show anything at all. Byron had had a girl like that once, a fiery young redhead whose family had moved to Illinois from Kentucky. She couldn't admit what she felt and so it hadn't worked out. Hell, if only it had he might not be standing here today!

And yet, he *was* standing here. Standing in the Missouri mud outside a place called Benton Barracks. What little he knew about the place he'd learned from Colonel Ingersoll on the ride down here. It could be summed up in just a few short sentences:

Benton Barracks was a training center for federal troops being readied for war; a place just west of the St. Louis fairgrounds where raw recruits would be armed with revolvers and sabres, and some even issued carbines; a place large enough to house and feed up to twenty-three thousand men at one time. In two or three weeks, when the ground thawed and the rivers were clear of ice, they would all be going south—and then north again. Down along the Mississippi River, then up the Ohio. To the mouth of the Tennessee. And then deep into Confederate territory to capture a railcrossing.

Byron was scared. And cold. But this John Lawrence fella seemed to have no fear. It was as if he had done this all once before, as if he knew exactly what to expect, as if someone had told him ahead of time how it would all turn out!

Nothing could be further from the truth, of course, but Byron had to keep reminding himself of that. All John Lawrence would say was, "Keep close to me, and you'll be okay." Byron would laugh and promise, and then John would say it all over again. Brave words for a man his size.

They say farmboys make good soldiers, but Byron had his doubts. These fellas lined up on the parade ground didn't seem to care much about slavery either way. All they cared about was saving the Union, and some weren't even sure about that!

Why had they joined then, if there was so much doubt? How had Colonel Robert G. Ingersoll of Peoria been able to raise twelve full companies of volunteers back in central Illinois?

The man was a good talker, for one. Everyone expected the war to be over by planting time, for another. And then there was the obvious. Winter in Peoria, this year or any other year, was long, wet and cold. Who wouldn't jump at a chance to escape it?

So here he was, freezing his hindside off, trying to learn how to be a soldier. Had he any idea what lay just ahead, Byron would surely have deserted right then and there!

38
On To War

Someone once said that war was the continuation of politics by other means. This was undoubtedly the case with the American Civil War. Not for another five hundred years—until the Great War—would more American blood be spilt for less reason. And Byron Matthewson and John Lawrence were caught right smack in the middle of it.

On March twenty-fifth, the Regiment of Illinois Volunteers proceeded to the Tennessee River where, on April 1, the First Battalion landed at Crump's Landing. The balance of the Regiment went ashore the same day at Pittsburg Landing on the west bank of the Tennessee River about ten miles above Savannah. They camped inland about two miles from where they put in. The Third Battalion, which included Byron and John's Eleventh Cavalry, encamped upstream on the north side of Snake Creek.

Knowing what he did about what was to come, Andu was amazingly calm. The losses would be staggering! In a mere two days of fighting, 13,000 Union troops and 11,000 Confederate soldiers would be lost. More than the combined total American casualties from the Revolutionary War, the War of 1812, and the Mexican War! And for what? Under five square-feet of ground!

Ridiculous, you say? If only it were.

Andu had been to the future, 1901 to be precise, and he had read the history books. Just before the turn of the century, Congress had authorized that a national military park be established here at the battlefield of Shiloh. Andu had been there, at the actual park. He had walked from monument to monument, from grave marker to grave marker. He had read the accounts. He had studied the time-lines. He had memorized the troop movements. He knew what lay ahead.

And what lay ahead was only one of the most brutal, most gruesome, most horrific battles of all time! Shiloh set the teeth and clenched the fist of the defenders of the Union. There, on the rolling, deeply-ravined fields of Shiloh, a great battle would be fought—and won—for the Union cause. On each side, great men would lead armies of youthful volunteers against one another, and after two days of struggle, one brave army would be sent whirling back along the road towards its stronghold at Corinth. When it was over, the Confederacy would be jammed back, and the Union army would be on the move, advancing south into Mississippi and vying for control of the nation's greatest waterway.

But it *wasn't* over; it had barely begun! There was still the small matter of those five square-feet of ground.

The Battle of Shiloh, fought April 6 and 7, 1862, was one of the great battles of history. It was a battle fought at such proximity as to rival the closeness of conflicts in medieval times, a battle where artillery duels were fought at simple musket range and where regiments and brigades of raw recruits showed in desperate struggle with one another what American courage really was.

To stand and fire, to fall back, rally and fall back again; to fire with comrades dropping all around you, then to close ranks, the few remaining touching elbow to shoulder, and then to fire again; this was the method, these were the tactics, which won the day. Shiloh was a battle fought on a rough, wooded plateau, up and down deep gullies, and amid thick underbrush and heavy timber. It was a battle saved only at the eleventh hour, and one so potent in its results that it very likely changed the entire course of the war!

As the year 1862 opened, the Confederacy was in command of practically every inch of territory south of the Ohio River. Its line of defense extended east and west across the state of Kentucky, from just below Cairo, Illinois, in the west to well beyond Bowling Green in the east. Directing this army was one of the ablest commanders the South would ever produce—General Albert Sydney Johnston. Fiery, impetuous, and magnetic, Johnston wanted nothing better than to throw himself and his combined brigades against the Union army. Under him were legions of capable officers, and together they'd seen to it that every strategic

MAP 1: THEATER OF OPERATIONS

UNION TROOPS
CONFEDERATE TROOPS

Scale in Miles

point was not only well-fortified, but garrisoned with heavy forces as well. Knowing that the North had but one plausible route open to them for an invasion of the region, Johnston had already moved months ago to foreclose that possibility.

The Tennessee and Cumberland rivers ran north and in a general sort of way, parallel to one another, emptying into the Ohio River at about the height of Paducah, Kentucky. Fear of their ascent by war vessels and an accompanying land force had prompted the Confederates to erect two forts, one on each river, at a point where the two waterways were but twelve miles apart, and where a force from one could be readily used to reinforce the other. Those defenses were Fort Henry on the Tennessee and Fort Donelson on the Cumberland. However, because of the daring stewardship of one man—General Ulysses S. Grant—by the end of February the situation had changed drastically, and to the South's disadvantage.

The man who would later become a central figure in the war had, at this stage, obtained only moderate recognition. Nevertheless, General Grant had asked for, and received permission to attempt breaking the Confederate line at Fort Henry, assisted by Commodore Foote and a fleet of his best gunboats. The story of the taking of Fort Henry and the subsequent reduction of Fort Donelson is a legend in its own right, but suffice it to say, when the battle was over, General Grant had accomplished what he'd set out to—shattering the practical center of the Confederate line of defense. Vanquished, Johnston had had no choice but to retreat and reestablish his line farther south.

This he did, and in short order a new front was established in Corinth along a railroad line which stretched across the width of the Confederacy from the Mississippi to the Atlantic. This was the line of the Memphis & Charleston Railroad, and as Johnston had no doubt already figured out, no better base of operations could have been chosen. The reason was simple. At this very spot another, even more important rail line crossed the first, one that ran north and south, one that ran all the way from the Ohio River to the Gulf of Mexico. *He who controlled this junction controlled the flow of troops, munitions, and supplies along* both *lines.* What's more, there were several strategic chokepoints along each line where the land surface was such that a few well-positioned regiments could easily defend themselves against an entire army.

Clearly, the importance of these two rail lines was not lost to either side. For, these two lines were the means for transportation: in times of peace—for all things in connection with commerce, and in times of war—for the hurrying forward from any point (north, south, east, or west) of all that pertained to war—arms, men, and provisions of every sort. Hence, the general who controlled those few square feet of ground where the two railroad lines met, owned absolutely all the means of swift transportation while his opponent had nothing. To possess such a vast advantage meant winning the war here in the west, and both Albert Sydney Johnston, the Confederate leader, and Ulysses S. Grant, the commander of the Army of the Tennessee, understood the strategic consequences quite well.

Thus, the queer, old town of Corinth became a killing field. Situated in the northern part of the state of Mississippi, not far from the Tennessee line and twenty-two miles from the Tennessee River, it should not have attracted much attention. But there sat this particular little plot of ground. It did not differ in any material respect from any other plot of ground in the vicinity, and it was not over five feet square; yet, it was for possession of this little piece of soil that more than twenty thousand men were killed, and many more wounded, in one of the most desperate battles of all time. What distinguished this plot of ground from every other, what made it worth such an awful price was that it was enclosed by iron rails:

	MEMPHIS & CHARLSTON R.R	
MOBILE & OHIO R.R.	WHAT WAS FOUGHT FOR— PLOT OF GROUND 4 FEET 8 1/2 INCHES SQUARE.	MOBILE & OHIO R.R.
	MEMPHIS & CHARLSTON R.R	

And so it began:

In the dying days of March, General Grant was to the north. He had made his way up the Tennessee and, utilizing every swift means of transportation at his disposal, had landed an army not many miles from that little piece of ground. It was for this reason that the sleepy town of Corinth became the object in the great scheme of military operations taking shape in western Tennessee. By the end of March there was assembled at or near Corinth some 50,000 men from each side, nearly 100,000 men in all, and John Lawrence and Byron Matthewson were among them.

Savannah, on the eastern bank of the Tennessee, had been designated by the North as the rendezvous point for the armies of the Tennessee and the Ohio to meet. But when General Grant arrived in Savannah, he immediately recognized the inherent strength of Pittsburg Landing some nine miles farther downstream, and adopted it instead as the place for the great encampment. The plain on which they camped came to be called Shiloh on account of a crude, log church which stood two and a half miles back from the Tennessee River. Gathered here were men whose names would rise from the maze of blood and battle and be remembered for generations. William T. Sherman, Albert Sydney Johnston, Lew Wallace, B.M. Prentiss, Braxton Bragg, WHL Wallace; generals all. Then there was Colonel Robert Ingersoll, and Generals Hurlbut, McArthur, and Polk. And of course, Privates Byron Matthewson and John Lawrence.

Given the great influx of men in the closing days of March, Pittsburg Landing was a busy place. Regiments and brigades were arriving daily. Many of the troops were newly-enlisted, undrilled, and in some cases, un-uniformed and unarmed. Others were armed only with old muskets of the pattern of bygone days. But along with the greenhorns, the victors of Fort Donelson were there as well. So was Lew Wallace and his Division five miles downriver at Crump's Landing.

Part of the Illinois Eleventh Cavalry was attached to Prentiss' Division on the front line, but the rest, including John and Byron's Company B, was attached to Lew Wallace's Division back at Crump's Landing. Because enemy movements were possible along a road which ran west from the river towards the little town of Purdy, Lew Wallace's men remained at Crump's

Landing and along the road to watch over both points of danger. Thus, at the outset of the battle, these troops—Byron's unit included—were not even engaged. They were connected, however, with the Union reserve by a road which ran parallel to the Tennessee River and then across a bridge over Snake Creek. It was perhaps a mile and a half from Snake Creek to Pittsburg Landing.

The Union position at Pittsburg Landing was naturally defended on all sides save one—the southwest, the side facing towards Corinth. On the east flowed the Tennessee River, its bank at the Landing a steep incline of more than eighty feet. On the north, the camp was protected by Snake Creek, a tributary which emptied into the Tennessee River a little below the Landing. To the southeast, and flowing into the river *above* the Landing, lay another creek, Lick Creek. Finally, enclosing the northwest side, was Owl Creek. All these streams were nearly rivers themselves, swollen with backwater from the Tennessee which itself was running high, fed by spring melt. With all other approaches covered, it would be from the southwest, therefore, that trouble would come, along that road running down from Corinth and on into Pittsburg Landing. This was the only quarter in which the Union Army was vulnerable to assault—in the front, between Owl and Lick creeks.

In the early days of April, 1862, the two armies lay little more than twenty miles apart. It was generally thought, by North and South alike, that the single best course of action for the Southern forces was to wait at Corinth for the attack by the advancing Northern scourge. But General Albert Sydney Johnston, perhaps the very "arm" of the South, had a different idea. Seeing how the Union army had but one weak point, he planned an immediate attack upon the main camp at Pittsburg Landing. If he could wipe out the Northern forces already landed there and about equal in size to his own, and if he could do so before General Buell and his Army of the Ohio could make it up from Savannah with fresh reserves, he could smash the entire Northern advance and change, perhaps, the face of history.

Seizing the opportunity, on the third day of April, 1862, General A.S. Johnston issued the order: Move on Pittsburg Landing!

39
Prelude To Battle

Sunday, April 6, 1862

It was a glorious spring morning! In the woods along the road from Corinth, and in the forest where the Confederates swarmed toward the point of engagement, and in the camp, too, of the Union army, birds were singing, spring flowers were blooming, the peach trees were in blossom, and every blade of grass underfoot was green and stretching upwards toward the sky. Early spring was upon every tree and spirits were high. Like the man said, it was a good day to die!

Just three days earlier, on April third, General A.S. Johnston of the South had issued the order to move forward. Northeast the army marched, straight northeast from Corinth. Steadily forward it tramped, the infantry on foot, the heavily-clanging artillery behind. They crept and floundered over muddy roads, the cavalry jealously guarding their flanks and their front. Onward, under their intrepid leader, the whole Army of the Mississippi advanced—horse, foot, and guns—trudging forward along the Corinth Road, still some eight miles from the Landing.

Johnston had planned his attack on Pittsburg Landing for sunrise, April fifth, but sunrise of that day did not see his army within striking distance. Indeed, it was nearly nightfall on Saturday the fifth—yesterday—before his weary soldiers had arrived and begun forming up in line of battle to await the next morning—*this* morning! When Sunday dawned, bright and glorious, the carefully-orchestrated movement forward resumed.

On they came, Hardee's corps first, spread out on both

sides of the road as far as the eye could see. On the left was Clerburne's brigade, its flank near Winningham Creek. Next was Wood's brigade, extending across the road. Then came Shaver's brigade on the right, with Gladden's brigade reaching all the way across to Bark Road.

On they marched, Confederates all. To the rear of Hardee's line came Bragg, with Chalmers, Jackson, Gibson, Anderson, and Pond behind, their lines overlapping beyond Gladden on the right and Clerburne on the left. Then came Polk's corps, and Breckinridge's, in columns by brigades, following along the road. Steward, Russell, Johnson, and Stephen were under Polk; Trabue, Bowen, and Stratham, under Breckinridge. Nearly 50,000 men in all—and every last one of them moving forward!

Away down in McCullar's Field on Lick Creek, on the extreme right of the advance, was Clanton's cavalry. Guarding Greer's Ford were the cavalry units of Avery, Forest, and Adam. On the left, guarding the road from Stantonville, was Brewer's cavalry.

In the very center, at the junction of Bark, Corinth, and Pittsburg roads, and less than two miles from Shiloh Church, General Johnston established his headquarters. From there he would prosecute the battle and press the Southern advantage.

Awaiting them, though not nearly so well organized, nor in so great a number, was the Union army. And inbetween the two lay the field of Shiloh, a rolling, untilled plain gashed by deep ravines and covered with trees plus the occasional patch of thick brush. Small roads crisscrossed the plateau. Here and there was the occasional open place where a log-house or else a half-cleared field let the daylight filter in through the otherwise tangled maze of forest and underbrush. Foot soldiers and horsemen alike would have trouble crossing the uneven ground.

On the road running out toward Corinth was the crude, log, meeting-house known to the locals as Shiloh Church. Here, and along the road leading from Pittsburg Landing to the village of Purdy, were fragments of the Northern army, the fifth division of the Army of the Tennessee, commanded by General William Tecumseh Sherman. His was a division of raw recruits, many of whom had never yet been under fire. As a leader, he had not yet distinguished himself from the other prominent generals of the

Union army. Today, that would change. On this field he would soon become a figure to compel the respect and admiration of an entire nation.

While, in the early morning hours, the main body of Sherman's troops were either in camp at breakfast or else mustered for Sunday morning inspection, his pickets and advance guard had engaged the enemy's outposts in distant fields and thick woods—places where the true strength of the attack could not be directly observed.

Thus, at first, there was no general cause for alarm, not even down at the Landing where some regiments were only now just disembarking from the riverboats. The situation would change, of course, later that morning when more than one regiment would be marched directly into action after coming ashore, but for now, at sun-up, there was no sense of urgency. Not until seven o'clock that morning would General Sherman's division begin to feel the full brunt of the invading Confederate forces.

The minutes ticked by and then, all of a sudden, glistening bayonets filled the morning air. *Heavy masses of infantry had emerged from the woods to Sherman's left!*

Any lingering doubts were now quickly erased: *The enemy intended a determined attack on the whole Union camp*!

All along the line of Sherman's division, even on the extreme right, the Confederates were advancing, every single man of the attacking force headed straight for the Landing. At the outset, a large body of Confederates even managed to cross the open field unchallenged, as they were wearing uniforms similar to those of the Union forces and displayed what was taken to be an American flag.

As the Confederates pressed impetuously forward, giving their rebel yell, some of Sherman's raw recruits turned and ran. But to their credit, most stood their ground and fought. General Sherman related afterwards, in his official report, that his division "was made up of regiments perfectly new, nearly all of them having only recently received their guns at Paducah. None of them had ever been under fire before, nor had they ever seen heavy masses of the enemy bearing down upon them as they did on that morning. Even so, they displayed the coolness and steadiness of older troops."

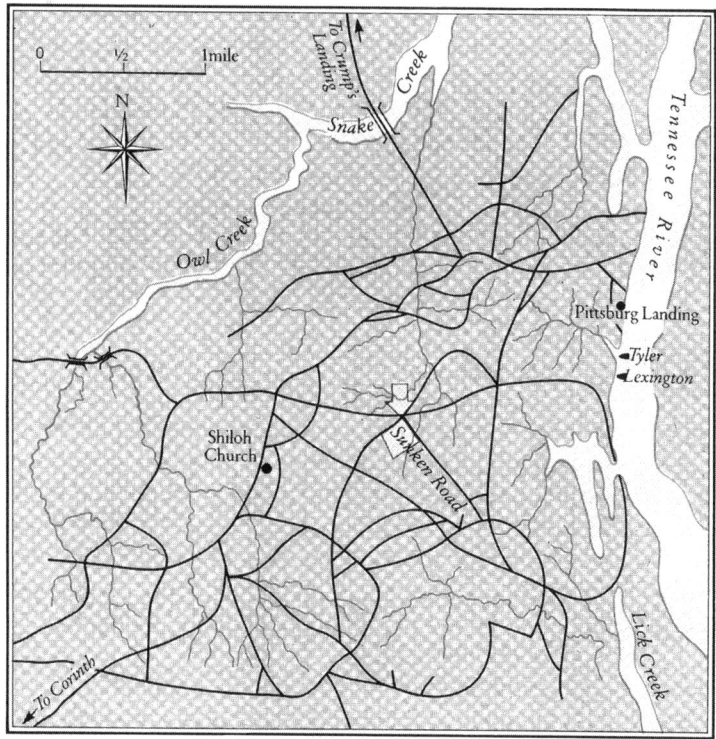

Strong words from a strong man, for Sherman's troops took a terrible beating in the opening salvos of the day.

The enemy advanced in overwhelming numbers, and with tremendous force. Nevertheless, Sherman's men met them with stubborn resistance. Holding fast, the soldiers in Sherman's command inflicted heavy punishment on the attacking Confederate forces.

Americans were now killing Americans with swift determination. Clerburne's Confederate brigade, in attempting to cross the marshy ground, received the brunt of the concentrated Union fire and was repulsed with heavy losses. Brigade after brigade of Southerners advanced, and time after time they were hurled back with severe losses, running in some units as high as seventy percent! But still they kept on coming!

Straight across the broken ground they came, through woods, and over ravines, and across gullies, every last one of them aimed like an arrow for the Landing. Every Southern soldier knew where he wanted to be and every Northern soldier knew it was his business to see that he didn't get there. This was the Grand Game of Poker, played at the highest level, and for the highest stakes. The cards had been dealt, the bets were down. It was winner take all!

The stubborn resistance of Sherman and his men was of untold value to the Union army. By disputing the direct road leading to the Landing, by almost singlehandedly holding back the enemy for a full two hours, he gave the forces posted nearer the Landing sufficient time to get onto the field of battle and into action.

Forced back several times, Sherman lost one battery after another. But each time he held tight, tenaciously rallying his forces, then making a new stand before being pressed back again. Driven from his own headquarters by the rebel onslaught, his losses were staggering, but once again he rallied, driving the Confederates back, recovering his headquarters, and then capturing a battery of Confederate guns. The man was nearly unstoppable!

Referring to Sherman long after the war ended, a veteran wrote: "I first saw him at Shiloh. He seemed disgusted and mad at the way the rebels came pouring out of the woods, world without end, and driving us back in spite of all we could do. Though he was wounded, the man kept riding around as if he despised the bullets and shells.

"My own squad leader, Captain Behr, had given the order to immediately unlimber and come into action, but immediately upon doing so, he was shot, and fell dead from his horse. The men abandoned five out of six guns, and fled in disorder. But General Sherman, he just stayed there in that saddle of his, defying the odds."

At one point, well back from the fighting, numbers of men, mostly without arms, were seen hurrying across the northern part of the field toward the Tennessee River. The confused appearance of these stragglers aroused officers and men alike, and a messenger was dispatched to seek an explanation for this flight of soldiers across the camp. The messenger quickly returned and reported that the fleeing men were from Sherman's command at the front, that Sherman's division was "all cut to pieces" and the "woods full of rebels." Seven brigades had been launched against Sherman with great vigor and tremendous force, and the messenger himself was urged to run for his life!

The situation was bleak, yet it would be impossible to give a complete account of the swaying tides of battle as they swept back and forth across Shiloh Field that morning. One surviving officer of the Twentieth Illinois infantry told Andu the next day that the regiment he was attached to passed backward and forward over its own regimental campground seven different times. It was as if two huge Titans were gripped in a wrestler's embrace, first staggering this way, now reeling back, then swaying blindly from left to right. The charges were swift rushes ending in fights at close quarters; the countercharges, the same.

Charge after charge was made by the Confederates, and more than once they were viciously repelled. But still they came—by the thousands—and before long, the attackers had no choice but to charge forward over their own dead and wounded! Finally, though, after repeated hammerings, their persistence paid off, and the Confederates were successful in dislodging the Union's most forward line. These were the forces commanded by General B.M. Prentiss.

Unable to withstand the deadly battering of overwhelming numbers any longer, at nine o'clock Prentiss withdrew his force, taking an advanced position in the left center of the Union line next to General WHL Wallace. Here was a wooded area matted thick with undergrowth, and running through it was a sunken road hidden from view by a narrow ridge. The natural entrenchment was so admirably suited for defense, the entire area in front of it became a killing field. In fact, it was so impervious to attack, Prentiss would never once have to abandon it and retreat further to the rear. In no time at all, the Confederates had christened the spot the "Hornet's Nest" on account of the intense gunfire that was stirred up every time they mounted an assault against it.

Thus began the long struggle to hold the center of Shiloh Plain. It was now between nine and ten o'clock in the morning.

Though it had not been chosen by Prentiss—only resorted to by immediate necessity—the position he now held in the sunken road was a strong one. For hours the Confederates dashed against this line, Prentiss at the center, WHL Wallace on the right, Hurlbut and McArthur holding them off on the left. Again and again the Confederates charged upon the Union line with infantry and artillery, but so far as they could see, their frenzied bravery was making little impression. Only as the day wore on and the Union ranks began to shrink from continuous hammering on both flanks, did the line start to bend at its southernmost point. By then, the tide had begun to turn against the North.

40
The Peach Orchard

It would be impossible to recite with grim detail every single thing that happened that bloody Sunday. Sherman became a hero, holding the center for hours on end; Prentiss, a POW, when after being the subject of a fierce assault, his battalion was surrounded; Johnston of the South, a martyr and a legend when he was shot in the leg and bled to death from a severed artery. But of all the battles within The Battle on that wood-clad and irregular field of Shiloh, the most deadly was the one in the so-called Peach Orchard. It was the first of the gigantic, deadly grapples at close quarters. Here came the first crucial test of the struggle between nearly ninety thousand Americans. Here, intelligent blood was shed.

Even before the start of that gory day, the brilliant Southern general in command had recognized that he had a golden opportunity. Albert Sydney Johnston had a plan—and it was a good one. By unleashing a firestorm of fighting against the unprepared Union line, he could turn the Union line to the left, thus opening the door for *his* men to seize the Landing. Then he would have the disheveled Union forces at his mercy and could drive them into the marshes to the north where he'd be able to chop the invading army into pieces. Ulysses S. Grant, with the remnant of his forces under Buell and Nelson still on the other side of the Tennessee River, would be an entity not to be feared, but to be pressed. The war would continue, not in Kentucky or Tennessee, but in Ohio.

Johnston could see it in his mind's eye, step after logical step. It all hinged, though, on step number one, crushing the army presently encamped at Pittsburg Landing. The rest would inevitably follow. Like a row of dominoes toppling over, all he had to do was give the first one a good shove!

One feels almost sorry that the light of a military genius so great as A.S. Johnston should have been snuffed out on that fatal day. Confederate or not, he was right in his conception of a once-in-a-lifetime opportunity. But there were other Americans on the battlefield that day, Northerners with military gifts as great as Johnston's. And there were rugged, plains-fighters from the farms and the workshops, men as ready to do or die as the splendid Southerners Johnston himself led.

In many ways it was a balanced fight. The chivalry of the South was to be met by the sturdy manhood of the North. There was bloody work at hand. Perhaps neither Gettysburg nor any other battlefield of the war furnished a greater scene of courage and carnage than that afforded soldiers in and about the so-called "Peach Orchard"—a field with but a few peach trees off to one side. It was an exhibition of American valor not yet tempered by discretion, or by any knowledge of the art of fighting. The result turned not so much on skill or cunning as it did on sheer obstinence.

Perhaps a mile and a quarter from the Landing was an open space named Duncan Field, and running directly through it was the all-important road connecting Pittsburg Landing to the city of Corinth. At eight a.m., General WHL Wallace, encamped near the Landing but hurrying forward to the front at first alarm, had taken two of his brigades plus three batteries of artillery and placed them in position just east of Duncan Field. He posted Sweeney's brigade north of the road and Tuttle's brigade in the woods and brush fringing the field. Then, using an old abandoned road which ran due south from the Landing-Corinth Road before bending east to meet up with the Hamburg-Savannah Road, he placed his three artillery units on a ridge to Tuttle's rear. The ancient byway made re-supply possible, as well as affording his men superior cover.

A few minutes after nine, Prentiss joined him there, taking up his third position of the morning, just to the left of WHL Wallace along that sunken road in what would soon be called the Hornet's Nest. A contingent of Missouri infantry arrived shortly thereafter, adding a badly needed six hundred men to the shattered remains of his division. Already that morning, under the weight of steady and continuous fire, Prentiss' command had dwindled in number to under a thousand.

General Hurlbut hurried out to support Prentiss as well, taking his artillery and his First and Third brigades along the Hamburg Road. Hurlbut commanded his troops in person, putting them in line of battle at the Peach Orchard, with one brigade lining up along the south end of the orchard, and the other along the west, its right flank extending into the timber and brush near the sunken road. To the left and upfront was Stuart, and to his immediate right, McArthur. His line stretched just east of the Orchard. Countless artillery pieces filled in the gaps between.

The fight opened with fire from three Confederate batteries. For the moment anyway, they were occupying camps Prentiss himself had been forced to evacuate earlier. A shell from one of these batteries blew up a Union caisson, stampeding the men. Terrified, they abandoned their guns and disappeared into the woods. Fortunately, cooler heads prevailed and volunteers from a neighboring unit moved in to rescue the frightened horses and spike the pieces. Lesson Number One of War: Don't leave a lost battery to the enemy where it might be captured.

Retreating forces from the rear of Prentiss' line now joined up with Hurlbut, and together, they dug in to hold that position. While ammunition was being supplied to Hurlbut's First and Third brigades, four regiments of infantry gave the rebels a sharp volley of musket fire. Completely re-supplied now, the remaining pair of batteries opened up on the Southerners, keeping up a steady and effective fire for several hours. The alert, brisk defense repeatedly sent the Confederates diving for cover, but not before leaving the field littered with dead and wounded.

Meanwhile, at the extreme left of the Union line, Stuart was bitterly engaged and overmatched by the attacking Confederate forces. General A.S. Johnston, having personally assumed command of his army's right flank, was determined to break the stubborn resistance of Stuart, and of McArthur, both of whom held on with a sturdy grip. To crush Stuart at the extreme left meant the turning of the Union line and the opening of a path to Pittsburg Landing.

Until about two o'clock that afternoon there was a

stubborn contest with unyielding vigor displayed on each side. But by then Stuart had been forced back and McArthur's left exposed. A new line was formed at the north end of the Peach Orchard with one of Hurlbut's brigades swinging left in support of McArthur. But it was already too late—McArthur was severely wounded. Then, at half past two, General A.S. Johnston—the Confederate leader—was struck by a minié ball.

With Johnston down, command of the Confederate advance fell to General Beauregard. But it was a bad omen. Beauregard was sick, and no other Southerner present understood as well as Johnston how to beat the North here at Shiloh. Shot in the leg and bleeding to death from a severed artery, the great general who had originally conceived the grand attack, died. The most simple care, a tourniquet, would have saved his life—but it wasn't to be.

And the battle he'd inaugurated here in the Peach Orchard? Having achieved now a life of its own, the ghastly struggle wore on without him.

Seven times over the next hour charges were made by the Confederates across that field. And seven times they were repulsed. But at long last, force in numbers eventually prevailed and Hurlbut and McArthur were compelled to retire, falling back toward the Landing with Stuart at the extreme left doing the same. What they left behind was a field literally carpeted with dead soldiers. General Grant, in his memoirs, described the holocaust:

"I saw an open field over which the Confederates had made repeated charges. It was so covered with dead, it would have been possible for a man to walk across the clearing, in any direction, stepping only on dead bodies and nothing else, his foot never touching the ground."

The colors of battle that day were many, and varied. The greens and yellows of the field. The Blues and Grays of the uniforms. The red of blood. It was this last color, the red of blood, that the soldiers would never forget. And in one place in particular, the Bloody Pond.

Somewhat to the left of the Union center was a small body of water that came to be known as the "Bloody Pond." The sheet of water wasn't large, no more than a city block in size, but what it lacked in circumference, it made up for in importance.

Shallow, sluggish, and still, it exists yet today, its waters bubbling up from one of the many abundant underground springs in and around Shiloh. Now no longer crimson, of course, back then its cool antiseptic waters undoubtedly saved countless lives. Here, to assuage their thirst and lave themselves, the desperately wounded—of both armies—limped, stumbled, or crawled. And as the tide of battle shifted to and fro, and the numbers of wounded mounted, the water became the color of blood.

Red is, of course, the color of stop signs in our modern world, but either the combatants were colorblind or else they'd reached the point of no-return, for the battle thundered on!

Solid at the center, but bending back at both ends, the Union line made its defense, holding off the attacking forces for five long, bloody hours. Four more times the enemy charged upon the Union position, four more times with a pounding accompaniment of artillery. Each time the attack was repelled with infinite spirit.

The Confederate losses were great, and between the looting of the abandoned Union camps and the sheer exhaustion of being under fire for so many hours, it had become increasingly more difficult for the Southern officers to rally their men for a renewed attack. But in the final analysis, the Union losses were greater still, and by four o'clock that first afternoon the situation had become untenable.

Sherman and his men had fallen back to the north and to the rear, selecting a new line along the Savannah Road. Here they had a view to guarding—and holding—the bridge by which General Lew Wallace and his forces from Crump's Landing were still anxiously expected at any moment. There was now desperation in the air, and from the most senior general on down to the lowliest private in the ranks, every heart was buoyed up by the hope of fresh reinfórcements, troops who were well-rested, well-drilled, and well-disciplined. But none arrived!

Every soldier in line of battle wondered where the men from Crump's Landing could possibly be. Had they bolted? Turned tail and run? Or had they been ambushed, their forces now decimated, and no longer to be reckoned with?

Throughout that whole long day of hard fighting the road and bridge had been kept open, and for what? At this late hour, the battle was nearly lost!

By five o'clock in the afternoon, Prentiss had been driven out of the Hornet's Nest and taken prisoner, along with what few of his heroic band of fighters remained. WHL Wallace had been mortally wounded. Sherman and his men were holding on by their teeth. They made their final stand of the day just at dusk when it commenced to rain.

This last battle of the day was neither a bloody affair, nor a long-lived one. Whereas A.S. Johnston might have pressed his advantage into the night, his successors on the field were not nearly so bold, preferring to retreat instead, and resume fighting in the morning. This misstep would prove to be the South's undoing.

Night closed in. The rain fell in torrents. The exhausted men of the First and Fifth divisions slept sitting up with their backs pressed against a tree. Only those tired to the point of collapse stretched out upon the soaking wet ground in merciful oblivion to everything that had come to pass during that long, shocking day of battle. In the morning it would begin again, but for the moment, the bloody fields and woods were quiet.

41
Reinforcements

Andu awoke in a cold sweat. It was the bird-beasts again. Every night now, for the past four nights, they'd visited him in his dreams.

Their ungainly heads, their vicious claws, their gaping beaks crushing those two poor innocent girls to death. The screams, the bloodcurdling screams. Andu, blowing them away with a single squeeze of the trigger. Somehow, he couldn't forget.

But why now? Why, after all this time, was he suddenly remembering?

The answer was obvious, and he cursed his stupidity. What a fool he'd been! He never should have let Margaret go in the first place! He missed her like crazy. Now, here he was, in an impossible situation, and with but one way out. First, he had to finish the job at hand. Then, damn it to hell, he'd go find her!

Andu shivered and tried to make the pain go away. His feet hurt, his back ached, and the rain came down in sheets. It was late Sunday night now, after midnight by his reckoning, and he hadn't slept a wink in over eighteen hours, not since sun-up this morning.

All around him were the moans of wounded soldiers. Andu himself wasn't hurt, nor was Byron—only beat up, like if they'd both been in a fistfight—or worse.

Andu felt like hell. The last war he'd been in, the one in Afghanistan, Andu had been a much younger man, better able to withstand the physical punishment. But now, at his age, hiking for nearly ten hours over uneven roads in lousy boots, was just too much. Cavalry or not, they'd been ordered to dismount early in the day to preserve the horses. It seemed that in this man's army, the animals ranked higher than the men! And why should that surprise him? This great big meat-grinder they called the Battle of Shiloh had already gotten the better of him, and he hadn't even discharged his weapon yet!

Andu took stock of himself. His knife. His musket. His tattered clothes.

In his beltpak, Jenny. In his breastpocket, the slender metal device to call the *Drift On* back from orbit. On his feet, boots. Rotten boots. Hardly up to the punishment he'd just put them through. A full day of hiking.

General Lew Wallace had marched with his columns at noon this morning from Crump's Landing, not quite six miles from Pittsburg Landing. Privates John Lawrence and Byron Matthewson were with him, along with the rest of the Eleventh Illinois Cavalry. Though their division made strenuous exertions to get onto the field of battle as soon as humanly possible, through misunderstandings as to which road was to be taken, as well as due to the poor condition of the roads themselves, their unit did not arrive at the front until nightfall, just a few hours ago. Indeed, at one point during the afternoon, their entire command was completely lost, wandering aimlessly around in the maze of swamps and winding roads north of Snake Creek. They were to have taken the river road, a road which in one spot came in more than two miles from the river. But after going some distance along it, they were met by officers General Grant had dispatched to hurry them along, and informed that they had taken a wrong turn.

Infuriated by the mix-up, Wallace turned back, thus delaying his arrival at Pittsburg Landing by more than half a day! Before it was over, he and his men had marched in excess of fifteen miles, and all of it over bad roads. In the end, though, they came in over Snake Creek on the Savannah Road, arriving at the Landing just after dark when Sunday's carnage and severe fighting was mostly over. To a man, they arrived exhausted, wet, and cold.

Not only had Lew Wallace's division been delayed getting to the front, but General Buell's army as well. Expecting Buell's arrival at any minute, General Grant had collected, and with careful precision, arranged the boats for transporting Buell's army across the river. All that bloody Sunday the boats sat there waiting on the east bank of the river—but no sign of Buell, or of his detachments! Not until two o'clock that afternoon, when a desperate and apparently losing fight was raging along every front—the right disorganized and nearly whipped, the left being driven in slowly, and the center on the verge of being overwhelmed by superior numbers—did General Buell arrive by boat in advance of his army coming up the wagon road from Savannah.

His first inquiry was, "What preparations have you made for retreating?" To which Grant replied, "I have not yet despaired of whipping them, General."

General William Nelson, commanding the Fourth division of Buell's Army of the Ohio, left Savannah at 1:30 p.m., Sunday, April 6th, and marched by land to a point opposite Pittsburg Landing. The anxiety of his soldiers to join in on the fight taking place on the left bank of the river enabled him to cover the entire nine miles in under four hours, a considerable feat given the mud and dreadful state of the rutted roads. By five o'clock that evening, the head of the column had been ferried across to the west side of the river, landed, and marched up the steep bank at Pittsburg Landing, immediately taking up a position in line of battle along that vital road. So close was the enemy, the situation could only be described as desperate. A semicircle of artillery—unsupported by infantry—was the only check upon the enemy's advance. Down along the riverbank a crowd of panic-stricken soldiers clamored to Nelson's arriving troops that the day was lost, that the Union army had been whipped. There were ten thousand or more of these runaways.

Though the Landing was defended, for the moment anyway, by little more than siege guns, and though there were barely enough men on hand to man them, Generals Grant, Buell, and Nelson were on the ground now, each cool, alert, and unshaken in their determination to hold the lines which were currently forming out of the chaos of earlier defeat.

For the first time since the battle began, the gunboats *Tyler* and *Lexington* opened fire from the river, throwing their great iron shells over and above the enemy's lines, doing little physical damage, but contributing mightily to demoralizing an already exhausted and weary Confederate army. The stubborn fight, waged since early that morning, had sapped the strength of the Confederates as they hung on in an uphill battle to subdue the spirited resistance of the Northern army. Though the rebels were being urged forward by confident and persistent officers who saw victory within their grasp, the impression that (assisted by the riverboats and their terrible guns) a mighty artillery defense would be made at the Landing, seized upon the minds of the Southerners, especially Beauregard. Whereas General Braxton Bragg, now on the field near the Landing, strained every nerve to form up his columns and continue the fight, Beauregard—ill with the flu—urged restraint. Bragg, filled with enthusiastic ardor after the triumphs of the day, saw only the remotest prospect of defeat. He gave the order: "Move forward . . . sweep the enemy from the field!"

Although greatly exhausted by twelve hours of incessant fighting without food, Bragg's Confederates responded to his order with alacrity. Over at the Landing, hurried preparations were already underway for a stubborn defense. Whatever few Union forces remained, were now massed behind the available batteries, and for the first time that day, they were in one continuous line of battle. The unbroken line reached from the Landing out to the Hamburg-Savannah Road, then stretched north and south along that road from Snake Creek nearly all the way down to the Corinth Road.

With calm determination, Grant, Buell, and Nelson waited for the attack. The boom of fire from the gunboats shattered the stillness. An occasional volley of musketry marked the movement of troops, both north and south. Only the expected assault never came!

At dusk, General Beauregard, the South's commanding officer now that General A.S. Johnston was dead, had done the unthinkable: sent orders to General Bragg and his brigade commanders insisting that they immediately withdraw. *All Confederate forces on the field of battle were to be pulled back out of reach of Union fire.*

Bragg was stunned! He had no choice but to comply, of course, though when he read Beauregard's directive to withdraw, all Bragg could do was shake his head and mutter that the battle was lost. Anybody could see that this was no time to give up!

While the great Union gunboats on the river threw their missiles far into the field all night long, a forlorn Bragg was reduced to brooding over the calamitous ruin of his hopes for an ultimate victory. It was a bitter pill for a man of his ability to take.

Night fell upon the field covered with dead and wounded, and the Confederates revelled in the rich spoils of all the Union camps they'd captured. In no small way the loot they scavenged contributed mightily to the demoralization of the victors, nothing breaking up an army's discipline and organization more effectively than the division of spoils among a band of victorious soldiers.

The Confederates and Federals alike counted their heavy losses that night, and in some cases, succored their wounded and prepared for the morrow. Lew Wallace's division, and Nelson's too, were now fully within the Union line. All evening long, even as a drenching rain fell, the transports on the river made their rounds from shore to shore. Without so much as breaking rank, Buell's army marched onto the vessels, were ferried across the river, and added to the quickly forming lines as soon as they marched off.

His head upon a saddle, General Grant passed the night under a tree. He had given orders for a full-scale attack against the enemy at daybreak!

42
Monday

The sun had not yet risen above the horizon and already there was a concerted movement forward by the entire Union army. Lew Wallace was at the extreme right; Sherman, McClernand, and Hurlbut at the left.

As compared with those who had fought all day Sunday, the reinforcing troops were fresh—but even that was only a matter of degree. The hurried march over muddy roads to the Landing had been extremely fatiguing, and the Army of the Ohio in particular, was in miserable shape. Many of them had marched some twenty-two miles yesterday, and a portion of them had stood shivering all night long in the streets of Savannah, the victims of a driving rain. Even the armies of Grant and Buell were soaking wet, having been without shelter during the drenching storm last night. Still, not a single word of complaint could be heard from the grim, stoney-faced fighters. They stood now at the ready, eager to redeem the fortunes of the previous day. It was dawn, Monday morning, April 7, 1861.

Down at the Landing and all along the banks of the river were stragglers and refugees whose shameful cowardice embarrassed the brave reinforcements. Indeed, there were so many runaways, the newcomers nearly had to fight their way up the road just to get to the battlefield! These deserters filled the air with their bitter complaints and pathetic cries, calling out to the arriving soldiers that the Union army was whipped, that it was suicide to even try. But the fighters of Buell were tough, and in contemptuous silence they passed them by. Who could have guessed that before the day was out, a victory as overwhelming as yesterday's defeat would be inflicted on the South?

Besides Buell's 20,000 men and Wallace's 7000, there were some ten thousand of Grant's troops who had fought the previous day—and survived—and who were once again in the line of battle. To meet this gigantic force Beauregard had no more than 20,000 men in total, for the Confederate losses had been heavy. Not only that, his regiments had been scattered and demoralized by the looting of the Federal camps captured the day before. There wasn't a man among them who hadn't been wearied by the terrific strain of Sunday's bloody encounter.

Like a carefully orchestrated dance recital, the North opened the battle precisely at daybreak. Nelson advanced along the Hamburg Road to attack Hardee in Stuart's camp out beyond the Peach Orchard. Then, according to cue, one Northern column after another advanced. Early in the fray was Lew Wallace's division, and Byron and Andu along with it.

By seven a.m. they had elbowed their way across Tighlman Creek and taken the heights south of it. Extending his right flank until it reached the Confederate left, Lew Wallace unleashed a tremendous fight in the same field occupied on Sunday by Prentiss and WHL Wallace. Again the Hornet's Nest became a scene of devastation. To everyone's amazement, General WHL Wallace was found, still alive, lying upon the ground where he had fallen the day before. Shot through the head, he had been left for dead when his troops were forced to retire at half past five yesterday afternoon. He was taken now to the Landing where he would be hurried onboard one of the hospital ships that had arrived during the night. Everyone was hopeful, of course, but Andu knew better. After so many hours laying out on the cold, wet ground, and after the loss of so much blood, his chances were slim to none. Still, it made the others feel good to try.

Strength on their side now, the Union line pushed steadily, and it pushed hard. All along the Corinth Road, from the Hornet's Nest out to Shiloh Church, the fighting was continuous and intense. Andu had seen war before—but never like this! The taking of territory, the taking of lives, and to what end? Five square-feet of ground? God Almighty!

What began with a noble purpose, ended as a slugfest, the winner being the one who succeeded in killing more of the enemy than they did of him. Some wars were proud, boisterous affairs with flying colors and gallantry; others, just acre after acre of blood with progress measured in yards or feet or inches, and pride a laughable matter after seeing your best buddy disemboweled by a bayonet right beside you there on the battlefield. Clemens had been right to defect, much as Fornax had before him. Men fought wars, yes; but blind men! If there were any heroes in the world, they were notably absent from *this* war.

Andu looked down at himself. He was a mess. He hadn't had a bath or a shower in more than two weeks. What should have been an inconsequential scratch had become puss-filled and infected. A sprain he'd suffered last week still hadn't healed. Bullets were flying all around him. Men were screaming. And yet, what was on his mind? None of these things. She was.

Each hour of each day now, he thought of her. Her eyes, her face, her smile. How long had it been since the two of them were together, since the two of them made love?

By her clock, nearly a year; by his, somewhat less. And for a great part of that time he hadn't been able to feel her. There had been a void, as if she were no longer a part of him. Now, though, he sensed her presence. No, not right there next to him; no, not even nearby. But closer than before. *She was searching for him with her mind!*

Andu caught his breath and looked around. Everywhere he turned he saw desperate faces. Young men, cold and dirty, scared and worried, afraid to die. And yet most of them would.

Andu felt pain. In his arm. Something told him he'd been hit.

Andu tried to get his bearings. He was in a confused, noisy, foul-smelling place. It was daylight, early morning, and the air was thick with smoke that hung, yellow and brown, above the ground. Around him, everywhere, far across the expanse of what seemed to be a field, lay groaning men. A wild-eyed horse, its bridle torn and dangling, trotted frantically through the mounds of men, tossing its head, whinnying in panic. It stumbled, then fell, and did not rise.

He heard a voice next to him. "Water," the voice said in a parched, croaking whisper. "Water . . . "

Andu turned his head toward the voice and looked into the half-closed eyes of a boy who seemed not much older than he himself had been when he was a soldier in Afghanistan. At first

Andu thought it was Byron, but it wasn't. Dirt streaked the boy's face. His blond hair was matted thick with mud. He lay sprawled on the ground, his tattered uniform glistening with wet, fresh blood.

The colors of carnage were grotesquely bright now: the crimson wetness on the rough, dusty fabric; the ripped shreds of grass, unexpectedly green, in the boy's yellow hair.

The boy stared at him with blank, cold eyes. "Water," he begged again. This time, when he spoke, a spurt of blood drenched the coarse cloth across his chest. It ran down his arm and dripped to the ground.

Andu's arm was immobilized with pain. He looked down. He *had* been hit! Andu could see now through his own torn sleeve. Something that looked like ragged flesh and splintery bone shown through.

He tried his other arm, and it was okay.

"Water."

Andu reached for his horse. He felt the metal container next to the saddlebag, and struggled to remove its cap. Cringing, he stopped the small motion of his other hand and waited for the surging pain to ease. Finally, when the canteen was open, Andu slowly extended his arm across the blood-soaked earth, inch by agonizing inch, and held it to the lips of the boy. Water trickled into the imploring mouth and down the grimy chin.

The boy sighed. His head fell back. His lower jaw dropped as if he had suddenly been surprised by something. A dull blankness slid slowly across his eyes. He was silent.

But the noise continued all around. The cries of 'the wounded men. The cries begging for water. For Mother. For Death.

Two horses lay on the ground, shot. They shrieked, raised their heads, and stabbed randomly at the sky with their hooves.

In the distance, Andu could hear the thud of cannons. Overwhelmed by pain, he lay there in the fearsome stench and listened to the men and animals die. As if he needed a reminder, he learned anew what it meant to go to war.

The minutes passed, and when he knew that he could bear it no longer and might welcome death himself, Andu opened his eyes and got painfully to his knees. His left arm hung lifelessly at his side. A troubled frown creased his face.

Going all the way back to the beginning at Camp Lyons in Peoria, Andu had never once left Byron's side, not even for an instant. The march to Benton Barracks a month ago, the subsequent trip downriver to Crump's Landing, the long and muddy hike through the swamps yesterday, the bivouac here today on the sunken road inside the Hornet's Nest. At each step of the way, Andu had been there at Byron's side, his guardian angel. Always wondering: Could he change history? Could he stop Byron from being shot? From being killed? Never once had it occurred to him that he, Andu, might be the one who was shot; that he, Andu, might be the one who was in danger; that he, Andu, might be the one who was killed! Only now, as it was actually happening, did it occur to him.

The morning air was so thick with the sounds of tracers, it made no sense whatsoever to try and take cover every time a barrage of bullets whizzed by. There were so many anguished yells—from both camps—it made no sense to look up every time someone cried out. There were so many bodies littering the landscape, it was impossible to tell who was alive and who was dead. In fact, when a slash of pain creased his shoulder, now, Andu wasn't even sure at first that he'd been hit for a second time. It could have been anything, he thought—a wood chip, a splintered branch, a wasp's bite. But when blood filled his shirt, then his hand, he knew.

A cold shiver ran down his spine. He didn't want to die, not here, not anywhere.

Byron had been crouching down in the grass next to him when it happened. He'd seen the earlier exchange with the dying boy. He'd seen John Lawrence risk his life by going to his horse for a canteen. He'd seen the boy expire, the color draining from his face. Now he saw John Lawrence stagger and fall.

The picture formed itself in an instant. Shattered arm, ashen face, red blood. Byron reacted immediately. Throwing down his weapon, he reached for his friend.

In a battle this crude, this medieval, there were no medics, at least not for the volunteers, and certainly not out here in the field near the front line. Medical help, if available at all, would be back at the rear, back by the Landing, where the hospital boats were docked.

Cradling Andu in his arms, Byron lifted the man from the ground and threw him over his shoulder. It was nearly a mile from here back to the Landing. He took off at a trot.

John Lawrence, née Andu Nehrengel, saw his life shrivel up and whither before his eyes. Everything was a blur now. A dead Union officer lay upon the field of carnage near a cannon. Keeping guard over the dead body was a mongrel dog. Teeth bared, it refused to allow anyone to approach the mortal remains of his master. That's what war was, Andu thought as he struggled not to give in to the pain: a long, bitter contest with stubborn bravery and valor to spare on both sides.

Then everything went black.

43
Panic

Desertion is an unfortunate fact of war, and Shiloh was no exception. General Sherman, twice wounded, had three horses shot out from under him during the two days of fighting. But despite his own injuries, it is worth noting for the record what he had to say about the men who flinched and ran away from him on that first day of battle. He did not rant and rave about cowardice, but reported the facts and made excuses for the runaways, telling how new and green they were, not drilled at all, some of their number not even acquainted with the proper use of arms. Sherman showed his grand qualities of mind and heart in the most trying circumstances a commanding officer could possibly face, not only in his handling of the situation, but also in his account of it afterwards.

Grant, like Sherman, took the disasters of the first day stoically. War was a grim trade, and retreat and defeat were a part of it. Men were sifted and tried in war as nowhere else. The veteran knew that some hearts would fail when the fiery test of battle came; thus, magnanimity was the mark of true greatness.

By General Grant's orders, the dead were to be buried on the field, Union and Confederate alike. As for the wounded, they were to be taken by boat to Savannah, with the worst cases being shuttled as quickly as possible on to hospitals along the Ohio River at places like Evansville, New Albany, or Louisville.

But there were so many wounded there was mass confusion at the Landing! Bodies littered the ground, and blood too. Shirts, pants, boots, caps, pieces of uniforms, cut off or torn off or simply thrown to the ground. And weapons. And eyeglasses. And bibles.

It was into this mayhem that a certain young soldier stumbled, exhausted and still lugging John Lawrence's limp body over his shoulder.

By now, Beauregard, the Southerner, had decided that his only course of action was to retreat, and he had begun a retrograde movement with great skill, keeping up a stiff fight to cover his withdrawal towards Corinth. By four o'clock Monday afternoon, the battle was over, though the cleanup to come was every bit as grisly as the fight just ended.

The body count was staggering—13,047 Union casualties, 10,699 Confederate. Plus an army of wounded. All headed for the river, all in desperate need of medical attention. At one point in time, at the height of the battle, it was so horrendous that every single boat which had been sent to transport the wounded downriver had to cut its ropes and swing out into the current to avoid being swamped by the throng of onrushing soldiers. There had been such a stampede of panic-stricken men, every steamer was at risk of being capsized!

The work of the hospital boats had begun almost as soon as the first shot was fired, and much of the work was overseen by the wife of General WHL Wallace. Something prompted her to go to her husband—she wrote later on—and without notifying him, she left her home in Illinois on the night of April first. Meeting up with some friends along the way, she journeyed up the Tennessee River onboard the steamer *Minnehaha* under the protection of the Twentieth Illinois Infantry, arriving at Pittsburg Landing just before daylight, Sunday morning, April sixth. She had with her only her Chaplain and a sweet young nurse who had shown up on her doorstep just the day before. The girl, known only to her as Margaret, had been told that a great battle was to be fought between North and South at Shiloh, and that nurses might be needed. How could she be of help?

Perhaps the appearance of this fresh, young face was all the prodding Mrs. Wallace required. Or perhaps Margaret herself had influenced the General's wife with a telepathic suggestion. Who could say? Either way, the next thing Mrs. Wallace knew, she was headed due south, straight into the eye of the storm. Her husband William had left weeks ago already; but at the time he had warned her that there was bloody work at hand. He had put on a brave face for his wife, as he always did, but she could tell that he was uncertain about their prospects for success.

Sending word to the General of her arrival Sunday morning, Mrs. Wallace and Margaret and the other nurses remained onboard the steamer waiting for him to make an appearance. At first they thought nothing of it, but as the morning sun rose ever higher over the spring landscape, they heard firing onshore. Their first hint that there was a raging battle just over the next hill came within the hour as dozens of wounded soldiers began arriving at the Landing before being brought onboard the *Minnehaha*.

The wounded were carried by twos and by threes and by fours until there were simply too many of them to be counted. Many of those who were brought in, pale and bleeding, were known personally to Mrs. Wallace, for they had grown up in Illinois. They all told the same story of the enemy's irresistible strength, of the awful slaughter of their comrades. The wife was told her husband was upon the field in the midst of a ferocious battle. She tried to send him a message with a captain who was going ashore to join in on the fray, but the captain was gone less than an hour when he himself was brought back to the Landing on a stretcher, suffering now from two painful wounds.

All day long the devoted wife remained onboard the *Minnehaha* waiting, and before noon the boat was crowded to overflowing with wounded. She tried to assuage them as best she could, assisting Margaret and the other nurses wherever possible. But many were beyond help, and she was no doctor.

As more hospital boats arrived on the scene, they too began filling with wounded, and before long Margaret left Mrs. Wallace's side to be onboard the *Decatur*. If history was any guide, that's where she would find Byron—and hopefully Andu as well!

By now Mrs. Wallace was sitting on the upper deck, every place below having been taken up by wounded. The mighty roar of cannon and musketry was almost deafening, it was so close. She had not heard from her husband in hours and was in deep despair. On the opposite shore, now, she could see the advance guard of Buell's army. Within minutes, her steamer was put into service ferrying the fresh soldiers across the river. With the newcomers arrived fresh hope, not only among the wounded soldiers onboard, but also among the stubborn and tenacious fighters onshore.

Over and back they went, over and back, ferrying Buell's advance guard across, the red-hot boilers working overtime. On one of these trips, Mrs. Wallace—hopeful and brave—was greeted at the Landing by the chaplain who had accompanied her on the way down here from Illinois. He brought her news too terrible to tell, though she read it in the faces of those who were with him. The woman was stunned by the blow, yet somehow she managed to hear the horrible story with stony calm. Her suffering, when it came, would come in private, later, after everyone else had left.

Her husband's division, they told her, had been falling back as ordered. But having already been flanked by the enemy, his command was still under a steady barrage of rebel crossfire even as they withdrew. Then, when Wallace's attention was suddenly called to an unseen pocket of the enemy, he rose up in his stirrups to get a better look. That's when it happened! Taking his foot from the stirrup, WHL prepared to dismount, then fell face-forward to the ground in full view of his men. Their leader had been shot, and no one around him even knew from which direction the bullet had come!

WHL's friends—among them an orderly who was like a son to Wallace—carried his body about a quarter of a mile towards the rear. Then, to avoid death or capture themselves, they laid him down where he would be out of reach of tramping feet, and left him. Nothing could presently be done to help him, as the enemy now held the very ground on which he lay.

All Sunday night long it rained. Mrs. Wallace nursed the wounded onboard the *Minnehaha*, finding small consolation in being able to help the sufferers around her. On Monday morning, about ten o'clock, word came to her that the General's body had been recovered. Miracle of miracles, the man was still breathing!

Left on the battlefield the day before, even the enemy had failed to recognize Wallace for who he was. Or to see that he was still alive. But now that the field was back in Union hands, the General would be brought to the river in short order!

Though mortally wounded, he who once was dead, was once again alive, and Wallace was taken to the boat nearest the shore. His beloved wife went to him, and although he seemed unaware of his surroundings, he knew her and remained conscious of her presence until his death four days later.

Meanwhile, Margaret searched frantically for Andu using every means at her command. Between the contentious roar of guns in the distance and the heartbreaking cries for help in the foreground, vocal communication was all but impossible. What good would it do her to scream out his name at the top of her lungs? In this crowd? None! Thus, it was with her mind that she searched. With her mind.

Margaret had come a frightfully long way to stand here on the pockmarked banks of the Tennessee River only to be drenched in blood. She had had to leave her newborn son behind, and in the hands of evil people no less; she had had to cross the mountains and the prairie alone, robbed once, and nearly raped; she had had to lie and steal her way downstream to St. Louis only to discover that the Moffetts were gone north on holiday and that Zebulon Leavenworth wasn't expected back for a year or more, not until the war was over anyway. In fact, if not for the recruiting poster she had spied nailed to a tree in downtown St. Louis, she might never have found her way to Benton Barracks and then on from there to the home of General WHL Wallace. He wasn't there, of course, but his wife was. Margaret had sent Mrs. Wallace the telepathic message that had brought them both here to Shiloh. But for God's sake, where was Andu?

44
Explosion

Lean and tall and blond she stood there, a vision of beauty if ever he'd seen one. Nothing at all like the farm girls he'd grown up with back home, nothing at all. Somehow he knew, though, that she wasn't interested in him, but rather in the man he was carrying. She spoke to him from across the deck, from across the dead and the wounded, from across the pained moans.

"If you're here, Byron, speak to me."

It wasn't possible, of course, but Byron heard the words just the same. He turned and looked in her direction, cautiously taking a step closer. By now the boat was pulling free of the dock, moving briskly out into the river. It had been sitting there a long time, tethered to the pylons, the boiler running at full steam. Along with several other boats—the *Kentucky*, the *Galena*, and the *Peru*—the steamship *Decatur* was taking wounded from the battle of Shiloh, first to Savannah, Tennessee, then on to other locations down and upstream, some as far north as Keokuk, Iowa.

Stepping over bodies on the blood-soaked deck, he came, moving ever closer to where she stood. The weight on his shoulder shifted and John Lawrence stirred for perhaps the first time since he'd been shot. It was as if the woman were speaking to him, to the both of them.

"Where are you, Andu? I've come all this way. Speak to me."

John Lawrence moaned. "Alpha . . . I'm here, Alpha . . . I'm here."

"*Where* are you?" came the voice in his head. "Give me a sign."

Byron came to a halt. Unbundling John Lawrence from his shoulder, he dropped him gently to the deck. "Nurse," he said, looking up at her, "this man is hurt."

Alpha Margaret came quickly to his side. "Oh my God!" she exclaimed, locking eyes with Byron. "How did this happen? You were the one who was supposed to get shot, not Andu."

The boat was a hundred yards from shore now.

"Ma'am?" Byron stammered, his face going white. "This fella's name is John Lawrence, not Andu. And what do you mean I was the one who was supposed to get shot?"

"You're Byron Matthewson aren't you?"

"Yes, ma'am," he sputtered, "but how is it that you know my name? I assure you, with a face as pretty as yours, I'd surely remember it if we'd ever met before."

"Oh, for heaven's sake, Byron, quit yapping! We can't let this man die!"

Andu moaned. "Drift . . . drift on." Reaching for his pocket with his good arm, he said it again. "Drift on."

"What's he sayin'?" Byron asked, the furrow in his forehead deepening. "Drift? Is the boat adrift?" he asked, looking anxiously back over his shoulder and out at the river.

At first Margaret didn't catch on, then it clicked. *They had to get back to the ship*!

Moving quickly now, Margaret reached across and unbuttoned Andu's shirt pocket. Inside was the slender, metal device he'd told her about when they first landed a year ago, the device they could use to call the *Drift On* back down from orbit to pick them up. It was caked with Andu's blood and she began to dutifully scrape it clean with her fingernails.

"What's that you got there?" Byron asked, thinking that she was just about to steal the loot of a dying man.

But before she could answer, the unthinkable happened: the boiler on the next boat over, the *Kentucky*, exploded in a fireball of heat and flame!

All night long and all day today, the paddlewheelers had been shuttling back and forth across the river with fresh troops coming one way and wounded troops the other. Each time they would make the short hop at full steam and each time they would keep that steam pent-up waiting on the next load. That is, until now. Finally, the boiler onboard the *Kentucky* couldn't take it any longer. Kaboom!

In a Krakatoa-style eruption, the boiler onboard the *Kentucky* exploded, sinking that ship and setting their own ship, the *Decatur*, on fire! Suddenly, the river was filled with bodies and the cold, rushing water began to drag them under!

As if united by a single force, Byron and Margaret dragged Andu's limp body across the burning deck and jumped into the churning black water. Their choices were stark: either burn to death onboard the ship or else drown in the swirling waters. The shore seemed close enough to make it.

The river was high with winter melt, and it was running fast. Margaret had no idea how cold it would be, nor did Byron, but the cold might have been enough to prolong Andu's life a few precious minutes.

As Margaret plunged headlong into the water, the first thing she thought of was Samuel Clemens and how his own brother had died under similar circumstances. That's when she realized how slim their chances really were.

Holding on to each other now, and to Andu, Margaret and Byron pushed for the shore. The muddy water was packed with lifeless bodies and burning cinders. Drowning soldiers clawed at them for help, but they barely had enough strength to save themselves, much less anyone else!

The river was littered with debris. They found a pair of floating woodplanks and held tight to them like two tiny life rafts.

It took every ounce of their energy, now, not to give up. But the worst was yet to come, for once they reached the shore and their cold wet bodies hit the wind, they began to shiver uncontrollably. Had Andu been conscious, he undoubtedly would have warned them that severe hypothermia could kill a person in under five minutes, a wounded person even quicker.

Tearing off their wet clothes before they froze, Margaret and Byron made their way up the steep bank. At the top they found dry clothes, stacks of them. Bloody, bullet-riddled uniforms that had been stripped from the dead and dying over the past two days as they were brought down to the Landing and put aboard the hospital ships. And horse blankets too. Woven on some medieval loom. Now both uniforms and blankets would have a chance to serve their country one last time!

Teeth chattering, Margaret led the way, the tiny metal

device still clutched in her hand. She was insistent, and Byron was helpless to disobey. Between them was a gurney, and in it, a wounded man wrapped in a coarse blanket. His face was white. No one would question them.

Faster she ran, her eyes unflinching. What she was looking for was a big, flat, open field where the runabout could land, one far enough away from the Landing not to attract any attention, yet close enough for them to make it in time, before Andu slipped into an irreversible coma!

They went north, away from Shiloh Field, into the marshlands near Snake Creek. Byron's mind told her which way to go. Only yesterday, his unit had hiked across a big open field on the way down here from Crump's Landing. He knew exactly where to take her!

45
Full Circle

The Year: 2433

The nurse was hysterical.

"Doctor Sydney, I don't know what to make of it!" she exclaimed at the top of her voice. "The woman claims she was bred *in vitro* in 2285 and has remained in stasis until just this past year. Only, according to her, she woke up in 2488. That's not for another fifty-five years yet! But wait; it gets better. The man in the funny-looking uniform with blood splattered all over it, well he claims his name is Byron Matthewson and that he was born in 1840. That's six hundred years *ago*! The other fellow, the one who's been shot twice and is still out cold, well the woman claims he's Andu Nehrengel, Carina's grandson. Only thing is, the *first* fellow, the one who calls himself Byron Matthewson, keeps saying the unconscious guy's name is John Lawrence, not Andu Nehrengel. For heaven's sake, Doctor Sydney, their stories don't even match! And look at the clothes they're wearing! Have you ever seen such stuff? Their uniforms—if that's what they really are—are riddled with bullet-holes and covered with blood. If I didn't know better, I'd say these three have been through a war!"

Doctor Sydney chuckled; he couldn't help himself. This particular nurse always tended toward the melodramatic. Not the best trait for an RN in the only medical facility on Mars, but then what could he do. Up here, it was damn hard to get good people.

Trying not to patronize her, he said, "Nurse Johnson, don't you think you're going a bit overboard? We get weirdos in here all the time. These people have obviously been through something, but exactly what, remains to be seen. The outdated clothes and the phony blood are probably nothing more than stage props and make-up. They're probably actors from that newly-formed guild; or worse yet, crazies. Clean 'em up and get them back out onto the surface."

His orders given, Doctor Sydney was just about to turn and walk away when Nurse Johnson objected. "But, sir, shouldn't we at least say something to Carina about this? And isn't Nehrengel Fornax's last name?"

"Look, I don't have the time to stand here today and argue with you," he snapped, obviously perturbed. "Patch 'em up if they're hurt and get 'em the hell outta here! If they're short on money, see to it that they get a job. I understand the company's looking for help over at the motor factory. And if they give you any more trouble or cause a ruckus, call Gunther down at Security. He'll know what to do. In the meantime, get ahold of Sister Siona and see if she can't be persuaded to come up here and calm that crazy woman down. After everything she went through back in Sane Lou, Siona's plenty capable of dealing with nutballs like these three."

Nodding her understanding, Nurse Johnson turned in the direction of the hospital's staff quarters. Sister Siona would either be down there or else across the valley in Newton at the Commons. Either way, Doctor Sydney was right. If anyone on the planet could handle this trio, Sister Siona could. Her life story was just shy of incredible!

Thirty-five years ago, in the titanic struggle for the North American continent, the United States was decimated. Yet, in spite of the destruction, some cities survived, though in a much reduced form. In time, settlers trickled back onto the ravaged land—Sister Siona among them. Part of a curious, offbeat order of nuns, she bravely met the challenge head-on. But, like all the newcomers, she had to be tough and resourceful just to survive in that tortured and blighted land. Even now, in her late sixties, Sister Siona was about as tough as they came. Indeed, if not for crossing paths with Carina Matthews at the Genealogical Institute that day, she might never have left Earth at all. Now here she was on Mars, at the Colony One Hospital, doing precisely the same job for them as she once had done for the hospital back in Sane Lou. Siona knew better than even Andu himself the story of Byron Matthewson, for along with Carina, she had heard it firsthand from none other than Brigham Smith. Now, she was about to come face to face with the legend they'd heard about so long ago.

• • •

The words came to him as if in a dream. She read them, but not out loud. He heard them, though not through his ears, through his mind. He heard them, but he didn't know how.

Margaret had found the Clemens of the past in the printbooks of the future, and she reveled in the discovery.

The book was old, very old, and the pages yellowed. But while Andu lay in bed and Byron paced anxiously about the room, and all three of them waited for whomever would appear at their door next, she silently read the passage, letting her imagination drift back over the centuries to the childhood Mark Twain later wrote of as a man:

"I remember the raging rain on that roof, summer nights, and how pleasant it was to lie and listen to it, and enjoy the white splendor of the lightning and the majestic booming and crashing of the thunder. It was a very satisfactory room, and there was a lightning rod which was reachable from the window, an adorable and skittish thing to climb up and down, summer nights, when there were duties on hand of a sort to make privacy desirable.

"I remember how very dark that room was, on a moonless night, and how packed it was with ghostly stillness when one woke up by accident and forgotten sins came flocking out of the secret chambers of the mind and demanded a hearing; and how ill-chosen the time seemed for this kind of business; and how dismal the hoo-hooing of the owl and the wailing of the wolf, sent mourning by on the night wind.

"I remember the 'coon and 'possum hunts,

nights, with the Negroes, and the long marches through the black gloom of the woods, and the excitement which fired everybody when the distant bay of an experienced dog announced that the game was treed; then the wild scramblings and stumblings through briers and bushes and over roots to get to the spot; then the lighting of a fire and the felling of a tree, and the joyful frenzy of the dogs and the Negroes, and the weird picture it all made in the red glare. I remember it all well, and the delight everyone got out of it, 'cept of course the 'coon.

"I remember the pigeon seasons, when the birds would come in the millions and cover the trees and, by their weight, break down the branches. They were clubbed to death with sticks; guns were not necessary and were not used. I remember the squirrel hunts, and the prairie-chicken hunts, and the wild-turkey hunts, and all that; and how we turned out, mornings, while it was still dark, to go on these expeditions, and how chilly and dismal it was, and how often I regretted that I was well enough to go. A toot on a tin horn brought twice as many dogs as were needed, and in their happiness they raced and scampered about, and knocked small people down, and made no end of unnecessary noise. At the word, they vanished away toward the woods and we drifted silently after them in the melancholy gloom. Presently, a gray dawn stole over the world, the birds piped up, then the sun rose and poured light and comfort all around, everything was fresh and dewy and fragrant, and life was a boon again. After three hours of tramping we arrived back wholesomely tired, overladen with game, very hungry, and just in time for breakfast.

"I remember . . ."

Then suddenly came a knock at the door and the trance

was broken. Margaret rocketed back to the here and now, and like an obedient soldier, Byron came to attention. Though he didn't know how, he too had heard Margaret's words, and this intrusion from the outside world seemed rude. It had come at just the wrong moment.

"May I come in?" the crusty old lady asked, entering the room without benefit of invitation. "Hello, little one," she said, reaching out to Margaret with her hand. "My name is Sister Siona. What's yours?"

"Prime Alpha. I mean, Margaret Hoolehan. Oh, I don't know what I mean."

"And yours?" Siona asked, turning to the handsome young man in uniform. Tattered clothes or not, there was no hiding his good looks.

"Byron Matthewson," came the answer.

"Yes, so I was told," Siona said, giving the lanky boy a quick once-over. "It's true then," she smiled. "I never thought we'd meet."

"Ma'am?"

"Oh, yes, I know all about you, young man. You're the boy from the first wife; all the other Matthewsons are descended from the second wife. Betsy something, if I remember correctly."

Flush and stammering now, Byron wheezed out the words. "How . . . could . . . I mean . . . where did you learn . . . I mean . . . "

"Oh, now don't have a conniption, Byron. If you don't settle down, you'll hyperventilate! Carina Matthews—that's your niece fifty-seven times removed—and I, visited a Mormon-run research facility west of Sane Lou, a facility where they archived all sorts of genealogical records. Histometrics and all that. She originally got hold of your name from her father, and he supposedly got it off some Civil War monument standing downtown near the river in Peoria . . . "

"*My* name? On a monument? In Peoria? Wow!" he exclaimed, his breast swelling with pride.

"Oh, yes, we're all so proud of you. Only problem is, you got yourself killed, you damn fool! Just like all the rest of the boys whose names appear on that monument. All dead!"

"I *died*?" Byron asked, suddenly white as a sheet.

Siona nodded grimly. "War's a terrible thing, Byron.

Lucky for you, the army's mustering records and all their enlistment reports survived into the future. Carina found them at the Genealogical Institute and recorded the pertinent information in her diary. I was there; I saw her do it. I remember the petty, little man who ran the place. First-rate pain in the ass, if you ask me. Obviously, that diary of hers went places we can only imagine."

"But *why*, for heaven's sake?" Byron asked, the color slowly returning to his face.

"Why did she keep track of this stuff, is that what you mean? 'Cause all the descendants of this Betsy something-or-other carried a genetic defect which caused them to die a premature death."

"Holcom. Betsy Holcom. That's my stepmother's name. But now wait a damn minute! This defect you're talking about—what kind of defect did you say it was?"

"Yes, of course, I forgot. You don't know anything at all about genes, do you? Well let me see if I can explain. A genetic defect is sort of like an inbred mistake. A disease you're born with. The way Carina had it figured, since you came from a different mother, you might be free of the disease. Only she had no way of traveling back in time to collect you up—or of transporting you forward to the future. Now, though, it seems as if *someone* has indeed figured that part out."

With this, Sister Siona went to the bed where Andu lay, still out cold. "And who might this be?" she asked, leaning over the bed.

Margaret answered. "Andu Nehrengel. Fornax's grandson. Is there actually such a person? Do you know a man by that name?"

"Indeed I do," Sister Siona nodded.

"So who, pray tell, was John Lawrence?" Byron asked, more than a little bewildered by the proceedings.

"That's anyone's guess. Probably just a name Andu made up. Someone whose identity he took when he went back looking for you."

"So Andu came back to save my life, and I ended up saving his?"

"Looks that way," Siona agreed, just now beginning to appreciate how confusing all this must be to him. "Now let me see if I have this straight: Andu enlisted with you as this John Lawrence fellow, got himself shot, and then what?"

"I pulled him off the battlefield, and then Margaret and I met on the hospital ship. I guess it was by accident, though at the time it was almost as if I'd been drawn to her. You know, like by magic."

"I see. And how did the two of you manage to get *here*? Was that magic too? God Almighty, you've time-traveled forward some six centuries. Pardon my saying so, but I find it hard to believe that either of you two characters has what it takes to pilot a spaceship, much less one warping its way through time! How did the two of you manage it? Andu must have been unconscious the whole way back. The truth now, and I don't want to hear any more crap about magic tricks or hocus-pocus!"

Margaret nodded her head knowingly and reached into her pocket. She pulled out the slim, metal device Andu had given her and handed it to Sister Siona to look at. "You're right, of course. Neither one of us has the first clue how to fly a spaceship. Fortunately, we didn't have to. Andu had already pre-programmed the ship's computer for the jump back. After our plunge in that freezing-cold river, he came to just long enough to tell me that all I had to do was hit the 'go' button when we got to the ship. I wasn't really sure where we were actually going until we got here."

"Smart man, that Andu. Definitely a Nehrengel. So you landed, brought him here to the hospital, and our Nurse Johnson patched him up?"

"Yes, first thing," Margaret said. "She injected him with some sort of red liquid."

"Acceleron, I should imagine. He should be coming around any minute." Then noticing the printbook Margaret had been holding onto ever since she first came into the room, Siona asked, "What's that you're reading?"

"Oh, just something I found in the ship's library. It's a volume by Mark Twain."

"One of my favorites."

"Mine too."

"Grew up near Sane Lou, you know."

"Yes, he told me that."

"You actually met the man?" Siona asked, surprised.

"Oh, yes. Onboard a riverboat. Only, he wasn't Mark Twain yet; he was still Samuel Clemens."

"You knew Samuel Clemens?" This time it was Byron speaking. Though he had long ago lost that clipping his cousin had sent him from the Keokuk *Gate City*, he would never forget the haunting words Clemens had written about that barren land he called Nevada. Come to think of it, his description could just as easily have been of Mars as of Nevada. Byron was just about to point that out when Margaret spoke up excitedly.

"Shush everybody, I think he's coming around!"

Andu's eyes fluttered once or twice, then he groaned.

Sister Siona leaned over him, her long white hair flowing alongside her face, giving her an angelic look. She put her hand to his forehead, then her palm to his cheek. The bright, overhead lamps blotted out everything else in the room.

His eyes came open.

He looked up at her.

"Is this heaven?" he asked.

She smiled. "No, this is Mars."